A NOBLE CALLING

+ AN FBI YELLOWSTONE ADVENTURE +

RHONA WEAVER

Two Oaks Press

Published by Two Oaks Press, Little Rock, Arkansas
www.rhonaweaver.com

GIRL FRIDAY
PRODUCTIONS®

Edited and designed by Girl Friday Productions
www.girlfridayproductions.com

Design: Paul Barrett
Project management: Sara Spees Addicott
Image credits: front and back cover photos © Bill Temple

Scripture taken from the New King James Version®. Copyright © 1982 by Thomas Nelson. Used by permission. All rights reserved.

Lyrics from "Nobody In His Right Mind Would've Left Her" used with permission from Dean Dillon.

ISBN (hardcover): 978-1-7347500-0-3
ISBN (paperback): 978-1-7347500-1-0
ISBN (ebook): 978-1-7347500-2-7

Library of Congress Control Number: 2020909076

First edition
Printed in the United States of America

A NOBLE CALLING

To Suzie

CHAPTER ONE

No, this day hadn't gone well from the git-go—even before the red and blue lights swirled in his rearview mirror. He'd driven the last 176 miles from Billings in an early-April snowstorm, not the sort of thing a southern boy handled real well. The low-hanging clouds were as dark as his mood. Just a few months ago, this spring had held such promise: the opportunity to move up the ladder a notch to a prize posting at the Bureau's New Orleans Field Office—so much white-collar crime and corruption in that city, it'd be like shooting fish in a barrel. The perfect posting for an up-and-coming agent ready to make a name for himself. Reasonably close to home and SEC football—not a bad city to start a family. . . . And then there was that. How had it fallen apart with Shelby? Had he been too focused on the job? Had med school consumed her passion? Had they—

"Sir, I need to see your license." Win heard the muffled voice through the frosty window. He hit the power button and the window dropped. The blowing snow and frigid air rushed inside as he struggled to form a coherent response. Standing in a near whiteout wasn't improving the ranger's mood. When he had to ask again, there was no "sir."

"I need to see your license. Do you know how fast you were going? The park is a forty-five-mile-per-hour zone."

"Forty-five? Out here? Uh, I guess maybe fifty-five . . . ," Win stammered.

"Well, try sixty-three miles per hour. That's borderline reckless driving here. Step out of the vehicle, sir." The cool blue eyes under the Smokey the Bear hat didn't look a bit friendly. The ranger was near Win's height and probably just past middle age. The close-cropped gray hair under his flat hat gave him a military bearing, and a deep scowl conveyed his thoughts. He clearly wasn't pleased with Win's lack of awareness.

Win stepped out of his ten-year-old SUV and the wind cut completely through his jean jacket.

The tall man in green now had a hostile stance that matched his tone. "Got your truck crammed full—one of the seasonal employees working in the park, are you? Guess you didn't notice the big '45 MPH' sign at the entrance? Or maybe you didn't notice you were entering Yellowstone National Park? Not paying a lot of attention, are you?"

The condescending lecture was jarring. *No*, Win thought, *this isn't going well at all.*

Another man in green approached from the other side of Win's Explorer and leaned forward against the hood, seemingly oblivious to the snow dancing across it. He casually rested his gloved left hand on the truck, but the wariness in his alert eyes contradicted his easygoing approach. The man's thin smile showed no warmth; Win knew his right hand was resting on his weapon. He was maybe in his early forties and much smaller than the first ranger, five eleven or so, but he moved with a quiet confidence that demanded respect. Self-pity and lack of sleep aside, Win quickly realized it was time to snap out of it or things could go downhill fast.

He sucked in an icy breath and shifted his eyes back to the tall, older ranger. "Sir, I'm sorry I was speeding. I'm Win Tyler, the agent assigned to the park's FBI satellite office. I just drove in from—"

"Well, isn't that special! Hear that, Gus? This boy is the new Fed they've assigned us. Where's that ID, son? Let's see . . ." He looked at the gold badge, then flipped open Win's credentials. "Hmmm . . . says Special Agent Winston R. Tyler. Coming to Mammoth Hot Springs from, let's see, license says Charlotte, North Carolina. Moving to the wilderness from the big city. What did you screw up to get shipped out here?"

A rhetorical question, Win supposed. He suddenly wasn't cold, and the snow seemed hardly a bother. This guy was hitting a little too close to home.

The ranger handed back the credentials and driver's license through the swirl of white and turned to the other figure in green. "Well, Gus, we've got real work to do." He glanced dismissively toward Win. "Speed limit is forty-five. No matter who you work for." He turned on his heel into the blinding flashing lights on his SUV.

The smaller man was still leaning on Win's old red Ford. "Slow it down, Sport. Oh, and welcome to Yellowstone. Mammoth is three miles up the hill." There wasn't a hint of welcome in the stern voice.

Win hunkered down in his truck seat as their large white-and-green SUV pulled onto the highway. Obviously, these rangers had never heard of the brotherhood in law enforcement. On the other hand, he didn't have a speeding ticket. Some consolation: It wasn't going well, but it could be going worse.

He shivered as the heater in the Explorer tried to keep up with the wintry air blowing in the open window. He hit the window's power switch and watched the tire tracks of the rangers' SUV rapidly fill in with snow. If he was going to make it up a three-mile hill in this weather, it was time to move on, as the highway was quickly turning white.

What did you screw up to get shipped out here? The ranger's exact words. Win tried to keep his mind from going there. No agent would volunteer to sit for two to three years in Yellowstone National Park unless they were on their way out. Nothing of note ever happened here. He'd joined the FBI to catch bad guys, save the country from terrorists and crooks, and maybe even build a successful career—not to be stuck in a two-agent office cut off from the world by snow and cold for seven months of the year, with only petty thieves and poachers to investigate.

The Explorer fishtailed as Win cautiously drove up the mountain, now at well under the speed limit. Even with the poor visibility, focusing on the road was far easier than focusing on his downwardly spiraling life.

* * *

Normally, Win wouldn't think of dropping in to any federal building, much less his new office, in anything less than slacks and a sport coat. But this wasn't a normal day; this was his first day of exile, his first day somewhere he desperately didn't want to be. He rolled the Ford into one of the many empty spots in front of the Yellowstone Justice Center. He'd looked it up on the internet, so he wasn't surprised to see a modern two-story building constructed to more or less blend in with the surrounding historic stone-and-frame structures. The setting might be pretty, he supposed, but today everything was shrouded by low clouds and bands of blowing snow.

Win had been told to check in at the FBI office and the resident agent would get him to his housing. He still had a few days of administrative leave remaining to get things settled. He drew a deep breath. *Let's get this over with.* The cold wind hit him as he sprinted up the steps to the front entrance. He made a mental note to find his heavy coat.

He passed through the metal-and-glass exterior doors and heard a click as someone unlocked a second set of more ornate, inlaid wooden doors. The lobby was empty—no one was manning the security system. His glance took in gray slate floors, gold stucco walls, and black ironwork on the light fixtures and upstairs railing. The design was meant to convey a western feel, but bright fluorescent lighting, sterile stainless-steel security features, and nondescript wall adornments negated many of the efforts at originality. Maybe it was his melancholy mood, but the building felt no different than other small, modern courthouses he'd visited. The ubiquitous black directory was beside the single elevator. Win's eyes scanned it quickly: Courtroom, Judge's Chambers, Assistant U.S. Attorney, U.S. Marshals Service, and several other offices, but no FBI. *That's odd.*

A short, portly figure in green and gray moved into his sight from an office near the entrance. "Hello there. Looking for someone?" At least the man had a friendly voice.

"Winston Tyler, FBI. Just been assigned here. I need to find the office and—"

"Oh, you're the speeder Chief Randall and Gus caught on the hill. Happy to have you here!" The man stuck out his hand and surprised Win with a strong handshake. He was wearing a Park Service uniform and carrying a firearm, but far past middle age and obviously not on a physical-training regimen.

"Sorry if the hand is sticky—lunchtime, you know." He pulled the hand away and wiped it on his pants. "I'm Bill Wilson, been here fifteen years, retired from the Nevada Highway Patrol way back when. I'm guarding the building till the U.S. Marshals and their security service get their contract worked out. Screwed-up mess in Washington! Supposed to have three contract folks standing guard here. Overkill, if you ask me. It's not like we're overrun with security threats."

The guy was a talker, and he'd already heard about the speeding stop less than fifteen minutes earlier. Win reverted to his southern roots. If nothing else comes to mind, talk about the weather.

"Good to meet you, Officer Wilson. Terrible weather driving here this morning."

The man peered out the double set of glass doors at the snow with disinterest. "They call all of us rangers here, law enforcement or not. . . . Oh, that little snow squall won't amount to nothing. We get those till June."

Win tried again. "So where's the FBI office?"

"You can call me Bill. Yeah, well, the FBI was supposed to be in this building, but there wasn't enough funding to finish out their office space. It's vacant. Couldn't even finish the jail. Building went two million over budget and they still didn't get it done." He shrugged. "Federal budgets, you know."

"So where *is* the FBI office?"

"Just down the street, in the Corps of Engineers Building, second floor. That little stone building was built in 1903 and used as the park's courthouse for over seventy years. It was the smallest federal courtroom in the U.S." The ranger glanced at his watch. "Let's see, it's after one o'clock. You can probably catch Johnson back at his office. No disrespect, everybody calls Agent Johnson 'Johnson.' He's been here five years, nearly a permanent fixture. I think he likes being in the old building. Over there, it sorta keeps him out of the action."

What action? Win thought. *It's quiet as a tomb in here.*

Win moved toward the front doors as the older man followed, now talking about how long it took to construct the Justice Center. Win said a rushed goodbye and eased toward the exit. The wind nearly jerked the outer door from his hand before he dove down the steps to his truck. He scanned his surroundings again as wind and ice pellets assaulted the windshield. A few huddled pedestrians were moving quickly into buildings, probably coming back from lunch, but largely the parking lots and sidewalks were empty. Ranger Wilson, Bill, was waving to him from behind the double glass doors. Win weakly waved back. Everyone knew everyone else's business here, same as back home. As an Arkansas boy, he was comfortable with that to a point, but today he felt a deep uneasiness. *Do they know why I was sent here?* He couldn't shake the gloom.

He drove up the street a couple hundred yards and pulled into the gravel side lot of a solid-looking, gray stone building with *United States Engineer Office* carved into the front cornice. There was nothing to indicate an FBI office was in the ancient structure. There was, however, a large black SUV with two antennas parked in the side lot—a promising sign.

Win had to admit he hadn't approached this posting with his usual attention to detail. Maybe it had been the shock of the disciplinary hearing or the suddenness of the transfer. He'd barely researched the FBI's Denver Field Office or the Jackson Hole Resident Agency, much less this out-of-the-way satellite office where he might have to spend the next few years. Agent Johnson had been on medical leave with shoulder surgery most of last month and hadn't returned his calls. Yellowstone had no FBI secretary or other support personnel to quiz. An agent in Denver told Win that Spence Johnson was considering retirement; he was a short-timer and wanted nothing to rock the boat. A second agent hadn't been assigned to Yellowstone in nearly a year. Word had it Agent Johnson thought that was just fine.

The snow was swirling in patterns across the wide concrete porch of the old building as Win climbed its granite steps. He braced to steady the wooden front doors from the gusting wind as he slid into the small space between the outer doors and the glass-and-oak French doors blocking his way to the lobby. He looked for a security keypad or intercom but found none, so he pushed on the inner doors. They silently swung open into the tiny lobby of the historic building. *So much for Bureau security features.* Walnut paneling was everywhere and the black iron chandelier in the high plaster ceiling gave off dim light. The narrow room smelled of polished wood and damp stone, and faintly of pine-scented cleaner. There was a stark contrast between this intimate, warm place and the modern courthouse he'd just left. Maybe Johnson's reasons for staying in the old building went beyond wanting to be left alone.

The constant hum of a printer was coming from somewhere up the substantial wooden staircase. Except for that sound and the ding of icy precipitation hitting the windows, there was silence.

The stairs creaked under Win's boots as he climbed them. The smooth oak handrail had brass fittings and good workmanship. He doubted they used the lowest-bid concept back in the day this was built.

The second door on the upper floor was open, and harsh fluorescent light poured into the wood-paneled hall. A faded plastic sign on the wall simply stated *Federal Bureau of Investigation.* It was hardly impressive. Win stopped at the open door. The office was good sized, but it was hard to tell its dimensions since boxes, files, and random pieces of office equipment were stacked everywhere, some head high.

"Geez, what a mess!" It was Win's involuntary reaction; it was also a mistake.

"Who the hell are you, Martha Stewart? Been here ten seconds and already bitching about your new office!"

Win flinched and backed away. He hadn't heard or felt the presence of anyone else in the room, yet from under the clutter rose a formidable man.

"Down here under the desk trying to plug in your phone! And me with a bad shoulder. You can do the computer yourself. A grand entrance you're making, Agent Tyler! You've already managed to tick off the Chief Ranger and his deputy by speeding. And I wouldn't worry about this mess—you'll have plenty of time to tidy it up. You can put up little yellow curtains when you finish, for all I care!"

The voice was deep and harsh, and the big man seemed to just be warming up—lots of pent-up anger there. The guy reminded Win of too many old-school coaches during his football days. *Time to brown-nose a little.*

Win stepped forward and extended his hand over the boxes on the desk. "Winston Tyler, folks call me Win. Thanks for the help with the phone. Heard about your shoulder surgery; hope it's healing well. I need to find my housing and, uh, get started in the office." He kept talking fast, hoping the anger would defuse. Johnson accepted the handshake, but his eyes remained in a tight squint. Even though Win and Johnson were technically equals in the Bureau, Johnson had been here for five years, was more than twenty-five years older, and deserved to be treated as the senior resident agent.

The big man kicked a box out of the way and moved past a pile of discarded printers. Win wasn't small at six-foot-three, but Agent Johnson was at least two inches taller and much, much broader. He had short, dark-brown hair flecked with gray, a ruddy complexion, and heavy brows over narrow brown eyes. He had the look of a middle-aged fighter—one who could still fight. He also looked more like a hunter than an FBI agent in his heavy twill pants, leather combat boots, and green wool shirt. He wasn't what Win had been expecting at all.

For a moment, the hum of the printer was the only sound filling the background; then, mercifully, a telephone rang from somewhere beneath an enormous pile of file folders. Johnson dug out the phone. "FBI!" he barked. Then his angry eyes left Win as he focused inward, hearing what the caller was saying. His responses were clipped. "Okay, out at the Hoodoos. . . . Yes, the abandoned trail. . . . Bordeaux? He's alone, they think. . . . Randall and Gus are there. . . . Okay. . . . Less than ten minutes."

Johnson hung up the landline and was all business. "Got a gunman up on the hill. Most of the park's law enforcement rangers are at firearms training, hours away. Chief Randall may need a little help coaxing the guy out. Want to go?"

Is he kidding? Given the reputation of Yellowstone, this might be his only real law enforcement encounter for the next two years. "Sure, yeah. My handgun is boxed in my truck."

"No time for that. You got your creds? You can use the shotgun or the MP5 from my vehicle. I can't use them with my bad arm." He moved out of the room, grabbed a dark coat from somewhere, and was jogging down the staircase before Win could react.

Johnson's black SUV roared to life and was backing out as Win closed the passenger door. They sped up the nearly empty road in the spitting snow, past a large, multistory frame building Win recognized from internet photos as the Mammoth Hot Springs Hotel.

Johnson talked as he drove. "The guy on the hill is a local named Luke Bordeaux. We suspect he poaches deer and elk in the park. He's from Louisiana—been here a few years. Had a run-in with us last year, but no convictions. Generally carries a rifle, a handgun or two, and a knife." He accelerated to pass a slower vehicle. "Some hikers reported an armed man near Snow Pass on Terrace Mountain, skinning out a deer, and Chief Randall hiked up a closed trailhead to try to catch the poacher. Now they're in a Mexican standoff and we're the backup."

Win never had the chance to visit Yellowstone as a kid, but he'd always imagined buffalo, wolves, and bears. Heavily armed bad guys didn't fit into his expectations.

Johnson steered past another carload of gawking tourists and kept talking. "Guns are in the usual spot. You take the MP5. It's fully automatic—we've got a Bureau exemption to carry automatics, since we're in the middle of nowhere. Let Chief Randall run the show. It's his deal."

They were gaining speed going up a wooded hill southwest of the building complex. Win barely glimpsed the white, steaming terraces that made up the area's namesake hot springs as they sped upward into a dark evergreen forest. The two-lane asphalt highway was steep and winding as it climbed the mountain. They'd covered more than three miles of switchbacks when Johnson abruptly swung off onto a narrow paved road that cut directly between two huge gray boulders. The rangers' big SUV was parked in front of them, almost blocking the single lane.

The metal safe for the long guns and Johnson's disorganized gear-box were in the rear of the SUV. Johnson unlocked the guns and eased his bad shoulder into a blue raid jacket as Win pulled on a bulletproof vest. He was digging in the tangled mess in the box for a raid jacket when garbled shouting from beyond the vehicles got their attention. Win stepped back and inserted a thirty-round magazine into the black submachine gun, while Johnson stuck an extra magazine into his pants pocket and pulled a Glock from under his coat.

"Sounds like Randall's in trouble, no more time to gear up. Move parallel to me," Johnson ordered.

The smaller ranger Win had "met" earlier on the highway into Mammoth had his handgun drawn and was crouched behind the Park Service Tahoe with two frightened-looking middle-aged guys in winter hiking clothes.

"The Chief's pinned down in the boulder field about a hundred fifty feet up the trail," the ranger said. "Shooter's higher in the rocks to the right. Been firing randomly. Our other folks are at least ten minutes out." Just then the sharp crack of a rifle rang out—everyone behind the SUV instinctively ducked.

"Well, looks like we're the cavalry. Gus, you stay put and keep everyone back."

The ranger accepted Johnson's order, but his eyes gave away his distaste for the backup position.

With a quick hand motion, Johnson sent Win to the right, around the rangers' vehicle and up the winding trail. Win moved in a crouch, dodging from one boulder to another, praying the rocks would provide adequate cover from the unseen gunman. The snow continued to taper off, but the low, grayish-white clouds hung close above him as he planted himself against the side of a huge rock.

The sharp crack of a high-powered rifle cut the air above his head and echoed off the walls of the surrounding canyon. The low cloud cover and close cliffs caused the single shot to sound like a dozen. The report reverberated through him like a rolling clap of thunder—he was keenly aware of the bullet's killing power. He edged himself deeper into a crease in the boulder where he'd taken cover and reminded himself to breathe. While his Quantico training had kicked in even before he heard the first shot, it did nothing to tamp down the adrenaline pumping through his system. His heart was pounding wildly as his eyes swept the unfamiliar landscape for any movement. He'd made the fifty-yard dash up the faint, snow-covered trail to this position as if in slow motion. Every sense was at its highest level: His sight was crystal clear, his hearing was acute, and his mind moved in a dozen directions at once. His first armed encounter after three years in the FBI, and he wished he'd be able to say he wasn't afraid. But that would be a lie. And Win Tyler didn't lie.

A brown, weathered *Trail Closed* sign leaned toward him, marking an indistinct path that peeked through the thin accumulation of snow and snaked its way through the towering boulders on a slight incline. The massive yellowish-gray rocks, some as large as houses, looked as if they'd been casually dropped there—randomly stacked and scattered up the slope toward a ridge that disappeared in the whirling, white clouds. Win hazarded a quick glance around his boulder. He could see the back of the park ranger about thirty feet to his left. The man was leaning into a smaller rock for cover. His felt hat was near his feet, and the wind was blowing his dark-green jacket open. A pistol was lying in the snow near the middle of the trail. It looked as if the ranger had been surprised by the shooter and had fallen and dropped the weapon. Not a good position to be in—the man was way too exposed.

Win peered farther to his left and caught a glimpse of the gold lettering on Johnson's FBI raid jacket. The agent had taken cover behind a rock the size of an elephant. Johnson raised a fist and pointed it toward Win: *Hold your position!*

Okay, got that. Win hugged his big rock even closer, whispered a prayer, and adjusted his grip on the MP5. He noticed his hands were shaking slightly on the hard plastic frame of the submachine gun. He didn't think it was from the cold. He heard the ranger call out something to the shooter, but the wind carried the shouted words away. He glanced again toward Johnson, acknowledged a second raised fist with a nod, then settled in to wait while the ranger tried to start a dialogue with the gunman. While he stalled. While they all waited for more backup to arrive. But it didn't take five minutes for Johnson's patience to wane; the older agent had tired of the waiting game.

"Luke!" Johnson called out. "Luke, we know it's you, dammit! Put down the gun and let's all get out of this cold wind!"

A loud retort from the rifle was the answer.

Geez, the guy is really close! Win huddled tighter against the boulder as the rifle's blast reverberated through him again. Despite the frigid temperature, sweat was trickling down his face. Johnson was signaling for him to move up. Win had a different idea.

He leaned into the icy rock and called out in a loud voice, "Hey, Luke! Win Tyler here! You from Louisiana? Well, either you're a lousy shot, 'cause I ain't seen no rounds coming in, or you're just firing off to celebrate LSU whipping Villanova in the regional finals last month! Where you from?" Silence for a minute, then Luke's southern manners kicked in—it might be okay to shoot at a guy, but you didn't ignore an invitation to talk basketball, or football, or, hell, anything else, when someone asked the central question in the South: "Where you from?"

"From Ferriday. Didn't the Tigers play a fine game! Fine game! Where you from, boy?"

"Grew up on a farm in Heber Springs, Arkansas. . . . Y'all had a great win! Program's on the way back!" He glanced at Johnson, who was staring at him as if he were an alien. Win intended to keep up the rhetoric and give the ranger a chance to retreat to better cover.

He called into the wind, "Do you know the Glovers from Jonesville? Knew them in Farm Bureau. Big rice farmers."

"Well, know of 'em. Daddy drove a truck fer old Mr. Glover when they still had cotton."

"Yeah, and how about Tucker Moses from the Moriah Plantation? He was my roommate in law school. Tucker played ball at Ole Miss."

"Sure, watched him play in high school—good people!" There was a brief pause as the wind gusted through the boulders. Then, "You a Fed?"

"Yeah, and speaking of that, how 'bout you drop your gun and come on down. I forgot my coat and I'm freezing out here."

There was silence for several seconds. "Well there, I ain't actually shot no one and it ain't a crime fer me to have a gun if it ain't loaded, is it?"

"Bordeaux, you're allowed to have a weapon in the park as long as it's unloaded." That was Ranger Randall piping in.

Who came up with these rules? Win was wondering.

"Alright, you boys stand down." Seconds later, Bordeaux appeared from thirty yards above Win and to his right, holding a scoped deer rifle high over his head with one hand and holding a pistol by the barrel with the other. Looked like he had done this before. Randall scurried to retrieve his handgun and moved back behind his rock. Johnson kept his Glock trained on Bordeaux's chest as the man moved down the trail toward them.

Luke Bordeaux was about Win's size, maybe slimmer, but it was hard to tell with the heavy, dark-brown coveralls he was wearing. A brown ball cap covered thick black hair that came nearly to his shirt collar and was blowing in the wind. His face was tan, with dark eyes and a short-cropped black beard and mustache. He moved like a hunter, without any noticeable focus on the trail. When Luke reached Randall's boulder, the ranger stepped out and took the weapons as Johnson moved to provide cover. Win stayed behind his rock with the MP5 pointed toward Bordeaux, then at the ground.

"Where's the feller from Arkansas?" Win heard Luke casually ask. Satisfied the gunman was alone, Win stepped out as Johnson lowered his pistol.

"Smart of you to give up, Bordeaux. This could have gotten real nasty," Randall was saying as he checked to make sure the guns were unloaded. The smaller ranger was jogging up the trail toward them with gun drawn. Win figured the two hikers would have a great campfire story to tell tonight.

Luke Bordeaux, totally ignoring the fact that he was now in handcuffs, was sizing Win up from ten feet away. "Did you play ball? You look like a ball player."

It was casual bravado and Win went along. "Yeah, played at Arkansas four years. Played quarterback then wide receiver. You played?"

The bluster disappeared from Luke's face and a flash of regret caused his eyes to drop. "Naw, never made it to college, but I played at Vidalia High fer three years. Went to every LSU game I could get a ticket to. . . . Miss it sometimes. I—"

"I'm really enjoying this reminiscing you gentlemen are doing, but Luke here is going to have an appointment with Judge Walters this afternoon. I'm sure you fine federal agents have better things to do than stand out here in the wind," Randall said. Two more armed guys in green were running up the trail. The older ranger continued, "We can handle it from here, Johnson." He didn't even glance at Win.

Johnson raised his chin to motion Win back down the trail, leaving the rangers to find the shell casings and the poached deer.

"See ya around, Win Tyler," Luke called after his back. The tone of voice sent a chill up Win's spine.

He and Johnson didn't speak as they made the short hike to the vehicles. Several other park rangers, an ambulance crew, and a small crowd of tourists were standing near the trailhead, waiting to see how the confrontation played out. After stowing his gear, Win climbed into the passenger seat to find the heater running full blast and Johnson on the satellite phone, reporting in to someone.

Johnson signed off the call, eased around the rangers' SUV, and turned the Suburban back onto the highway. He maneuvered around several parked vehicles as he spoke. "For a guy who just got here on a LOE transfer, you've had a pretty good day. A little unorthodox maybe, but you did a nice job talking that fool down. Bordeaux could've put a bullet in Chief Randall at any time."

Win wasn't hearing the praise. He heard Johnson say "LOE transfer" and a sick wave hit his stomach. "Loss of Effectiveness." It didn't get much worse than that in the FBI. He clenched his jaw, stared out the window, and pretended to take in the scenery.

Johnson didn't notice his discomfort. The man continued to ramble on. "Randall wasn't too grateful to you. Embarrassed he let himself get into that position, I'd think. Probably thought the poacher was further up the slope when he headed up the trail. As Chief Ranger he wouldn't normally be in the field, but since most everyone was at training, I guess he was filling in."

Win tried to regain his composure as he listened. He kept his hands stuck in the pockets of his light jacket. They were still shaking a little. He slumped back in the seat as the adrenaline began to dissipate. He'd tried to act as if facing up against an armed man were an everyday event. In reality, he'd never held a loaded gun, much less a submachine gun, on anyone, ever.

"Will he actually get off? No laws against an unloaded gun?" he finally asked.

"Probably—this is the Wild West. Everyone hates gun laws out here, even the Federal Magistrate." Johnson scowled down the highway. "Actually, most anyone can carry a *loaded* gun in the park. The only reason Bordeaux is restricted to unloaded weapons is his previous run-in with the legal system. And we can't prove he was shooting at anyone, as you pointed out to him. He was just rattling some nerves. Might get him on discharging a weapon in a national park, but that's just a rinky-dink charge. Judge would probably give him a lecture and dismiss it. If the rangers find the bullet in the deer he was skinning out and match it to the rifle, they could charge him with poaching." Johnson frowned as he finished the thought. "Many folks in this part of the country consider poaching a far worse offense than shooting at a federal officer anyway."

Seriously?

CHAPTER TWO

Win awoke in the dark with a moment of panic—not remembering where he was or why he was there. Sad, confused dreams darted toward the edge of his consciousness. Dim light filtered in from under a curtain, and dark shapes in the room began coming into focus. His head was still throbbing slightly, and he feared that any movement might bring on the terrible headaches and nausea he'd experienced throughout the night. He slowly raised himself on one elbow, then dropped his head back to the worn sofa pillow and closed his eyes. *So far so good.* Altitude sickness. That was Agent Johnson's diagnosis yesterday afternoon, when he dropped Win off at the old stone house that would be his home in Mammoth Hot Springs. There hadn't been any sympathy.

"Too much activity, too fast. We're above 6,300 feet here. Drink lots of water, take some aspirin, and sleep. I'll do the paperwork on the incident with Bordeaux. We can both initial it later. I may be shipping out for a while, so be at the office 8:15 Saturday morning. Your first day at your new duty station, Tyler—April 12th."

Then he'd left Win to collapse on the grungy, stained couch. Late yesterday afternoon, after a couple bouts of nausea had passed, Win had taken off his boots and wrapped up in a wool blanket his mother had packed in his truck "just in case of emergencies," as she'd put it. He figured this qualified.

When he opened his eyes the second time, more light was coming through gaps in the curtains. There was the faint sound of vehicles starting in the distance. His breath rose in the early-morning light—he'd forgotten to turn on the heat. He guessed he'd alternated between violent sickness and sleep for about fourteen hours. A scratching sound came from the corner, then a quick scurry of motion across the floor. *Oh, geez! Mice, rats . . . something moving.* The current residents checking out the new tenant, he supposed. His eyes narrowed in resolve; he wouldn't room with rodents.

More scuffling, this time from outside a large wooden door that was emerging from the room's gloom. Footsteps on the porch, a light knock on the door. "Yoo-hoo! Hello! Agent Tyler? It's Maddy Wilson. Hello?"

Win launched off the couch with the blanket wrapped around him, tripped over two boxes, and found a light switch. He inched the door open. A short woman with tightly curled gray hair smiled up at him. She was encased in a blue down coat that made her look nearly as wide as she was tall. A pink fleece scarf was wrapped around her neck—its color perfectly matched her plump cheeks. Steam rose from the wicker basket she carried.

"Oh my, I hope I didn't wake you." Even though it was obvious she did, her soft, singsong voice continued uninterrupted. "I'm Bill Wilson's wife. You met Bill yesterday. He hated he missed all the action. I understand you single-handedly talked that rascal down off the hill. Bill was so impressed! Well, I wanted to bring something over. . . . . My, you must be freezing standing out here in your sock feet." It occurred to him how awful he must look, but she kept talking. "No, no I don't need to come in. Made these a minute ago and there's hot coffee in the thermos. We'll have you over for dinner after you've settled in." She handed him the basket and was moving across the wooden porch and down the steps. "If you need anything, just call. Our number's in the basket. So glad to have you here!"

He managed to mumble a reasonable offer of thanks before moving back into the living room, which was already feeling more like home as the scent of warm muffins filled the air. The headache had retreated to a dull throbbing, and he knew the hot coffee would go a long way toward curing that annoyance.

After two cups of Mrs. Wilson's coffee and three still-warm muffins, Win was feeling more like himself. A glance in the bathroom's cracked mirror confirmed his fears about his appearance: nearly three days of stubble, matted hair, and bloodshot eyes. A long, hot shower would have been nice, but the water wasn't even lukewarm. He couldn't get the thermostat to respond with heat either; his breath was still visible. He reluctantly retrieved clean clothes from his travel bag, braved the cold water, and set about making himself presentable.

It was closing in on 7:30 when he finally turned on his phone and heard the numerous tones for missed calls, voice mails, and texts. *Yes! Cell service at my house!* He smiled down at a recent text from Will, his fifteen-year-old brother: **dude mom has not heard from u in 3 days. she thinks ur kidnapped on the high plains and will call cops or fbi. wait, u r fbi. give her a break call her.**

He dutifully called his mother and made an upbeat report on his uneventful trip across half the country. He didn't mention the near shoot-out on the mountain, the less-than-friendly new coworker, or the altitude sickness. She wanted pictures of his new house, his office, and Yellowstone. He promised to send some, but it occurred to him he'd been so sick yesterday afternoon and last night that he had no idea what his new place looked like.

His thoughts were interrupted by the morning's second knock on his door. This time it was firm and direct. *Okay, maybe Johnson decided I might die last night and is finally checking to see.*

Instead, he opened the door and looked down on a slight young man dressed in green—obviously the color of choice here. "Hi, hope it isn't too early, I'm Jason Price, Assistant Facilities Manager for National Park Service Housing." Win raised an eyebrow in disbelief; the kid couldn't have been over sixteen or seventeen years old. Apparently, he got that response a lot. "Well, uhhh, my father is the actual facilities manager, but I homeschool and work part-time since staffing's been reduced. Federal budget cuts, you know."

The kid looked official enough, with his thick clipboard and uniform, so Win opened the door wider. It was nearly as cold in the dreary room as it was outside, where, as if on cue, the snow began to fall.

"So sorry about the condition of the unit," the young man was saying. "We weren't expecting you until Friday, but I've got a six-man crew lined up to go to work at eight o'clock. The last tenant moved out two months ago, and this unit has been scheduled for an upgrade for, like, thirty years, but, you know—"

"Let me guess, federal budget cuts?" Win interjected, smiling.

"Yeah, yeah, but this is a real sweet house. It was built in 1894 as the park's seat of justice. It's in the Fort Yellowstone Historic District. Constructed of Yellowstone sandstone—the walls are eighteen inches thick, two beautiful fireplaces, oak floors and paneling—all original to the early 1890s. The Federal Magistrate wanted a modern place, so he lives down in Lower Mammoth. Lots of our employees want to live in newer houses, but units like this have real character." He was talking and writing on the clipboard as he walked through the living room. "Needs paint, lighting . . . bathroom needs lots of work, plumbing issues. Kitchen needs new appliances and counters, polish the hardwood floors and woodwork . . ." He paused and gave Win an expectant look. "The last tenant used the big southwest room as a bedroom and office. It gets a little late-afternoon sun in winter and looks out over the Lower Terraces of the hot springs. We got those rooms and the upstairs bedrooms and bath shipshape last week. What did you think?"

"Uh, didn't feel well last night," Win admitted. "I haven't made it past this room and the bathroom. I—"

"Altitude sickness, I'll bet," the kid interjected. "Pretty common. Drink lots of water and rest."

"Yeah, I got that. Feeling much better. Wanna show me around?"

"Sir, if you don't mind, my guys will be here in a few minutes. Why don't you pick out your new living room furniture from my photos." He handed Win his phone. "I'm planning on installing Wi-Fi today. Want satellite TV? I've got two 42-inch flat-screens in the warehouse you can have."

He had Win's attention now. He'd been told there was no television or internet service in park housing. "You can do that? Yeah, sure."

"The rental units for tourists don't have TV or Wi-Fi, in keeping with the park's rustic, back-to-nature concept, but hey, you're here for the long haul. We can make this house totally awesome." His thin face took on a determined look as his eyes ran over the stained sofa, sagging curtains, and scuffed floors.

Win was starting to realize the assistant facilities manager would be a good man to know. Unfortunately, his headache was making a reappearance. He sat down on the old couch and cradled his head. It was obvious that staying in the house wasn't a good option for the day.

"I might check out the park," he offered.

"Hmmm," the boy said, "tell you what, this will take two full days, then there'll be things to tweak. The park roads are all closed because of the snow except for the Gardiner entrance. Won't be any snow issues on the main roads north of here. You might want to get down to a lower altitude anyway, maybe run to Walmart and stock up on stuff. Maybe spend the night at the hotel or in town. Could meet you here at 5:30 tomorrow afternoon and let you inspect the place. Is that a plan?"

Lower altitude was sounding like a wonderful idea. Win stowed the few possessions he'd unloaded the day before back in his truck and leaned his head against the frigid steering wheel to let the nausea pass. According to Jason, Walmart and civilization were about ninety miles north in Bozeman, Montana. He drove out of the park down the same slick mountain road he'd driven in on—this time he remembered the forty-five-mile-per-hour speed limit.

*   *   *

As Jason predicted, all signs of altitude sickness left him as he descended over a thousand feet in elevation from Mammoth into Gardiner. The snow had stopped by the time he drove the five and a half miles into town, and except for the low, gray clouds, there was no sign of winter. There was no sign of spring either, but he was in Montana's mountain country; he couldn't expect the seasons to be the same as in the South.

When he'd left his childhood home in Arkansas late on Easter Sunday, the dogwoods and redbuds had been in full bloom. He shook his head to clear the homesickness and tried again to appreciate his new, very different surroundings.

He'd blown through Gardiner on his way to the park the day before, but he'd been in too much of a funk to really notice it. This trip, he slowed and meandered through the sprawling community of about nine hundred that straddled the high banks of the Yellowstone River. The old downtown lay south of the rushing river; its stone and clapboard buildings had once fronted a long-abandoned railroad. The structures now faced the iconic stone arch heralding the north entrance to Yellowstone—the town literally sat at the doorstep of the world's first national park.

A couple of bars, a café, and a few businesses were open, but most of the storefronts were dark and sported signs promising to reopen in mid-May. Win turned north off the main drag and drove across the river bridge, passing an assortment of convenience stores, motels, and tourist shops lining the highway leading out of town. Many of those businesses remained shuttered as well. Apparently the little town hadn't shaken off winter just yet.

As he drove north toward Bozeman, the low clouds met the tops of the rolling gray and brown hills, giving the countryside a claustrophobic feel. From the photographs he'd seen on the internet, he knew there were vast mountain ranges and forests in the area, but the snow clouds obscured any view of them. Clumps of low brush and an occasional stand of evergreens or bare cottonwoods dotted the landscape. The Wyoming-Montana border region would have to grow on him. His first impression was of its barrenness.

He was expecting Bozeman to be a sleepy, declining little cow town, but was pleasantly surprised to see a city of almost fifty thousand that appeared to be in a bit of a renaissance. Montana State University sat near a bustling main street that had an upscale college vibe. The modern airport had nonstop commercial flights to a few major cities. Shoppers were friendly and outgoing. He couldn't figure out what was fueling the economy, but something sure was working. His new home in Mammoth, Wyoming, was within two hours of Bozeman. Maybe he hadn't been exiled to the far side of the moon after all.

Win had already decided his usual attire of a dark suit and tie wasn't going to cut it in Yellowstone. He'd stick out like a sore thumb. After an hour of relaxed surveillance outside the local courthouse, he could see that attorneys and law enforcement officers dressed more casually here, with a bit of a western flair. Stops at two outdoor supply stores and a couple of western-wear shops provided the needed additions to his wardrobe.

Driving back into the park the next day, he felt a bit of his natural optimism returning. Some of the apprehension had left him, and his better nature was trying to reframe his new posting as more of an adventure than a trial. His overloaded SUV eased up the final mountain onto the plateau where Mammoth sat and into the same winter weather he'd left thirty-two hours earlier. The low clouds still hung over the hills, and a thin dusting of snow covered everything.

He was running early for his meeting with Jason, so he took a few minutes to look over his new hometown. The internet told him Mammoth had a year-round population of fewer than three hundred people, which swelled to more than two thousand with additional park employees, contractors, and temporary workers during the short tourist season. A retro post office and a medical clinic sat on the opposite side of the divided street from the Justice Center. Vintage stone buildings contained the park's headquarters. The massive stone Albright Visitor Center was just across the divided street from the FBI office. Several large two-story brick-and-clapboard houses extended to the south from the Visitor Center. The tourist brochure he'd picked up called the big houses *Officer's Row*, and said they'd housed Fort Yellowstone's Army officers and their families back in the late 1800s. Many of the historic buildings faced an open area, which had served as the cavalry's parade grounds more than a century ago. Just beyond the houses, on the southern end of the historic district, was a pretty gray-stone church. It pulled at his heart for a moment, before he looked away. *I have to get back into church.*

A hundred years ago, someone had the good sense to plant dozens of trees in this area. Their towering bare branches now rose above the chapel and many of the nearby buildings. It would be green and shady here if spring ever came.

Win looped back toward the FBI office and then turned west on the highway toward his house. He passed the expansive Mammoth Hot Springs Hotel and two restaurants. There was a general store, an old-fashioned gas station, and a small number of other buildings, all in the cream-and-gray paint scheme of the historic district. His house stood slightly apart from the others; it was the last structure before the Grand Loop Road climbed past the Lower Terraces and southwestward into the western part of the park. When Yellowstone's roads fully opened, that highway would lead to Old Faithful and its famous geyser basins, fifty-two miles away, and to West Yellowstone, a town of fourteen hundred, fifty miles away on the western boundary of the park.

The brochure said his new house had been the residence of the park's first judge, as well as a courthouse and jail. It was a solid-looking gray-stone structure with one and a half stories; the upper level had double dormers and a snow-covered wood-shingle roof. Two stout red-brick chimneys rose from the center of the house. Large evergreens shielded its covered front porch from the highway and the open parade grounds. A porch swing and two Adirondack chairs had appeared on the porch since his earlier stay. Every window glowed brightly in the dwindling light of the gloomy afternoon—the house, his house, actually looked inviting.

Having tourists nearly on his doorstep would take some getting used to, but the view from one side of the house was the trade-off. The cascading white terraces of the hot springs dropped off a mountain in layers for several hundred feet toward the side of the house. Shallow streams of scalding water, colored orange by bacteria, flowed less than seventy feet from the driveway. Raised wooden boardwalks meandered around some of the features, but no tourists were braving the weather this afternoon. Steam rose from the hot pools on the terraces and blended into the spitting snow, creating a floating curtain of vapor and fog. Win figured few folks had such a fascinating next-door neighbor.

Workmen were hauling tools and ladders out the back door as Win pulled into the gravel parking area between the rear of the house and a small wooden shed. When he stepped out of the truck, Jason beamed. This kid clearly loved his work.

"We finished right on time, sir. Still have a few things to do. But come on in and let me show you around."

There was new tile and paint in the mudroom, laundry room, and kitchen—and new appliances and countertops, polished wood floors and paneling, even curtains on the windows. Stained French doors led from the kitchen into the room where Win spent his first night in Yellowstone. He wouldn't have recognized the room. The vintage light fixtures were burning bright against the stamped-copper ceiling. The brick fireplace looked freshly scrubbed and was outfitted with substantial-looking black-iron hardware and screen. A cream-colored sofa, with matching chair and ottoman, had taken the place of the dilapidated couch where Win had slept. A large flat-screen TV sat on an antique credenza against the opposite wall.

"It's all hooked up, sir. Let me show you how the TVs and Wi-Fi work here."

Win was liking this little guy more and more.

The large first-floor bedroom was where the judge's office and a portion of the jail were located when the house was built in 1894. Although Win hadn't seen the room earlier, he suspected Jason had worked his magic on it as well. There were antique wooden bookcases and a leather reading chair with an ottoman in the corner, and a large walnut bed faced the structure's second brick fireplace. A flat-screen TV dominated the space above the fireplace's mantel—his mother would hate that, but he loved it. The comforter on the bed, the curtains, even the wool rug in the room proclaimed the colors of nature: greens, blues, browns. The bedroom and office were outfitted exactly as he would have done it if he'd had any talent at interior decorating— which he did not. He decided he owed the assistant facilities manager a steak dinner.

After Jason finished the grand tour and left, Win walked back through the house. He was accustomed to having his own things, but almost everything he owned was now in storage. His high-rise apartment in Charlotte couldn't have been more different from the piece of history he now occupied. Back in Charlotte, Shelby had selected modern furniture. She'd also picked out the twelfth-floor apartment with the city view, in a building with a gym and a pool. He'd lived there for nearly three years, but had never really felt at home. Now that he thought about it, he wasn't even sure she'd asked him what he preferred. He'd let her make so many of their decisions. . . . He'd gone with the flow.

He fought back a wave of emptiness as he ran his fingers over the kitchen's new granite countertop. *Goin' with the flow isn't who I am. Nearly thirty years old. . . . Shoulda figured that out before now.*

* * *

Win's phone was buzzing the 5:15 a.m. alarm and he hit the snooze. As his head fell back on the pillow, he realized he'd been holding her soft hand; it was warm and comforting and so painfully real he immediately felt moisture come to his eyes. He blinked the beginnings of tears away and tried to swallow the lump rising in his throat. She'd never been big on sleeping too close to him at night, but whenever he awoke he would always touch her hand. Often he'd held it when he drifted to sleep. Someday maybe he'd actually wake up and not have dreamed of her, or felt her touch, or longed for her. But the heavy tightness in his chest and the gripping pain in his heart told him "someday" hadn't come quite yet. He forced himself to crawl out of bed and face the morning. One more step toward moving on with his life. Eventually it had to get better; everyone said it would.

He wondered if that was true.

* * *

A little later that same morning, seven miles as the crow flies northwest of where Win sat in his kitchen, drinking his second cup of coffee, a man stood staring out the window into the falling snow. The man was a little past middle age and of medium height. His dense brown hair was in a short cut, and heavy brows hooded his eyes. There wasn't anything particularly remarkable about his appearance; he was still fairly slender and strong for a man his age. He wore the uniform of his age group in the West: black Roper boots, sharply creased Wrangler jeans, and a white snap-button long-sleeved shirt. A gray Stetson hat sat on the desk nearby. A large silver belt buckle from one of his son's rodeo wins anchored his leather belt, *The Lord Lives!* engraved along its length. His face and hands were weathered and tan, and his mouth seemed to be permanently set in an almost-smile. The look could change in an instant from a genuine smile to a threatening snarl—it was a perfect reflection of his heart.

He was looking out his second-story office window over the grounds of the new church. They'd only been here eleven months and already had ninety-eight adult members. And membership did have its requirements: church services three times a week, tithing of income, and commitment to some service for the church at least twice a week. Adherence to the church's doctrine left little time for other pursuits, which was just the point. Eventually it would become a self-contained community. It was destined to be the spear tip of the Lord's return in glory.

The church building was actually a large, wood-frame hunting lodge whose original owners hadn't weathered the latest economic downturn. After the seventy-five-acre tract with its substantial improvements slid into bankruptcy, the federal government tried to buy the land. It was one of the few inholdings within the boundaries of Yellowstone National Park, but funding requests at the Park Service moved at the pace of cold molasses, and the bankruptcy trustee finally sought another buyer. The church's cash offer had quickly been approved. The renovation of the main lodge, manager's house, twelve log cabins, and barns was now complete. And the location was perfect. The church was only four miles by gravel road from the main highway and the national park's north entrance at Gardiner. Their land was in the foothills of the mountains. It was isolated, but not remote.

Providence had led him here, no doubt. Southwestern Montana was the ideal site for his church. The ruggedness of the region drew men and women who valued their independence and had low tolerance for a government that continually tried to meddle in their affairs. They were God-seeking souls who needed a strong leader to guide them.

His reflections were interrupted by a soft knock at his door. Two tiny little girls in long cotton dresses and snow boots were standing in the doorway, smiling up at him and holding out yesterday's art project. Sister Jenny gently nudged the six-year-olds into the large office. The man's face lit up with pride and joy, and he quickly closed the distance to the shy youngsters.

"What do you beautiful girls have there?" He leaned down close to them and wrapped his arms around their shoulders. "For me? You colored those for me?"

He admired the artwork as the girls overcame their shyness and began pointing out animals, rivers, and, of course, angels. He sat them in the big chairs and let them pick a Bible story for him to recite. Their teacher beamed at her pigtailed charges and thanked him for his time as they moved out the door a few minutes later.

A thick man in a heavy coat leaned against the doorframe and watched as the children walked down the hall. "David and Goliath. Always was one of my favorites! You tell a great story." He laughed softly as he walked in to shake hands with his prophet.

"Brother Ron! You're back sooner than we thought." The Prophet shook the man's hand and then closed his other hand over it. "A successful trip?"

"A very successful trip. Walk downstairs with me and I'll show you. Came early to unload a few things—thought I could drive you down." Ron moved along the hallway to the stairs. "I see we have more children in the school now. You'll have to hire another teacher."

The older man caught up as they started down the oak stairs.

"We've also had several join the men's prayer group this month," he said. "Three served in Afghanistan. They're fine, patriotic men, seeking the Lord with all their hearts. God is bringing the right men to us."

Outside the front door, he stopped to hug one of the sisters who was standing on the wide front porch, watching the younger kids play kickball in the early-morning snow. Ron was standing beside the covered bed of his silver pickup, and the older man hurried to join him. He pulled his gray Stetson down tighter in the wind and light snow. He wished he'd taken the time to grab his coat.

Ron pulled the waterproof tarp back on several boxes labeled as Bibles and schoolbooks. He called two of the older girls over and handed them several large plastic sacks of big white teddy bears, all with *God Is Love* stenciled across their chests in pink and blue.

The Prophet was thrilled. "Give them out to all the little ones, girls! This will make their day!" His gleaming eyes turned back to the treasures his assistant brought: two more boxes to examine.

His gaze met Ron's, and the stout man grinned. "Twelve Bibles in each box, twelve bound copies of the Bill of Rights and the Constitution, $50,000 cash, and twenty pounds of Semtex."

"Hallelujah!"

CHAPTER THREE

W in had always finished projects; he wanted one job done before another was started. Of course that never worked in real life and certainly not in the Bureau. There were always starts and stops, new cases, new priorities, new leads to follow, but he tried to compensate for the uncertainty of the job by fostering a sense of completion in his private life. So when Jason's workmen had arrived at 7:30 this morning, he'd already been up for two hours, hauling in his boxes and his new purchases from Bozeman. He wanted the house finished, then he'd move on to other things.

It was still snowing off and on, although the coldest air had moved away; it was predicted to inch above freezing by late morning. The workers were putting new mirrors in the downstairs bathroom as Jason drove Win to the outskirts of Gardiner to the Yellowstone Heritage and Research Center to peruse the art and other treasures the Park Service had collected over the last zillion years at Yellowstone. Those riches were sitting unused in the basement of the modern three-story building. It seemed so wasteful to Win; they'd spent seven million on a building that would preserve paintings, drawings, and records of the historic buildings in Yellowstone National Park, but they couldn't get a few hundred thousand each year to keep those same structures from decay and decline.

"Some of these paintings were given to the park by the artists. Most hung in one of the lodges or hotels—all the way back to the late 1800s,"

Jason was saying as he keyed in the combination to a climate-controlled area. The required one course in freshman art appreciation at the University of Arkansas was the extent of Win's art education, but he did appreciate beauty when he saw it, and there was plenty of beauty sadly stored away in these vast, nondescript rooms.

Jason kept talking. "At least we have a proper place to store the art and artifacts—that's something, I guess. Look here, sir, I pulled a few paintings out of their crates last night so you could see them better. The house deserves some authentic Yellowstone art, don't you think?"

Jason's enthusiasm was contagious, and Win could have easily spent all morning sorting through the paintings, but he had other work to do. He chose a large oil painting of buffalo in the Lamar Valley to go over the fireplace mantel in the living room. It was painted by a French artist and had hung in the Old Faithful Lodge for seventy years. They picked several pieces for various rooms, mostly waterfalls and landscapes. Then Win found the bear picture. It was actually an oil painting as well, dating back to 1904, the tag said. A huge brown grizzly bear towering over a fallen elk, painted by some German guy. It was so powerful it seemed alive.

"Hey, could I hang this in the office—the FBI office?"

"That bear is totally awesome! Sure, it's government property. It has to hang in a historic building. The older agent was never interested in any of our inventory, but sure!" Jason seemed thrilled to have a prospective new project.

After they unloaded their haul back at the house, Win watched Jason pull out of the gravel parking area and was just beginning to appreciate the slightly warmer temperature, the rising cloud level, and the tapering snow flurries when the rain began. He ducked inside, where the workmen were still at their tasks, but he felt a bit in the way, so he decided to drop in on Johnson a day early. Win was annoyed that the older agent hadn't checked on him. The man knew how sick he'd been that first afternoon, yet not a word from him. And the senior resident agent should be the one showing him the ropes in his new post, not some seventeen-year-old kid who might or might not actually work for the Park Service. Hospitality was definitely not Johnson's strong suit.

The agent's office door was open. Win leaned in and knocked lightly. Johnson glanced up with a squint and a scowl. He answered the intrusion with one sentence: "It isn't Saturday yet."

Win wondered if this was his office persona—a way to hold others at a distance. It was certainly working. Win had seen brief flashes of quickness, efficiency, and focus in the agent during the episode with the suspected poacher, but he saw none of that now. Instead, he saw a graying, overweight bureaucrat hunched over paperwork in an office that was beyond cluttered.

"Hey, didn't mean to bother you—workers at my house. Thought I'd drop by and see if you wanted to catch lunch." Win hated being so deferential to this jackass, who clearly had no intention of being welcoming, but if they were going to work together for months if not years, they might as well be civil.

There was a long pause. The only sound was rain hitting windows hidden somewhere in the room behind piles of files and boxes. "Well, hell, might as well get this done now. I got the final call yesterday and I'm out of here for in-service training at Quantico for two damn weeks. You can report anything that happens, not that there'll be anything, to Jim West, our supervisor in Jackson, Wyoming."

"Does he get up here often? Any of the brass?"

Johnson snorted. "Hell, they never darken the door. No one's gonna look over your shoulder here or give a rat's ass about what you do or don't do. It's a seven-hour drive to Jackson when the park's roads are closed—about three to four in summer, with all the tourist traffic and bear jams. Takes a day to drive to Bozeman and fly down. And Denver? Our home office? Well, that's a seven-hundred-mile trip." Win saw a hint of sadness cross the man's face. Then, "We may not be on the far side of nowhere, but you can damn well see it from here."

So Johnson feels some remorse for his banishment as well. Win quickly changed gears to keep his own emotions in check. "What about the case with the poacher?"

The older agent cleared his throat. "Won't have the preliminary hearing on Bordeaux until after I get back, if they have one at all. The rangers can't find any poaching evidence." He glanced down at his desk. "The caseload's light . . . two open cases of felony drug violations, an assault case, and a theft-of-government-property investigation. I'm letting Park Service folks handle most of the legwork on those."

Win interpreted that comment as "I'm not doing any more work than I have to."

Johnson was still talking. "Your keys, phone, and codes are in an envelope on your desk. Let's go see your vehicle; it arrived yesterday. The only damn perk of this office is a good vehicle. Can't do lunch. Busy."

Win moved back into the hall and flipped on the light in the adjoining office. He stepped around boxes and retrieved a large manila envelope from atop the stacks of files on the shoddy metal desk. Johnson was already walking down the hall toward the stairs. Win pulled up his parka hood as Johnson swiped his badge on the rear exit door.

"Security system is back on for this door. It doesn't work half the time, and the front-entrance keypad was never installed."

Win saw an opening. "The assistant facilities manager offered to help with the office. Any problem with that while you're gone?"

"Knock yourself out. Just get all the old working files shredded to confidential trash, to be shipped to the Jackson Hole RA. Scan anything that needs to go into the Sentinel system. I never did upload everything to our new digital system."

New digital system? The Sentinel computerized case management system was in place long before Win joined the Bureau.

Johnson kept talking as he walked toward the vehicles. "I got written up on that at the last inspection. Damn stuff has accumulated for years. Got written up on all the technology crap and the security system too. You younger agents love that stuff. Have at it!"

Two weeks without Johnson was beginning to look real good.

Win's new ride was a dark-gray Ford Expedition. It had all the bells and whistles: FBI-encrypted digital radios, analog radios to communicate with everyone including the state police and local law enforcement agencies, and a satellite phone system. Three antennas, but two were concealed. The blue police lights were well hidden within the grill, mirrors, and back window. *Good, not too obvious.*

The SUV had Wyoming tags with the little emblem of a cowboy on a bucking horse—very inconspicuous. As Win memorized his fabricated license plate number, he smiled to himself. *Can't sneak up on the bad guys with government plates.* Johnson had already placed a Remington 870 short-barrel shotgun, an MP5 submachine gun, and extra ammo inside the SUV's metal gun safe. They spent the next fifteen minutes standing in the drizzle, checking off the truck's required equipment: raid jackets, body armor, flashlights, first aid kit, ax, rope, survival gear. All the mandatory stuff for more isolated FBI postings had to be in their proper places. Any FBI agent would know exactly where to find each piece of equipment in his vehicle. Win liked that structure. His Bureau car in Charlotte had contained a whole lot less gear, but backup in Charlotte was minutes away; backup here might be in another state.

Johnson tromped back into the stone building with hardly a parting word. Win wanted to check out other areas of Mammoth, but the rain had picked up again and the temperature was dropping instead of rising, so he camped out in the lobby of the Mammoth Hot Springs Hotel and began setting up his new Bureau phone. He called or texted anyone who could be annoyed with him for having been out of touch for days. One scolding from little brother about not calling home was enough. His melancholy mood reemerged as he keyed in contacts and skipped over *S*. No Shelby on this new phone, none of her family; even some of their mutual friends were gone. Five years in a relationship and not seeing her name in his Favorites brought the hollow feeling in his chest back with startling suddenness.

He leaned back in the chair and stared past the comfortable furniture in the vintage lobby, through the large windows, into the gray rain. It occurred to him that the low clouds were identical to the dark ones hanging over him these last several months. He'd been right in there, working with the lead agent on the biggest political corruption case on the East Coast: the Brunson case. Less than three years out of the FBI Academy at Quantico, he was making his mark—then it all fell apart and he'd been told he was lucky to still be in the Bureau. Some agents lost their jobs, others were forced to retire. There'd even been death threats. He knew he'd handled his part of the case strictly by the book, but here he was at a dead-end duty station, where the powers that be were hoping he'd flame out and quit—or worse. He just wasn't sure what worse looked like.

And Shelby. Shelby picked her timing perfectly. He'd desperately needed her support, but she'd come unraveled like a cheap sweater. *"Your career with the Bureau is over! Quit now!"* His mind's eye saw her rage, saw her shake her long blond hair back over her shoulders. *"How could you put your Bureau friends ahead of our future? We can still be together in New Orleans! My residency starts in April. Quit now!"* He could see her storm out of the apartment and slam the door as if it were yesterday.

How had she loved him for five years and not known he wasn't a quitter, or that he wouldn't turn his back on friends who needed his testimony to keep their jobs or at least keep their pensions? How did they drift so far apart that they no longer knew each other's hearts— each other's souls? He slumped farther down in the chair and stared vacantly toward the room's tall ceiling. He knew those were just the painful symptoms, the superficial torment masking the real crisis in his soul. *Have I brought this on myself by straying from God?* He closed his eyes to silence questions he couldn't yet answer. *I have to get beyond this.*

Lunch wasn't an interest any longer, so he bought peanut butter crackers and a Coke at the gift shop and drove his old SUV back to the house. He tried to dig himself out of his funk by dodging workmen and unpacking boxes in his bedroom. Two mice scurried from under the bed and into the closet, where they promptly disappeared into some secret mouse place he couldn't locate. He made a mental note to buy lots of mousetraps.

Oak dining furniture, rugs, more lamps, and a wooden antique desk and chair had appeared. Various painters, electricians, carpenters, and housekeepers were swooping through to finish numerous details. He wondered if everyone on the post got this type of service. He wondered if little Jason had an agenda. He was stacking his legal books in a tall walnut bookcase when Jason appeared in the late afternoon. When he saw the boy's eager face, he regretted his cynicism. The kid was just passionate about his job. He knew it had been far too long since he'd felt that way.

Jason carefully wiped his wet boots and walked through the house, checking the items on his clipboard. Win could tell the boy was proud of himself, and even though he hadn't fully seen the "before," he had to admit the "after" looked amazing for a 120-something-year-old house. He gave Jason the go-ahead on the FBI office makeover and smiled as the boy's face lit up. They waded through a mountain of government paperwork on employee housing, with Win marveling that he would only be paying a tiny fraction of the rent he'd paid in Charlotte.

Jason placed his paperwork into its folder as he leaned back against the kitchen counter. "Hmmm, one more thing today, sir, uh . . . I guess you noticed the mice."

"Yeah, if you could call the exterminator, I'd really appreciate it. Two mice were in the bedroom this afternoon."

"That's the issue, uh, the exterminator. Since we're on national parkland we aren't allowed to use any chemicals to get rid of bugs or rodents—environmental rules, you know. Snap traps just get rid of the stupid ones, and sticky traps are inhumane."

This conversation was not moving in the direction Win had hoped. "Is it against the park's rules to shoot them?" he asked, smiling.

Jason didn't miss a beat. "Well, maybe not technically, but—"

"I was kidding, Jason. So how am I gonna deal with the mice?"

"There's a cat that goes with this unit."

"Seriously? A cat?"

"Yeah, a great cat! Born in this house. The last tenant didn't care for cats. He wouldn't let him stay. That's why the mice have taken over. The cat moves in and the mice split. This cat's been in our heated garage for three months, waiting for the new occupant—that's you!" Jason said it as if Win had won the lottery. He was talking quickly now and walking toward the back door. "He's in my truck; brought him over for you to check out. Not allergic to cats, are you? Great cat! His name's Gruff."

"Nothing against cats, but I'm more of a dog person." *Why am I letting this teenage kid talk me into taking an animal I don't want or need?* His eye caught some movement from the corner of the kitchen floor. Well, maybe he did need it, but he sure didn't want it. "Look, I don't have any cat stuff. Food, cat box—"

"No problem. My mom sent over a whole sack of food, plus a litter box and litter. You're set for a week. You'll hardly ever see him. Big house to roam." He saw Win's hard face and dropped the charm offensive. "If you don't take him, sir, he'll have to go to the pound in Gardiner. We have two inside cats. It's here or the pound—and you know what that means." Jason looked so pitiful Win thought he might burst into tears.

Win made the mistake of pausing long enough for Jason to get the cat carrier out of his truck and onto the washing machine in the mudroom. Win leaned over to peer inside and jerked back when a large, yellow, furry mass of teeth and claws lunged against the carrier door.

"Whoa!" He looked in from a bit more distance. The big green eyes narrowed and the cat let out a long, low growl and hiss. It reminded him of Agent Johnson. No doubt the mice would move out when this big guy moved in.

Jason was standing by the door and seemed to be holding his breath.

"Alright, I'll give it a try, but just one week. And then you may be trying to find him another home. Does he bite?"

*   *   *

About the same time Friday afternoon that Win was being introduced to his cat, 449 miles by road to the southeast on the windswept Great Plains, a different meeting was about to commence. They were supposed to meet at 1800 hours at the Super Z Truck Stop off Interstate 90, one mile west of Spearfish, South Dakota, and just a few miles across the Wyoming state line. The small, wiry man was early; he always came early, couldn't be too careful these days. He pulled his dirty black Stetson down tighter and dropped his head against the wind. He was leaning against the still-warm grill of a Peterbilt 379 loaded with steel pipe destined for the North Dakota oil fields. He'd hitched a ride with the driver this morning and they'd come across two states. He pulled up the collar on his ranch jacket. The chill was setting in as the sun faded behind a wall of clouds. He nursed the rest of his beer. Better to drink it slowly; he didn't have the money to buy much more tonight.

The driver was walking toward him from the truck stop where he'd taken a shower and eaten an early dinner. "Hey, Bronte, I'm gonna get two, three hours of shut-eye in the sleeper—you can sit in the café. Don't have to stand out here in the damn wind."

The small man almost didn't respond; he'd forgotten he'd been going by the name of Bronte today. He nodded and took the last swallow of beer. "Appreciate it, but no, this is where I get off." He threw his chin toward the cab. "I'll get my gear and move on." He turned and dropped the bottle to the gravel.

"Okay, suit yourself." The driver moved faster than the smaller man expected and was climbing into the cab, blocking the steps. "I'll just hand it out to you. Hell, what you got in here? Bricks?" He passed the heavy military duffel bag down to Bronte's waiting hand and retreated into the big rig's cab.

Bronte eased the bag on down and heard the locks latch on the truck's doors. Smart man.

As he headed into the wind toward the café's white lights, he folded the nine-inch switchblade back on itself and slipped it into his jacket. Just as well, he was thinking. It might have complicated things. The men he was meeting would have money and if they didn't, well . . . something would come up. Always did.

The oily gray gravel crunched under his worn boots as he made his way past dozens of parked tractor-trailer rigs toward the front entrance of the bright café. Most of the trucks were idling, and the low rumbling noise and diesel fumes were strangely comforting. The sounds and smells took his mind back to an earlier time when he'd walked in sandy gravel past rows of tanks and armored personnel carriers, not trucks. The rumbling had been much the same, just louder; the smell of diesel and grease had been almost intoxicating in the intense heat. The screaming mortar rounds had come in just then, and nothing had been the same since. Not one damn thing.

He spotted two of them from across the lot. They were getting out of an older Ford pickup; looked like Iowa . . . no, it was Nebraska tags. Both men were tall and stout. You'd figure them to be brothers even if you didn't know they were. Both with dark crew cuts, both in combat boots, both with bad dispositions that got worse with a little drinking. He hadn't seen them in well over a year. They'd been lying real low, which meant whatever they were all meeting up for had to be worth the risk. *Them boys wouldn't be showing up here if the stakes weren't right high.* He leaned against the side of the building and dropped the duffel bag at his feet. One of the brothers raised a couple of fingers to him and nodded in recognition. The late-afternoon sun poked from around the clouds and made another stab at warming up the barren landscape, but the cold wind cancelled it out. He glanced at his watch; it was almost 6:00 p.m., 1800 hours. Bronte knew the younger man approaching him from behind. He hardly turned his head when the newcomer spoke.

"Ain't seen you since that last stint in Leavenworth. You doin' alright?" The younger man didn't wait for an answer. "This better be worth it, I come all the way from Kansas City—hell of a lot warmer down there!"

The younger guy pulled up beside the small man, and they both watched the brothers finish fueling their truck. The collar of the younger man's heavy coat didn't quite cover the dagger tattoo on the side of his thick neck. He was the only one of the group with a heavy beard, and his was striking: It was reddish orange, the same color as his short-cropped, spiked hair.

"Damn, its cold up here. . . . Where the hell is Chandler?" The redhead dropped a ratty bag on the pavement and kept talking. "Hey, man, I hear Buck, Little Man, and Pedee have already been embedded. Buck's in with some high-class security firm, and who the hell knows what Chandler's got Pedee and Little Man set up doing in that Podunk town we're headed to." The man's voice went up an octave and he grinned a sideways grin. "Yeah, boy! We're putting the band back together!" He laughed that high-pitched, evil-sounding laugh of his.

The smaller man cut his eyes toward the redhead and sighed. He was thinking, *This job better be good if I have to deal with this ass for very long. How in hell did he get out after only six years on two murders?* Some "I did it when I was so young" or some "I had a sorry childhood" lawyer excuse, he figured. Not the real reason, the "I did it 'cause I'm a raving psychopath" real reason. *Our justice system is going to hell.* He wished he had another beer.

A late-model blue Cadillac pulled into an empty spot down from them, and a well-dressed cattleman type got out of the passenger side, settling his hat. The small man generally hated surprises, but this one turned out to be appealing. He pulled himself up straight and sucked in his stomach.

"What the hell!" It was the fool redhead.

"Watch your mouth around the Prophet," the smaller man snarled.

The Prophet was pulling on a black leather coat. He was moving toward them. The brothers had parked their truck and were closing in on them—both had expectant looks on their broad faces.

Ron Chandler was grinning as he stepped out of the Cadillac and leaned an arm across the open door. "Hello, boys! Get ready to find some religion—you're fixing to join the army of the Lord!"

CHAPTER FOUR

W hoa! Geez! Whoa!" Win flattened himself against the storm door in the dim light as a huge dark shape materialized between him and his truck. A massive black head swung up as the animal rose to its full height of over six feet—it was *waaay* too close. He'd already locked the heavy wooden door at the house's rear entry and he was now trapped on the top step, unsuccessfully balancing his coffee cup in his left hand while holding the keys with his right. The bull arched its back and stretched its 2,200 pounds of pure power. *This monster probably has muscles in its ears!* Condensation rose from its dark nostrils, and it snorted a sharp warning at the intruder. It shook its head again, the menacing black horns glistening in the cold, damp air. Win was sure the dark eyes were searching for a convenient target. He froze against the aluminum storm door and held his breath as hot coffee streamed down his hand. This situation was most decidedly not covered at Quantico. *Panic button on the truck keys?* Nope, the animal was between him and the SUV; the truck alarm could stampede the creature right into him. *Shoot it?* No, he couldn't shoot the thing. . . . He probably didn't have enough firepower to bring it down, for starters, and even if he could, well, it would be downright un-American to shoot an animal in Yellowstone. *Warning shots?* Gosh, how embarrassing for the new FBI guy to wake the rangers with gunshots his first week at work. Many FBI higher-ups already thought they'd sent a loser out here—he wasn't about to prove them right this morning.

He was hoping all the reports of bison having extremely poor eyesight were true. There was no doubt if this big guy spotted him, he'd squash him like a bug. Win's knowledge of this beast extended only to the Discovery Channel, but he did remember hearing that most of the visitor injuries in Yellowstone were caused by bison, or buffalo, as he'd grown up calling them. Seconds passed, and the gurgling of the small stream and the steady drip of water off the roof were the only sounds. Then with a quick flick of its short tail and a parting snort, the bull slowly ambled away into the early light of the rainy dawn. *Okay then, time for a tactical retreat.*

"Well, Toto, we're sure not in Kansas anymore!"

The big yellow cat gave him a distrustful, quizzical look; his cat wasn't much friendlier than the huge bull. Win stood at the kitchen sink, ran cold water over his stinging hand, and dabbed the coffee off his coat sleeve. *Yes sirree, talking to a snarly cat at 5:50 a.m. on a Monday morning. . . . Highlight of my day will likely be near-death by buffalo.* He exhaled a deep sigh. *I really need to get out more.*

He'd worked all weekend and managed to clear a few paths through the upstairs storage room and the mess that would become his office. He'd made an introductory phone call to Jim West, his new supervisor at the Bureau's Resident Agency office in Jackson, which for some reason the Bureau referred to as the Jackson Hole RA. Jim seemed like a nice enough guy, but he appeared totally disinterested in anything related to Yellowstone. He clearly had bigger fish to fry dealing with DEA and an influx of Mexican meth in the Jackson area. Win knew Jim West would have heard the sordid details of his fall from grace that led to his transfer to Yellowstone, but the man had the professionalism to welcome him to the FBI's Denver Field Office. He rubber-stamped Johnson's "suggestions" that Win reorganize the satellite office and hurried off the phone to whatever issue had brought him to his office on a weekend morning.

Win had also researched the four FBI cases Johnson mentioned as being active—four very routine cases. Even as a first office agent in Charlotte, Win had handled five to seven cases of much greater complexity at a time. He made phone calls to the two Park Service special agents whom Johnson had listed as lead investigators on those active cases. *Who knew the Park Service had special agents?* He hadn't really expected them to be in their offices on a Saturday, but both agents' voice mails stated they were out of Yellowstone indefinitely, working at some national park in Alaska. *Oh, well.* It occurred to him that once the office reorganization project was completed, he could very easily die of boredom.

*   *   *

With Johnson back at the FBI Academy at Quantico for two weeks of training, Win attacked the chaos at the office with a vengeance. By Tuesday morning, Jason's craftsmen were at work performing their magic on the FBI's long-neglected office space. On Wednesday there was a break in the weather's awful snow-to-rain-to-ice routine, and Win decided it was way past time to get in some exercise over a long lunch break. The high-altitude headaches had become few and far between, and running had always cleared his mind and lifted his mood. After four and a half straight days of organizing and shredding files, he sorely needed that. He waved to the workers who were giving the wooden garage behind his house a new coat of paint as he started up the mountain highway leading past the hot springs terraces.

Win slowly jogged past the *Road Closed—No Vehicles* sign and then set a faster, steady pace up the winding mountain highway. He hoped to run two miles before he hit the snowpack. With the earbuds in, he didn't hear his phone. He was just beginning to enjoy the freedom of the run when a ranger in a white-and-green Tahoe pulled alongside him and waved for him to stop. It was the same stern-looking ranger who'd been with Chief Randall during the events of Win's first day in the park.

"Hey, see the sign back there?" Gus Jordon called out.

"It said *no vehicles!*" Win shot back, annoyed at the interruption.

"What do we have to say, *no vehicles or idiots?*" the ranger yelled back. "What do you think you look like running on a deserted road in the mountains?"

Win leaned back with his hands on his hips, trying to catch his breath. *What obscure rule have I violated now?*

The ranger answered his own question. "You look like lunch to every mountain lion or bear in the area—you can't run up here alone this time of year! You don't even have bear spray!"

"You've got to be kidding!"

"Dead serious, Sport!" Gus's tone quickly changed. "More important matters. Chief Randall sent me to get you. Couldn't reach you on your phone, but the painters at your house saw you head this way. The Secret Service has called a spur-of-the-moment powwow on a potential terrorism threat, and the Chief thought there should be some FBI presence there."

"What? I haven't heard anything . . . from our office in Jackson. . . . Someone would have called me." Win tried to slow his breathing. "I . . . I didn't get the impression Chief Randall cared much for the FBI."

"He cares even less for the Secret Service, so hop in and I'll get you back to your house. The meeting's in an hour at the Justice Center."

* * *

Win walked into the large, modern conference room at 1:00 p.m. His supervisor had been livid when Win called to tell him about the meeting. There should be FBI agents from Denver's Joint Terrorism Task Force attending, not some relatively new agent who'd only worked white-collar crime. Obviously, the Secret Service was stepping into the Bureau's jurisdiction and a turf war was brewing.

The Special Agent in Charge of the Secret Service in Montana lived up to his billing as an arrogant, condescending jerk. He wore a dark suit and drab tie. Maybe late forties, with thinning brown hair. His name was Jonathan Lomax, and Win disliked him immediately. Gus Jordon had told Win the guy was known for making a mountain out of a molehill and ramping everyone up for nothing.

"Glad you could join us, Agent Tyler. Been here since last week? Well, fine. We knew Agent Johnson was out of town. Didn't realize the Bureau had another boy up here." Lomax said "boy" with just the wrong tone, gave Win a lukewarm handshake, and dismissed him with a wave to the far side of the conference table.

Everyone in the group of seven was studying their phones and drinking coffee as they waited for the last few latecomers to show up. Win introduced himself to each person, collected their business cards, then settled in to take notes. His orders were to lay low, pay attention, and report back to Jim West ASAP when the meeting was over.

Win hadn't met any of the others except for Richard Randall, the Chief Ranger, and Gus Jordon, the Deputy Chief Ranger. The local U.S. Marshal, Paul Robinson, walked in, threw his winter coat over a chair, set his black cowboy hat on the table, and shook everyone's hand. The man looked exactly as Win pictured a U.S. Marshal from the Old West: tall and lean, with a handlebar mustache and thick, graying hair. Win wondered where he'd stashed his horse. They killed an extra five minutes waiting for the two guys from Alcohol, Tobacco and Firearms, who showed up too casual and too late to be impressive. Both in their late thirties, in jeans and windbreakers, both wearing blue ATF ball caps—they looked more like trucking-company employees than federal agents. A slight Park Service employee eased in last and found a chair next to Chief Randall. Her pale eyes darted around the intimidating group as if she were thinking of running from the room.

The Secret Service SAC finally stood and got right to the point: Three sightings of groups of armed men had been reported by Park Service employees and other credible witnesses during the last seven days. The sightings had been of twelve to fifteen individuals in the northwest part of the park, in fairly inaccessible areas. Each of the witnesses described the subjects as carrying "assault rifles or machine guns." That comment got everyone's attention and the meeting's mood took on a heavier tone. A projection screen dropped at the far end of the room, the lights dimmed, and Lomax nodded toward the nervous young woman.

"Virginia McCoy, a trail technician with the Park Service, took several photos late last week, on Friday afternoon. Ms. McCoy, give us a little background on the photos before we put them up."

She took a deep breath and gave them a brief report. She'd been snowshoeing while checking the condition of cross-country ski trails when she saw movement on the opposite ridge, less than three hundred feet away. She'd taken the photos with her phone in light snowfall. None of the armed men acknowledged her, although she knew they saw her—the area she was traversing was high meadow; there was no cover. She seemed embarrassed that she hadn't called out to them—questioned who they were, why they were there. She admitted their numbers and their armament made her fearful. She said the men had moved on snowshoes in single file along the opposite ridge and then disappeared from sight. Six grainy photos of several men atop a snow-covered ridge appeared on the screen.

There was an audible response from the group of federal officers when the photos appeared. Everyone was apparently expecting to be underwhelmed by the Secret Service's evidence of bad guys roaming the hills of the country's most storied national park. The photos were chilling. The men in the pictures wore military-style camouflage uniforms with backpacks. They carried rifles similar to AR-15s—those guys were not out elk hunting. Each of the group of twelve had a mask over his face and a formidable bearing. They looked like the real deal.

A second group of photos had been taken by two members of a bear research group working ten miles south of the spot where McCoy took her photos. Those pictures were taken mid-week but only received by a Park Service ranger on Saturday. Their quality was poorer, but the pictures clearly showed fifteen men in military uniforms with packs and assault rifles. The researchers told the ranger they were within one hundred yards of the men in a remote area near a backcountry trail.

A snowplow operator and his assistant also reported a brief sighting at mid-afternoon on Monday, less than forty-eight hours earlier. No photos were obtained, but they counted fifteen individuals with military-type equipment about six miles northeast of the bear researchers' position, in an area of mountain roads they plowed every other day.

In no case had the unidentified men acknowledged the witnesses or confronted anyone.

Lomax asked the group if they had questions for the trail technician. There were several general questions, then Win asked the ones he saw as obvious.

"How often in April do you hike that particular trail, Ms. McCoy?" he asked.

"Once a week, normally Friday if the weather's okay. The snow is still deep in that area, so we snowshoe in three miles and then backtrack to the road."

"You said 'we.' Were you alone when you saw those individuals?"

"No, this time of year we always travel in teams. Ben Okahio was with me."

"What did you carry with you that Friday—anything noisy?" Win saw Chief Randall's face and the U.S. Marshal's eyes. They both knew where he was going with this.

"Yes, we take a light chainsaw to clear any fallen timber or limbs off the trails. That's why we go up there."

"Did you use the chainsaw near the time you saw those guys? If so, when?"

McCoy thought for a second. "Yes, sir, maybe ten or fifteen minutes before we saw them."

"Those are all the questions I have. Oh, and I probably wouldn't have called out to them either. You were seriously outgunned. Good job getting the photos." Win gave her an approving nod.

SAC Lomax quickly dismissed the trail technician and assured her he was "ninety-nine percent sure" the armed men she'd seen were U.S. Army Special Forces on a training exercise. "Nothing to worry about at all," he said. "Just let someone in Park Service law enforcement know if you see anything else out of the ordinary. Nothing to be concerned about," he repeated as he escorted her from the room.

A moment later, Lomax leaned against the closed door and looked back at the photos on the screen. "Well, folks, we're one hundred percent sure they're not our military. We have several high-level dignitaries scheduled to visit the park soon, and the Secret Service is the lead agency for their protection. Of special concern is the mid-May dedication of the Saul Benjamin Cohn Monument by the Israeli Ambassador.

Our Ambassador to Israel will also be in attendance, along with several Senators and cabinet-level folks. As you may know, the Cohn Monument is to be dedicated to one of the earliest Jewish explorers in Yellowstone. The dedication site is in the general area of the park where the sightings of armed men have occurred. Several of the white nationalist and separatist groups are strongly anti-Semitic. There's already been considerable online chatter from right-wing extremist groups about soiling an American park with a Zionist monument." He paused for a bit of dramatic effect. "Any one of those visiting VIPs would be a high-value target. We may have a real problem, folks."

Lomax took a chair and kept talking. "We'll hand out enhanced copies of the photos and our initial analysis of the armed men. Locational maps are in the handouts." He scanned the group. "Any thoughts?"

Chief Randall pointed out that the lead man in the enhanced photos appeared to be the same individual, and that he resembled a suspected poacher named Luke Bordeaux. "No way to be absolutely certain because of the distance and the masks, but the person in the photos has the same build as Bordeaux. Bordeaux also knows the northern part of the park and its surrounding national forests like the back of his hand," the Chief concluded.

The U.S. Marshal spoke next. "Agent Tyler, you asked the young lady some interesting questions. What were you getting at?"

"Well, it seems to me that whoever they are, they're moving in remote locations, yet in areas where they expect to be seen. And not just be seen, but seen by two credible witnesses in each instance," Win said. "They would have heard Ms. McCoy's chainsaw and could have avoided detection. The trail technicians were in a predictable location, and so were the snowplow operator and his spotter. An approaching snowplow could have been heard from a mile away and easily avoided. I assume the bear researchers also make their locations known to someone. In each instance there were two witnesses in locations that, while remote, could be predicted."

"What significance does two witnesses have?" one of the ATF agents asked.

"It's scriptural. It's in the Bible. If they're part of a domestic militia having a religious foundation, such as God's Sword or the Righteous Brotherhood, they'd base everything on scriptural dogma. If their mission was to be seen, they'd want it grounded in Scripture, so there would need to be at least two witnesses to each occurrence. There would also need to be three sightings, because the number three signifies completeness—a completed mission."

There was a very long pause after Win completed his analysis. SAC Lomax sighed. "Or it's a coincidence there were two witnesses to each of three sightings. It makes no sense they'd want to be spotted."

After hashing it out for an hour, the group agreed that there was a very real possibility some domestic terrorist group, or at the very least militia wannabes, were in a position to cause damage to the interests of the United States. Something had to be done about it without causing panic among the thousands of tourists who'd be descending on Yellowstone in the near future. It was decided that ATF and the U.S. Marshals Service would run their traps and see if any of their informants had intel on a new threat moving into the area. The Secret Service would work to get drones and other intelligence assets into the park to better assess the danger. Since it was possible one of the armed men was Bordeaux, the Park Service and FBI would focus on him, since they'd recently filed charges against him.

Chief Randall summarized their problem. "Bordeaux is out on bail on poaching and firearms violations, but we honestly don't have much of a case. A bear ate the evidence before we could get a slug for ballistics to work with on the poaching charge, and we can't make the case he was shooting at us unless we can prove he was targeting someone. With our evidence so weak on those charges, I don't think we could get a search warrant to go on his property."

"We need to move on this now." Lomax was anxious and it showed. "Is there no way we can get to him?"

"I could drop in on him for a visit. I just moved here." Every head in the room turned toward Win. It seemed so simple to him, just drop by; people back home wouldn't be surprised. Apparently not so out West.

"Do you know what you're saying?" It was one of the ATF guys. "This guy may be crazy. He could be harboring a group of heavily armed whackos. And it's almost impossible to run effective backup for anyone out here in the sticks."

Lomax stared hard at Win. "You've been on duty here less than a week? Correct me if I'm wrong, but I'm guessing you have no specialized training in this type of work."

"Hold on there, Lomax." It was Chief Randall coming to Win's defense. "I'm not so sure this is a bad idea. Agent Tyler handled himself extremely well against Bordeaux last week; it could have easily gotten ugly. Bordeaux had me pinned with a rifle and Agent Tyler talked him down. He's about the same age as Bordeaux, and they're both from the same part of the country. Bordeaux wasn't threatening toward him." He looked at the others around the long table. "I wish there was another way, but I don't see any other good options—we need some intel and quick. We have nearly four million people coming to this park in the next four months, and we have to know if we really do have a problem."

The Chief paused to let the group digest that, then he continued. "Bordeaux lives about three and a half miles northeast of Mammoth on an inholding within the park boundary. Our agency can help with backup, but there's no way to conduct surveillance on his house without being seen. Not with this time crunch. It would be blind going in there, but it may be worth the risk. I say we go in this afternoon, if Agent Tyler is volunteering."

So much for Win's orders to lay low in the meeting—it appeared that Special Agent Winston Tyler had volunteered.

CHAPTER FIVE

Win changed from suit and tie into jeans, flannel shirt, boots, and parka, and was in Chief Randall's conference room at the Park Service's huge stone Administration Building within thirty minutes. Win's supervisor, Jim West, came on the video feed and Chief Randall briefly explained the situation to him. Jim West was not a happy camper. He was furious the Bureau was being placed in a highly unpredictable situation without time to plan—no way to jump through the hoops to get formal approval from the field office in Denver. Jim said he'd call their bosses, but without more information they'd likely defer to the agent on the ground. That meant if Win was willing, it was a go.

I need to prove myself, a small voice whispered in Win's head. Another voice cautioned him not to be stupid, not to be reckless. He ignored the internal warning and nodded to Chief Randall. "I'll do it."

There was no way to wear a wire because of the distances involved, nor was there time to position a support team near the Bordeaux house without being seen. Those were the conclusions of the group of green-and-gray-clad rangers who were huddled together at the rear of the conference room. Aerial maps of the forty acres the Bordeaux owned showed a house, a barn, and a couple of mobile homes, all sitting on a plateau surrounded by dense woods. The gravel access road dead-ended at the house after meandering for over two miles from the highway. It was three miles to the nearest neighbor. The Yellowstone River was one-quarter mile north of the house, in a deep ravine. One of the rangers pointed out the obstacles to Win on the aerials. He remarked that if Win had to get away from the house on foot and Bordeaux pursued, Win would be toast. *Great confidence builder,* Win thought.

The rangers who were most familiar with Bordeaux were in Grand Teton National Park doing search-and-rescue training, but the folks who were briefing Win said Bordeaux had lived on the land for about five years with his wife and one or two kids. He drove a late-model Ford F-150 twin-cab pickup, and his wife drove a smaller truck. He'd worked as a commercial hunting and backcountry guide, and although he'd lost his guide license about a year ago, he had no criminal record. He was an expert marksman and was known to have a quick temper. *Terrible combination,* Win was thinking.

There were nearly fifty permanent law enforcement park rangers stationed in Yellowstone, and it seemed like a good number of them were milling around outside as Gus, Chief Randall, and Win walked out of the building to Win's SUV. The Chief patted Win on the shoulder and told him not to take any chances. "Turn around and drive out if it doesn't feel right."

"If you need backup and can't get to your truck's satellite phone, dial 911 on your cell phone. The call will go directly to the park's call center," Gus Jordon remarked as Win climbed into his new SUV.

"Cell service out there?"

"Naw, probably not, but I thought it might make you feel better," the seasoned ranger quipped. "We'll sit along the highway. There'll be two other units near Gardiner and some of our Special Response Team here with the helicopter. I don't know how long you southern boys like to visit, but you should be getting to his place about 1700 hours, and if you aren't out of there in four hours, at 2100, we will come in. Follow my rig on the highway, I'll pass the road to his house and hit my signal. Buy you a drink later?"

"Sure, thanks." Win felt the comfortable rumble of the SUV's big engine come to life as he nodded back at the ranger. He was certain the guy knew he was working hard to put up a good front. *Putting up a good front—story of my life.* He tried to counter the insecurity he suddenly felt with logic: *They have confidence in you, you're well trained for this. You are ready.* The thing was, he didn't feel ready. He'd spent most of his short career with the Bureau shuffling papers and solving bank and securities fraud. Yes, he'd helped solve some important cases, and yes, he'd saved the citizens from some scumbags, but those scumbags weren't terribly dangerous—those criminals didn't carry guns. As he followed Gus's Park Service Tahoe down the mountain toward Gardiner, he quoted Scripture under his breath: *"The wicked flee when no one pursues, but the righteous are bold as a lion."* Problem was, he didn't feel particularly righteous either.

The nicer weather was holding for the moment. The temperature must have been near fifty, and the low clouds were showing signs of breaking up. Win tried to keep his mind on the weather, the landscape, or the road. He told himself he needed to be calm and focused when he got to the house. *Just drop in on him.* It had sounded like such a good idea at the time. His second thoughts were tying his stomach in knots.

At the bottom of the long mountain, the ranger's Tahoe hit a straight stretch of highway and its right signal briefly flickered. Win turned and crossed a short wooden bridge. The winding dirt and gravel road to Bordeaux's house was in bad shape from the spring thaw. The first mile was barren scrub grass and low shrubs that were the same gray-brown color as the muddy road. The narrow track then disappeared into a dense forest. Lodgepole pine, maybe? He made a mental note to learn the names of a few western trees. The climb up the hill was not steep, just steady, and the road improved once he reached an upland plateau.

He came upon the house quicker than he expected. The ranch-style frame house was sitting at the edge of a stand of towering evergreen trees. It looked older and needed paint, but it wasn't shabby. A thin cloud of smoke was coming from a stone chimney, and the lights were on in the deep shade of the trees. The yard wasn't much and there was no landscaping, but it was tidy. He could see covered porches on the front and south sides. The top of a barn was visible to the rear of the house, but trees blocked the view of the mobile homes. There was no sign of a person or animal. *Surely the man has a dog.*

He pulled up beside a small dirty pickup of some type; the larger truck was not in sight. *Maybe Bordeaux isn't home.* He turned off the ignition and scanned the yard as he let the occupants prepare for company, since he'd arrived unannounced. No one came to the door. He reached under his coat to his right side for the comforting feel of his Glock as he opened the door to step out of the truck. Every sense was focused on sounds, movement, anything out of the ordinary. He heard only a squirrel in the trees to his left and the sharp popping of the SUV's hot engine; he smelled only the pine and the woodsmoke from the chimney. He stepped off the running board and closed the truck's door loudly so that anyone inside the house would hear.

A large woodpile was to the left of the house, and a chopping block with a chunk of wood sat on top. A heavy ax was embedded in the larger block of firewood; several pieces of split wood had fallen to the side. Only a lazy man would leave his wood scattered with the ax out. Judging from the appearance of the house and yard, Luke Bordeaux wasn't a lazy man. A sick feeling swept through Win's stomach as he realized someone had to have been chopping wood in the last few minutes, and someone was now standing less than twenty feet behind him.

He froze in place. He still had one hand on the side of the truck, and he kept it there. He could see Bordeaux in his side mirror. The man was directly behind him with a rifle pointed at his back. Win moved his left hand slowly away from his body and reminded himself to breathe.

"Not very neighborly to be holding a gun on company, Luke." He didn't move as he said it, and he tried again to remember to breathe. He was surprised his voice was steady despite his fear. "Just came by for a friendly visit, I don't know many folks out here yet." The gun behind him didn't move. For some reason, it occurred to Win that he'd served nearly three years in the FBI in Charlotte and he'd never seen a gun pulled in a hostile situation. He'd been in Yellowstone a little more than a week and it had already happened twice.

"I don't have many friendly visits from Federals out here," Luke softly replied.

Well, that's probably true, Win supposed.

"Friendly visit?" Luke's tone was biting. "I don't reckon that's right. I figure you come snooping around to see what you can get on me since you've got nothin' with that last foolishness up at Mammoth."

"That could be it, I'm not gonna lie to you, but apparently that ain't working for me, so how 'bout you put the gun down and we talk."

"I'm talking just fine. . . . Don't you move those hands, boy."

Win had always been able to talk with anybody—he'd prided himself on that ability. He was afraid this was gonna put that to the test. "Luke, has anyone ever told you it's a federal offense to point a loaded gun at an FBI agent?"

"You wanna find out if it's loaded! Out here, it don't make nobody any difference iffen you shoot trespassers! You see the 'No Trespassing' sign comin' in?" The man's voice was louder now.

"C'mon, you can't shoot someone for driving to your house! No place has laws like that!" *Man, I hope I'm right—could the law be that skewed out West?*

"You'd better be coming up with a real good reason why you're standing in my driveway, boy!"

Win's palms were starting to sweat and Bordeaux's tone was getting harsher. Win needed to stay calm, but fear was fighting him for control. He could taste the bitterness in his mouth. "Quit calling me 'boy'! I've heard that once too many times today! Put down the gun and I'll go back where I came from!"

"Might be a bit late fer that, Win Tyler!" Luke was advancing from behind him, quick as a cat. Win whispered a silent prayer.

* * *

The answer to Win's prayer came in a screaming, laughing little whirlwind racing across the yard to his truck. She gripped his pants leg and squealed with delight as only a three-year-old can. Right behind her was a whooping little boy in an Indian bonnet swinging a wooden hatchet. Win immediately saw the gun barrel drop in the mirror. He went down on one knee and grabbed the hand of the tiny girl.

"Well, well, now! Aren't you cuter than a speckled pup!"

She grinned, hid her face in her free hand, and swung her dark ponytail with delight. Win let out a deep sigh of relief and smiled into her flushed face.

"Who are you, darlin'?" She transformed into sudden shyness and studied her feet.

"Tell the gentleman your name, baby."

Luke was now standing beside Win, as calm and polite as could be. Out of the corner of his eye, Win saw the front door open and a tall young woman step out and call to the wild little Indian. This could be a cordial visit among friends anywhere, except that the man had just slung an assault rifle over his shoulder. Win turned his attention back to the little girl, who'd managed to answer "Abby" and then dissolve into a puddle of giggles.

"How old are you?"

Three little fingers went up and she beamed at him. "Three! Nigh onto four!"

"Luke, it's nearly time for supper. . . . Does the gentleman want to stay for supper? We have plenty," the tall woman called from the porch.

Well, at least part of the Bordeaux family still has their manners, Win thought. Luke gave Win a hard look as he straightened up. Little Abby immediately reattached herself to his pants leg, hiding from her hatchet-waving big brother.

"Expecting anyone else?" Win asked. "I'd hate to intrude."

"No, not as I know." Bordeaux shifted the rifle's strap on his shoulder. "But then . . . I wasn't expecting you."

* * *

Three hours later they were sitting in their coats on the south porch, with the side door to the house cracked just enough to hear if the kids awoke and called out. Win was cradling a cup of very hot coffee. Luke got up to stir the coals and add a log to the fire he'd built earlier, in the pit beyond the porch. The clouds had broken for the first time since Win had been in Yellowstone, and the stars were so bright and close they didn't seem real.

As he sank into the warmth of his heavy coat, he thought back on the evening. He'd felt dishonest being in their home at first, but Ellie Bordeaux was raised proper—she'd welcomed him with a disarming southern hospitality that set him at ease within minutes. Win's grandmother used to say any southern girl worth her salt should be able to entertain the President or the Queen of England if they dropped by unannounced. Ellie Bordeaux was definitely worth her salt. She'd offered him sweet tea or coffee even before he'd finished wiping his boots on the front mat.

Their house was warm and cozy; it smelled of cornbread and simmering stew. His eyes had taken in the main room, kitchen, and adjoining dining room in one casual sweep. There was the kids' crude crayon art on the refrigerator door, clean floor and rugs, relaxed furniture, and flames licking at a single log in the huge stone fireplace. He saw books that looked well read rather than placed for decoration, framed pictures of the children and of family back home. A half-finished puzzle was on the hardwood floor near the television, and toys were stacked under the coffee table. Win felt comfortable with the lack of pretense.

He had to make a conscious effort to keep an investigator's open mind. A heavy camouflage coat hung next to the rear door, its pattern perfectly matching those of the armed men in the photos he'd seen hours earlier. He'd watched Luke put away the Wilson Combat Recon Tactical Rifle—an expensive precision weapon identical to the one carried by the lead man in the photos. There was no doubt Luke Bordeaux had been trooping around the forests of Yellowstone leading a lethal-looking platoon. The question now was why.

He'd felt Bordeaux's wary eyes following him, even as the man marshaled the children to clean up before supper. He felt the dark eyes on him as he bowed his head for Abby's big brother's lengthy stab at saying grace. He had to bite his lip to keep from laughing as the five-year-old told God how his life would improve if only he had a puppy. When Ethan finally pronounced "Amen," Win raised his head to see Luke grinning at his little son—then a nod and a quick smile toward him. The man had decided to call a unilateral truce for the night. Luke Bordeaux transitioned into the perfect host.

Ellie was a very good cook, but Win found himself wondering if the thick elk stew was the byproduct of a legal hunt. He had to continually remind himself to ease up, to not get too caught up looking for hidden crimes. Let them reveal what they would. As the evening went on, it became easier. Win played his horsey kid games with little Abby and Ethan. He watched as Luke read to them before they went to bed. Luke and Ellie both seemed to be good parents, attentive and gentle. Intellectually, he knew better than to let that sway his opinion of their overall character. Some of the cruelest gangsters and Nazis had reportedly been caring parents—still, on the surface, these folks seemed really decent.

"You must have young children." Ellie had smiled at him as he bounced Abby on his knee for at least the tenth time during the games.

"No, no children, but my younger brother, Blake, has four-year-old twin boys and a two-year-old girl. I try to be a good uncle, but I don't see them as often as I'd like because of my job." He remembered Shelby used to say he was a kid magnet. She hadn't really wanted children—said they'd interfere with her medical career. *Strange that thoughts of Shelby would drift through my mind tonight.*

Win and Luke looked over a compound bow Luke was making and went through the list of who they knew or knew of in their respective states, where they'd both hunted or fished, and when they'd attended major college games. It was a comfortable ritual establishing them as Sons of the South—it set out common denominators that kept them both rooted in a homeland far away from the barren hills and snow-topped mountains of this place.

"Your name's Bordeaux, that's French. But you don't have the Cajun accent."

Luke shrugged. "Daddy was Cajun. Ellie's folks are mostly Cajun, but we both grew up over 'round Ferriday. Not much French influence on that side of the state. Just talk like a Louisiana country boy, I reckon."

Ellie chimed in. "Don't let him fool you—he can drop back into Cajun talk when he's around his daddy's people. I can't even understand him!" She flashed Luke a playful smile.

Win had formed some conclusions about Luke Bordeaux early on. The guy was sharp, real sharp. He appeared outgoing and was probably fun loving and social. He seemed to have the Cajun *"Laissez les bons temps rouler"*—"Let the good times roll"—attitude. But there was a tension beneath the surface that made Win wonder if his initial impression of Luke's easygoing nature was misplaced. And the guy was definitely physically imposing. He was about Win's size, but he had a palpable aura of strength and quickness about him. Win had a tendency to judge other men's appearance and temperament by what Shelby would say about them. She'd always had an opinion on such things. As the evening wound down, he wasn't real sure what she'd say about Luke Bordeaux—maybe that he was intriguing, possibly that he was edgy, certainly that he was good-looking, in a Caribbean pirate sort of way. For sure that he was deceptively intense.

Earlier, Win had asked about living in Montana, and Ellie said it was sometimes hard and sometimes wonderful, just like life anywhere, she supposed. Her mother had told her to bloom where she was planted. She wanted so badly to do that, but she'd found it hard to feel included since she and the children spent part of each year back in Louisiana. The new church they'd begun attending this month was helping, she'd said.

"So where are y'all going?" Win asked her.

"Prophet Daniel Shepherd's new church outside Gardiner, the Arm of the Lord Church. They're Luke's clients—ahhh, becoming his friends, I suppose. They invited us. I've got some literature on it. It's a small congregation, but it's growing." Luke took the flyer from Ellie's hand, giving her a warning look, but handed it to Win, who scanned it quickly.

"I don't think it would fit your style, boy. It's working-class people who don't see no need for government interference in their lives."

Win's eyes narrowed at Luke's insult. Thankfully, Ethan made a timely escape from bed and had to be rounded up. The uncomfortable moment passed.

Win switched his focus back to the present and watched the red sparks fly from the firepit through the steam rising from his coffee. The sparks seemed to melt into the star field above. The adjectives coming to his mind weren't adequate: *awesome, magnificent . . . spectacular?*

One of the children cried out and Ellie motioned Luke up. "Your turn." She smiled at him, and he touched her shoulder lightly as he went inside. Win envied them that casual intimacy. He felt very relaxed for a moment and then very sad. He was a force of destruction here. He was an adversary.

It was as if she could read his thoughts when she spoke. "My husband is a good man. He's doing the best job he knows how to take care of us. He's bitter toward the government about losing his guide license last year. . . . He hasn't made peace with it yet. So you can't be anything 'cept his enemy, and his enemy has to be my enemy. Do you understand?"

She was sitting only a few feet from Win on the porch, and he realized how beautiful she was in the firelight. Her hair was nearly as black as Luke's and fell well below her shoulders. She had an almost-olive complexion, with the high cheekbones, fine features, and deep-brown eyes common among Louisiana's Cajun women. She also had their fiercely independent nature. She was warning him off—she would do nothing to compromise her relationship with Luke. She would not be a source of information.

She didn't give him time to answer her question when she continued, "Since the children and I came back from home a few weeks ago, it's been different. Luke has more of a purpose and is doing more of the things he loves now. His friends may not be the ones I'd choose in every way, but they're God-fearing men."

Win knew exactly which "friends" she was taking about.

"Ellie, my grandmother, who was far wiser than me, would say that God-loving men are far better than God-fearing men. Some situations aren't as they first appear. I don't want either one of you to come to any harm. Test the spirits and see if those men are good or evil."

"And you, Win Tyler, which one are you?"

Before Win could wrap his mind around that rather heavy question, Luke came through the door with Abby bundled in a blanket and handed her off to Ellie. "Here, Mama, this one won't go to sleep," he whispered to her.

Abby spotted Win. "I like you best!" She squealed and grabbed for him as he playfully dodged back in his chair, thankful the dark mood had lifted.

"Best of what, lil darlin'?" Win asked her.

"Best of Daddy's friends! You happy! You good! Be my friend?" She sang it over twice like a song, and he put his hand on her head and told her he would. He looked at Ellie's face. Even in the flickering firelight he could see that she looked troubled.

Win glanced at his watch and realized he was pushing it on time. He thanked Ellie again for the great dinner, and he and Luke stepped off the porch and walked out of the firelight into the darkness toward his truck.

Luke was talking softly. "Been nice having someone from back home come over. Good fer Ellie and the kids. But you ain't gonna be safe droppin' by fer a while—neither snooping nor visiting."

"Luke, I know you're trying to make a living, but you need to know who you're dealing with—"

"You're fishin', you don't know nothing."

"I may be fishing, but if we're gonna talk in idioms here, you're playing with fire and I think you know it or at least suspect it. You've got a great family. Think about them." Win handed him a business card. "My personal cell phone number is on the back, if you want to call it instead of a government phone. We pay for information."

"Yeah, and you can bet I ain't a snitch." Luke dropped the card.

Win didn't want to see an example of Luke's temper. He lowered his voice and eased his tone. "I know. I know. Just want you to think about what you may be getting yourself and your family into, that's all."

He retrieved his gun and his phones from the front seat where he'd left them when he was invited into their home. He holstered the hand-gun as he got into the truck.

"I appreciate you not shooting me this afternoon. . . . Other than that, this has been the most hospitality anyone has shown me since I've been out West. Take care of yourself, Luke."

"You too, Win Tyler."

*   *   *

Gus and his three guys were waiting in the Tahoe behind a low rise along the highway. Win lowered his window and nodded in greeting as he pulled close beside them.

"Well, Sport, you cut it pretty close. They had the rotors turning on the chopper," Gus remarked. "Glad you're back in one piece. The Chief and all the heavy hitters are waiting for your debrief back at the office. Follow us." Gus pulled his vehicle away, and Win tried to sort out his conflicted feelings on the short drive to Mammoth. He thought back to little Abby's song and wondered, *Am I happy? Am I good?*

CHAPTER SIX

During the debrief, Win had shocked the group with the news of Prophet Daniel Shepherd's cult encamped four miles from the park's north entrance. Well, actually he'd shocked everyone except Gus and Chief Randall, who'd been dealing with the church since it purchased the inholding within the park over a year ago. The Park Service folks had no idea the "church" was likely a front for criminal activity, but Daniel Shepherd's various churches had been on the FBI's terrorism watch list for years. Win knew little about domestic terrorist groups, but even he'd heard of this guy. Shepherd was a hate-mongering proponent of the anti-government New America Movement—operating under the guise of religion. He'd once been based in South Dakota but had dropped out of sight months ago. He was former military, and a high percentage of his cult's membership through the years had been disenchanted ex-servicemen. There'd historically been a strong criminal element in the group; they were suspected of carrying out bank robberies and other illegal activities to support their operations. The Arm of the Lord Church was apparently Shepherd's latest enterprise, and no one in federal law enforcement was jumping up and down to welcome them to the neighborhood.

Over the following hours, the senior levels of several federal agencies fought among themselves over the extent of the threat that the armed men in Yellowstone posed. Win was learning that politics often trumped common sense when it came to such things. The FBI would normally be the lead agency in any perceived threat involving domestic terrorism, but the Bureau's bosses at the Department of Justice were reluctant to get involved in a situation that could appear to infringe on religious freedom, even if the centerpiece of that religious freedom involved yahoos with semiautomatic rifles and a history of violent crime. So the DOJ kicked the prospective investigation over to the Department of Homeland Security, where the Secret Service brass began to squabble about the budget issues related to bringing aerial surveillance assets into the area. The U.S. Marshals Service was relegated to running warrant checks on anyone remotely involved in the church group. The Interior Department's National Park Service was totally sidelined—no one was even including them in the conversation.

Thursday afternoon they got a bit of a break. ATF had an informant come through who confirmed there was a well-equipped militia of at least thirty men drilling on the land owned by the Arm of the Lord Church. The militiamen were all former military and employed residents of the area.

The bigger news was what the snitch wasn't saying. The ATF informant refused to turn over the dirt on four additional men who were now living in the mobile homes on the Bordeaux property. The informant told his ATF handler that those four men were the real heavyweights, but he was demanding more money before he began naming names. Two possibilities: The informant could be talking big to leverage more cash out of the government, or the long-suspected criminal element behind Daniel Shepherd's cult could be sitting in the park's backyard. Unfortunately, there was too little evidence of wrongdoing to obtain a court order for a Title III, so the Bureau couldn't conduct phone taps or any type of invasive surveillance.

The FBI's Denver Field Office, which would ultimately be held accountable for whatever happened, decided to at least open a preliminary investigation and run limited ground surveillance on the Bordeaux, Daniel Shepherd, and some of the church members. So within twelve hours of Win's contact at Bordeaux's home, eight agents from the Denver office were on loose surveillance detail around Gardiner and Mammoth Hot Springs.

* * *

Before dawn broke on Friday, Win was jogging up the stairs to his office. He was on a mission. He waved a half-hearted greeting to one of the surveillance guys, who'd set up shop in Johnson's renovated office, and started another pot of coffee in the gleaming new break room. Johnson was scheduled back a week from Monday. When he arrived, progress on the office might come to a screeching halt. In less than one week they'd made tremendous strides on the renovation, and Win wanted to keep the momentum going. As an added bonus, the near-frantic construction made it far easier for him to dodge the Denver agents and politely decline their offers to socialize. He was sure they knew he'd been shipped here on a disciplinary issue—no one transferred to Yellowstone voluntarily. He'd lectured himself this morning for his lack of courage in interacting with them, for his refusal to face what he figured was their veiled judgment of his failures, but his self-lecture did no good. He kept his distance.

During his digging through the files, Win discovered that the FBI had leased the entire Corps of Engineers Building from the Park Service the year after the 9/11 attacks. Back then, Bureau offices were expanding to meet what was perceived as an impending global terrorism threat and the FBI's isolated Yellowstone satellite office was established. There were never enough felony cases in the park to justify one permanent FBI agent, much less two, but as in most government operations, once money was appropriated, the funding continued. The Yellowstone office became the FBI's dumping ground for unwanted agents who couldn't be fired for whatever reason but certainly weren't welcome in the mainstream Bureau. One long winter in this isolated place with nothing productive to do had been enough to convince most of Win's predecessors to resign and seek employment elsewhere. Johnson was an exception. He stayed for years and did next to nothing. Win thought that was the saddest situation of all.

Having the entire building under FBI control was a huge advantage for Win's plan to meet Bureau standards for office security and utility. Jason's carpenters and tradesmen were converting unused space to extra offices, a communications room, a break room, and a locker room. The original historic courtroom was being renovated into a conference room. Jason came through with antique furnishings that had been stored and forgotten. Historic artwork would hang in every room. Win could expand the FBI's usable office space from three cluttered second-story rooms to the entire old building by removing a few walls, getting rid of years of accumulated hard files and unused junk, and utilizing twelve-hour shifts from a group of very talented craftsmen.

It was shaping up to be an amazing transformation in such a short time. Agent Johnson would think he was in the wrong building when he came back to Mammoth. *No, he won't think that.* Yesterday they'd affixed a shiny brass plate to the front entrance of the building. It proudly proclaimed: *Federal Bureau of Investigation – Yellowstone National Park.*

Win was hanging his framed diplomas and cleaning drywall dust off the bookcase in his personal office when Jim West called at eight o'clock. Twenty minutes later, Win found himself pulling into sleepy downtown Gardiner in an attempt to develop Ellie Bordeaux as a source. He'd had very little training in targeting an informant, and he really didn't have a clue what he was going to say. The idea was to develop the trust of the prospective "confidential human source," as the Bureau called its informants. Win could say nothing about the situation or the potential case. No questions, no disinformation—the Bureau's way of saying *no lies.* Ellie needed to think the contact was purely coincidental. Of course, nothing was ever coincidental with the FBI; an agent had been trailing Ellie every time she'd left home since Win's visit at their house two days ago.

There was little traffic on Gardiner's Park Street. Few of the storefront buildings had come to life for the day. Much of the little town wouldn't wake from its winter hibernation until more tourists began arriving next month; only a few places were open for business. Win entered Hampton Hardware and the soft jingle of bells announced his presence. He pushed his hat back and nodded to the woman behind the front counter. He breathed in the mixed smells of cattle feed, weed killer, and lumber as he scanned the cluttered aisles of dry goods and tools for Ellie Bordeaux.

She was in a conversation with a second clerk near the back of the store. He watched her as she tucked a strand of silky hair behind her ear, cocked her head, and furrowed her brow as if trying to understand what the thin young man was telling her. She looked good. When she glanced up and noticed him, he had no trouble producing a genuine smile. She was carrying her tan parka and wearing a heavy, blue flannel shirt over a white top; her faded Wranglers were tucked into snow boots. *Yep,* he thought again, *she looks real good.*

"Hey, Ellie, building something?" He moved down the aisle next to them.

"Hi, yeah. Luke promised Abby and Ethan a tree house this summer, so I'm starting to gather the materials." There was no suspicion in her eyes, no distrust. She glanced down at the paper in her hand, "Not sure what Luke meant when he wrote down these six . . . nail sizes? And the young man here"—she nodded to the clerk, who looked lost—"he just started in hardware and doesn't know either. Had no idea there were so many kinds of nails."

"Want me to see what I can do with it?" He gave the clerk an *I've got this* look.

She smiled back and handed him the crumpled sheet of paper with Luke's very precise list of building materials.

"Okay, uh-huh, one pound coated sinker twenty-penny, one pound exterior galvanized sixteen-penny . . ." Win efficiently moved through the open nail bins, sacking and weighing each type. "Nails done!" He glanced back at the list. "What about the hinges, lumber, and other stuff?"

"Just the nails today. I'm getting what we need little by little. Working part-time as a substitute teacher at the elementary school. Things are tight, but maybe by summer . . ." She let that trail off. She blushed and dropped her head slightly when she realized she'd admitted their poor financial situation to him. Then her pride kicked in. She raised her chin and forced a smile. "You don't want to hear about that. Tell me what you're looking for."

What am I looking at? What am I looking for? Thoughts floated in his mind for a millisecond before he got himself back on track. "Embarrassed to admit it, but I'm shopping for cat toys. Cat came with my place, and I'm afraid he might be bored." It sounded lame, but Win was thinking it wasn't a lie—he'd intended to get Gruff something to play with, since the cat wanted nothing to do with him.

Ellie's good humor quickly returned, and she helped him pick out several silly cat toys. They talked about the kids for a couple of minutes, then they paid for their purchases and he walked her out to her pickup. A cold east wind off the Absaroka Mountains had kicked in; it blew straight down the row of old storefront buildings and hit him square in the face as he grabbed his hat, opened her truck door, and braced to keep a gust from snatching both hat and door. They said their goodbyes and he watched her drive toward mountains hidden behind a shroud of dark clouds.

He tucked the cat toys into his coat and walked across the nearly deserted street to a white, late-model pickup with highway department logos, where a fictitious surveyor sat in the driver's seat, studying a street map. The early-forty-something guy in the orange reflective safety vest and yellow hard hat barely glanced his way as he eased into the passenger seat.

"Good contact, Tyler—you even opened the door for the gal." He cocked his head and gave Win a sly look. "Yessir, if she'd lose that country-girl vibe, she'd be one hot number! Got some great photos. Hell, you two make a nice couple!"

"Not funny." Win shifted to get comfortable in the seat. "Cut it out."

"Just saying. You're a single guy. . . . Long, cold nights . . ." The guy arched his eyebrows and smirked.

"Cut it out. She's married." Win's reply was angry.

"Yeah, well, married to a thug who could be spending a few years in the federal pen. You know damn well she could get a little lonely."

Win quickly leaned over the pickup's center console, put his right hand on the steering wheel to block the man's right arm, and caught the surveillance agent behind the neck with his left hand. He squeezed just hard enough to get the guy's full attention. "What part of *cut it out* don't you get? You think you can show some shred of professionalism here!" Win's strong hand and arm had him pinned in a painful nerve lock.

"Okay, okay, let go! Let go, damn it!" He was gasping for air. "Where'd you learn that trick? Damn, that hurt!" The guy sat rubbing his neck and shoulder after Win dropped his hands and leaned away. The agent stared down at the camera in his lap and made no attempt to meet Win's narrowed eyes. "Hell, didn't mean any disrespect." He blew out a breath. "Okay, okay, I was out of line."

Then the agent whined a little. "I just hate screwing around doing next to nothing, following housewives around, while I've got real cases to work in Denver. If they keep us up here long, I'm gonna get so far behind I won't have a weekend off till mid-summer." He paused and looked warily toward Win. "I'm sorry, alright? Are we square here?"

Win briefly met the guy's eyes, then stared out the front windshield. He was wondering why he'd gotten physical. "Yeah, we're cool. I don't normally have such a short fuse. Maybe I'm feeling a little dirty approaching her. She hasn't done anything wrong."

"You know the drill, this is part of informant development; might help us get closer to the bad guys." The agent laughed. "Hell, Win, if this lightweight stuff bothers you, I sure wouldn't recommend you put in for undercover work—you *do not* have what it takes!"

Win grinned to lighten the mood and assured him undercover work wasn't in his career plan at the Bureau. He found himself only half listening as the man outlined their surveillance strategy for the day. He knew his earlier anger was directed more at himself than at the other agent's crude banter. There was no harm in noticing and admiring a good-looking woman. None at all. But he knew he'd crossed the line with Ellie this morning. In his mind, there'd been more than admiration, and he was disappointed in himself. He was also thinking the surveillance agent might be more right than he knew. *Maybe I don't have what it takes to do the job.*

* * *

Much later that same Friday morning, a burly man sat slumped in the driver's seat of a Ford sedan, watching the front of the old engineers building. The locals called the building "the Pagoda." Maybe its shape? He wasn't sure why. But he did know the area's FBI office was located in the gray stone building. It was nearly noon, and almost every day for the last several days, the young man who was the new resident agent would come out the front door to walk two hundred yards up the sidewalk to the building housing the Terrace Grill and the Mammoth Hotel Dining Room. There were few choices for lunch in Mammoth this time of year, and the young man seemed to have a tendency to follow a set routine. Routine was a dangerous thing to develop in the older man's line of work. It was dangerous for the young man too—he just didn't know it yet.

The sun suddenly stuck its head out of the dense gray clouds and bathed the surroundings in unexpected bright light. It had been so gloomy the last few days that the sunshine was an unaccustomed visitor. The patches of snow and ice on the green tile roof of the Pagoda building caused a near-blinding reflection in the dazzling sunlight. The man hadn't needed his sunglasses for days and now cursed himself for not having them.

Just after twelve noon, right on time, the front door opened and the agent came into view. As usual, he was alone. He stood on the granite steps, smiling at the sunshine. He was maybe late twenties, tall, with the broad shoulders and chest of an athlete. He was trim and fit with a capable, confident air about him. Not quite cocky, but close. The young man generally had a friendly expression, smiled easily. He was polite to a fault—always opening doors for people, speaking to most everyone he met. Probably a good-natured kid, the man thought. He watched him pull a pair of dark sunglasses from his jacket pocket and put them on. Then the agent ran a hand through his thick brown hair, put on his Indiana Jones–style hat, and adjusted it to a bit of a rakish angle. The older man chuckled to himself. He was thinking any woman alive would find Yellowstone's resident FBI agent to be one handsome man.

The agent usually had the look of a prosperous young rancher. He wore his khaki twill pants, western-cut jacket, cowboy boots, and leather belt with a little silver on the buckle as if he'd grown up in them. Always starched shirts, usually a tie—nothing flashy, nothing to identify him as a federal officer. He was dressed to fit in with the locals, albeit the better dressed of the locals. The older man had seen him only once in traditional suit and tie, and he'd worn that look just as easily as the western garb. He was obviously comfortable in his own skin—probably any set of clothes would have suited him fine.

The agent was taking his time to bask in the welcome sunshine. As he stretched his arms behind his head, his jacket pulled back and the older man could clearly see the black handgun holstered to his belt on his right-hand side. He knew it was a Glock 22, a .40 caliber semi-automatic pistol, not the FBI's newer standard-issue Glock 19M. The older man idly wondered why the young man carried the more power-ful weapon, wondered if he was accomplished with it. He knew the FBI spent considerable time training their new agents with handguns and that they were required to pass marksmanship tests every few months during their careers. He doubted if this young man had ever drawn the pistol in a confrontation. He doubted he ever would.

He watched him walk up the sidewalk past the hotel, scanning the sparse trees and bare bushes in front of the historic buildings for wildlife. Even during miserable weather, he'd seen the agent turn his back into the wind, pull his heavy parka tight around him, and observe ground squirrels, ravens, or magpies going about their business in the cold drizzle and sleet. He was obviously a curious fellow. The older man saw so many of his generation with their eyes only on their phones. He was thinking it was a shame this contract was for one who actually seemed to look at the natural world with interest.

The older man raised a worn crime novel into sight and pulled the new cowboy hat down lower to hide his face as the agent finally walked past his rental car and up the sidewalk toward the Terrace Grill. The waiting was becoming tedious; it had been six days. Complacency could set in if one waited too long. Worse yet, he could develop an affinity for the target. The younger man appeared to be a decent sort. He had to admit, this assignment was shaping up to be a bit distasteful.

He lowered the book and shifted in his seat as the sun warmed the interior of the car. He'd make the long drive to Spokane this afternoon and tonight. Time to spend a day or so working on the complex extraction component of this job. It was high risk dealing with law enforcement; they all seemed to take it so personal when one of their own was involved. He shrugged a little. *High risk—high reward.* Still, he knew he had to have everything solidly in place well before he pulled the trigger.

His pale gray eyes never left the agent. The young man had slowed and was watching some rodent-like thing scurry through the frozen bushes. The older man let out a deep sigh. He had played out numerous scenarios in his mind and on the ground. He had well-rehearsed short- and long-range options. He was waiting for his employer to choose one. He was waiting and way past ready for the thing to be set in motion.

CHAPTER SEVEN

Saturday dawned damp, foggy, and miserable. Yesterday's sunshine had evaporated like the vapor from the thermal springs, and Win's heavy gray sweats were barely keeping the chill at bay. He stopped to catch his breath and watch a stream of scalding water trickle down the mountainside. He moved off the trail to explore the water's source and thought back over last night's dinner with Maddy and Bill Wilson. Her visit with coffee and muffins his first real day in the park was still a good memory. Bill was hoping to retire soon from his second career as a ranger, and she was looking forward to moving near the grandkids. A home-cooked meal and a legitimate excuse to avoid the Denver surveillance agents were a winning combination.

He'd also managed to get away from the office long enough yesterday afternoon to meet with the park superintendent, a thin, studious-looking gentleman who seemed to be nervously awaiting the coming of the tourist hordes when the roads fully opened in a few weeks. Nobody mentioned the "armed men," and Win got the distinct impression the superintendent believed if the issue was ignored, it might just go away.

Win pushed aside a bush and squatted beside a plate-size iridescent blue opening that was coughing up spurts of water.

"Wouldn't touch that iffen I's you."

Win froze with his fingers inches above the steaming water of the small cobalt pool. Luke Bordeaux's thick Louisiana accent came from

behind him—very close. He'd seen no one on the last two miles of his
jog up through the boardwalks and trails of Terrace Mountain. No one
was out sightseeing in this weather, except him and, apparently, Luke
Bordeaux. Win took a deep breath, stood up slowly, and turned toward
the voice. He squared his shoulders toward the man.

"And why shouldn't I touch it?"

Luke was casually leaning against one of the car-size gray boulders
on a slight rise a few feet away, near the hiking trail. His drab-green
hooded jacket kept the light drizzle off his head. A canister of bear
spray hung from his belt, and Win could clearly see the grip of a handgun through the open jacket.

"That little un there will burn the crap out of ya. Made that mistake
only once when I first moved here. Them little blue uns are bad hot."
Luke looked down at Win's running shoes. "You might wanna move
away from it. Ground tends to be thin there where it looks real white.
You kin break right through the crust into the hot water."

Win followed Luke's eyes down to his track shoes, took two steps
forward to the darker ground, and stood looking into the man's face.
Luke had a friendly, amused look in his eyes.

"You following me around for any specific reason?"

"Other than to keep you from afallin' in a spring and boilin' to
death? C'mon, I'll show you some things about 'em to watch out fer.
There's a new thermal area that sprung up three years ago just over
that ridge. Easy walk. Take 'bout two hours to look 'em over. . . . Got
that much time?"

"Need to make some office calls, but not till this afternoon. Yeah,
I'll go."

Win noticed Luke hadn't answered his question, but he was curious about the man's intent. It wasn't just coincidence they'd run into
each other in a park nearly three times the size of Rhode Island. Maybe
Luke had decided to provide some information on the Prophet's group,
or maybe he was just trying to size him up. Those were the potential
positive possibilities. But as they trooped through the thick evergreen
forest up a narrow game trail toward the higher ridge, it occurred
to Win that he was following an armed suspect well off the marked

hiking trail and he'd told the man he wasn't expected at the office until much later. No one would miss him for several hours. He had no cell service and no weapon. And he felt like a fool. Win silently asked God to forgive his stupidity and to keep him safe anyway.

He was relieved when the trail finally crested the hill and they stood side by side, staring down at a small area of white earth and thick steam. The new thermal area was within a narrow ravine surrounded by lush forest. Luke hadn't spoken during the fifteen-minute hike to the site, but when they reached the area of dead shrubs and dying trees surrounding the hot spot, he switched into teacher mode.

"You know most of Yellowstone is sittin' on top of one of the world's largest volcanoes, right? There's a forty-five-mile-wide caldera, and the lava from the underground volcano sits from three to twelve miles below the surface." Luke glanced at Win. "You seen the caldera rim?"

"Naw, never been here before," Win admitted, "but I got the volcano part from TV."

"Well, the north rim of that caldera is 'bout twenty-five miles south of here. There's a fault line from the underground magma, or lava, at the Norris Geyser Basin that runs all the way up here to Mammoth. That's what heats the water in this part of the park and causes the thermal features here. You wanna really watch yourself if you see white crust on the ground—that tells you there's a hot spring underground or an old one has died out. They kin pop up from day to day.... Pretty things, the little pools—blue, green, orange, blackish, mostly. Sometimes you can sorta tell the temperature by the color of the pool, sometimes you can't. They're fascinating to see, but you gotta show 'em some respect— they kin kill ya."

Win made himself comfortable on a damp rock and settled in for more of Luke's lecture. After a short course on Yellowstone's geography, wildlife, and vegetation, Luke circled back to discussing the thermal features.

"I've studied up some on the geology of this place. Mammoth doesn't have geysers like other parts of the park. That's because the Mammoth area sits on top of limestone instead of igneous rock, uh, hard rock, like granite. The hot water dissolves the limestone into calcium carbonate, and it bubbles through cracks in the rocks to the surface as a mineral called travertine—that's the shiny white stuff you see around here. The travertine holds the hot water, and as it cools it forms the terraces. They kin grow a foot or two each year. The water pressure decreases here because the limestone is soft and gets broken up. There's nothing to trap the pressure like at Old Faithful, which sits on top of igneous rock. So, this hot water forms terraces instead of being forced into the air as geysers."

"That isn't a geyser?" Win was eyeing a two-foot-high jumble of grayish-brown rocks spewing hot water and steam into the air.

"Nope, these here are steam vents, or fumaroles. Can get right active and throw water a few feet, but they don't do much more'n hiss and stew. Some of 'em smell like sulfur, some have boiling mud surrounding 'em. Isn't it amazing to think this little spot that sprung up a few years ago could look just like the hot springs terraces in a couple hundred thousand years!"

Luke seemed almost embarrassed by his exuberance. "Guess I get a little carried away with the magic of this place. It is magical . . . you know. I reckon I get into a zone talking 'bout it." He was smiling as he stood up, and the white swirl of the blowing steam enveloped him, partly obscuring his dark features. In that instant Luke Bordeaux seemed bigger than life—his eyes twinkling in good nature, his smile radiant and genuine. Still, there was something about this man that challenged Win's soul. He couldn't decide if that was a good sign—or a very bad one.

After Luke's half-hour introductory course, they sat down on the dry part of a log beneath a huge tree that Win now recognized as a Douglas fir. The drizzle had picked up, and Win pulled the hood of his sweatshirt over his head. Luke dug a ham and cheese sandwich out of his jacket pocket, unwrapped the wax paper, and handed half to Win. They unclipped their water bottles and shared the early lunch.

Luke turned his head just enough to watch Win's eyes when he spoke. "Ellie was real impressed with you when you was out at our place last week. She thinks you're honest."

"What do you think?"

Luke reflected for a while and chewed the sandwich. "Welp, reckon that's partly why I followed you out here this morning. Wanna get a better feel fer you. Not working today, and Ellie was taking the kids to a birthday party in town, so I had some time on my hands." He paused and studied the spitting fumarole. "After us visitin' the other night, it seemed sorta important that you know I didn't poach that deer. I was cuttin' up a deer a bear had killed—wanted to see what kinda fat reserves the deer had after winter. I reckon the hikers thought I was skinning it out. Didn't shoot that deer. Don't hunt out of season or in the park. Never have."

Win considered that while he munched for a few moments longer on one of the better sandwiches he'd had in a while. "Okay, then. Why shoot at Chief Randall?"

Luke glanced away and grimaced, then looked back and sighed. "Alright, that wasn't the smartest move on my part. I wasn't expecting anyone to be comin' up the trail with a gun drawn." He sighed again. "Ahhh, I blame that ranger fer part of the mess with my guide license— decided to put the fear of God in him. Don't guess he was expecting me neither, so it sorta went downhill from there. . . . But ya know, Win Tyler, I never shot at anyone that day."

Win was thinking back to the reports he'd heard on Luke's marksmanship skills and figured that was true. The man could have easily shot Randall. Win just grunted, nodded a little, and finished the sandwich. He took a sip of his water before he continued the discussion.

"Suppose that'll be up to the court to sort out." Win pulled his damp hood back a little. "I'm guessing here, but I'd think as a condition of you posting bail on poaching and federal firearms charges, you wouldn't be allowed to carry a weapon into the park. Or anywhere else, for that matter."

Luke smiled slightly and stared straight ahead at the little steam vent that was sputtering to life a bit more. Then he shifted on the log as he slowly pushed the right side of his rain jacket back and dropped his right hand to the top of the pistol grip. "Yeah, well, maybe I shoulda read the fine print in that release a little closer." He narrowed his eyes. "You gonna have a problem with me carrying out here?"

Win hesitated as the man pushed back his hood. Luke's look was suddenly menacing. The mist and steam formed little silver flecks that lighted on his dark hair and close-cropped beard. His eyes were coal-black in the gloom under the tree's canopy. Luke's quick change in demeanor reminded Win of a snake that had awakened and instantaneously coiled to strike. He was acutely aware that he was sitting within three feet of a man who was capable of killing him in a heartbeat. He was also aware that he had no weapon to defend himself.

Luke let the tension build for several more long seconds. Then he slowly moved both of his hands to his knees and his gaze back to the hissing fumaroles. Win struggled to breathe normally and to slow his heart's pounding. He wanted to swallow, but his mouth was too dry. He was thinking Luke's efforts at intimidation were very effective—he was scared. He was also thinking he was fixing to find out the real reason Luke Bordeaux had followed him up this hill on this dreary Saturday morning.

Luke seemed to be studying the clouds of rising vapor in front of them. He spoke softly, just over the sound of the steam spewing from the small vent. "Yeah, Ellie was mighty taken with you the other night." He nodded and paused for a second. "She said she run into you in Gardiner yesterday mornin' and you was right friendly."

Should have told him I saw her in town. Uh-oh . . .

"Might just be a coincidence, you running into her at the hardware store—just like me running into you up here on this hill." He spread his hands in front of his knees and shrugged before he continued. "Ellie is a trusting woman. I wouldn't want it no other way." He paused for a long moment, turned his face back to Win and locked eyes with him. He dropped his voice a notch. "But I ain't so trusting, not with a Fed, that's for damn sure. So it would be real smart of you not to run into her again when I ain't around—coincidence or not. Don't much matter to me what you might be after—information or . . . or something else. You keep your distance, boy!"

He held his piercing gaze until Win dropped his eyes and looked away. Win felt more anger at himself for allowing Luke to shame him than fear of the man's threat. The worst of it was he knew he wouldn't feel the shame if there weren't some truth in Luke's veiled accusation.

Win cleared his throat and finally answered, "I hear what you're saying, Luke." His voice sounded guilty even to him, but he plodded on. "I respect your relationship with your wife." He finally met Luke's eyes again. "As for information, as you put it, that's in your hands. You're the one putting Ellie and the kids at risk by hanging out with suspected criminals. I could likely do something on the poaching charges if you're willing to talk to me about—"

Luke's quick movement cut him off in mid-sentence. Luke was leaning toward him, and Win had no idea how the man had drawn the gun so quickly. A Beretta 92FS had appeared in Luke's right hand. The black barrel of the 9mm weapon shimmered in the blowing steam; for the moment it was pointed toward the fumarole. Win's eyes jumped from the gun back to Luke's intense face. He had no clue where this was headed.

"You're not *really* hearing me, Win Tyler! Some of the men I'm working with have made mistakes, but they've paid their dues, and all of them been good soldiers—put their lives on the line fer our country. Now you and the federal government think you kin dictate how we worship, what we believe, who we associate with! Told you the other night I was no snitch. You see anything that's happened to change my mind?"

"I'm not gonna talk civics or theology with you, Luke, not, uh, not while you've got a gun in your hand!" Win heard his voice shake just a little.

Luke twisted to face him and leaned in even more—they were less than two feet apart. The Beretta was still pointed away, but Win watched Luke's finger move to the trigger. Win wanted to move back, but there was nowhere to go. He felt completely cornered. He forced himself to breathe, but beyond that he had no idea what to do.

"You threatening me? You trying to scare me?" Win knew he sounded afraid. The guy had caught him totally off guard.

"Damn right! Is it working?" Luke spoke forcefully, but the deep-brown eyes had softened and there was a hint of a playful smile at the corner of his mouth. Win felt Luke's anger lifting with the mist.

"Yeah, yeah it is!" Win summoned his courage and forced himself to grin back at Luke as he raised his hands in mock surrender.

Luke leaned back, nodded in response, then faintly smiled. "It's hard not to like you, boy." He holstered the Beretta nearly as fast as he'd drawn it, but Win saw the flicker of a conflicted look in his eyes as he secured the gun.

Win managed to swallow hard before he spoke again. "Can I ask you to think about something?" He went on before Luke could answer. "I'm betting your daddy taught you to never draw a weapon unless you were gonna use it, same as my daddy taught me. So what is it in you that makes a weapon one of your first responses? Rather than think it through, talk it through, or pray it through? Happened with Chief Randall, happened twice with me—liable to not have a good outcome one of these times. You have no intention of shooting me."

Luke stood up, flipped up his hood, and blew out a deep breath. "No. . . . Not today, anyway." He arched his eyebrows and shrugged. "Follow me down to the main trail. We'll be gettin' on back."

Luke kept up a pretty good pace going back down the ridge to the main trail. They were halfway down before the adrenaline in Win's system began to level off. The drizzle and wind had picked up, and big cold drops continually fell on the men as they moved through the deep woods. Win spoke first as he stepped onto the main trail. "I suppose we've both got some things to think on, you reckon?" He watched the rain slide off Luke's hood. Bordeaux's dark eyes were veiled and impossible to read.

"Yeah, seems that we do. It's a damn shame, really. . . ." Luke took another deep breath and blinked a few times, but never finished the thought. "Behave yourself, Win Tyler." He raised a hand, turned up the trail, and disappeared into the steady drizzle and fog.

* * *

Win knew that Jim West wasn't going to be thrilled with his Saturday-afternoon telephone report on his unexpected visit with Luke Bordeaux. That was an understatement.

"You were unarmed, but you willingly hiked miles off the public trail into the wilderness with an armed felony suspect—no one knew where you were—no communications, no possibility of backup? What were you thinking!"

Win knew it wasn't really a question, but he meekly tried to answer anyway. "I just had a gut feeling the guy wasn't a physical danger to me—"

"Were you still thinking that when he pulled the Beretta? Good Lord, Win!" His supervisor took a deep breath before continuing. "Look, I know you're at a disadvantage up there. Johnson won't be back in the office for another week, and you haven't had any advanced work in informant development or violent crime. I know I approved your contact with Mrs. Bordeaux yesterday. That was a mistake on my part, considering you have so little support up there—not to mention the fact that her husband obviously knows exactly what we're up to. And instead of us having surveillance on him, he's got it on you! As for your gut feelings, it's important to pay attention to them, but you've got to realize that good instincts come in large part from experience, and you don't have the experience with armed subjects to put yourself in that kind of danger on a hunch."

He went on like that for a good two more minutes. Win held on to the phone, scribbled on a notepad, and acknowledged from time to time that he was listening. Jim finally wound down with the suggestion that they arrest Bordeaux for violating the conditions of his bond on the poaching and firearms charges, not to mention witness tampering, assaulting a federal officer, and several other pertinent charges. Win didn't agree.

"I know I wasn't real smart today, Boss, but Bordeaux is probably our best chance at developing an informant in this deal. Nothing may come of it, but if those militia guys are up to no good, Bordeaux is right in the thick of it."

Jim had apparently finished chewing on Win and he switched to the situation at hand. "Well, something may actually come of it. I had a videoconference with Denver this morning, and the ASAC says the Secret Service and the Park Service folks in Washington are jumping up and down because so little has been done to investigate the possible threats the group poses to the park. Everyone's been a little out of pocket the last few days, but with the Attorney General coming back home from his European tour tomorrow, we could get the go-ahead to do more serious surveillance on Shepherd's group—as early as next week. So maybe we leave Bordeaux out for the time being. You manage to stay clear of the guy, okay? Do you know how much extra paperwork I'd have to generate if my new agent in Yellowstone got shot?"

Win hadn't met Jim West in person yet, but he knew he'd like the guy. Jim had given him a pretty thorough reaming out over this morning's adventure with Bordeaux, but he hadn't been harsh or gone overboard. In any normal Bureau office, he'd be sitting at a desk or cubical within a few feet of the guy. There'd be lots of interaction, lots of opportunities to learn the ropes from the supervisor and other senior agents. As it was, they were more than 150 miles of mountains and impassable roads apart. Getting to the six-agent RA in Jackson was a daylong excursion, and the Denver office might as well be on another planet. An unexpected wave of loneliness swept over Win. Given his low standing in the Bureau, the distance he felt was far greater than could be measured in miles.

CHAPTER EIGHT

Gus Jordon, the Deputy Chief Ranger, made good on his offer to buy Win a drink and took him to dinner that Saturday night at one of the few open spots in Gardiner, the Bull Moose Bar and Grill. Gus pulled off his coat and moved through the loud, crowded room to an empty table in a quieter spot near the corner. Win trailed behind, checking out the huge elk and moose heads adorning the rough wood-paneled walls, while the ranger ordered a bourbon and Coke from a waitress with purple hair and more earrings than Win could count.

In this setting, Gus was laid back and easy to be around. Win thought he looked much younger than his forty-four years in hiking boots, jeans, and a heavy wool shirt. He was bareheaded and the wind had blown his short, light-brown hair in every direction. He had a scrubby, half-grown beard; apparently the Park Service had no grooming code. The Bureau no longer required a clean shave either, but that memo had never made it to Charlotte's White Collar Crime Squad. Win knew the rugged, outdoorsy look appealed to the women. Shelby would have said Gus was "*just darling.*" Win ran a hand along his smooth chin, sighed, and ordered a beer.

Gus leaned back and surveyed the crowd before he spoke. "We didn't exactly give you a warm welcome when you first drove into the park."

Win shrugged it off. "No problem."

"Well, actually it was—not that it makes much difference, I suppose. But you ought to know that isn't Chief Randall's normal way of doing things."

Win nodded. "He came over and apologized on Monday."

"I'd been surprised if he hadn't. Randall's a good man, a good boss. He wasn't supposed to be working that day—it was the anniversary of his wife's death last spring. He was having a hard time with it. Shouldn't have been in the field."

The colorful waitress arriving with their drinks interrupted the emotional topic. Win took a sip of his beer and nodded again to acknowledge the explanation.

He and Gus ate their tamale dinners as they rehashed last week's adventure at Bordeaux's house and the lack of anything solid on the mysterious militia that had roamed the park until six days ago, but hadn't been spotted since.

Win wanted a little background on his prospective informant. "What do you know about Bordeaux's issues with the law?"

"An FBI agent named Harper arrested Bordeaux on federal poaching violations, maybe fourteen months ago. Alleged he'd conspired with some well-heeled trophy hunters to kill park elk and bears. I transferred here right after it all went down. Bordeaux always maintained his innocence. There was no physical evidence any wildlife were killed. No real evidence of anything, really, other than Bordeaux being a convenient target for an overly ambitious special agent. Maybe I'm talkin' a little outa turn here"—he gave Win a hard look—"but every charge against the guy was later dismissed. Still can't get his hunting-guide license back, for some reason."

Win could tell Gus was trying to not step on the Bureau's toes as he recounted what he knew and what he'd heard. "The park was really shorthanded when that case started. Chief Randall had to be a lot more involved than you'd normally see. It kept looking like Bordeaux was getting railroaded, but the guy didn't help himself any with his hot temper. Agent Harper was a young guy, like yourself. He was the one pushing it—pushed it hard. Agent Johnson seemed content to just stay on the sidelines. Harper left right after I got here. . . . Heard he'd quit the FBI."

"The Park Service went after Bordeaux too?" Win asked.

"Park rangers assisted in the arrest and investigation, so I'm sure Bordeaux blames us as well as the FBI for putting him out of business. There was no love lost between your agency and our rangers over that case, that's for sure." Gus swirled his drink in his hand, "I don't know much about Bordeaux except what I've heard from other rangers who've been around him. He's former military, was a Green Beret or some kind of special ops. I've heard he's extremely capable as an outdoorsman. One of my rangers called him a ghost in the field; says he can shift from easygoing to downright dangerous in a split second."

That's for dang sure, Win was thinking.

Gus took a sip of the bourbon and kept talking. "We've got to tread lightly on this whole thing—regardless of what the Secret Service wants. This country has a gun culture; there are no laws against carrying firearms, even loaded firearms, into the national parks. Unless they're convicted felons or under court order not to be armed, we can't do a thing to prevent them from trooping around in the woods with their weapons. You can't legally pick a flower or pocket a rock in Yellowstone, but you're welcome to carry an assault rifle with a thirty-round magazine most anywhere you want to go." He shook his head slowly. "Strange world we live in, isn't it?"

They finished their dinners and watched the weekend crowd of off-duty park employees and a few locals. The lights had been dimmed, the drinking was getting heavier, and the bar was getting louder. Win volunteered to be their designated driver and Gus settled into his fourth bourbon and Coke. Win was still working on his first beer as Gus moved the topic to his personal life. There was a failed marriage, the long drive to visit his kids and dog, and lonely duty in remote outposts. The pain in his slurred voice was real. After a pause, Gus smiled into Win's face. "Still, I've got the best job in the world. Our agency stays screwed up. There's fewer than 1,300 permanent law enforcement park rangers in the whole country and the number keeps dropping. We never have the resources, staff, or money we need, and it's hard on the people. But even with all the hardships, it's the best damn job in the world."

Gus straightened in his chair and met Win's eyes for a brief moment before glancing away. Win caught just enough in those brown eyes to realize that even after four drinks of hard liquor in the last ninety minutes, the guy was nowhere near tanked. It occurred to Win in an instant: Yellowstone National Park was a dead end for FBI agents, but it would be the opposite for the Park Service. This guy had to be one of their top men in the country just to be here. Gus could be playing him, digging for information by appearing to be a little intoxicated and very transparent, to lull him into talking about the Bureau's plans on the armed men case.

It was no secret that several federal agencies were in competition over what could become a major domestic terrorism investigation. Win knew entire agency budgets got bumped up or down depending upon who did what in those kinds of high-profile cases. On the other hand, Gus Jordon might just be a really friendly guy who honestly wanted to build a positive relationship with a younger brother in law enforcement. *Who am I kidding?* Win tried not to let his face reflect his thoughts. *Why can't everyone just play nice?*

Gus leaned back in. "This your favorite method of interrogation, Sport? Get a man drinkin'? You now know more'n you'd ever wanna know about me and I still don't know a damn thing 'bout you, 'cept you're gutsy and smart. Tell me about Special Agent Winston Tyler.... Tell me what's happenin' with the FBI."

Not gonna happen. Win smiled and tipped his half-full beer bottle toward the man. He settled into his standard diversionary topics of sports and general law enforcement stuff. Interagency politics and intrigue aside, Win liked the ranger. Despite his obvious personal conflicts, the guy seemed to genuinely care about this place and its people. Win couldn't fault him or his agency for aggressively wanting to protect the park from any threat. But the good guys' response to the threat in this situation, if there was a real threat, was lost somewhere in the depths of the bureaucratic morass.

* * *

Lost? It wasn't hard to get lost in the vastness of the place. It wasn't like there were a lot of roads to meander down, not even many trails. He'd read once that less than one percent of Yellowstone National Park was developed; most of it was still a true wilderness. Around four million tourists would come traipsing through, almost all in the three months that passed for summer. Only a tiny fraction of those would wander off the main highway that made a figure-eight loop through the center of the park. There was plenty of room to get lost . . . or to lose something or someone. On this crappy-looking Thursday afternoon, he intended for someone to get permanently lost.

He didn't reckon that losing Wayman Duncan was any great loss for humanity in the first place. The man was a damn weasel; a sorry excuse for a human being if there ever was one. He'd served in some low-rent unit in the Air Force—probably stood around for four years smoking cigarettes and spitting on the tarmac, pretending to guard planes to get his service time in. That was the only thing that got him accepted into the church. The service time also ushered him into the military prison at Leavenworth when he screwed up and got caught stealing MREs by the caseload and selling them on the black market. Not weapons, not ammunition, not explosives, but damn Meals, Ready-to-Eat—what a half-assed effort at crime! And then to get caught, no less, and convicted. He'd joined up with the guys off and on during the two years they'd been on the same cellblock at the big prison. He'd heard the Prophet. He'd claimed he'd converted to the Covenant's Sword, as they were calling it back then. But more'n likely he was just using his professed newfound faith and the daily church meetings as a way to get out of his cell. The military was good about that—letting them meet as often as they wanted.

He hadn't seen Wayman in a couple of years when he suddenly showed up full of religious fervor and wanted to rejoin the church about a month ago. Wanted to join the Prophet's militia too, but thank goodness the boy Dan Shepherd had in charge of training had the good sense to smell out a slacker and kindly declined the offer. If he'd put on their uniform, he mighta actually caused some damage. As it was, he was just a damn nuisance. They were coming down to the wire on the deal and there wasn't any room for foul-ups. There were Feds popping up like weeds after a spring rain, and now he had to contend with the likes of Wayman Duncan.

Word was Wayman had cozied up to someone at ATF. Word was Wayman had taken money to rat them out. The man didn't know anything harmful at this point, but he could stumble onto something, so it had to be handled. He'd considered giving him bad information to confuse the Feds, but that only worked when you were dealing with someone with a little intelligence. Wayman didn't qualify on that point. That being the case, there wasn't any other way to go. Dan Shepherd didn't want to know the details—he just wanted it handled. It was gonna get handled today. Wayman Duncan was gonna get real lost.

They'd parked Wayman's old Buick in three inches of snowy slush at the edge of the park highway at a little pull-off where the brown wooden sign said *Phantom Lake*. Had a nice ring to it, given the purpose at hand. The Park Service was making an effort to keep the highway passable between Mammoth and Cooke City, but it had been open less than half the time since early April. The little thaw they'd had the last three days was the only reason they'd gotten this far. Supposed to snow another foot tonight, and that'd cover up what went on at Phantom Lake this afternoon.

They'd only met one car and a couple of Park Service vehicles in the ten miles since they'd left Mammoth, and the pull-off was screened from the highway by a grove of evergreens. Couldn't be too careful, though, so they'd dressed like winter hikers. He fished a couple of hiking poles out of the back seat, zipped up his heavy coat, and stretched as he climbed out of the front passenger seat. He pulled the ski mask down over his face and smiled to himself. He'd never worn the black mask to keep out the cold, but it'd seen a good deal of use in several real lucrative bank robberies and yeah, that time with the armored car. Wearing it for its intended purpose was kinda nice—silly thing would keep him real toasty in this weather.

"Damn cold!" Red was unfolding his long frame out from behind the wheel. He pulled a knapsack out of the back seat and helped himself to a couple of the aluminum hiking poles. There hadn't been much conversation on the way over here; never was when you were around Red. The boy was a few bricks shy a load in most every way, but he was a freaking genius with plastic explosives. *Prophet says the Good Book teaches the Lord gives each of us a talent. . . .*

Red tossed the car keys up high and caught them in his gloved hand. He laughed a wicked-sounding, high-pitched laugh and his breath formed a cloud of condensation above his head. "Hell, I ain't nearly as cold as ole Wayman's gonna be—you hear that, Wayman? You comfortable in there?" Red rapped hard on the car's trunk.

He swung his head toward the fool. Even from behind the black ski mask, the dark intensity of his eyes carried to the redhead.

The younger man backed a step away from the car in the slush and shrugged. "Just playing a little. . . . Damn cold out here."

"Not another word from you till this business is done. Hear me? If you don't hear me, there'll be hell to pay!" He knew that little tirade oughta keep some of the foolishness at bay. Of all the things the redhead feared, he knew his anger topped the list.

He checked his watch: 1500 hours. The boys would swing by to pick them up in less than an hour. He listened for any sounds of approaching traffic. It was quiet. All he heard was the motor popping and the steady drip of slush off the undercarriage of the car.

"All right."

They yanked Wayman out of the trunk and kept the zip ties on him. They trooped past the north end of the little frozen lake, about half a mile up the slick, slushy trail to the crest of a tree-covered ridge and halfway down the other side. The wind was picking up in the tops of the lodgepole pines, and ever so often there was the sharp snap of small limbs breaking. Wayman's heavy breathing and their boots in the icy mud were the only other sounds. Wayman had offered them money, drugs, you name it, but he'd known damn well the die was cast as soon as they pulled guns on him back at the trailer.

He'd told the snitch he wouldn't sic Red on him if he'd come clean. Wayman tearfully told them about his meeting with the ATF boys and where he'd hid his payout. He'd sent one of the brothers to Wayman's shabby apartment in Gardiner to get the $2,500 in crisp new bills ATF had paid the man for next to nothing in information.

It didn't take long.

He glanced back at the bright-red flecks that patterned the hard crust of the huge snowbank. There was a raven nearby carrying on with an irritating *caw! caw! caw!* Just a damn fancy crow, that's all they were. . . . He watched the silly redhead swinging the camp shovel as the fool slipped and slid his way back up the trail toward the ridgetop and the lake and the car.

He stopped to admire the beauty of the small valley below him. The cold snap today was turning all the snowmelt to ice on every wisp of tall grass that tried to stick its head above the scattered drifts. The clumps of evergreens were covered with thin coats of ice, and the little stream that cut through the meadow was sparkling, even in the flat light. Wayman had a picturesque resting place, that was for damn sure—more than the scumbag deserved. Once the big snowbank melted in June, he'd be food for the animals, but that wouldn't be such a bad thing either. Least he'd serve some purpose in death. He'd never served any useful purpose in life.

He smiled as a small herd of elk eased out of the forest across the valley and trotted toward the stream. The snow was beginning to fall in soft, pretty flakes. Someone had asked him once if killing folks got easier the more often you did it. . . . Hell, it never was hard in the first place.

* * *

There was light streaming in the window across the room near Win's desk. He'd forgotten to close the blinds when he fell asleep. The red numbers on the clock read 4:23. He'd been sleeping, what? Nearly five hours. *Long enough for this night? Naw.* He rolled over and stretched and pulled the down comforter up higher. But the light was pulling

at him, and he opened his eyes again, gave up, and moved across the
room to pull the curtains. The whole world looked white outside the
window. The big snowstorm they'd predicted for Thursday night had
finally arrived. It was snowing big flakes, clumps of flakes, and all the
while a huge full moon poured down silver light. *No, that can't be*—but
it was. A full moon bathing his little corner of the world with soft light,
while snow clouds hovered over the mountains to the south and the
high winds carried the snow to this place. *What did Luke Bordeaux
call Yellowstone the other day—magical? Geez, it's beyond magical!*

Win pulled on his heavy sweats and a parka and eased out the
back door in his insulated boots. He glanced around for anything large
that might gore or eat him. *Coast is clear!* This was the downy, gentle
snow he remembered from those infrequent snowfalls back home in
Arkansas. This deep, soft snow brought happy memories, a sense of
awe, a feeling of peace. He was hard-pressed to find words for it. It was
a spiritual thing.

His boots displaced the fresh powder as he walked past his Explorer
and the Bureau SUV and jumped the little stream flowing beside the
driveway. The snowfall encased Mammoth in a blanket of quiet. No
sound except for the flowing water and the almost imperceptible hiss
of steam rising as clumps of snowflakes struck the scalding water in
front of him. The shiny white surface of the travertine terraces and
the glistening layers of draping ice added to the wonder of the scene.
He wanted to capture it somehow, but a picture wouldn't do—not one
he'd take, anyway. So he leaned against one of the wooden rails on the
boardwalk and became a part of it.

Then, sure enough, Shelby intruded, and the tight grip of loss filled
his chest. *How dare she haunt me here!* He raised his eyes to the moon
and felt the soft flakes settle on his face and hair. He fought down the
intense desire to share this wonder with her. For as long as he could
remember, he'd been able to pull out the phone and call. Didn't matter
what time it was, didn't much matter where he was, he called. He told
her how things looked—how things felt. How he felt. It was ripping
him apart that he couldn't do that now. *I have no one to call.*

He tried to regain his focus on the beauty around him, but his mind wandered away from his anguish in a more familiar direction. He thought about work. The last several days had been barn burners. He'd talked the Denver surveillance agents into helping him babysit the Park Service's workmen off and on so he wasn't tied to the office every minute. Bureau rules prohibited contractors, office cleaners, maintenance men, basically anybody, from being in the FBI office alone without authorized personnel on-site. He just happened to be the only authorized personnel around until the eight Denver agents hit town last week. Even with those folks taking some of the load off, he'd still been in the old building from early morning till late evening most days. Jason's crew had been at it full tilt for ten straight days now. Some rooms only had minor touch-ups remaining. Another day and the renovation would be wrapping up. Then what would he do?

Well, there was the "armed men" issue, which was going nowhere fast. Everyone was scared to death of DOJ coming down on them for infringing on the group's right to worship. The Prophet had proclaimed a "New America" would spring from the mountains of southwestern Montana, but no one in the federal government had a clue what that meant. Since there'd been no hint of illegal activity in days, the FBI surveillance agents had pulled out this afternoon. They were back home in their beds in Denver tonight.

He'd gotten word that two of the Charlotte agents who'd been fired over the Brunson case had appealed their terminations. All the folks on his old White Collar Crime Squad were keeping their heads down waiting for a new supervisor to be named, waiting for the appeal hearings to begin, waiting for other repercussions. One of the Charlotte agents had texted him to watch his back. *What does that mean?* He had an awful sense of foreboding about it. Good men's lives had been turned upside down. The bad guy had friends in high places, and those places included the DOJ and the FBI. It was a hard lesson, a sickening lesson in the workings of the world. The good guys didn't always win—not in this life anyway.

A diesel engine starting near the main housing area jogged him out of his melancholy thoughts. Black wisps of clouds swept across the moon for a moment and plunged the sparkling world around him into darkness. The moon reappeared in little slivers that sent shafts of light through the heavy snowfall. God was whispering to him, *Focus on the good.* His thoughts turned to small accomplishments, little positives to pull him back from the undercurrents of depression.

Well, he hadn't yet broken the Park Service's strict rule on not feeding the animals, although it was killing him not to feed the chipmunks and ground squirrels that made his backyard their home.

And he'd come to treasure his hour-long lunches, when he'd wander to one of Mammoth's two restaurants, eat his one decent meal of the day, and text or call his brothers, his buddies, or friends in the Bureau.

Plus, he'd hired a housekeeper, Tia, who'd come once a week and keep the dust from accumulating in the house. She'd also drive sixty miles into Livingston every week to pick up groceries and dry cleaning for him and for several other single men and women who lived in Mammoth and didn't have the time or desire to shop for themselves. She was a kind, middle-aged woman who liked his cat and would even iron his shirts.

And he'd bought a dark-brown felt hat from the Mammoth General Store that suited him. It was a mix between a cowboy hat and a fedora, and it kept the rain and sleet off. He'd never worn anything on his head to work, but most men in this region seemed to wear some kind of cap or hat when they were outside and the weather was bad—and the weather always seemed to be bad.

He'd also signed up for the ten-dollar membership at the hotel's sports club, a gym of sorts that was open to employees and contractors at the park. It had a basketball court and a reasonable assortment of weights and exercise equipment. It was in a historic building directly behind the hotel and just over a hundred yards from his office. Now he had no excuse for not getting back in shape, especially since the Bureau gave their special agents three work hours a week for physical fitness. He'd let that slide during the last six months. It was way past time to put the hammer down on working out.

Maybe most important, he'd revived his once-long-standing habit of calling his folks and grandparents every Sunday afternoon or evening. For most of his life they'd been his anchors. No one had chided him for his self-centered sinfulness of the last two years. No one had said, "I told you so." He was so grateful for those examples of unconditional love.

And last night he'd pulled out the big file folder that held all the job proposals he'd received since law school. Those who didn't know him well always assumed he'd move from a successful college football career directly into the pros. Win loved the game, but he'd never felt the draw toward pro football. Oh, the money was great, but he never pictured his life there. He'd had solid offers from several top-flight law firms and corporations. His one-year stint as an Assistant U.S. Attorney bolstered his already-impressive résumé, but settling into a traditional law firm or a corporate environment didn't fit his style.

The FBI had appealed to his desire for public service while offering something different—the chance to work with a team, the chance to make the world a better place, and maybe have some adventure along the way. He'd seen the Bureau as his life's calling. He'd never had one regret, never one doubt, about his chosen life's work until January 25th, when the U.S. Attorney in Charlotte, North Carolina, announced at a press conference that several FBI agents were under investigation for misconduct relating to the alleged entrapment of Congressman Eric Brunson—a pillar of virtue in the U.S. Congress.

CHAPTER NINE

As Thursday night's big snowfall slowly melted into an icy mess, Win was spending his third consecutive Saturday in the office. Johnson would be back on Monday and Win wanted everything in place. He was wrapping up the highlight of his day: ten minutes of FaceTime with the world's cutest niece and world's greatest nephews and a recap of Razorback football recruiting with his brother Blake. He closed out the call, pushed off from the chair, and admired the newly hung bear painting on his wall as he reflected on the renovation's progress.

FBI technicians from the Salt Lake City Field Office had installed the new computers and other electronics, which had sat in their boxes for well over a year. Those guys stayed two extra days reconfiguring the building's security system and installing updated satellite communications systems to enable videoconferencing. They still wouldn't have coverage over the entire park, even with new systems, but it was a vast improvement over the outdated junk they'd relied on for years. Win had offered the technicians several nights at the Bureau's two visitors' cabins at Mammoth—both had sat empty the last two summers. Bartering the two cabins in one of the country's most popular parks, where it could be nearly impossible to get a room, turned out to be an easy sell. He knew if he'd waited for work orders to go through the proper channels in Denver, it would be months before the technical updates could be accomplished. Horse-trading went a long way, he'd found, even in the federal government.

The steady, freezing drizzle and fog drifting by his second-story window at 1:30 in the afternoon was one more reason for working in the office this Saturday. Win plopped back down in his chair, logged into his secure email, and discovered that Johnson had decided to prolong his getaway by taking a couple of weeks of annual leave after he left Quantico yesterday. As much as he didn't like the man, Win felt a sinking feeling as he reread the message. Two more weeks alone. . . . He knew he wasn't real good at "alone." Most of his life had revolved around a team: his close-knit family, football in junior and senior high school, college football, then Shelby, his FBI squad in Charlotte—his teams. He let out a deep sigh, turned away from the computer, and thumbed through the sparse files on his desk. He could read through the "armed men" working files again, or he could go home, change into his sweats, and watch a TV movie. He picked up the files.

It had been ten days since Win had visited the Bordeaux home. FBI background checks on Luke and Ellie sat on his desk; he basically had them memorized, but he glanced through them again. Luke grew up in a low-income family of four children in a rural area south of Ferriday, Louisiana. His father worked at a chemical plant in Vidalia and drove trucks for log companies or area farmers on his days off. He died five years ago in a log-truck accident. At thirty-two, Luke was the eldest son. He'd been a very good student and an outstanding athlete until the middle of his junior year in high school, when he dropped out to work at a local sawmill.

"Looks like he quit school to help support the family. What a shame." Win added his own commentary to the factual report.

A second Bordeaux son had served time in the state penitentiary for various minor drug offenses and now worked at a local grain elevator. A third son joined the Army and was killed in Afghanistan. That would have been around the time Luke started running into trouble in his own Army unit. He'd been released with an honorable discharge, but it was clear he was forced out. Until that time, Luke Bordeaux was an outstanding soldier. He'd served with distinction in Iraq and

Afghanistan. *Silver Star, Bronze Star, Purple Heart—wow, this guy's a hero.* After nine years in the service, he'd moved up to staff sergeant and was an instructor for special operations at Fort Bragg, North Carolina. He'd been selected for Delta Force right before his separation from the service. Delta Force was the Army's equivalent of the Navy Seals, the best of the best. Win thumbed back through the service documents. He wanted to know what happened to end what appeared to be an exemplary Army career, but Luke's military records were incomplete and Win's requests for more information had hit a wall.

There wasn't much information on Ellie. She was thirty years old. Born and raised in Vidalia. Her mother was a schoolteacher and her father worked as a foreman on a local farm. There were two sisters who had families and still lived in the general area. Ellie had been an excellent student and an all-state basketball player. Her degree in elementary education was from Methodist University, near Fort Bragg. *Bet she went to college while Luke was stationed there.* She and Luke had been married since she was nineteen years old. *Childhood sweethearts, maybe?*

They'd moved to Montana just over five years ago, but both children were born in Louisiana. Win smiled. They may live out West, but they were trying to make sure they raised little LSU fans.

There was information on everything from credit scores to traffic tickets to every single incident with any law enforcement agency. Nothing interesting until the last fourteen months, when Luke's run-ins with the local FBI agent began.

Win stretched back in his chair, put his hands behind his head, and closed his eyes for a moment. He thought of these "subjects" as the living, breathing people he'd shared dinner with, told his stories to, and laughed alongside just a few nights ago. He pictured Ellie's smile when she saw him in the hardware store, and Luke's menacing eyes in the mist as the guy turned toward him with gun drawn. . . .

He let his mind wander to probe various scenarios. Could Luke Bordeaux have been involved with Daniel Shepherd's group before they made their move to Gardiner? In the suspected bank robberies?

Could Bordeaux have known them through his military connections? Could—

The ringing of his personal phone interrupted his thoughts. He didn't recognize the number, but it looked local. Probably a wrong number, he thought, but he answered it anyway.

She had been crying—he could tell it in her voice.

"Win Tyler?"

He sat up straight in his chair and answered calmly. "Hey, Ellie, you okay?"

"Wouldn't be calling you if I was okay, would I? I found your card in the yard a while back. I . . . I think I need to talk to you. I can't talk on the phone long . . . I'm using a lady's phone in Gardiner."

Smart girl. She isn't using her cell phone to call me. Good. "You in any danger?"

"No, no, not now—but it might get to that, and I'm afraid for Luke."

"Okay, when is a good time to meet?"

"I can get someone to keep the kids tomorrow after church. Luke won't be home until tomorrow night. . . . Luke doesn't know I'm calling you."

Yeah, figured that. "Where do you want to meet?"

"Fewer folks know me in Mammoth, I suppose. More tourists there, could blend in." She sounded like she was fixing to cry again.

"How about the chapel here at Mammoth, two o'clock. Will that work?"

"Okay . . . okay, I'll come."

The call went dead and Win stared down at the four short paragraphs that, according to the FBI, summed up the life of Mary Ellen "Ellie" Bordeaux. Just the facts. Not the soul. He'd never developed an informant before, but he was already sure he wasn't gonna like it.

* * *

The powers that be at the Bureau, the Park Service, and the Secret Service declared a full-court press for Win's meeting with Ellie. The higher-ups were on a videoconference within twenty minutes of her call. Even though the agencies had nothing concrete on the church group, the grainy photos of a military-type militia in Yellowstone just ahead of some very high-level diplomatic visits still had Washington a little shaken. Prophet Shepherd's rants on the ultra-right-wing radio circuit had become increasingly anti-Semitic, and that wasn't helping calm nerves. No one had been able to get any reliable intel on what was going on within the group. The ATF informant was suddenly off the grid. Win's contact with Ellie was critical to advance the investigation, and Chief Randall seemed to be the only one who believed Win could pull it off.

Tom Strickland, the Denver Field Office's Special Agent in Charge, knew about the Brunson fiasco in North Carolina. He knew Win had been exiled to Yellowstone instead of being fired. But he also knew enough about the politics of big-time political corruption cases to acknowledge the possibility that Agent Tyler might have simply been in the wrong place at the wrong time and hadn't gotten a fair shake by the Bureau. Still, Win's big boss was very hesitant to put a relatively new agent, even a good one, in a situation where the information he needed to gather was so essential.

SAC Lomax, of the Secret Service, thought they were nuts to even be considering it. He wanted to immediately bring Ellie Bordeaux "in" when she showed up at the chapel and pressure her to reveal what she knew—through threats of putting her children in state custody and indicting her for harboring fugitives. He wanted to play hardball, and he certainly didn't think Win was up to the task.

Chief Randall pointed out to both of them that Mrs. Bordeaux had contacted Win on his personal phone, and so it was very likely she would only meet with him. If a more experienced agent appeared instead and she refused to cooperate, the entire investigation would be derailed.

It was finally agreed that park rangers in civilian clothes would clear the chapel and secure its entrances. FBI agents from Denver would run Win with a wire and video feeds. The Secret Service guys would just have to stand around and fret. Lomax hated it, but he finally agreed. Win spent half of Saturday night on the video feed being coached by various FBI tutors on informant-management techniques. When he finally got home, he ate a peanut butter and jelly sandwich, remembered to feed the cat, and lay down on the bed with his Bible. After a few minutes of reading, he knew how he'd handle it.

When the FBI contingent walked into the office the next morning, Win was shocked to see that the Denver SAC and the National Security ASAC had accompanied their two wire technicians and the support agents. The FBI jet from Denver had also landed in Jackson and picked up Win's direct supervisor, Jim West. They'd flown into Bozeman, the nearest large airport, and arrived in Mammoth mid-morning. There was no pep talk, no chitchat. After brief introductions, they left Win to do his job as they huddled downstairs with Lomax and Chief Randall in the conference room.

SAC Strickland reminded Win of one of those big-shouldered English bulldogs: medium height, barrel-chested, with small, watchful eyes and a clean-shaven head. He'd been one of the first African American agents to serve as an FBI Assistant Director. He'd stepped down from that job in January and taken the Denver SAC position because he'd grown up in southern Colorado and planned to retire there. The last thing he needed was a major screwup in a national park on his watch. He'd been in the Bureau for twenty-five years, was former military, and had the reputation of being organized, direct, and fair. He'd never been to Yellowstone National Park, and while he had no illusions his young agent would score much on the informant meeting, he saw the trip as a good chance to be out among the troops.

Denver's Assistant Special Agent in Charge, or ASAC, for National Security, Wes Givens, had the tall, slim, Ivy League lawyer look. The guy could have been a model for *Town & Country*. An expensive tan trench coat was perfectly folded across his left arm as he shook Win's hand.

Win's quick assessment of his immediate boss, Jim West, confirmed his impressions from their phone and video calls. The guy was in his early forties, about five feet ten, with blondish-brown hair in a short cut. Jim's eyes were alert and friendly when he introduced Win to the higher-ups.

All three men had a competent, professional air about them. They were here on serious business and their demeanor reflected that fact. They *looked* like FBI agents. Win was thinking the Director would be pleased.

Just before the two o'clock meeting time, Win was sitting in his SUV in the small parking lot across the highway from the Yellowstone Chapel, listening to the radio chatter and watching the surroundings. Several civilian vehicles had been parked in the lot so that Win and Ellie's vehicles wouldn't stand out. A female ranger in hiking garb was lounging near the front of the chapel's white double doors, pretending to read a map in the light drizzle. Win thought that was weak, but at least she could prevent anyone from entering the building. Two plainclothes rangers were near the rear of the church, trying to look nonchalant. It occurred to Win that the church's chiseled stone was the same pale-gray color as the low-hanging clouds.

Since leaving her house for church early that morning, Ellie had been trailed by two cars of FBI agents out of Bozeman who'd been brought in to help. Win watched one of the surveillance vehicles slowly drive by as Ellie pulled into the lot. She parked the silver Toyota pickup three spaces down from Win's SUV at 1:58 p.m.

The chatter on the radio stopped. *Time to saddle up.* Win took a deep breath and got out of the truck. He walked to the chapel and went in—he could feel her eyes on him. The small front foyer was adorned with two beautiful stained-glass windows that carried the themes of the park: waterfalls, geysers, and wildlife. Polished beams anchored the vaulted wooden ceiling in the main sanctuary. A carpeted center aisle led to the raised chancel with its tall wooden cross and altar. Everything was spotless. This vintage house of worship was obviously much loved. He moved slowly down the rows of oak pews. He didn't have to remind himself he wasn't there to see the 1913 architecture today.

He was surprised at how calm he felt. His bosses might not like it, but he was going to handle this his way. If it worked, fine. If not, well, at least he could live with himself. There would be no pressure, no threats, no blanket offers, no attempts to turn her against her husband. She came in the door of the sanctuary a couple of minutes behind him.

The audio feed on the wire Win was wearing and the video from the hidden cameras were being transmitted directly into the park's Dispatch Office, a compact building 250 yards away. Chief Randall, SAC Strickland, and SAC Lomax all stood directly behind the large screens relaying the live feed and watched the show. Their number twos took up positions on the sides of the room.

Win walked to the front of the small sanctuary and looked at the gleaming brass cross, open Bible, and twin candlesticks on the altar. It wasn't an ornate church by any means.

He turned and faced her.

"Hey, Ellie, I appreciate you coming. How's Abby and Ethan?" He said it as casually as if he'd just run into an old friend in the produce aisle in Kroger.

She smiled at his question and stopped in front of the chancel where he stood. They talked about the weather and the children for a minute. Then she turned her head to the side, watched his deep-blue eyes a moment, and shook her head. "You're waiting for me to decide what to do, aren't you, Win Tyler? Is that how you people do these things?"

"Naw, that's not the way it usually goes, but I've never done this before. You're an intelligent, resourceful woman. You tell me what you need me to know and we'll go from there. Did you test the spirits like I asked you to?"

SAC Lomax shook his head and looked at Strickland. "Where did you *get* this guy!"

Randall's annoyance showed. "Be quiet and watch how he works. He's honest with her. . . . Paying attention to how she's feeling. He let her know she's calling the shots, then asked a question. He's smart."

She sat down on the front row of pews across from where he stood, and looked down at her hands. "Some of the men are evil, but some are just grasping for anything that makes them feel a part of something bigger than themselves."

"I'm most interested in the evil ones, Ellie. Luke's one of the other ones, isn't he?"

"You know that. I . . . I wouldn't be here if I didn't think you saw who he is. Only he's been going to Prophet Shepherd's church for a couple more months than I have—he's spending more of his time with the men at the church now. He's let four men move into the mobile homes on our place. They moved in the day after you came by. We used to use the trailers for Luke's hunting clients, but business has fallen off." She looked up at him and paused. "They're paying rent, cash we need, and Luke says I'm silly to worry about them influencing him to be too extreme. But they're not good men."

"Well, here's the downside you and I both know right well: You sleep with dogs, you're liable to get fleas."

"And Luke knows that too. But it's like he's being brainwashed at the church. The Prophet's sermon today . . . he said a few truths, but then he twisted the truth to hate. Talked about reclaiming America, about bringing the government down, taking over the park. Preached hate! Luke can't see it. I'm afraid he's letting the bitterness he feels consume him. It's clouding his mind!" She started crying softly.

Win sat down beside her and handed her a Kleenex from the pew rack. "Well, renting the mobile homes right next to you and the kids to a bunch of lowlifes certainly isn't sound thinking." He waited a moment and then asked softly, "Well then, Ellie, what's the Lord telling you to do about it?"

The folks in the Dispatch Office exchanged glances. Where was Agent Tyler going with this?

"I've been praying about it, and I think the Lord has sent you to us as a deliverer. You came to our house just as I'd come to realize something awful was fixing to happen. I don't have proof . . . ah, it's more a feeling . . . but there's meanness brewing. At first Luke thought they were just trooping around like soldiers, maybe reliving old times. No real harm done. But he knows something is going on now—he isn't sure what—and he's too proud to get out." She wiped away more tears. "Are you going to ask me their names?"

"You'll tell me if you want to. . . . I trust you to know what you should do."

"I think the men at our place have been living in South Dakota and Nebraska somewhere. When they first showed up, they all had fresh haircuts, brand-new clothes, boots, everything. And it was like they'd been schooled in the Prophet's doctrine. Not taught truth, just schooled in what to say, you know? I don't even think they use their real names."

"Any idea on the real names?"

"Sometimes I'll hear one of them slip up and call someone by a different name. . . . They actually do that pretty often."

"Not the sharpest knives in the drawer then?"

She laughed softly. "Luke said almost the same thing the other night." She paused for a moment and studied the wadded tissue in her hand. "Do you want me to write this down for you?"

"No, the FBI is recording us, so just tell it to me."

"Someone's recording this now?" Her eyes darted around the sanctuary. "That makes me a little anxious. . . ."

"It keeps you from being here too long, and it keeps others from saying you said something you didn't say." *Not to mention it allows us to use everything you say against you and the people you love,* he thought to himself.

She accepted that and spent the next several minutes giving him a tremendous amount of information on the four men living on their place.

"Who's their leader? Who's running the show?"

"Luke says everyone's a follower of the Prophet, but these four seem to answer to a man named Ron King. I heard someone call him Chandler once. He turned on the guy like he was gonna hit him when that name slipped out. He came here with the Prophet to establish the church several months ago. He really is an evil one—you can see it in his eyes. He was over at our place all morning yesterday. I picked up a pen he'd been writing with and put it in a ziplock bag, like I've seen them do on the police shows. Maybe y'all can get fingerprints on him." She pulled the baggie from her pocket and laid it on the pew.

"You're afraid of him?" He already knew the answer to that question, and before she could answer, he asked her if she and the kids could go back to her mother's for a while till this all blew over. She said she'd been trying to arrange for the children to go back, but she was now convinced that whatever the men were up to was happening soon. She'd heard them refer to a mission in May several times.

"Yesterday I was behind the trailers, rehanging the clothesline that fell down in the snow. They didn't know I was out there, and I overheard some things I probably wasn't supposed to hear. Ron King said something about,"—she glanced back down at her hands—"about a 'hit,' about a 'target.' They were talking about explosives . . . and . . . 'bringing in the big guns.' Whatever that means." She looked away, then tried to smile. "Maybe I've been watching too many *CSI* reruns on TV."

Win shook his head. "No, no I don't think so. . . . Anything you can tell me is helpful."

Then her nerves got the best of her. She stood quickly. "I've got to go get the kids." He walked behind her to the foyer door, where she stopped and turned to him. "Has it occurred to you that Luke would want to kill you if he knew you'd met me?"

"Well, if he just wants to kill me, that's okay by me—if he decides to do something about it, then I've got a problem." He smiled down at her. "Okay, seriously, it did cross my mind. Why do you think I suggested we meet in a church?" He tried to sound reassuring. "It wouldn't be a good idea to tell Luke we met, and I'm glad you didn't call me from your cell phone. But if you need help, you call any way you can, you hear? Don't put yourself in harm's way to get information, but if you learn anything interesting, I'd like to hear about it." He gave her a small white card with a phone number and told her that it would be answered 24/7. That she should ask for him or tell whoever answers that she needs help.

"You need a code word to use if there's ever a situation where you or the children are in real danger and I need to get you out fast. Pick a word or a phrase you would never say in conversation. Something you would never think of saying."

She lowered her head and thought for only a second or two, then replied, "Roll Tide!" No one from Louisiana would ever say the University of Alabama's battle cry.

"Perfect!" He grinned. "I like your style, Ellie."

"Do y'all have a plan?" Her eyes were fearful. Her eyes were on his.

"The FBI? Probably not yet, but you need to remember the Lord does. Jeremiah 29:11 says that the Lord knows His plans for us. And His plans are for good and not for evil, to give us a future and a hope. You've got to have faith, Ellie."

"I'm trying to hold on to that, Win." She looked down and then asked, "Is there any way to keep Luke out of trouble in this?"

He knew that would be the central question. He knew that was coming.

"Ellie, he can talk to me and we can work something out, maybe even get the poaching charges dropped. I've talked to him about it. Maybe he's thinkin' on it. I hope so."

They walked into the small foyer and he held the heavy outer door open for her.

"Remember, Ellie, He has a plan."

"Thank you, Win Tyler." Then she walked out into the spitting rain.

* * *

The brass and their entourages had moved from the Dispatch Office to Chief Randall's conference room by the time Win made the short walk from the chapel.

"You hit it out of the park! That was one of the best informant contacts I've taped in years. Really creative!" The lead FBI wire technician was obviously impressed. Win figured the guy needed to get a life.

"Mr. Strickland said to tell you they'll be back over to your office after they finish the wrap-up with the Park and Secret Service folks." Win handed off the ziplock bag containing the pen to another technician. The last thing he wanted to do was get ready for a conference with his superiors. He'd been so focused on the meeting with Ellie that he hadn't spoken to any of them except for the initial formalities hours ago.

He walked over to the FBI office and made a fresh pot of coffee. He was sure glad little Jason and his crew had gotten the bulk of the remodeling finished. The renovated courtroom actually looked like a first-class conference room—not junk storage space. It wasn't large, but it would easily accommodate ten to twelve people. Jason had come through with an American flag and large Bureau seal for the back wall. The room's historic artwork was jaw-dropping. He sat down at the long oak table and closed his eyes for a few seconds. He didn't want to relive the meeting with Ellie . . . not yet. He couldn't shake the feeling he was using her. Well, it wasn't just a feeling. It was a fact. On the other hand, Luke was the one who'd gotten his family in this mess by becoming involved with those yahoos and allowing some of them to move onto their land. Maybe the intel would show this bunch was just a group of misfit wannabes and the FBI could go out and scold them and every-one could go back to their normal lives. He knew there were a lot of possible outcomes. He knew that wasn't one of them.

CHAPTER TEN

H ey, buddy! You ready to pack it up and c'mon down and practice a little law with me? Got ya a big-dollar client all lined up!" It was Tucker Moses's upbeat voice on Win's personal phone at 5:00 in the morning.

"What are you doin' up at this hour? It ain't even hunting season! Let me guess, you aren't up, you just haven't been down yet."

"You think I stay up and party all night every night?"

"Uh-huh."

"Damn straight I do! But it's Wednesday morning, six o'clock here, and I drug myself up early so's I could catch you before you got off nabbin' criminals. Hadn't really talked since you got out West. Texting don't count for much. . . . You thinking 'bout my offer?"

Win yawned and grunted into the phone. He'd detoured to spend four days at Tucker's family home on the Moriah Plantation in Louisiana when he drove from Charlotte to Arkansas last month. He and Tucker had shared an apartment for their three years of law school at the University of Arkansas. He didn't have a closer friend in the world. After school, Tucker had joined his uncle's law firm in Oxford, Mississippi; it was a perfect fit for him. He'd been the kicker for the Ole Miss Rebels for his four years of undergraduate school, and the name recognition from his college football career propelled his law practice in the university town. Tucker was doing real well for himself.

"I'm not kidding, Win! Got a Boston pension fund owns pert near half of Chicot County needing a sharp agricultural lawyer. You're the man! Can get you a $20,000 retainer today! That's just one client. Hell, they'll be thicker'n ticks when folks hear you're hangin' out your shingle."

"Un-huh. First off, I'm not an agricultural lawyer. . . ." Win yawned again.

"Close enough! You grew up on a farm. Hell, you kin even ride a horse. Those Yankees won't ask too many questions; besides, you sure got the sharp lawyer part down pat! C'mon, quit hangin' back on me. What with your brains and good looks and my astute business and marketing sense, we'll be the hottest little law firm in the Mid-South fore you kin bat an eye!"

"Reckon that'd be right, but I'm not feelin' it just yet, you know. . . . Maybe I need a few more weeks to get myself back running between the ditches fore I start making big decisions."

Tucker eased back on his sales pitch. "Well, I reckon I can spend this twenty grand. . . . But you still think on it, you hear. Besides, seeing as you're single again and I haven't had a take-her-to-meet-mama girl-friend in a coon's age, I could use a few of your castoffs."

"For real, Tucker?"

"Well, I haven't exactly been beating off the women lately. Hit a bit of a dry spell." He paused, then his voice took on a serious tone. "Don't suppose you and Shelby have talked?"

"No, no . . . haven't called. Haven't heard from her. . . . No."

They both breathed a deep sigh. During their visit last month, he and Tucker had talked over his breakup with Shelby with their typical depth of emotion: Tucker had told him he was real sorry and Win had replied that he'd make it. Then they'd gone out and shot five rounds of skeet at Tucker's daddy's hunting club. Afterward they'd sat on the club's big wooden deck overlooking the cypress swamp on Bayou Cocodrie. They'd drunk a couple of beers and discussed next fall's football season. Nothing else had been said of Win's broken engage-ment or his broken heart.

Tucker ended the somber mood. "Gotta go get ready for the read-ing of a will—can you imagine how thrillin' my morning's gonna be! Anything exciting going on in Yellowstone?"

"Well, a guy held an assault rifle on me the other evening, then pulled a Beretta on me a week ago Saturday, and I nearly got into a shoot-'em-up my first day out here. 'Cepting for that, it's been pretty slow."

"Hot damn! Told you it wasn't gonna be any fun out there! Hey, did you ever wonder why we morph into talking like rednecks when we get with each other?"

"Maybe 'cause we *are* rednecks?" They both laughed at their fool-ishness and punched off the call. Win smiled at the phone as he pulled on his sweatpants. He'd done a few things right in his life—being best friends with Tucker Moses was one of them.

* * *

After he'd finished his early-morning routine, and done a few extra stretches against the wall of the old garage, he was setting a pretty good clip up the winding trail behind his house. The lousy weather had moved out on Sunday night; it had been clear and cool ever since. He'd made the run up Beaver Ponds Trail the last two mornings to the top of a remote overlook that gave him a great view of the hot springs' terraces and the mountains to the south and east. He didn't know where the trail went, but exploring it in earnest would have to wait for more snow to melt. He could jog about one and a half miles steadily upward to a level bench area before he hit the snowpack—that would do for the time being.

The guy at the gas station had suggested the "hike" but warned Win to carry bear spray, which they conveniently had for sale for for-ty-five dollars a canister. Win hadn't seen a bear yet, but the trail signs all carried sobering warnings, so he paid his money, took the one-min-ute "how to use the stuff" lecture from the filling-station guy, and wore it clipped to a web belt with his water bottle. It was a hassle running with the stuff, but at least he was running again.

It woulda been nice to focus on the sounds of the small stream, the birds, or an occasional interrupted squirrel on those early-morning runs, but his mind was filled with details of the False Prophet case, as they were calling it now. It'd been three days since his meeting with Ellie and two weeks since he'd driven to the Bordeaux house. At the debrief on Sunday afternoon, SAC Strickland told him they'd gotten enough credible intel from Ellie to open a domestic terrorism case, and then shocked him by naming him the case agent. Win's bosses had been lavish in their praise of him, not only for the informant interview with Ellie, but also for his other actions on the case. And all the men seemed blown away by the satellite office's dramatic makeover. As they'd left Sunday afternoon, ASAC Givens had told him how pleased they were to have him as a part of the Denver Field Office. Win was still trying to get his head around the unexpected elevation in his status within the Bureau.

The False Prophet case—*my case*—was ramping up big-time. Analysts in several federal agencies were grinding out the background information on any possible suspect who could match the information Ellie had given him. The fingerprints on Ron Chandler, or Ron King, as he was calling himself, turned out to be a real winner. Chandler had been dishonorably discharged from the Army for two vicious assaults in Iraq and had spent considerable time in the military prison in Fort Leavenworth, Kansas. Since his last release from prison, he'd become the prime suspect in several bank robberies and at least four murders. The man was smart and ruthless—there was strong suspicion of heinous crimes, but not enough evidence to arrest him.

Specialized teams of armed FBI surveillance agents, or MST-As, from Minneapolis and Salt Lake City had arrived, and the eight surveillance folks from Denver had reappeared. With eighteen agents now in the field, their coverage of the Arm of the Lord Church had intensified considerably. Denver had flown in a supervisor on Monday to coordinate the surveillance effort. Watching suspects in the sparsely populated backcountry was far more challenging than anticipated, even with the surveillance teams' three airplanes in periodic use.

The Jackson RA was nearing the takedown phase of a major meth-amphetamine investigation and FBI manpower on the Violent Crime Squad was stretched thin for at least another week. Win was in desperate need of clerical help, so Chief Randall sent over a Park Service clerk with top secret clearance, Janet Swam. She'd been helping him handle the logistical stuff, getting lodging and vehicles for the incoming agents and keeping the office running. Janet reminded Win of his second-grade teacher. She was ancient in a timeless sort of way, with severe hair, prim dress, and a ridiculously serious expression. She did, however, appear in his office with treats twice a day, so all was good.

Bureau intelligence analysts were laying out chilling scenarios for Win to review. Everything from an armed takeover of park buildings with hostages, to the destruction of irreplaceable natural wonders with explosives was being considered. Then there was always the very realistic possibility that nothing would happen at all. Problem was, it was now his job to prevent a catastrophe, while at the same time not over-reacting. Win was quickly learning that being the case agent on an investigation of this size was both exciting and incredibly exhausting. He knew he had to get his exercise and his sleep if he was going to stay on top of it.

He slowed to leap a deep mudhole in the path and forced his mind back to the run. He hadn't seen anyone else on the trail any higher than the cascading hot springs, now far below him. All he could see of the terraces this morning were pockets of fog mixing with the rising steam. He slowed to a walk as he crested the hill's steepest point. He moved off the trail toward a clearing containing a sloping gray boulder that God must have put there just for folks to sit on and stare in awe at the wonder of the mountains in the mornings. On Monday, the first day that he'd made the run, he'd been stunned by the splendor of the view. Gray, purple, and blue mountains stretching to the horizon—their colors giving clues to the distance. In this clear air, at this altitude, he was guessing he could see for over forty miles. He slowed his breathing, unbuckled the bear-spray belt, and dropped it to the side as he walked to the boulder. He had a few minutes to kill before he started down the hill, so he sat down on the large rock and took off his sweaty knit cap. He leaned back on the cold granite and waited for the sun to clear the distant hills.

He felt eyes on him before he heard anything. He sat up slowly and silently cursed himself for leaving the bear spray forty feet away. Win slid off the rock and saw him standing at the edge of the clearing. He'd probably seen more frightening sights in his life—but he sure couldn't remember when. Luke Bordeaux was in full camouflage and armed to the teeth.

"I aim to teach you a lesson, damn you." He didn't say it loudly and he didn't say it with emotion. He said it as a fact.

Luke knows. He knows I met with Ellie.

"Threatening a federal agent isn't real smart, Luke." Win was amazed his voice wasn't shaking.

"This ain't between me and the FBI. This is between me and you. We're gonna see how well they taught you to fight in your FBI school." He leaned the assault rifle against a tree and pulled off the large military backpack and his holster belt. He threw his canvas field cap down on top of the pack and ran a hand through his black hair. His eyes never left Win, and Win could feel their hostility even from the distance.

At least he's not gonna shoot me. . . . Some consolation.

Win hadn't been in a real fistfight since junior high school. It sure wasn't his preferred method to settle disputes, but it was a whole lot better than gunplay. As Luke began moving slowly toward him, Win crouched slightly and waited. They were about the same size. Win might have an advantage in reach, but that was about it. Win thought of the huge stack of firewood at Bordeaux's house—*This guy is probably strong as an ox.* And he knew there was little chance of his prevailing against a man who'd spent several years in the Army Special Forces. Win's eighty hours of FBI defensive tactics training, which didn't include a whole lot of actual fighting, would have to be supplemented by divine intervention and some creative thinking. *Maybe the guy will get overconfident,* Win thought. Luke Bordeaux certainly had every reason to be overconfident.

Win lunged at him when Luke was just outside swinging range. Win came in fast and caught Luke with a blow to the face that turned him, but Luke landed a glancing strike to Win's jaw, sending him hard to the ground. As he sprang up, Luke sidestepped and dropped him again with two clasped hands to the back of Win's head.

Damn! All Win could see for a moment were brilliant, flashing lights amid the sharp pain.

He gave up on conventional boxing and lunged upward toward Luke's middle from the rocky ground. Luke sidestepped again and brought him back to the ground with a solid kick to the ribs. Win shook off the blow and rolled to the side, bringing Luke down with a twist of his legs. *Something I learned has worked!* He went for Luke's hands while he had him down, but Luke was quicker and knocked him back with a knee to the stomach. Win tried to back away, gasping for breath, but Luke was on him in less than a second and knocked him flat on his back with a right fist to his jaw. Luke said nothing, but stepped back while Win staggered to his feet.

It clearly wasn't over yet. Win stumbled over a bare sagebrush, spit out some blood, and waited for Luke to move back in. His head was spinning and he was having trouble knowing where to focus—Luke solved that problem by pulling a deadly-looking knife from somewhere and moving it slowly in a circle in front of him.

"That isn't fair!" It was all Win could think to say as he took a step back and fought to clear his head.

"Who told you life is fair?" Luke was in no hurry now. He balanced on the balls of his feet, just out of Win's striking range, slowly moving the knife and waiting for an opening.

Win couldn't back up any farther. The boulder he'd been sitting on earlier was right behind him. He crouched a little and tried to focus on the knife. *Watch the weapon,* his Quantico instructors had said, *the hand with the weapon will tell you where the person will strike.* It was so hard not to focus on the man's eyes, but nothing in Bordeaux's eyes could kill him. The knife surely could. He saw the silver blade reflect the sun's early rays. He was aware he was holding his breath, and he tried to breathe. *Being shot is not looking so bad compared to this.*

Win sighed deeply and turned his palms up slightly. Among his brothers at home, this was the sign of surrender. He had no other options. "Why . . . why don't you tell me why we're fighting, Luke?"

That was all it took. Luke was on Win before he could blink, throwing him against the boulder—his left hand pulling Win's arm behind him and his right hand drawing the knife to Win's throat. Win was pinned against the rock, staring right into the fury in Luke's eyes. He felt pain as the knife touched the side of his neck.

"Damn you! You leave Ellie out of this mess!" Luke hissed between clenched teeth. "You've got no right to drag her into your plots against me, against my friends! You're trying to turn her against me! You're trying to take everything I have—"

"She called me, Luke." Win closed his eyes; he knew this could go either way. "She. Called. Me." He said it in a whisper, as if saying it too loud would make it sound more wrong than it was.

Luke reacted as if he'd taken a body blow. He stepped back, blinking rapidly, and brought his free hand across his chest. He knew instinctively Win was telling the truth, yet accepting that truth was devastating.

Even unarmed, Win knew he had the upper hand now. "She's afraid, Luke! She's afraid for you, for the kids, for herself! She doesn't know what to do. She doesn't want to lose you, but she thinks they're pulling you away. She says you're too proud to ask for help. Maybe I can help you both."

"You ain't out to help anyone but you! If you go near her again, I will kill you!" Luke's voice shook when he said it. He turned on his heel, silently donned his gear, and blended into the forest.

The man appeared and disappeared as if into thin air. There was no sound, no movement on the trail or in the trees. For a few moments Win thought the fight could have been imagined. But his head was throbbing, his legs were shaking, and his ribs ached. He moved a hand to his neck and felt the blood. *All too real.* Win glanced down at his skinned knuckles; he'd only gotten in one good lick on Bordeaux.

Where do I go from here? He could press charges against Luke for assault. Luke would get arrested, Ellie would pull back, and they'd have no possibility of an informant within Daniel Shepherd's cult. Just based on what they had now, if warrants started hitting on the men who were staying in the mobile homes at the Bordeaux place, Luke and Ellie could both face harboring fugitives charges. That would be bad enough, but things could easily get much worse for them if the agents were able to tie them to any type of conspiracy against the Israeli Ambassador or other dignitaries who would be visiting the park next month.

Win tried to think about the logical, practical side of this problem: building a strong case for the Bureau. But his heart kept going in another direction. These were real people whose lives were very likely to be torn apart, and he would be one of the driving forces in that destruction. He folded his arms across his eyes and leaned against the cold boulder as the sun burned away the last of the fog below. His heart ached worse than his head. He didn't even know what to pray.

*   *   *

Win was glad no visitors were expected at the office today. He had angry-looking red scrapes from Luke's fist on the side of his jaw and above one eye. The shallow knife cut was visible on his neck. He entered the back door of the office after 7:45 a.m. and set about checking messages and reading all of the morning's required FBI bulletins from Denver and Jackson Hole. Mostly routine stuff today, thank goodness, nothing dramatic on the case. The surveillance supervisor was locked away in a downstairs office, probably frantic over the frequency with which they were losing their subjects. With any luck Win could dodge her till this afternoon. Three of Jason's carpenters were putting finishing touches on the new downstairs locker room and gun safe. Janet was in the conference room, organizing his hard copies for the working files on the subjects. She was the least-inquisitive person he'd ever met; she didn't even comment on his obvious injuries when she came upstairs to offer him two doughnuts from her daily box of goodies.

He took the scheduled call from his supervisor at 9:30 and was glad they weren't on video. Win could tell Jim West was preoccupied with the impending meth bust in Jackson, so he said nothing about the fight with Bordeaux. He was supposed to be developing Ellie Bordeaux as an FBI source. He reasoned that dealing with her volatile husband was just an unfortunate part of the process. Was Luke a danger to Ellie? No, nothing he'd seen in the man made him think that—Luke Bordeaux saw himself as Ellie's defender, her protector. Win would write up an innocuous incident report for the online file and leave it at that. Hopefully, Jim would be too busy to peruse it closely and it wouldn't come back to bite him.

Somehow, deep down, Win felt Luke's attack was justified—a bit excessive, but justified. He hadn't felt right talking to the man's wife behind his back, especially after the guy had already warned him off. Knowing it was for the Bureau and the greater good hadn't eased his conscience. After Luke whipped him, he actually felt better about it, as if he'd paid his penance. He knew it wasn't a logical feeling, but it was no less real. Win also knew Bordeaux could have killed him bare-handed this morning. Luke had roughed him up, but he'd deliberately pulled his punches so no serious harm was done. Luke Bordeaux was sending a message, man to man.

*   *   *

"Hey, Sport! What happened to you?" Gus Jordon was topping the stairs as Win crossed the hall to the communications room just before noon.

"Ran into something on my run this morning. No big deal." Win shrugged it off and shook hands with the Deputy Chief.

Gus walked from room to room, admiring the results of the renovation, then they took coffee into Win's office. They talked about the welcome spell of fine weather before Gus stated the reason for the visit. Chief Randall had run into the Montana ATF supervisor at a luncheon in Missoula yesterday, and the ATF guy wanted to quietly get the word out that their informant at the Arm of the Lord Church had missed a couple of scheduled contacts. It had been nearly a week since he'd last been seen, and ATF was getting concerned. The man was a drifter named Wayman Duncan. Gus had his latest mug shot, a physical description, and his vehicle information. Could be a real problem or the guy could have skipped out with ATF's money. Gus laughed and said ATF was notorious for losing informants right after they'd paid them.

Win grinned at that, and pain shot through his jaw. He gingerly placed a hand on it and nodded. He'd get the word out to the FBI surveillance agents in the field.

Gus was weighing whether to intrude into the agent's business. He finally spoke. "I think I can guess what you ran into on the trail this morning, Win," the ranger said. "I've been in this business a long time. That's a knife cut on your neck—a warning, I'd say. Was it only Luke?"

"Yeah. But Luke was enough." Win managed to smile.

As they walked out of the building, Gus made him an offer. "We don't have any special agents assigned here now, so tomorrow I'm going to interview the bear researchers who saw the armed men and took those photos. I'd be pleased to have you ride along. Roads aren't anywhere near clear yet, so I'll be following a snowplow into the park at 6:30 in the morning and following it out late. You'd get to see some of your new stomping grounds and interview two more of the case witnesses."

Win jumped at the opportunity to get out of the office and away from that stress for a day. "Sure, sure, I'll get the surveillance supervisor to cover the office."

"I'll pick you up at your place at 6:15. Wear warm hiking gear. I'll bring the coffee."

CHAPTER ELEVEN

The next morning, for the first time in months, Win actually found himself excited about doing something related to work. He was a little sore from the fight with Luke. Okay, he was a lot sore, but his cuts and bruises weren't nearly as noticeable. He did his push-ups and sit-ups, read his Scripture, had a cup of coffee, and was showered and ready to go before six. He tried to coax the cat to him with one of the new toys, but gave up and was content with watching Gruff stalk the light from his cell phone across the hardwood floor. He was feeling more like himself this morning. Maybe he was coming out of his three-month slump. He told himself it was about time.

Gus picked him up before sunrise, and the ranger's Tahoe slowly followed a huge snowplow up a steep, icy road any southern boy would have considered impassable. They entered an area Gus called the Golden Gate, where the highway extended around a sheer rock cliff. The road was suspended here and the drop was hundreds of feet. The snowplow's V-shaped steel blade sent tons of snow cascading over the side of the cliff. Win's anxiety over the road's condition was suddenly overridden by the stunning beauty of the sun clearing the eastern mountains and pouring golden light onto thousands of draping icicles and small frozen waterfalls. Ice hung from every crevice on the surrounding yellowish cliffs. The wondrous scene was topped by a silent fifty-foot waterfall of ice suspended above a stream near the highway. They were less than five miles southwest of Mammoth, but they'd already climbed nearly a thousand feet in elevation, and ten-foot piles of snow lined much of the road. They'd climbed back into winter.

The road crested the mountain pass and entered an upland valley surrounded by even higher mountains. The valley floor was covered with low, barren brush; swaths of evergreens dotted the rolling hills, and broad patches of snow filled shallow ravines. After following the plow for another mile, Gus pulled off at a snow-covered parking area and pointed out a shimmering lake. "Ice is breaking up, so there's usually some wildlife around Swan Lake. Got extra binoculars if you need them." He turned the crackling radio down low and they sat in the warm truck, poured coffee from Gus's thermos, and looked to the west.

As Win dug his field glasses out of his day pack, he spotted two coyotes loping along through the barrens only twenty yards from where they sat. "Coyotes in front of us. . . . Ah, what's the scrubby little bush that sticks up everywhere?"

"Sage, that's sagebrush. It'll be green and fragrant in a few weeks. It takes hold in most of the cleared areas between four thousand and ten thousand feet elevation. It's not related to the type of sage you cook with, but it smells real good."

As Win made another sweep of the area with the binoculars, he was thinking he had no idea anyone cooked with sage, but then if it wasn't grilled, fried, or breakfast, he was pretty much clueless about cooking. He made a mental note to get a plant identification book.

"This country's so different from what I'm used to. . . . Wow! Elk at two o'clock."

Six large bull elk with velvet antlers were making their morning pilgrimage to the lake. Their deep-rust-colored heads and chests contrasted sharply with their golden coats and white rumps. Their heads were up, ears alert, antlers swinging in step, as they moved through a snow-covered meadow with a dignity proclaiming them sovereign over this valley. *Awesome!* Win was running out of superlatives.

They kept up the watching and the talking for over an hour, and Gus dug out some of yesterday's doughnuts, which were still plenty good, and they had another round of coffee. The sun gained ground on the valley and turned every frost-covered blade of grass into crystal.

Two bald eagles swooped in and soared through the steam rising from the surface of the lake. A group of buffalo bulls crossed the road within ten yards of them and lumbered past. The massive heads swung to acknowledge the SUV, but it caused them no alarm. The frost and snow had frozen to their shaggy brown-and-black coats, and the sunlight made them sparkle with every movement. The condensation from their deep breaths formed foggy rings above each head, and they moved away like huge, shrouded ghosts through the barren sage. Win felt overwhelmed by the wonder of it all. He decided if he wasn't in Heaven, he was pretty darn close.

* * *

"Catch him! Catch him! Stop him!" a woman was screaming as she ran up the steep trail toward them. About twenty feet in front of her was a flying brown furball that was also squealing at the top of its lungs. Win was hiking the point down the backcountry trail, and he immediately kicked into gear. He hadn't spent years in fumble-recovery drills for nothing! The cub made a dodge to Win's left off the trail, and Win dove for it into a snowbank. He came up with the squirming, crying rascal in his left hand and triumphantly held it up. The cub immediately bit his hand and continued squalling. Win nearly dropped it.

"Hold it like a cat! Scruff of the neck!" Gus yelled to him. The cub bit again and Win stuffed it inside his open coat and hugged it tight—the crying stopped. Win could feel its little heart racing and beating hard against his own. He sat up in the snowbank and smiled down at the little critter. *I'm holding a real live wild bear—this is so cool!*

"Nice stop!" The woman called down to him from the trail. She was trying to catch her breath from the uphill sprint and was leaning toward him with her hands on her knees. Win slowly maneuvered to kneel in the snow. The woman was standing uphill above him, and when he stood, they were nearly eye-to-eye. Seeing her face brought him to a complete stop. She was flushed—both from the run and from the cold air—and her thick, long brown hair had fallen loose from its ponytail. She was looking into his coat at the little bear, and smiling one of the most beautiful smiles he could ever remember seeing. Then she looked up and met his eyes.

He pulled off his ball cap and nodded to her. "Howdy, ma'am, you lose this little thing?" *Cheesy, yes*, but she smiled at him. Her soft-brown eyes were locked on his and she straightened, nodded, and blushed even more. They both seemed at a loss for words, but she recovered faster than he did and motioned him down the trail.

"Do you want me to take him?" Her voice had a subtle southern accent.

"No, no, he's not even moving now."

"Got to get him back to his mama. She'll be waking up soon," the girl said. They rounded a house-size boulder and approached a tranquilized grizzly bear lying in the snow outside a round, culvert-shaped metal cage. A second cub was leashed to the trap. Five researchers were bustling around the bear in practiced activity. A bearded man, in shirtsleeves despite the cold, was drawing a blood sample from the adult bear's front leg, and a second man was doing measurements on teeth that looked to be over two inches long. A petite older woman approached the newcomers with outstretched hand.

"Hello, Gus, it's great you could get with us on a day when we've had such good luck. We'll wrap up here in a few minutes and move out so the animals can recover. Tory, where's the little male that got away?" The woman had a precise northeastern accent and a tone of authority. Win was guessing she ran a tight ship.

"I've got him," Win volunteered and walked closer so she could peer into his coat. The tiny bear was mewing softly, almost like a kitten.

"Do you mind holding him for a few minutes? We'll be finished here as soon as we weigh her and the cubs and get a few more samples." She turned back to her work.

Win really was interested in the research techniques, but he was much more interested in the young lady named Tory. She looked to be in her mid-twenties and she was tall, maybe five eight or five nine. She was dressed like the other researchers, in green insulated overalls and hiking boots. Her leather gloves and a red bandana were stuffed in her back pocket, and she was carrying a can of bear spray on a web belt.

No earrings and, most importantly, no wedding band on her hand. She pulled her hair back into the ponytail and continued to go about her work. In less than five minutes, Win and the older woman were extracting the cub from inside his coat. It weighed fifteen pounds—ideal for four months old, she said. Win was surprised when the woman handed it back to him.

"He seems to enjoy your company, best to keep them as low stressed as possible until we finish. We'll get the female cub now."

Win put the cub back into his coat and saw Tory give him a quick smile from her position on the other side of mama bear. It took everyone to lift the adult bear into the sling for the weigh-in. The bear weighed 405 pounds; a fairly large female, someone said, above average for this time of year with two cubs.

Gus held up a huge paw for Win to look over; the claws were at least three inches long. "This is one reason we don't jog in the woods this time of year." He gave Win a serious look. Win glanced back at the claws and remembered Gus's earlier warnings about not running alone in the mountains. He definitely needed a different exercise plan.

"Okay folks, let's pack up here!" the petite woman commanded as mother bear stirred, making a weak attempt to rise.

Win took the cub out of his coat and held it up to face him. It made no attempt to bite this time, but kept mewing softly. "See you, Bubba, you grow up big and strong." He passed it off to one of the researchers, who placed the cub next to its sister and mother. They quickly gathered equipment and backpacks and began the trek up the trail away from the bear family.

They hiked the switchbacks upward for well over a mile at a fast pace, finally pausing in an open meadow to rest. The small gray-haired woman, who had to be in her late sixties, wasn't even winded. She turned to Gus and introduced two of the men as the witnesses they were to interview. Gus, in turn, introduced Win to Dr. Catherine Kane from Northwestern University, the lead researcher for this year's Interagency Grizzly Bear Research Project.

"Gus, why don't you and Agent Tyler plan to have lunch with us at camp. It's nearly eleven o'clock now. You can do your interviews at your leisure," Dr. Kane suggested.

The researchers' camp, composed of canvas and nylon tents, was about four miles from the trailhead where Gus had parked the SUV. It was four miles of rugged territory, and while the trail was mostly open, the deeply shaded areas still contained large amounts of snow. Dr. Kane said their group had been at this site for three weeks and would be leaving within a few days. Some of the project's researchers would go back to Mammoth and Bozeman for seminars and a well-deserved break, then the camp would move to the Roosevelt area of the park.

The case interviews didn't take long. They sat at a sheltered camp table with each man and learned little more than what had been disseminated in the original report. Both the witnesses were wildlife biologists with the U.S. Fish and Wildlife Service, and neither of them seemed to think heavily armed gunmen roaming the wilderness was any big deal. They'd sent in the photos and report to the park's rangers only upon Dr. Kane's insistence.

While the group waited for the soup to warm on the Coleman stoves, Gus continued to visit with Dr. Kane, whom he'd known from his stint at Glacier National Park. Win dabbed alcohol on the tiny bites on his hand as he maneuvered close enough to the young woman to introduce himself.

"Hey, thanks for letting me hold the cub. That was a neat experience. I'm Win Tyler."

"Well, thank you for catching the little bugger. I'm Victoria Madison, everyone except my mother calls me Tory. Where you from?"

Thank you, God! Another southerner! And a darn pretty one at that.... "Heber Springs, Arkansas," he answered. "And you?"

"Just south of Nashville, Tennessee—a town called Franklin. I'm working with Vanderbilt University on this project for the Park Service."

They went through the usual exchange of information that comes so naturally to southerners, and he learned she'd recently obtained her doctorate at Vanderbilt in ecology and environmental sciences. This was her first year to be accepted into the Interagency Grizzly Bear Research Project, which was apparently a coveted position for anyone in her field. She clearly had an abundance of enthusiasm for the assignment. He was thinking she had to be a smart girl if she went to Vanderbilt. Too bad their football team was usually terrible, but then their former players probably all ran big law firms or Fortune 500 companies. A trade-off, he supposed.

Everyone ate together in a large heated tent, and most lingered over coffee after lunch. As they were finishing their coffee, a thin, scholarly-looking guy walked over and stood across the camp table from Win and the girl.

"Tory, I need you to come help me catalog some of the morning's samples." The man's tone had just the right amount of edge to suggest he did not like her keeping company with Win, however briefly.

"Ah, sure, Dave, let me introduce you to someone. Dr. David Crowder, this is Special Agent Win Tyler. He's here to talk to—"

Dr. Crowder didn't glance at Win. "Yes, yes, I heard we were having law enforcement people here today. Much ado over nothing, if you ask me."

Win started to respond with the usual "No one asked you" and put the guy in his place, but he let it pass. This arrogant guy might be Tory's boss or boyfriend. *One way to find out.*

Win ignored Dave and leaned in closer to Tory. "I know you've got to get back to work, but give me a call when you get to Mammoth next week. I'd like to hear more about what y'all are doing." He spoke loud enough for Dave, the jerk, to overhear him. Dave screwed up his mouth to speak but thought better of it. He turned and walked out of the tent. Definitely not a boyfriend—not yet, anyway, judging from his reaction to the challenge. Boss? Maybe.

"Sure," she was saying, "I would like that. Call you at your office?"

"Yeah, or call my cell. Here's my card. Either way would be good. Nice talking to you." He smiled when he handed her the card and felt encouraged by the interest in her brown eyes as she took it. *Things might just be looking up.*

* * *

"Was gonna try to show you the Norris Geyser Basin today. It's one of the park's main hot spots. Some great thermal features and geysers there, but we've got a little slide blocking the highway. We'll drive up and check in with the plow operators before we head back toward Mammoth," Gus was saying as Win fastened his seatbelt.

They'd stowed their gear in the back seat after the hike from the bear researchers' camp. Gus started the SUV and waited for the heater to warm up. "Noticed you visiting with a girl back there. . . . Heard her name was Tory. Very pretty gal," Gus remarked.

"Uh, yeah. She seems nice. I'd like—"

Gus interrupted. He seemed to be talking out loud to himself. "She might be a little young for me, but I don't know, maybe not. Catherine said she's a hard worker, very sharp. And man, is she a looker!"

Win stared out the passenger-side window. He couldn't decide if Gus was teasing him or actually interested in Tory. He drew in a breath. *What single man wouldn't be interested in that girl?* His chest tightened and he knew his eyes had narrowed as he turned back to Gus and forced a smile. "I was thinking I might ask her out."

The man shot a smug grin back as he pulled the Tahoe out of the trailhead's snow-covered parking area. "Think you can compete with me for the women? I'm a park ranger, Sport! Cool job, great uniform . . . women love all that! You're just a G-man, dime a dozen! No uniform. You work behind the scenes. Hell, you can't even brag to the girls about what you're doing. Compete with me? Not a chance!"

He does have a point. . . . The concern must have shown on Win's face.

Gus was laughing at him now. "Relax, Win! Just messing with you—trying to get you to lighten up! You are wound real damn tight. I can see you're interested in her. No problem!" He was still grinning. "Hey, our jobs can be really taxing. You deserve to have some fun—go for it! And if this gal doesn't work out, I know for a fact there are half a dozen women back in Mammoth who've been trying to figure out a way to meet you."

Win knew his ears were getting red, and he felt his face flush. Gus swung into storytelling—not really off-color stories, but close. He'd gotten himself into some hilarious situations. Win found himself laughing with the man in spite of himself. The ranger kept it up for the next thirty minutes of slow driving through some of the most beautiful country Win had ever seen.

* * *

"Days like today are what I was talking about at the bar in Gardiner—can you imagine a better job?" Gus cut his eyes toward Win as he drove. He looked back to the snow-packed road and nodded. "Yeah, I know you made me that night. I must be slipping, damn it. Was trying to get a feel for where the FBI was going with the militia case. . . . I wasn't up-front with you, and it's bothered me ever since."

Win raised his eyebrows knowingly and looked over at the man. "And this field trip today was your way of making up for that, or . . ."

"Or more interagency spying?" Gus laughed. "Nope, no spying! Today was more to ease my conscience and get to know you better. We should be on the same team. My experience with the FBI has been good in other parks: professionalism and respect. If it gets any more out of hand with this church militia, we're going to need all that and more. But our agency brass thinks those boys have had their fun and are just gonna fade away. No sign of them in the park in days. A few scary dudes staying at Bordeaux's place, but we've got nothing big on them yet. Everyone's thinking it's over and we can all fall back into our routines." Gus slowed the Tahoe on the icy road and eased to a stop behind a huge yellow snowplow.

Win took all that in and stared through the windshield. Gus had called it a "little slide," but the wall of snow blocking the highway looked every bit like a huge avalanche. The two snowplows were idling in front of them as a large bulldozer maneuvered around to the front.

Win said what was on his mind as the ranger started to open the SUV's door to step out. "So you don't see a threat. . . . Is that your honest opinion or the company line?"

Gus cocked his head and grinned as he pulled on his gloves and grabbed his cap from the console. "What do you think, Sport? They pay me to worry."

* * *

"Target in motion at 300.2 yards, wind northwest at 5, elevation 472 . . . now wind northwest at 7 . . . 301.1 yards. . . ." The man whispered the coordinates to his shooter. His gloved hands were steady on the optical range finder, the best civilian piece money could buy—over $2,900 at Bass Pro Shops.

The shooter raised his head above the black Leupold Mark 5HD scope. "Damn, he needs to move from behind the plow. . . . Hold!" he whispered back in a frustrated tone. The shooter tugged at the white hood covering his military field cap. It was actually part of a white no-iron sheet set his niece had bought at Walmart; she'd done a real nice job making the white jacket and pants. Pretty good waterproofing on it too. But he was ready for the high-country snow to melt so he could shed it. Wearing a damn sheet—helpful as it was for camouflage—it just didn't seem right.

"Reset! Reacquire target." The hushed voice behind them had a lethal urgency. He wouldn't tolerate any screwing around.

"Reacquired at 298.7 yards, wind northwest at 3, elevation 472.2," the spotter whispered in response. They were lying on top of a limestone bluff, 470 some-odd feet above the snow-covered park highway. Their heavy packs for overnight winter camping were seventy feet behind them—this was the sixth ambush set in a day and a half, and it was by far the most promising group of targets. The spotter liked to think of them as targets. It was easier that way. They weren't living, breathing human beings who were out here earning a living, same as him. On any other day he might help them buy new tires at his regular job at the automotive shop in Gardiner. Today, however, they were targets.

The shooter whispered a question to the instructor, who knelt close behind him. The spotter thought it was silly for them to be whispering.

The noise from the idling snowplows and bulldozer below them would have drowned out a bullhorn. But he had to remember there was a protocol, a set method, and stealth would be a huge factor in their future success. He took a deep breath and wished he'd brought along another Snickers bar. It wasn't horribly cold on the ridge, but he'd been lying on the snow-covered ground for nearly an hour, and he knew chocolate would go a long way toward easing his discomfort.

The shooter was making another adjustment to the scope. His rifle was a Remington M40 with a fiberglass stock, the same type he'd trained with years ago in the Marine Corps—an excellent long-range weapon. He knew there were newer, whiz-bang sniper rifles the military had now. Hell, the new scopes could measure and calibrate themselves. But those fancy guns didn't shoot themselves. You still had to have the marksman. And he was a marksman. He had the service medals to prove it. He shifted slightly on the waterproof tarp. Yeah, well, he might be older and a little slower, but he was still good, real good. Soon he'd get the chance to prove it. This shot was only three hundred yards, almost no wind. Piece of cake.

The stretch of highway below was notorious for snow and rockslides, and the park's plowing crews had brought in a big Caterpillar bulldozer to pull the two snowplows through the roughly eight feet of slide and new snow blocking the highway. They'd go through this routine day after day from late March until late April or early May—sometimes much later. The northwestern part of Yellowstone usually received over six feet of snow, half of which often arrived during the time of year other parts of the country called "spring." Clearing all 310 miles of paved roads for tourist traffic wouldn't be completed until later in May, another nine or ten days at least. That was typical for this time of year in Yellowstone National Park. What was not typical was the sniper team lurking less than five hundred feet above the plows.

The shooter sighted in on the man below who was walking back toward the second snowplow. He watched through the scope as the driver stopped between the plows to light a cigarette. The man had on green insulated overalls, a fluorescent-yellow safety vest, and one of those winter Park Service caps with the earflaps—made the guy look like a damn Russian. The shooter whispered a clipped, "Acquired! Permission to take one target?" He eased his breathing for the shot—

"Hold!" It was the stern voice behind them.

A perfectly clear shot. Why in hell ain't I pulling the trigger? The shooter kept his impatient thoughts to himself. He wasn't stupid enough to challenge the man behind him.

"Higher-value targets . . . at three o'clock," came the whispered explanation a second later. "Acquire!"

The shooter shifted his tall frame a bit to his right on the rock-solid ice. "Acquired," the shooter whispered back as his scope found the park ranger stepping out of his SUV. He used the scope to scan for a moment; a second man was in the vehicle. The spotter gave the new coordinates while the shooter recalibrated the rifle.

"Permission to take two targets?"

"Permission to fire."

The shooter eased his breath to slow his heart rate. He lined up the scope's crosshairs on the front of the first target's dark-green coat, right on the gold badge. His finger eased back the trigger . . . and he whispered, "Boom!" He realigned in less than a heartbeat and "fired" through the windshield at the man in the Tahoe.

The tone of the instructor behind the team softened. It was now an easy southern drawl. "Well, brothers, you just struck a blow fer America—took out two of the oppressors. Nice set, well done. Let's see an ordered withdrawal. We'll do a debrief a hundred yards to the rear, then we'll be gettin' on back."

CHAPTER TWELVE

It had been a long day. Win was paying for yesterday's "day off in the woods," as his supervisor called it. It was May 2nd, and arrests had finally been made in a big meth bust in Jackson. The culmination of that case freed up a significant amount of Bureau manpower—they were bringing in several of the Denver office's Joint Terrorism Task Force agents to get a better surveillance rotation. Win was scrambling to get more operational rooms set up in the park's Justice Center for them; he'd long since run out of office space in the smaller FBI building.

It was nearly 8:45 p.m. when Win finally walked in his back door, pulled his gun out and laid it on the kitchen counter, and tried to flip on the lights to the den, as he'd taken to calling his front room. *No lights!* Well, maybe Jason's electrician hadn't been so thorough after all. He pulled his personal phone from his pocket; he needed to touch base with his brothers tonight before it got too late back home. He walked into the dark room to turn on the TV and absently noted the blinds in the room had been pulled. Friday wasn't the day the housekeeper came, maybe he'd just forgotten she'd be—

"You ain't a quick learner, are you, Win Tyler?"

Win gasped as he hit the record button on his phone, then stood there trying to get his eyes adjusted to the dark room.

"Turn around and sit down on the couch." That put Win looking back into the bright light coming through the open French doors from the kitchen. All he could see was a tall silhouette. It was impossible to see the man's eyes or whether he was armed.

"This is getting a little old, Luke—you trying to scare me to death." Win tried hard to keep a steady voice. His heart was pounding so loudly he was afraid Bordeaux could hear it. *Is Luke here to finish what he'd started on the mountain the other morning?* That frightening thought flashed through his mind. He tried to focus on what the dark shadow was saying.

"In any of these times when I've had a weapon on you—which is gettin' pretty regular—if I hada wanted you dead, I wouldn't had to scare you to death, now would I? So where's your weapon now? Sittin' in the kitchen. The bear spray the other day—thirty, forty feet away. Got to give yourself some sorta fighting chance. You can't even tell if I've drawd down on you. You don't have many options."

"How 'bout if I get my Glock from the kitchen, go outside, come back in, and we try this again?"

Luke laughed softly and began screwing the light bulb back into the floor lamp. Win didn't move. As soon as the fear had passed, he'd realized this could get pretty interesting.

"Nice place you got here."

"Thanks, you been here long?"

"'Bout fifteen minutes."

"Want a beer?"

"Be right nice."

When the light came on, Win saw no weapon in Luke's hands. The guy was dressed in black coveralls and gloves with a black ski mask and wool cap. He would've been invisible in the dark, and he looked scary as Hell. Luke pulled the cap and ski mask off as Win walked past him to the kitchen. He saw two holstered handguns and a knife on the back of Luke's black web belt. Win got the beers from the refrigerator and didn't dare touch his gun.

They sat in the den, sipped their beers, and passed the customary couple of minutes discussing the weather. Then Luke got down to business.

"It's situational awareness," Luke began.

"What?"

"It's bothering you that I ain't had any trouble gettin' the drop on you all these times."

"Well, I have been giving some other job offers a little more serious thought since I met you."

"That ain't it. . . . Kin tell it in your eyes. You ain't afraid of me." Luke smiled a wicked smile. "No more'n you oughta be, that is. No, you got somethin' else stokin' those restless fires."

"Maybe so." *How does he know? Can he see through me that easily?*

"But the situational awareness—you're right good at sensing what's in front of you. Even to the side of you. You're not worth a damn at feelin' things out behind you. Might come from all them years playin' quarterback. Might work out fine on a ball field, all the action is in front and to the side of you, but it ain't real handy if someone's after you in real life. You kin learn it; gonna take some effort. I'd make that effort iffen I's you."

"So you're here to give me pointers in self-defense?"

Luke set his beer down and cleared his throat. "Partly, but mainly I come over here 'cause Ellie says I owe you an apology."

Win wasn't expecting that. "How so?"

"I ran into a lady we know from Gardiner Sunday night at the gas station, and she mentioned seein' Ellie up near the church in Mammoth that afternoon. . . . Just made me sick, but I figured she'd met you. After we got into it Wednesday morning, I was gonna confront Ellie again about callin' you and meetin' with you, but she dressed me down fer not takin' my responsibility to protect our family seriously. Fer allowing a bunch of trashy ex-criminals to live in our trailers just fer the money." He paused and let out a long sigh. "You been married?"

Win shook his head *no*.

"Well, someday maybe you'll understand. You don't *ever* want to get called out by a good wife fer not being the man of the family."

Win could see that.

"So, I'm sorry I went off half-cocked after you up on the mountain the other day. I kin have a temper. Probably my Cajun blood."

"Apology accepted, Luke, but I'm having a hard time believing you showed up looking like a dang ninja just to apologize to me."

"I did, but yeah, well, there's a bit more." He dropped his eyes for the first time and seemed to be struggling for the exact words. "Ron King, uh, the Prophet's main man, he brung in three more men this mornin' fore dawn to our place. Your boys out there been stretched a little thin, and I don't think they caught it."

Well, he knows about our surveillance. So much for the FBI's tactical advantage, Win thought.

Luke kept talking. "Don't know who they are. They have prison tats from some white supremacy bunch and they came in packin' fer bear. I didn't think Brother King would be mixed up in any real meanness, but with those new boys he brung in . . . I ain't so sure 'bout it now."

"Packing for bear? Heavy weapons?"

"All three of them carrying brand-new Daniel Defense M4s with over five hundred rounds each." Luke paused. "Then there's a 82A1 Barrett .50 caliber rifle."

"Geez." Win whistled softly.

"Yeah, I was thinkin' the same thing. That rifle could take down a helicopter and drop a man at more'n a mile."

Win knew the powerful weapon was a very difficult rifle to shoot accurately. "Anybody you know who can shoot one of those?"

Luke smiled. "'Cept for me, you mean. Don't know. . . . We have a guy in the church group who's had sniper training. He might be able to handle it." He shrugged. "Maybe one of the new guys who brung it in this mornin'."

Win hoped his phone battery wasn't dead and the phone was still recording this. "So what's going down?"

"I don't know. The church is paying me to get the militia in shape and on target: traipsing around in the woods all day, practice shootin' and such. But those other boys are mostly holed up at our place, doin' their own training. . . . Somethin' ain't right. Now there's seven men at our place—all rough men. And Brother King wants me to integrate them into our militia. I'm hearin' bits and pieces 'bout an ops mission in the park. It's kinda changing my thinkin'. I'm sending Ellie and the kids back to her cousin's in Oklahoma City tomorrow. Ellie swears she's gonna drop off the kids and come back up here in a few days. I hope not, but she can be a stubborn woman." Luke smiled a shy smile.

"Sending them away is a good move." Win nodded his approval. "That's a huge relief to know they'll be out of there."

"Ellie ain't gonna be talkin' to you 'bout this anymore. You got that?"

"I hear you." *He's protecting her. He wants her out of the loop.*

"Then there's a couple more things."

Uh-oh.

"I overheard some chatter on the CB radio right after noon, between the men at our place and King over at the church. Wasn't real clear—they're using some code—but there's a dirty cop involved in somethin' with the church. I wouldn't count on any reliable local backup, if I's you."

"Who?"

"Deputy sheriff is all I know. Never seen him or heard a name."

The Secret Service was supposed to be intercepting all radio communications between the subjects. *Why aren't we getting this?* It was sounding worse by the second.

Luke took a slow drink from the beer and paused for a long moment.

"You said there were a couple of things," Win finally said.

Luke set the beer down, stood up, and stretched. Win noticed his cat had been sitting beside Luke. The cat had never gotten within five feet of Win.

"Win, you got a gun by your bed?"

"What? You didn't check that when you came through the house?" He said it a little sarcastically.

"I wouldn't go through a man's things."

Didn't seem to bother him to break in, but he drew the line at pilfering, it seemed.

"Uhhh, heard one of the new boys mention your name. Said someone's gonna take you out."

"What? Why? I'm just doing my job here." Win's voice echoed his shock.

"In case you ain't noticed yet, we're not in the South, where even the most redneck white trash have some regard for the law, especially the FBI. Up here lots of folks don't see it as you doin' your job. They see it as you interfering with their right to be left alone to do as they damn well please. It probably isn't anything against you—you ain't been here long. More'n likely it's your badge. Don't know who's pullin' those strings, but far as I know none of the militia boys are mixed up in that meanness." He drew a deep breath. "I'd bet it ain't personal."

"Sure makes me feel better to know it isn't personal! Or then it could be another diversion. You boys trooping around in the woods hoping to be seen a few weeks ago was the first one," Win countered.

"Yeah, I never understood the purpose of that, but it seems to be pulling a lot of your resources toward one area, don't it?"

"I suppose killing an FBI agent would consolidate resources even further, but none of this really makes any sense."

Luke shrugged with his eyebrows. "Well, there are the obvious conclusions: Either you're dealing with madmen who have no logical plan 'cept to cause as much disruption and chaos as possible, or they're settin' up two significant diversions to run the third play."

"What do you think?"

"Well," Luke said, shaking his head and standing up, "reckon if there is a third play, it ain't likely to go down real quick." He walked to Win's front door and stopped, hand on the doorknob. "The Prophet and Brother King left fer somewhere today and won't be back fer a few days. I doubt if your folks over by the church caught that either."

Luke opened the front door and stepped onto the dark porch. "You'll have to fiddle with the breaker box to get the rest of the lights to work in your livin' room and out here. I shut 'em off when I came in the house." Luke seemed to be having a hard time saying what was really on his mind. He shifted near the door.

"Win, how 'bout you try harder not to let *diversion number two* go down. . . . I came here partly to make a point. You're an easy target." He paused again and took a deep breath. Then, "You promise me you'll make sure Ellie and the kids get back safely to Louisiana when this is over? Ellie said you treated her with total respect on Sunday. I have a brother who went to the pen. I know it ain't always handled that way."

"You could get them back South yourself, so where you gonna be?"

"I may be too deep in it at this point. I'm still trying to sort it out."

"You could work for us," Win offered, as he stepped outside.

"Hold it right there! I have a payin' job with the Prophet that I aim to finish unless things get totally out of control. I'm a man of my word."

"There's your pride getting in the way of good sense."

They stood there in silence in the cold darkness for a few moments. Then Win stepped close to Luke and nodded. "Luke, I promise, within my power, to do right by your family."

"That's all I can ask. . . . Be careful, Win Tyler." Luke had taken off his glove and he shook Win's hand. Then he vanished off the porch into the night.

* * *

What had been a long day turned into a very long night after Luke left the porch. Win grabbed the still-recording cell phone, his coat, and his weapon and ran out the back door toward his vehicle. He paused for a second in the darkness right outside the door to consider Luke's last warning, but he knew for the moment he was safe. Luke was still lurking somewhere in the night. He could feel it. In Luke's mind, Win's promise was the only thing preventing Ellie from being criminally prosecuted, the only thing keeping her and the kids together if this all went down badly. And it was certainly shaping up to go down badly.

He headed to the office, calling the Jackson Hole RA as he drove. Fifty-five minutes later Win was waiting for the Park Service's technician to finish digitizing the recording from his personal phone. The Denver FBI bosses had returned to their offices for the teleconference, as had Jim West down in Jackson. Randall, Gus, and the FBI's surveillance supervisor were sitting in Win's conference room, drinking coffee while waiting for the audio feed to begin. Win leaned against the doorframe to listen. The tech guy had it coming in loud and clear.

It started after a long beep, with a chilling voice: *Turn around and sit down. . . .* They listened to the entire twelve minutes or so in silence. The recording picked up the initial cold, calculated cadence of Luke's Louisiana drawl. Win was surprised to hear himself sound confident and casual. He was glad the others couldn't tell from the recording how frightened he'd felt at first. As the recording played on, the tone of both of their voices became mostly cordial, even supportive. It was an interesting piece of intel for sure. Nobody would complain about being pulled back to the office for this one.

It was quiet for a few moments after the recording ended. The Park Service tech guy moved to another office to let them talk. Win sat down at the table with his notebook. The poor surveillance supervisor shook her head several times during the recording. Now she looked like she wanted to crawl into a hole. Luke's comments on the FBI surveillance misses were going to create a firestorm in Denver. As Win knew better than most, the Bureau hates mistakes.

"Evening, everyone—Tom Strickland here—well, this will take a little time to digest. Very, very good work, Win. Obviously your plan with the wife on Sunday was right on target in getting her husband to turn—at least to the degree we've got him now."

Sad that being honest and sensitive with a person was a "plan," Win thought.

Chief Randall gave his initial thoughts. "This could, of course, be disinformation to point us in the wrong direction, but I'm inclined to believe it's accurate, given the, shall we say, unique relationship Agent Tyler and Luke Bordeaux seem to have developed. On the surface, Bordeaux's own stated conclusions—that we're either dealing with madmen who have no set plan, or with a sophisticated force that's creating limited diversions in order to achieve a larger goal—seem reasonable."

Win was thinking that killing him didn't sound like such a limited diversion.

Wes Givens summed it up. "If either of those two scenarios is correct, given what we know about the group's makeup and capability, we now have an imminent domestic terrorism threat and I think we need to declare it as such to Washington. It's sounding as if Daniel Shepherd's group is planning an armed assault against someone or some part of the park. We've been severely limited on the actions we could take up to this point, but Bordeaux's comments give us the leverage we need to get wiretaps authorized."

They spent the better part of the next two hours going back over parts of the tape and addressing specific issues. ASAC Givens was on and off the teleconference, making calls and taking calls from various other FBI offices, ATF, the Marshals Service, and other agencies to consolidate resources. They broke at about the one-hour point, and SAC Strickland put a call in to the Deputy Assistant Director for Counterterrorism in Washington. Chief Randall did the same with his respective higher-ups. To say that some serious marshaling of counterterrorism assets was going on was an understatement.

Strickland's final remarks came down to the apparent threat on Win's life. "At this point, Win, we have to consider the threat credible. Could be those militia types are blowing smoke, but we can't take that chance. I'm sure Chief Randall would be willing to provide security for you until we can get more of our people up there, and pull you out."

Win wanted to stay on the case, and he was ready with his response. "I appreciate the concern, Mr. Strickland, but as Bordeaux said himself, it's not likely personal; it's the badge. I don't think it would matter who the case agent is. They aren't coming after me, they're coming after the Bureau. I've developed some informants who may be able to break this open. We can't afford to lose momentum, and our time frame may be closing. I want to stay on the case."

"Your points are well taken. We'll talk some more about this tomorrow. In the meantime, I'll ask Chief Randall to provide you with security."

As the teleconference wound down, the SAC asked Win one last question. "I should have asked this earlier, but Win, was there anything in tonight's encounter with Bordeaux that wasn't on the recording?"

"Yes, sir, at the beginning, when I walked into the dark room—into his ambush—he said something like, 'Win Tyler, you ain't a quick learner.'"

"See that you prove him wrong, Win."

*　*　*

Win was still at his desk an hour later, working on the Title III affidavits for the phone taps they'd request for Bordeaux and several others at the Arm of the Lord Church. He sat back and calculated the time back home. It was 2:20 a.m. in Arkansas. Way too late to call, but Blake would catch his text early the next morning. He sent a quick text to his younger brother and was surprised when his cell rang almost immediately.

"Hey, Bubba, what's up?" It was a silly private joke they had. Blake, who was two years younger but had grown an inch taller, had been calling Win "Bubba," the southern equivalent of "brother" or "little brother," since his growth spurt in high school.

"What are you doing up so late? Sick cow?" Win asked.

"Naw, don't you people have the Weather Channel out there? Thought that might be why you're texting, concerned about us and all. It's springtime in tornado alley!"

"Bad there?"

"Has been, but the folks down around Little Rock are gettin' the worst of it. I'm sitting on the porch watching it move past. Put all of 'em to sleep in the basement a few hours ago, after we lost power. You should see the lightning to the south! Miss you, Win. You weren't really here when you were here last month. You gettin' better?"

Win drew a deep breath. "I think so. I hope so."

"Well, if you end up happily married to Shelby let's forget this conversation, but I'm okay seein' that girl move on. She was high-maintenance, and she got more self-centered and more selfish as time went by. Someone who's gonna be your wife oughta be building you and your dreams up. You and her—well, it shouldn't be so much work. Hey, isn't this the same advice you gave me about ten times before I met Rachel?"

"Easier to give advice than take it," Win answered.

"Suppose so. . . . Other than girl problems, why are you texting me in the middle of the night?"

"Got an issue here. Part of a case, so I can't say anything specific, but Big Brother will be listening in on my personal phone for a while, so you might want to tone down the humorous messages and such, and maybe pass that on to Will."

"Dang, and I thought they were already listening in! Okay, but no worries about Will calling you anytime soon. He's suddenly discovered girls, or maybe it's they've discovered him. Comin' out of the ugly duckling stage. Granny says he may end up being the best-looking one of the litter."

"Lordy!" Win laughed and tried to picture his skinny fifteen-year-old brother with a girlfriend.

"Okay, let's cut to the chase—this call ain't about Shelby or visiting or whatnot. Can tell in your voice. What's up?"

"Got some dangerous things going on here. Some serious bad guys. I . . . I wanted you to know how much I love you." Win sighed. *There, I said it!*

Blake paused a long time before he responded; Win could hear the thunder rolling in the background. He suddenly felt very homesick and alone.

"The bad guys in the FBI or outside?" Blake finally asked.

"For a change, they're on the outside. They're for real."

"Got anyone there you can talk to?"

"Well, weird as it sounds, I seem more inclined to open up with a fella who may be one of the bad guys."

"Uh-huh. You know what Daddy says, 'The only difference between the good guys and the bad guys is often just some poor judgment along the way.' But still, sounds like you need to expand your circle of friends."

"Yeah, I was thinking that too. I just can't seem to bring myself to trust anyone. Can't bring myself to trust my own judgment of people right now."

"Well, Bubba, I'm betting ninety-five percent of the folks you're dealing with are good, decent people. Most of the Feds are wanting to do the same thing you are: make a real difference in people's lives and make the world a better place. As you always said, a noble calling. You got gut-kicked by the FBI and your girl, right about the same time. It's only been a few months. I think you might be pushing it. Give yourself some slack."

"If I get myself killed in the meantime—"

"Hey, you got some premonition about dying out there?"

"No, not at this point. No."

"Good . . . good. You want me to tell you what you'd say to me? Well, here it is . . . 'Yea, though I walk through the valley of the shadow of death, I will fear no evil; for You are with me; Your rod and Your staff, they comfort me.' The Twenty-Third Psalm. God's watching over you, Win."

"I know . . . I know."

"Not gonna dissuade you from calling the folks and telling 'em how much you love 'em, but just know it ain't necessary. We know it already. It's who you are, brother."

"Appreciate you saying that. . . . But you know, I've been a little out of touch these last two years," Win said softly.

"Well, sounds like it'd be a darn good time to get your head back in the game, as old Coach Stewart would've said."

"He'd said it a good bit stronger than that, but yeah, you're right. Need to get back to work too, I suppose. Thanks for calling me back."

"Hey, Win, we all love you too. Be careful."

The call ended and he sat staring at the framed picture of his two brothers and himself that sat on top of his oak bookcase. The photo had been taken back home on a trout-fishing trip on the White River last fall. It had been a perfect morning. If there were going to be other perfect mornings, he knew he needed to follow the advice he'd been given tonight by two men: *Get your head back in the game!* Blake's words and Luke's message.

CHAPTER THIRTEEN

Three of the FBI's surveillance agents were still meeting in Johnson's office as Win finished the affidavits and hit the send button to get them to Denver. Soft footsteps on the stairs told of a visitor. Win moved away from his desk to the door, rested his hand on his holstered handgun, and waited for the newcomer. He'd never liked the FBI's policy of closing off their offices from the public with locked doors and security systems, but tonight he could sure see the need for it. Rationally, he knew whoever was coming up the stairs at 1:45 a.m. had the office's keypad number—still, he kept his hand on his Glock.

The park ranger who appeared at the top of the stairs looked to be early thirties. He was decked out in a dark-green tactical uniform. A small mobile radio dangled from his darker body armor. He wore a dark-green Park Service ball cap and his black helmet, a Sig Sauer handgun, clips, a Taser, and who knows what all hung from his web belt. He was not as tall as Win, but he had an athletic, solid build. He removed the cap as he topped the stairs, brushed his short blond hair forward, and cut his eyes toward Win. Those gray eyes were just short of hostile.

"U.S. Park Ranger Hechtner to see Special Agent Tyler, sir."

A none-too-friendly voice, either.

"I'm Win Tyler." Win held out his hand and the man did return the firm handshake, but his less-than-cordial manner remained.

"Chief Randall has assigned our team to you until your security people arrive. I'm the park's Mammoth District Ranger and the Special Response Team Leader. I'm one of the officers on the Joint Terrorism Task Force, and I have top secret clearance, so I'm authorized to be in your offices. I have two men guarding this building and two at your house."

"Well, U.S. Park Ranger Hechtner, I'm not familiar with your agency's protocols. How do you prefer to be addressed?" If this guy was going to get all formal with him, he could throw it right back.

"You can address me as Ranger Hechtner, sir."

"You can call me Win. And you don't need to call me 'sir.'"

Win left the man standing in the hall as he stuck his head in the office next door to tell the other agents there were armed guards outside. He grabbed his coat and followed the ranger to his Tahoe for the short ride to his house. The man didn't say a word, but on the positive side, he seemed alert and watchful. If the ranger could keep him from being harmed, why should he care how much personality the guy had. A man in the same SWAT gear, wearing night-vision goggles and carrying an assault rifle, emerged from the darkness outside Win's house as they pulled up.

Ranger Hechtner killed the vehicle. "My men will do a sweep of the house's interior. When that's clear, two men will be outside and I will stay inside. May we proceed?"

"Uh, sure—there's a cat inside. I appreciate your help tonight."

"That's our job, sir." He said it with a little too much edge.

Oookay, so no thawing this guy out.

After the sweep came back clean, the other rangers moved to their guard posts, where Win hoped they wouldn't freeze in the twenty-five-degree weather. Ranger Hechtner unlatched his Remington 870 from the SUV and took up a spot in the den while Win fed the cat and made a pot of coffee.

"Coffee in the kitchen if you or your men want it. See you in the morning—I'll need to leave for the office at six o'clock." Win closed his bedroom door without waiting for a reply.

Remembering Luke's question from earlier in the night, he slept with his gun on his nightstand. He'd never done that in his life. He also slept with the Twenty-Third Psalm in his heart—he'd done that hundreds of times. The Scripture brought him a lot more comfort than the gun. He was up at 5:30 and grateful for the three hours of sleep. Several hours of standing guard in a dark house hadn't improved Ranger Hechtner's mood. Win warmed up a cup of the hours-old coffee in the microwave and asked the ranger if he'd care for any. *Nope, he is all business.*

Hechtner was stone-faced. "We'll exit the house from the front. There are clear shot avenues from the barren ridges to the northeast above the rear of the house. Always use the front entrance."

Okay, got that. Being aware that someone wanted him dead, and thinking through the possible ambush points, was a surreal and unwelcome experience.

The night-shift supervisor for the surveillance guys handed Win a stack of messages when he got to the office. No matter it was a Saturday morning; there would be plenty of company coming to town. The field office had chartered a large jet, which was leaving Denver with the office's supervisor for domestic terrorism, Emily Stuart; ten FBI SWAT guys; and a bunch of other folks on board. Jim West was taking a private flight into Bozeman rather than drive the seven-hour, circuitous route to Mammoth from Jackson, avoiding the park's closed roads. A full-blown command center would be set up in the vacant space within the Justice Center. Analysts, technicians, and portions of Denver's Domestic Terrorism and Violent Crime Squads would be en route tomorrow. The FBI's super-sophisticated Nightstalker surveillance plane and its support group would arrive in Livingston, Montana, before noon. Black Hawk helicopter support from the Wyoming National Guard had been approved at the highest levels in Washington. The Denver office was coordinating the delivery of those assets.

Win started working the phones with the Marshals, the U.S. Attorney's office, and the Federal Magistrate to see if warrants could be pulled together for a preemptive takedown if DOJ decided that was the best course to take. If there was an imminent threat, it might be more prudent to raid the church and Bordeaux's trailers and round up the suspected bad guys before they could launch any type of attack. They'd probably end up charging the suspects with relatively minor offenses and parole violations, but if bloodshed could be averted, that might be the way to go. Preventing acts of terror on American soil counted more with the FBI in this day and age than building a case for trial. It would be great to do both, but protecting the public was job number one.

When Janet Swam appeared at 7:00 a.m. with a huge box of muffins, Win remembered that he hadn't eaten since yesterday at noon. He was at his desk, working on his second blueberry muffin and sorting priorities, when Ranger Hechtner, still in his SWAT getup, made another appearance.

"Sir, we've rotated two more men at your house and two here at the office. They're in civilian clothes and will blend in with the visitors. For your information, we call the tourists 'visitors.' You need to close your window blinds—keep them closed until this threat is over. My orders are to stay with you until your people relieve us."

His point on the window blinds was well taken, but he said "your people" a little too sharply. Win didn't like his tone or his surly attitude. He left the ranger standing in his office doorway as he finished the rest of the muffin, downed half a cup of coffee, and decided to get serious about getting his head in the game, as his brother had put it. He looked straight into the ranger's eyes and raised his voice a notch.

"Ranger Hechtner, close the door and sit down." That seemed to catch the guy off guard; his chin came up and he cocked his head slightly to look down at Win from the doorway.

"Do it now." Win didn't say it with a raised voice, but there was no doubt he expected his order to be followed. Hechtner closed the door and sat down.

"Now, it's real obvious to me you're not enjoying this job of watching my back. But I don't care what you think about me or the Bureau or whether I've wrecked your weekend plans, or whatever is going on with you. We both have jobs here. I need you to keep me alive while I do mine. It is our job, and I mean *our* job, to protect the public and the interests of the United States government. Do you get that?"

Hechtner's gray eyes dropped to the front of Win's desk for a moment, then he straightened in the chair and slowly nodded. "I'm sorry—you have my apology, sir. I've let some personal feelings get in the way. You can call me Trey."

"Apology accepted, Trey. Please call me Win, and don't hesitate to point out anything you see me doing or not doing that's going to impact your job or my life. I appreciate you being here." Win smiled as he stood and moved to shake hands with the ranger, who then left the office to take his post downstairs. The handshake was strong, and Win had a sense of the strength of the man as he stood next to Trey's broad shoulders. He reflected a little as he moved back to his desk. Within the last twenty-four hours he'd received formal apologies from two men, either of which could beat him like a yard dog in a fight. He made a mental note to get to that gym and hit the weights again when this mess was over.

* * *

It was nearly noon that same day, and two of Ranger Hechtner's plainclothes rangers were watching him and the surroundings from a reasonable distance. Win stood on the concrete landing outside the entrance to the Mammoth Hotel Dining Room and watched the arrival of the lady who would be his new boss for this operation.

Supervisory Special Agent Emily Stuart was slowly getting out of the back seat of Johnson's black Suburban. The vehicle had been picked up by Jim West and their little group of higher-ups at the Bozeman airport and commandeered for their use while Johnson remained on leave. Jim nodded to Win and stayed in the driver's seat, talking on his phone. SSA Stuart was struggling to pull on a heavy coat while continuing to hold her phone to her ear with one hand. She was of medium height and build, with frizzy orange-reddish hair. She wore gold metal-rimmed glasses and quite a lot of makeup. He was guessing her age to be early forties, but it was hard to tell. Her gray business suit was stylish, complete with high heels; she looked completely out of place in Yellowstone.

She kept her eyes on her phone as she walked up the concrete steps leading to the landing at the restaurant's entrance. Win opened the door for her, and that act of chivalry suddenly seemed to awaken her to her surroundings.

"What do you think you're doing!" It was a sharp, nasal voice. Win thought the angry comment was directed at her phone or at someone else, but she was staring up into his face with a scowl. "You think I can't handle a door, Agent Tyler? You think that *gentleman* crap is going to impress me?"

Win stood there, holding the door open. He was speechless, which was probably a good thing. He was thinking he would forgo asking to take her coat or pulling out her chair at the table. She blew through the door and confronted the tiny hostess. Jim West watched the whole scene unfold as he followed her up the steps. He was grinning at Win as they trailed Emily and the hostess from a safe distance.

"I see you've met Ms. Stuart." Jim was almost laughing.

"Well, actually no, I haven't been introduced to her. . . . She, uh, knew who I was. . . . She seems to be having a bad day."

"Emily never has good days. Just keep your head down."

* * *

The next morning Win was leaning against the frosty windowpane in his office, staring out at a brilliant orange sunrise. It was as if someone had repainted the parade ground during the night. How had he missed the gradual greening of the lawns or the first buds on the trees? It was Sunday, May 4th. Spring in Yellowstone had snuck up on him. No, there weren't actually leaves on any of the trees yet—certainly no flowers. A late spring, he'd heard several folks say, but there were little inklings of it. The patches of snow were becoming few and far between, the wind didn't have quite the same bite, and there was even a silvery-green tint to the sagebrush that populated most every open space.

He normally loved the spring. Back on the farm it had always been the season of promise. New calves, new crops, new life—hope for a good year. He'd always been an optimist, he'd always been one to look on the bright side, but this delayed spring, in this foreign place, was bringing more foreboding than joy. *Someone wants to kill me.* He pulled the blinds and moved away from the window as he replayed Ranger Hechtner's warnings in his head. *Maybe I should take a little more annual leave . . . or take Mr. Strickland up on his offer to go to Denver. Maybe . . .* He drew a long breath. He wasn't one to run away. The SWAT Team guys from Denver had taken over as his protection detail late Saturday afternoon. They would watch his back. He had a job to do. He breathed in another deep breath. *I have a job to do.*

His desk phone rang again at 7:15 a.m. and he began to recite the subject profiles of more than a dozen different church militiamen to one of the Critical Incident Response Group supervisors back at FBI Headquarters. Eastern time was two hours later; it was 9:15 in Washington, D.C. This morning he'd already been on the phone with four different Headquarters or Denver supervisors reporting on various facets of the case. The Bureau higher-ups were still waffling on which tack to take. There was clearly enough concern for an aggressive investigation, but nowhere near enough evidence for terrorism indictments. The Arm of the Lord Church was blaring out a steady stream of anti-government and anti-Semitic rancor online, and the first of the park's dignitary visits was only days away. The Israeli Ambassador and a group of prominent Jewish leaders were scheduled to dedicate a monument in Yellowstone on May 12th. They were coming down to the wire.

*   *   *

At 8:15 Win was on his third cup of coffee and deep into Washington's analysis of the Prophet's possible funding sources when he felt someone's eyes on him; he looked up to see a woman leaning against his office doorframe, watching him. Manners kicked in and he immediately stood up. She moved forward into his office with a smile and outstretched hand.

"Hi, Deborah Mills from the Denver office. Call me Deb. Wes asked me to give you a hand on the case file overload on False Prophet—catchy name for the case, I like that. I understand this case is not a one-person job." She had a good handshake and an easy smile. Her eyes stayed locked on his the entire time she moved toward him.

"Good to meet you, Winston Tyler. I go by Win. Can use the help. Mr. Givens said he'd call some folks in. When'd you get here?"

"Several of us flew into Bozeman last night and drove in kinda late. They've got us staying in those little cabins behind the hotel. They don't have TVs, radios, or Wi-Fi in the rooms here, and the cell phones don't work half the time." Her brown eyes widened in shock at the primitive accommodations.

"Some of the many charms of the place."

He was thinking she was maybe early forties, maybe five four or so, short brown hair, sort of plain, but well dressed in casual snow boots, wool slacks, sweater, and jacket. Her jewelry was modest: tasteful gold earrings, necklace, and wedding band. She looked like an upper-middle-class lady out to see the nation's premier national park—except for the gun. She was wearing a Glock on her belt under the jacket. She was an agent. *Good*, Win thought.

As he found out during the next several minutes, she was one of three senior agents in the Denver Field Office's Domestic Terrorism Squad. She'd been in the Bureau for sixteen years and at the Denver office for seven years. She'd read Win's entire case file and listened to the audios on his informant interviews. She seemed to know all about his background, and she also seemed to sense that he was more than a little uncomfortable with the concept of her working for him given their vast differences in experience in the FBI.

"Win, you're the lead case agent—you know that gives you tremendous power over the direction of most aspects of this case. I'll be assisting you. I've been at this for a while longer than you, so don't hesitate to ask me questions. This is a huge case. . . . I can only remember a few other things our office has been this ramped up about since I've been in Denver. Plus it's out here in the middle of nowhere. I'm here to take some of the weight off you by working with the other agencies, making sure the paperwork flows, and helping with the analysis. Plus I know the other Denver folks in our terrorism squads, so maybe I can help you utilize their skills. Actually, you and I are authorized to pull any of them up here to work with us on any aspect of the case if we need additional bodies. On a case this big, we will need additional bodies. I brought a clerical assistant and two intelligence analysts here with me."

She shifted in the wooden chair and quickly glanced down at her phone before she continued. "I want to be near your office, so our little group will pass on the space over at the Justice Center. I'm having phones and computers installed in your spare storage room today— we'll work out of there. The technicians will be here from Denver mid-morning. You okay with that?" She didn't wait for him to answer. "You *are* my boss on this case, and from what I've heard about you, I think we'll work together really well."

Win was wondering what she had heard about him. He was also thinking Wes Givens had brought her in to make sure his new agent didn't screw anything up too badly. He would have done the same thing had their roles been reversed, but it still stung his pride a bit.

She kept talking. "Why don't you come back and see what I have in mind for your extra storage room, and then we can go over your current assessments of the various aspects of the case and our deployment of resources and assets. . . ." She was already out of the office. He sighed as he followed her down the hall. Even with her declarations that he was still running the case, he was getting the distinct impression that with Deb, he was just gonna be along for the ride.

* * *

"Agent Tyler! Win!" It was just after noon the next day, and a heavyset bald guy in his early fifties was calling through the open passenger window of a big tan SUV as it pulled alongside Win in the street. The two plainclothes SWAT agents who were shadowing Win started to move in, but he gave them a quick okay sign when he recognized the man's clipped manner of speaking. Win walked across the sidewalk from the post office steps to the SUV's open window and leaned in toward the driver.

"Hi—Stan Marniski. Deb Miller said you were going this way after lunch. Good to finally meet you in person. Just flew into Bozeman and I'm driving out to the main surveillance site. Want to ride along?" It didn't sound like a question.

The man's accent was decidedly northeastern, maybe New York. The Unit Chief Win had been talking with on the phone off and on for the last two days talked fast and had the urgency of the big city about him. Marniski was way over Win's pay grade and he'd been more than a little intimidating on the phone. Win had told him at length about the difficulties of surveilling the church compound from the perimeter: large expanses of open sagebrush cut by deceptively deep ravines with thick evergreen and aspen pockets; boulder fields; acres of old-growth forest; two limestone hillsides pocked with caves, small streams, and dangerous crevices. The church's entire seventy-five acres was crisscrossed by dozens of game trails. Only one gravel road into the church compound, but a zillion ways out. Anyone familiar with the difficult terrain could just blend into the landscape and disappear— which unfortunately had been happening with regularity as the FBI's surveillance teams tried to keep their subjects under watchful eyes.

The portly man was talking nonstop. "Understand there's been more surveillance glitches." He casually waved it away. "Gonna clean that up! You know Tom Strickland wanted me out here from Washington to deal with it." The honcho's sharp look dismissed Win's SWAT guards. "I'll be your security this afternoon. Hop in! Let's go."

He drove Win back to his Bureau SUV and leaned his considerable bulk against the side of the truck as Win geared up. Win changed his cowboy boots out for insulated hiking boots as he listened to the Bureau's Unit Chief for Surveillance ramble on and on. Win was having a hard time getting a word in edgewise. He pulled the lighter version of body armor out of his truck and started to key in the gun box for his MP5 when Marniski spoke up.

"No need for the flak jackets or the long guns. We're just doing a little recon this afternoon so that I can get a better feel for the terrain. . . . No chance of running into the bad guys."

This dude does not know the territory, Win was thinking. Based on his experience after less than four weeks in Yellowstone, he knew there was real potential for the bad guys to be anywhere at any time. He ignored the senior supervisor's command and pulled the body armor on under his brown parka and pocketed two extra magazines for his Glock; he left the MP5 in the truck. *Marniski isn't the one under a death threat, but no reason to be totally insubordinate.*

"Need to see the lay of the land for myself." The man was still talking. "No room for mistakes. Weather isn't too bad today—supposed to snow again later this week. Can you believe that? I've got the maps, GPS, binoculars, everything. . . . Can't screw up and get over their property line. DOJ will have a fit if one of our guys dares infringe on someone's religious liberty. Can you believe how damn touchy everyone is about this deal? Talk about having to be politically correct—never mind that those nuts are planning an armed revolution!"

He switched topics without losing a beat. "Haven't been out in the field for a couple of years, maybe a little rusty . . . but hey, bought a pair of hiking boots in Bozeman on the way in. Need to get a picture of me hiking around the woods in these. My kids won't believe it." He stared down at his new boots. "Who'd thought I'd be outa Washington today, hiking miles on surveillance. . . . It's not like I'm a field agent anymore. But, hey,"—he slapped Win on the back—"I've been sitting behind a desk in D.C. way too long. Let's go have a little adventure!"

* * *

Win had just hiked around a massive boulder on the muddy downhill trail. Stan stumbled up beside him as Win froze in place. Two men in tan and green stood less than ten feet away. They'd been waiting for the agents to step around the huge gray boulder. Both in full camouflage, with camo face paint below their field caps. Both armed with scoped AR-15s that were aimed square in the center of their intended targets.

Win was afraid his heart had stopped for a moment. The black assault rifles looked especially deadly from the business end. Both men had them at the ready, fingers on the triggers—it would be over long before he or Stan could clear their coats to get to their holsters. *Federal Agents Killed by Fanatical Church Militiamen*—a potential headline for tomorrow's newspaper flashed through Win's mind.

"Whata you doing out here?" the younger of the two gunmen hissed.

"Bird watching." Win motioned toward the high-powered binoculars hanging around Marniski's neck. It was the first thing that popped into his head.

The second man spit to the side. "Sure you are."

Win swallowed hard. He felt Stan put a hand on his coat sleeve; the older man probably feared the younger agent might make a Rambo move. *No chance of that! Just be cool. . . . Be cool.* They were seriously outgunned. "Bulletproof vest" was a misnomer—he knew 5.56mm rounds from those rifles at ten feet would slice the vest he wore like a hot knife through butter. The tension that hung in the air between the four men was so thick you could cut it.

"You're standing too near our boundary! This is our land—the Arm of the Lord Church! You're spying on us! You think we don't know what you're doing? You're damn federal police!" It was the younger man talking in a loud, irate voice.

Win was sure hoping Luke was right about the militia having no part in the threat against his life. But even if the death threat wasn't in play, this was still a dicey situation. It had the potential to turn into a fatal confrontation if any one of the four men made a mistake or overreacted.

Stan had talked nonstop during the hour-long drive from Mammoth to the FBI's surveillance staging site in the wooded foothills more than a mile southeast of the church compound. He'd kept up the chatter on the three-hour trek to the various surveillance posts hidden in the ravines and forests on the fringes of the church's property line. Now, for the first time all afternoon, Marniski wasn't saying a word.

Win tried to get his focus off the gaping muzzle of the nearest rifle as he made his best stab at a conversational tone. "Well, that's not real nice of you to say. First off, we're standing within the national park. Secondly, America doesn't have federal police. We work for the FBI. We're investigators. We're here to solve crimes and prevent terrorism. We work for you just the same as for any other law-abiding Americans." *Never mind that you frigging yahoos are holding automatic weapons on federal agents—committing at least two felony offenses.*

The younger man interrupted Win's calm reply and frantic thoughts. "We ain't like any other Americans—we're patriots! Defenders of the nation! You work for the oppressors: the Jews and that bunch of internationalists who took over our government. You do their bidding! Don't tell me you work for us!"

The younger guy was clean-cut under the war paint, maybe mid-twenties, maybe six feet, but Win was thinking he looked bigger than that. Might have had something to do with Win's perspective being on the wrong end of the guy's gun. Both militiamen looked plenty capable, and the younger one was getting himself all worked up.

Somehow Win's voice remained steady and relaxed. "There's folks around who would threaten the peace of the nation. We're just making sure that isn't gonna happen here. You could help us out, you know." Win paused and looked at them expectantly.

Both men raised their chins a little. "Yeah, right. . . . And how is that?" the younger one asked suspiciously.

"Lookie here. . . ." Win slowly moved his left hand into his coat pocket and pulled out the two crumpled wanted posters he'd intended to hang in the post office after lunch. "Two more thugs made our Ten Most Wanted list this week. These men are Middle Eastern. Seen 'em around?" He held the flyers up so that the militiamen could see them.

"Hell no! No Arabs around here! You kidding me?" It was the stocky man answering.

"For real, guys. Our Ten Most Wanted list—there's a $500,000 reward for either of these two. They're dangerous enemies of our country and they could be anywhere. We have to be watchful. You could help us keep an eye out for them." He shrugged. "Just thought I'd ask."

He hoped he'd talked long enough to defuse some of the men's hostility. He hoped they'd see a little common ground. He hoped they'd realize this didn't have to end badly. As he folded the flyers back into his pocket, he cut his eyes sideways toward Stan. The agent was staring hard at the armed men; his face was pale and tight.

Win glanced at his watch. "Geez, look at the time—we need to be moving on. We still haven't spotted a red-throated ground grouse or a yellow-speckled warbler yet." He saw the younger militiaman suppress a smile. The guy obviously knew Win was making up the bird species. Win felt Stan relax just a bit. The tension was easing.

Win allowed his shoulders to drop slightly, to transition to a less-aggressive stance. "I'm Win Tyler, resident agent over in Mammoth. We didn't mean to bother you boys. No intention of coming on the church's land." He spread his hands out a little to his sides, palms up. "No harm, no foul." He looked into the younger man's blue eyes and saw him make the right decision.

"Alright, alright. . . . No harm, no foul," the younger one said and nodded. "I'm Corporal Jeffery Shaw, church militia." He smoothly moved the rifle into the port arms position. The corporal nodded to his companion, and the stocky one's finger came off the AR-15's trigger as the barrel swung downward. "You men stay away from our boundary, you understand me?"

"Got it," Marniski answered as he took a step back.

Win nodded to the men, then turned and double-timed it around the massive boulder with Stan on his heels. He stopped behind another large, solitary rock about a hundred feet up the trail in the tree line. His adrenaline level was dropping some and his heart rate was a little steadier. He turned toward the Unit Chief and noticed the color coming back into the man's face. Stan blew out a long breath, shook his head, and raised his eyebrows. He pulled off his ball cap and ran a hand across his bald scalp. Despite the forty-two-degree temperature, there was a sheen of sweat on his scalp and face. The senior agent leaned against the boulder and glanced back to make sure they weren't being followed. "You warned me that getting in close wasn't a good idea." He shook his head again. "Man! You got that right!"

Win couldn't help but grin back at him. "Just a little adventure. How's that desk in D.C. looking now?"

CHAPTER FOURTEEN

Marniski dropped Win off at his house later that afternoon and Win shed his field clothes and rushed to shower. He needed to get back to the office and file a report on the unintended run-in with the church's militiamen. He peered through the blinds in his bedroom to watch one of the plainclothes SWAT agents shoo away a couple of tourists who'd decided they'd break the rules and hike the trail beside his house.

There'd been a noticeable uptick in the number of tourists since the weather had hit a mild streak the last few days. With so many more people around, Win was grateful the Park Service had closed off the hiking trail and a couple of the boardwalks that were nearest his house; they'd even blocked a good part of the parking lot between the house and the highway. All the signs said something along the lines of *Closed for Ecological Study* or *Closed for Wildlife Habitat Protection* or some other innocuous lie intended to not tip off the public to the fact that someone might want to kill the resident FBI agent. While the park superintendent seemed genuinely concerned with the danger to Win, he clearly didn't want to alert his visitors to a threat he hoped would simply disappear. Win was thinking the guy needed to remember the old saying "Hope is not a plan."

As he waited for the SWAT Team leader to show up and take him back to the office, he checked a short text on his business phone from Jason, smiling at photos the boy had sent of potential Yellowstone art to hang in the storage room that Deb had appropriated yesterday for their intelligence analysts. The kid was clearly fascinated with all the recent FBI activity, and Win hated having to keep him out of the office for the time being—way too much sensitive stuff floating around right now. They still hadn't made it to Win's promised steak dinner, but they'd shared several quick suppers in the office with the workmen before the FBI's domestic terrorism effort really got ramped up. Win had made it his business to encourage Jason to apply for college, and Jason had made it his business to bring Win into the twenty-first century by way of social media.

Win watched the SWAT agent through the slit in the blinds while he thought back on his last conversation with the kid.

"Said you grew up on a cattle farm, a small-town guy, but you were one of the best high school quarterbacks in the country. A four-star recruit—big-time player. Quarterback at Arkansas, did awesome in five games and got hurt. Never came back as a quarterback, uh . . . played receiver and was second team All-SEC your junior and senior years. Big-time player." Jason's eyes were wide with admiration.

Win, who was digging into a bag of chips, stopped eating and cocked his head to hear Jason out. "Where'd you get this stuff?"

"ESPN search, Google search. What? You never did a search on yourself? There's all sorts of cool stuff. Photos, everything! Said you won rifle marksmanship competitions in high school, and you're a Sigma Chi, went to law school. Uh, there are two *Law Review* articles you wrote—couldn't make much of those—but man, you are legit!"

"Whoa, whoa!" Win was blushing and laughing. "Yeah, okay, I googled my name a few years ago and it embarrassed me, so I never did it again. I don't do any of the social media stuff. Never did. My coaches wouldn't allow it in high school or college. I saw some friends get hurt by it. I figured you might learn some things about a person, but you could also get some wrong impressions. Can't really know a person from the internet."

Jason seemed honestly puzzled there could be things about a person that couldn't be gleaned from an online search. "Like . . . what do you mean?" he asked.

"Well," Win dug deeper into the bag of chips and looked at him. "C'mon now, it didn't tell you I'm scared of spiders and heights, I was shy around girls forever, I can't dance worth a hoot, and I'd've never made it out of college without spell-check."

"That's the stuff you'd put on Facebook, Snapchat, or Instagram! Dude—I mean, sir, you need to get out there!" Jason had railed on and on about the wonders of social media and the advantages of knowing everything about everybody with the click of a keypad.

Win shook his head as he moved away from the window to go meet his ride. Nothing like being declared outdated at the ripe old age of twenty-eight by a seventeen-year-old, home-schooled, part-time employee of the National Park Service.

*   *   *

SSA Stuart had taken over Johnson's office while he was on leave, and her eyes were on the computer screen when Win knocked on the open door. She glanced up at him in anger. "As a result of your little romp with Marniski this afternoon, Wes may call in the Hostage Rescue Team to consult—*consult*—HRT! They won't just consult, they'll deploy! They'll take the case over and marginalize our squad's impact and visibility! And as for you—I know your type. Big man on campus during your jock days in college, brownnoses your way through law school, decides to go on some crusade to rid the world of evil, and ends up in the Bureau on the fast track based on your good looks and our ever-present good-ole-boy network! I'm hitting the nail right on the head, aren't I, Agent Tyler?"

Win stood in the doorway, holding his paperwork, too stunned to answer. She was standing now, leaning toward him over Johnson's large antique desk. She never lowered her voice.

"Then, it all came crashing down, huh, Tyler? Got on the wrong side in the Brunson case and held on to this job by the skin of your teeth. So I'm stuck with having to deal with you on what could be a major domestic terrorism case—stuck with working with some cowboy who thinks he's a stud and has no idea how to handle these types of high-level operations!" She gave him an imperious wave and sat down at the computer as if he weren't even there.

Deb and another agent were standing in the hall when Win backed out of the open doorway. Their shocked expressions told him they'd heard every word of Ms. Stuart's rant. Win didn't even pretend to know how to respond to his supervisor, much less to his colleagues who'd overhead.

"Never thought of myself as a cowboy." It was all he could think to say. The agent just raised his eyebrows and shook his head. Deb stood there and closed her eyes for a moment. Win moved past them down the hall to his office, threw the file on the desk, and sat down hard in his chair.

The light knock on his door was Deb. She moved inside his office and closed the door before he could even acknowledge her. Raw anger, humiliation, and confusion were competing for his top emotion.

Deb rested her hands on the back of one of the wooden chairs and didn't sugarcoat it. "You came here on an LOE transfer. So you're not getting a lot of respect from some of our people. So what? What did you expect?" Then her tone softened. "I read your reports and listened to the audio on your informant meetings with the Bordeaux. All of it real good work. You've got the attention of the big bosses. They're impressed and Emily feels threatened. She's on the fast track to a promotion at Headquarters, and she doesn't need anything or anyone making waves."

"I can't figure out what I've done to cause her to lash out like that. . . . I was fixing to give her my report on the contact with the two militiamen. She's been here less than three full days. I need to be able to work with her. She's my boss on this case," he stammered.

Win expected Deb to leave. But she didn't.

"You don't know, do you? I guess there's no reason for you to know, you've only been assigned to the Denver Field Office for a few weeks. You have a right to know—it's no secret. Emily has been, ahhh, seeing Samuel Cushing for over a year now. Probably another reason she isn't keen on you."

Win's eye's widened as his stomach dropped. "Are you serious? Cushing from Headquarters? The Deputy Assistant Director over Public Corruption?" Samuel Cushing was the driving force behind the Bureau's reversal on the Brunson case. In Win's view the guy was probably dirty. Samuel Cushing had banished him here and would like nothing more than to find a reason to end Win's short career with the FBI.

"Yeah, one and the same. Emily has her eye on a job at Headquarters, and Cushing has been greasing the rails for her. But if this operation falls apart for her, even he won't be able to get her to Washington. Mr. Strickland won't take any crap from Headquarters, and he won't recommend anyone who he doesn't think is up to the job. So Emily has two reasons to hate you: You're in Samuel Cushing's gunsights, and you're showing her up on this case."

"Whoa." Win leaned back in his chair. That put a different spin on things. And not in a good way.

Win didn't ask Deb what he should do, but she told him anyway. "Just do your job, cover your ass with memos and emails, and try to stay clear of her. She's so hyped up she'll probably hang herself on this deal if you give her enough rope. And come join some of us for dinner and a beer tonight. You can't work every minute of the day. Several armed agents can surely cover your back this evening. Besides, Emily did get one thing right—you sure aren't hard on the eyes!"

Win felt himself blushing as Deb turned, opened the door, and walked out of his office.

*　*　*

One reason he'd been avoiding spending free time with the Denver agents was his fear that they'd discover why he was sent to Yellowstone and look down on him. Based on Deb's comments, they all knew about the Brunson disaster anyway, so there was no reason to avoid them. He couldn't hide behind work forever. He needed to make connections. *Expand your circle of friends,* that's what Blake had suggested. He knew his brother was right; most folks in the Bureau were really good people. Deb seemed nice enough. Pushy, for sure, but in sort of a maternal way.

At the hotel's bar that night there were nine Denver agents gathered, all of whom had several more years in the Bureau than Win. Mr. Strickland was clearly not sending inexperienced agents to Yellowstone to work the case. Win's worries about being ostracized for perceived past sins in Charlotte were soon forgotten—the agents were all welcoming and friendly. Most everyone in the group had changed into more casual clothes and settled into a night of leisure. Win wished he had the same luxury, but he knew the lure of new intel on the case would call him back to his office tonight. One thing for certain about the Bureau, you could actually work 24/7 if you were so inclined. He had to remind himself again that he needed a break. He needed some down time, some time to unwind.

Deb introduced him to an agent named Ramona Gist, a petite, black-haired woman who managed to sit beside Win at dinner and immediately take an interest in everything he had to say. She wore a brown leather jacket over a tight white sweater with skinny jeans. He was thinking they looked sorta spray-painted on. Her big silver earrings spun when she shook her long black hair, which she seemed to do a lot. She was maybe mid-thirties and fairly attractive, with a good figure and large brown eyes. She was on the Domestic Terrorism Squad in Denver and said she just loved the West. Ramona was also recently divorced with two small children—something one of the men mentioned but she hadn't brought up. He couldn't figure how she could show him phone photos of her golden retriever and forget the pictures of her kids.

Win felt a little panic creep in when he realized Ramona was set to interrogate him on his private life with the same intensity he might use on, say, a bank robber or kidnapper. She had also done a little research and knew way more about him than he would have liked. It occurred to him, as most everyone else ordered another drink after dinner, that he hadn't been with a woman except Shelby in well over five years. He'd forgotten how this was done. *Well, there was the bear girl the other day. . . . I did* alright *there, but then I'll probably never see her again.* He felt his confidence begin to slide.

Before Shelby, there hadn't been many romantic relationships; he'd always been busy with sports, school, and work. His parents had been ruthless in drilling into him his responsibility toward women. He was to be a protector and provider. A man who respected and cherished women. He would never take advantage. Since junior high school his mother had told him his football prowess and his good looks gave him an even greater responsibility to be a role model for his brothers and his friends. He was cut very little slack when it came to dating. He had a duty as a Christian to be above temptation—not that he got that right every time, but he sure did try.

It wasn't that he was never hit on or didn't have the urge from time to time to proposition some woman—those things happened but were never acted on, because for the last five years he'd had Shelby to fall back on. He was taken. He was engaged; he'd be polite and gently deflect any admirers. He'd buck up and resist any temptations. He was taken. It occurred to him as Ramona leaned into him, laughing at someone's joke . . . *I'm not taken anymore.* There was no safety net. He was on his own, and this aggressive woman had a bead on him.

He'd also been told at least a million times that he was naive about girls. That unfortunate trait was definitely not coming in handy with Ramona. She kept maneuvering closer to him and he began to notice how nice she smelled. But one thing he did know for sure about himself, he liked being the hunter way more than being the hunted. And one thing he knew for sure about Ramona was that there were enough red flags with her to start a parade. When Ramona casually touched his leg for the second time, he started looking for an escape strategy and found it sitting directly across from him. The older agent sitting across the table from them was watching Ramona's less-than-discreet flirting and Win's occasional deer-in-the-headlights looks with equal amusement. He finished his second beer and asked Win if he'd looked over the park's collection of missing person's files.

The guy paid his tab and continued, "It's been a curiosity of mine the last several years. A missing person file, per se, doesn't rise to a criminal investigation, but there could be a pattern in several of those files—maybe, maybe not." He shrugged. "If you have a few minutes sometime, I'd like to visit with you on a couple of the most recent cases. Doesn't have to be tonight, but I've got some time."

Win knew the guy was giving him an out either way. He could go back to the office with him and escape Ramona or decline and let the budding romance play out. He took the first option in a heartbeat.

"Yeah, I noticed those files. I actually read through several of them. If you've got time tonight, that would be great. Gee, Ramona, good meeting you. . . . I'll see you around, I'm sure." She said something Win was glad he didn't quite catch. He stood up to leave, and she smiled and threw her hair back again, shaking those earrings. Her eyes said he would definitely see her around.

He said his good nights to the agents who remained at the table or at the bar. Pulling on his heavy coat, he met the other man at the dining-room entrance. They walked down the dimly lit street toward the office and Win noticed two of the SWAT agents had dropped into step several yards behind them. He hadn't noticed them in the restaurant.

"Your name's Murray, right? Thanks for bailing me out in there," Win said.

"Yeah, I go by Murray. Ken Murray, Violent Crime Squad Supervisor. Been hearing real good things about your work. Listened to your informant interview with Ellie Bordeaux this afternoon, all those references to the Scripture and prayer—thought Ramona might not be your type." Win was glad it was dark; he knew his face was red.

The man chuckled. "Ramona is a good gal in lots of ways—a real good agent by the way. Don't let her after-hours behavior fool you; she's a sharp investigator with great analytical skills. But in her private life, I'm afraid she has the subtlety of a bull moose in rut and the single-mindedness of a heat-seeking missile, so don't be shy about telling her where you stand. She's had three husbands that I know of and is in the process of destroying two or three marriages in the Denver office. None of us knew she was going to be in Mammoth tonight, so Deb sort of got strong-armed into introducing you two."

"Appreciate the heads-up." He could still smell her perfume on his shirt and felt grateful his loneliness hadn't grown to the point where he was tempted to cross his own lines of behavior to ease that void. He couldn't imagine a worse basis for a relationship. But there he was, being naive again. He knew it wasn't a relationship Ramona was interested in tonight. He shook his head to clear those thoughts and turned back to Murray.

"So you're the supervisor over the missing persons cases? I actually kept the hard copies of those working files here in the office when I scanned everything into our digitized system. Some of the cases are very compelling, really tragic. Don't know if you're aware, but ATF has a missing informant who was last seen here at Mammoth twelve days ago. The rangers found his car abandoned at a trailhead last week. No sign of the CI—that guy could end up being added to the missing persons list."

Someone slammed a car door in the darkness and Win flinched at the sound. The older agent didn't break stride. His words in the cold night were reassuring. "Win, there hasn't been an FBI agent specifically targeted and killed on American soil in over twenty-five years. Oh, once in a great while there's a threat, but as dumb as criminals can sometimes be. . . . They aren't dumb enough to bring the wrath of the Bureau down on their heads by taking out one of our people."

CHAPTER FIFTEEN

It was a text from a number he didn't recognize and Win didn't bother to read it. His personal phone was being monitored, and if it were anything of interest, he'd get a quick call from the Bureau's communications folks—so he just let it slide. It had been another in a long series of nights at the office. He'd gotten maybe five hours of sleep last night. Win fiddled with the dining room's window shade while he waited for his ride to the office. He hated living in the house with the blinds drawn all the time. He figured it must be driving the cat nuts. But then, he'd never know, since the cat still wouldn't get near him. He peered around the shade at the early-morning light. The days were getting longer, and at 6:03 a.m. there was plenty of daylight. A clear, sunny morning was starting to materialize.

He pulled on his jacket, topped off his coffee, and moved into the mudroom at the sound of a vehicle driving up. His ride was running a little late, and while he was impatient, he knew Denver's SWAT agents on security detail outside the house must be climbing the walls awaiting their shift change. At least he'd slept in a warm bed, while they dealt with the freezing temperatures and the monotony of guard duty. The SWAT Team's SUV pulled up and parked on the gravel area behind the house, just as it had the last two mornings. Ranger Hechtner wouldn't approve, Win thought. Be unpredictable, he'd said. Maybe they were getting a little complacent. Today would be the fourth day since Luke's warning of the death threat and nothing had happened.

He started out the back door and had reached the first step when he remembered the text on his personal phone. The SWAT guy was leaning out of the Suburban's window, talking to one of his men near the old garage. He was obviously in no hurry. Win stood on the back step, holding the storm door open with his shoulder as he tried to balance his coffee mug and pull out his phone. The new text read: **#2— Play is on—am—LRR**

What? What! In an instant he knew it was from Luke, and in that same instant he knew he was in grave danger. He glanced toward the barren hills to the north, dropped the coffee, and dove back into the house.

The .50 caliber bullet tore through the storm door just as he let it go—glass and aluminum shattered under the impact of the huge round. Shards of glass and metal exploded against the freshly painted walls of the mudroom. Win landed on his stomach amid two sacks of cat litter. He closed his eyes tight as projectiles ricocheted though the small room, shattering both windows. When he opened his eyes, he saw thick red liquid covering his left side. He felt no pain but realized he must have been hit. He blinked in shock at the widening crimson stain on his starched white shirt. Then he smelled the familiar scent of the laundry detergent. The bullet fragments had obliterated the plastic bottle on top of the washing machine.

Thank you, God! Thank you. . . . He kept repeating his thanks under his breath as a mantra as he scooted toward the relative safety of the dining room. Before Win cleared the mudroom's tile floor, the shooter got off a second round into the engine of the SWAT agent's SUV. A heavy thump and small explosion erupted from the damaged engine block as the vehicle died. The reports from the rifle came less than a second later—two distant, sharp cracks few would recognize as gunfire.

The dining room's eighteen-inch-thick sandstone walls offered him protection. At some point in the chaos of the last five seconds—he had no idea when—he'd drawn his gun. He'd dropped his phones in the mudroom. *No going after them now.* The SWAT agent guarding the front of the house called out that he was entering and came through the front door, moving low to stay below as many windows as possible. He was communicating with the others in the rear and with the SWAT Team leader at the Justice Center on his personal radio. He crouched beside Win with his short-barrel MP5 clutched in his hand. He looked as scared as Win felt.

"No one's hit in the back. . . .They're scrambling. . . . Long-range rifle . . . Got the truck, we're supposed to hang tight—oh my God!" His eyes widened as he took in the dark-red stain on Win's side.

"Laundry detergent. No kidding!" Win was grinning.

"That thug is gonna be ticked! Killed a Suburban and a bottle of Tide!" The SWAT guy was grinning.

Then they both leaned into the wall, laughing—a release of the intense tension and fear both men felt. When they finally got themselves together half a minute later, Win felt his emotions turning to anger. What kind of coward tries to assassinate a man with a gun that can cut a person in two! An underlying rage was boiling up at the unseen enemy. He needed to temper the powerful emotions by focusing on a response to the attack, but since he was the target, he was ordered to stay put.

The FBI reaction was swift, thank goodness. Win heard a helicopter in the distance within five minutes of the shots. Several agents arrived outside the house even more quickly. They weren't too worried about blending in with the tourists at this point, and most had assault rifles at the ready. The SWAT agent's radio crackled with updates. Park rangers were shutting down two nearby trails. Nearly half the FBI's surveillance force had been called in from the field or repositioned. It wasn't yet 6:30, but nobody even remotely connected with law enforcement was sitting this one out. The house shook as a second helicopter thundered low over them about ten minutes into their wait. Someone reported that a sniper rifle and ghillie suit had been found northeast of Win's house. After what seemed like an eternity, the guy's radio finally signaled an all clear. Gus Jordon and the FBI's SWAT Team leader rushed in the front door moments later.

"What the hell!" the team leader yelled at the agent standing with Win in the dining room. Win was sure the Denver SWAT Team leader was a very articulate man, but most of what was said in the first couple of minutes were words Win would never repeat. The guy was furious with his team for giving the assassin an easy, predictable shooting lane. Somebody in the Bureau was gonna catch hell, and it was looking like it was gonna be him.

While the SWAT guys were focused on their internal "How could this have happened?" tirade, Gus put a hand on Win's arm.

"You all right?"

Win nodded and looked away. His hands were gripping the back of one of the oak dining room chairs. He scanned the mudroom floor, which was littered with pieces of glass, aluminum, plastic, and shrapnel. He knew the mess in the backyard from the remnants of the door and windows would be worse—coulda been him in pieces when that massive round hit. *Coulda been me.*

"Nothing on the shooter?" he asked.

"Not yet—everyone's on it. Got the hills behind the house covered with responders. Your SWAT Team will get you back to your office. Chief Randall is in Billings; I'm standing in. I've called our evidence-response folks in to tape the house off and supplement your people on the crime scene investigation. It's been nearly twenty minutes since the shots—we oughta be good to get you out of here now." The ranger looked down at Win's stained side. He glanced at the mudroom and managed a thin smile. "At least you smell real good. . . . Want to change before you go?"

Win nodded. "Yeah, just be a minute." He was glad Gus was giving him some privacy. He'd have to have his game face on when he hit the office. He wasn't at all sure he had the emotional strength to pull that off. He was still having to remind himself to breathe.

He splashed cold water on his face and washed the sticky liquid soap off his side. He pulled on a clean shirt, tie, and jacket. The cat was peering out from under his bed, watching his every move with frightened eyes. The sounds of numerous vehicles arriving and loud, strained voices outside his windows filled the bedroom. Win directed his comments toward the cat. "You may be wishin' you had a different roommate before this is over, buddy. You're gonna be stuck in this room for a day or so." The big orange cat pulled back. Win's tone became gentle. "It's okay, Gruff. . . . It's okay. Don't be afraid. . . . Nobody's gonna hurt you." He looked back into the mirror, into his own deep-blue eyes. He straightened his tie and was thankful his hands had quit shaking. *It's okay, Win. . . . It's okay. Don't be afraid. . . . Nobody's gonna hurt you.*

* * *

They filed out the front door of the house and hustled Win into the SWAT Team leader's Suburban with the agent who'd been driving the disabled SUV. That man was slumped in the front seat, keeping his head low. Win figured either he was blaming himself for the protection foul-up or he hadn't recovered from the shock of the attack. Win could see two Black Hawk helicopters maneuvering above the barren hills to the north of the hotel. The heavy, rhythmic thumping of the powerful military copters' rotors pounded the high-country air. *Won't be any guests sleeping in this morning.*

There were no structures in the hills behind the hotel's cabins except a small utilities complex. There were, however, heavily used hiking trails and a gravel road that meandered northward for five miles to the park's north entrance at Gardiner. Based on the constant radio chatter, it appeared the gunman had taken the two shots, slipped out of the sniper suit, walked to the main trail, and blended into the early-morning walkers and hikers who were taking advantage of the beautiful weather.

Gus climbed into the other side of the back seat and followed Win's eyes to the activity on the hills. "Without a witness who saw something suspicious on that knoll, or a description of the suspect, finding the bad guy is gonna be a long shot. . . ."

Win turned in the seat and forced a reluctant grin at the ranger. "Really? A long shot. Little early for cop humor, isn't it?"

"Gotta keep your sanity any way you can, Sport. I'd vote for Kentucky bourbon, but hell, it is a little early for that."

The SWAT Team leader started the SUV and eased it away from Win's house. Bureau and Park Service vehicles were still arriving, but none had sirens blaring or lights flashing. It was intentionally low-key. In keeping with the Department of Interior's desire to keep this whole unsavory business a secret, there was no general alarm at Mammoth. That seemed totally bizarre to Win, with heavily armed FBI agents milling around his yard and about a dozen gawking tourists, the early risers, just yards away at the thermal features. A couple of rangers were sent over to assure everyone the police were simply conducting security drills. Nothing to worry about.

SSA Stuart had assembled the FBI's on-site supervisors, a few of whom looked like they'd just rolled out of bed, in the office's conference room. Win could hear the commotion of voices on phones or in animated conversations as soon as he came through the old building's back door. Everyone in the conference room was standing. Everyone was tense. Everything stopped when Win entered the room with the SWAT Team leader, Gus, and the other agent following close. Win felt all eyes swing to him. It went quiet.

Jim West finally moved to him and put a hand on his shoulder. He met Win's eyes and his tone was low, as if he were fighting to control his anger.

"Glad you're all right. We will get him. We're going to throw everything we've got into finding him."

Win nodded to his boss and scanned the intense faces. Jim moved to the shaken SWAT agent and spoke quietly to him.

The debrief was quick and dirty at this point. They needed to fill any gaps, hear what the victims saw; there would be time for hand-wringing and recrimination later. Win told the hastily assembled group that as soon as he read the text he knew it was from his confidential source and he knew it was a warning of an imminent threat.

"Tell me how you knew that?" Ms. Stuart asked.

"The text read, '#2—play is on—am—LRR.' What it meant to me was that the second diversion the source and I talked about last Friday night—killing the resident FBI agent—had been set in motion. I believe L-R-R referred to long-range rifle and a-m was obviously the timing of the attack. If I'd read the text earlier, when it came in, I wouldn't have gone out the door, and we might have been able to locate the shooter."

Unfortunately, locating the shooter still hadn't happened. The shots had been taken from a spot 2,932 feet from Win's back door. A long shot—not a tremendous distance, but a very long shot. The bad guy was no amateur. The gunman had been concealed behind a small boulder near a desolate graveyard on top of the hill. The shooter's location would have been well hidden from the park buildings and the trails below, but it would have been clearly visible from the air. After the threat on Win's life had been communicated last Friday, one of the Bureau surveillance planes had flown a visual watch pattern over Mammoth beginning at daybreak each morning and periodically during each day, looking for anything out of the ordinary. But today's plane wasn't even in the air from Livingston yet. The Tuesday flight wasn't scheduled to arrive over the area until nearly 7:30 a.m. because of a switch-out in pilots. It was as if the assassin knew the FBI's flight schedule. Win tucked that unsettling thought back into his consciousness.

Ken Murray may not have made it to the shower this morning, but he had a laser-like focus on their problem. The man ran a hand through his ruffled hair. He turned hard eyes on Win and leaned across the conference table. "We retrieved your personal phone from the scene. We're trying to find out why the text didn't trigger an alert to you from the communications staff. It's possible that way out here there may be gaps or delays in some of our communication feeds. Initial intel tells us the phone that sent you the text is a basic throwaway. I sent a text back on your phone as soon as I got it. No response yet, and no way to trace the original text back to any individual." He leaned back in his chair, his eyes still intent on Win's. "If the text was from your source, you need to touch base with him or her ASAP. We don't have much to go on."

Referring to Luke Bordeaux as his confidential source and not naming names was a calculated move on Win's part. This case was strictly a *need-to-know* operation, and at this point in the investigation, Bordeaux's involvement wasn't general knowledge, even among the FBI contingent. Chief Randall and Gus were the only non-Bureau officers with that information. Win wanted it to stay that way for the time being. One informant had already gone missing since this case began; he didn't intend to put another man at risk.

SSA Stuart spoke again before breaking up the meeting. "Mr. Strickland has been briefed by phone. He informed the Director of the shooting shortly after it happened. Wes Givens will be flying here later today to take charge. Our Hostage Rescue Team could be mobilized, but at the very least they'll have someone from HRT here for consultation by tomorrow. We can't be one hundred percent sure today's incident is related to the church group, but everything is pointing in that direction. The .50 caliber rifle we recovered is probably the one Win's source mentioned. Win, I need you to reach out to your source now. Coordinate your informant work and your 302 statement with Jim and Ken." She paused and looked around the crowded room. "Let's get on it! We have to find that shooter."

Win moved to the privacy of one of the small downstairs offices and tried Luke's cell phone number. He wasn't expecting an answer and he didn't get one. He left a message pretending to be an old friend wanting to talk about LSU football. *C'mon, Luke, call me.* He leaned against the wall and closed his eyes. If Bordeaux had enough information to send him a warning, he might know significantly more about the shooter. But what if Bordeaux was playing him? What if he was the shooter? Win's mind went back to Friday night's conversation. He'd asked Luke, "Who could use one of those long-range rifles?" What had the man said? "Except for me, you mean . . . maybe a guy in the church group . . . maybe one of the men who brought it in." *Except for me . . . geez.*

The next hour was a blur. Win gave his FD-302 witness statement to two agents from Murray's Violent Crime Squad. He glanced at his watch as he left the interview, only 8:35. It felt like days had passed since the shots at his house.

Jim West caught Win's eye and motioned upstairs toward Win's office. Jim and the bulk of the FBI contingent had been spending most of their time in the Justice Center since they'd hit town, but today the old stone building was crawling with agents. Ms. Stuart was still encamped in Johnson's office. Win knew Johnson had been called back early from his leave; when the agent arrived later today, he might have to work out of the broom closet. As the case agent, Win got to keep his office—one of the pluses for shouldering that responsibility.

Win's supervisor closed the door to the office and settled into a chair. He quickly checked his phone. "Sorry, just checking the text traffic. . . . No breaks finding the thug yet," Jim began as he pocketed the phone and turned his attention to Win. "Probably not what you were expecting when you got the Yellowstone posting, huh?"

"No, sir, not at all."

"Listen, Win, there is no dishonor, and I mean none, in asking to be pulled at this point. We can have you in Jackson by tonight—or Denver, if you'd rather be there."

"I'm fine. I appreciate you considering my request to stay on the case, sir."

"You've done good work here. . . . Murray and I took it upon ourselves to override Emily on this—we're leaving you on the case. That said, I don't think it would be wise for you to stay at your house until we get a better handle on our security lapses. Maybe Bozeman for tonight?"

Win gave a single nod, and Jim continued. "Tom Strickland and Wes Givens are real high on you. A single-handed conversion of the office space in less than three weeks! We're not even going to ask how you got unauthorized support from the Salt Lake City Field Office to help set everything up. Your informant development has also been outstanding, and I like how you work with people. Maybe one exception there. Win . . . don't let Emily get to you so easily. You're both driven, and she's more than a little hard-nosed, but try to trust her judgment."

"I know. . . . There's been some friction."

"Well, just tread lightly with her. Maybe try being less formal with her, use her first name. Not so stiff." Jim shifted in the chair and tried to get Win to make eye contact again. "You sure you don't want to head down to the Jackson RA? Just for a few days?"

"I'm good. I still have last night's surveillance reports to review. Then I need to—"

"The SWAT agent said you have ice water in your veins. You haven't missed a beat—you're eerily calm. It's a little spooky, Win. It's not like someone unloads on you with a .50 caliber rifle every day."

Win glanced up and managed a thin smile. *Me? Calm? If only you knew.*

As Jim stood to leave, he dug in his jacket pocket and produced a note. "Oh yeah, the technical folks still have your personal phone. A call came in while you were in your 302 interview. From a woman . . . here's the phone number. She wants to see if you can meet for lunch."

Win blushed at his boss reading his personal message. "Probably a girl I met last week. . . . Bad timing."

"Why not go? This may be the best opportunity you'll have to get out with a civilian in public until we take these yahoos down. They've had their shot at you this morning and missed. Chances of anything else happening to you today are slim and none. I'll send a man along to sit in the background." He was holding the message and smiling down at his young agent, trying to ease Win's discomfort.

Jim did have a point. The shooter was on the run and wouldn't likely be thinking of another attack. After the supervisor left his office, Win returned Tory's call and set up an early lunch. If he ever needed something positive to occupy his thoughts, today was the day.

* * *

Win could see the activity on the rocky, barren hill from where he stood at the window inside the foyer of the hotel's dining room. The big cottonwood trees standing behind the hotel hadn't leafed out yet, and his view of the high knoll through their outstretched bare limbs was unobstructed. His people were up there trying to figure it out; a shot from that distance would have taken serious planning. Had the shooter just lucked out with today's delayed aerial surveillance from the Bureau plane? How had the bad guy known his routine? Win wanted desperately to be up there working, but Bureau rules relegated him to the sidelines. He pushed his frustration down and forced himself to refocus on other matters. He forced himself to watch for Tory Madison.

The restaurant was in a large frame building across the street from the entrance to the hotel. Both buildings had the same soft yellowish-gray paint; they were both constructed in 1936. With a few exceptions, Win had eaten at the restaurant every day since he'd arrived in Yellowstone. He was usually comfortable here. *Not so much today . . .*

He nodded to Agent Dillard, his shadow, as the man moved toward the bar area to observe the growing lunch crowd. He saw her walk out from under the wooden canopy in front of the hotel. *Wow. She is beautiful.* His knees went a little weak; he suddenly felt nervous and self-conscious. *Geez! Win! If you can tamp down your nerves after a near-killing, you can surely deal with meeting a girl for lunch! Get a grip!* He responded to his internal lecture with narrowed eyes and shallow breathing. It had always amazed him that others saw him as totally calm and collected, never anxious, never out of control. Win Tyler might be having an internal meltdown, but no one around him would have a clue. It was a handy little defense mechanism that had the downside of making him seem distant and detached at times.

He watched her coming across the street from the hotel. The heavy hiking boots and overalls were gone. She was wearing black cowboy boots, dark jeans, and a gray sweater. A black coat and scarf were slung over her shoulders. She had the look of a confident woman, and he noticed she either nodded or spoke to everyone she met on the crosswalk. She looked like a genuinely nice person, not too focused on herself.

He held the door open for her, and she smiled that beautiful smile and shook her head in an attempt to tame her blowing brunette hair as she walked into the foyer.

"Glad you called, was hoping you would," he told her.

The tiny foreign hostess seated them against the far wall. Agent Dillard found a table in the near corner and seemed content with sipping ice tea and scanning the room for bad guys.

"Did you hear all the commotion early this morning? Around six? My one day in weeks to sleep in—ugh! Helicopters flying low, people yelling. . . . It sounded like an invasion!"

He pulled out her chair for her and moved to sit down. "Uh, yeah." He fumbled with his napkin.

She narrowed her eyes slightly under perfect brows and pulled her chin down a little. "So what was going on? You work for the FBI. Don't y'all know everything that's going on?"

"The FBI only knows everything that's going on in the movies and on TV." He adjusted his napkin again. "So, did the hotel folks tell you what was happening?"

"They finally sent a guy door-to-door—he said the police were conducting drills. I'm not buying that." She took a sip of her water and met his eyes. "Oh, so you can't say. . . . I get it. Okay, you needn't say."

The waitress showed up beside them, and he broke eye contact while she ordered. *Uh-oh, this girl is reading me like a book. Don't telegraph everything you're thinking, Win! Curious girl . . . smart girl . . .*

They worked their way through their sandwiches while hitting the high points of their brief time in Yellowstone. She told him about her weeks in the field. Tory looked very feminine, but she was obviously tough. That much time in a nylon tent, much of it in snow and icy rain, didn't sound like Win's idea of a good time. But she made the various outdoor hardships sound adventurous, even fun. As he'd suspected, Dr. Kane was very serious about her research and expected everyone to pull their share of the load. Tory sounded like a worker; she seemed enthusiastic about everything. *Reminds me of me not so long ago.*

"You wouldn't believe all the wildlife!" Her eyes were bright and she laughed softly when she told him about frantically climbing boulders to escape a herd of hundreds of bison flowing toward the center of the park two days ago. "I was desperate to get away from them." Her eyes widened. "They were moving toward the valley, toward the new grass. They had no interest in me. I'll never forget it—the sound of the cows grunting to their babies, the musty smell of earth being churned up under so many hoofs, the big bulls snorting to each other. . . . I was high on the rocks, safe. I was so silly to be afraid." She cocked her pretty head. "I'll bet you're not afraid of anything."

Nope, not going there. He fought the urge to glance at his armed guard as he grinned back at her. "Ah, everybody's scared of something, but I've got some awesome angels looking out for me. . . ." He eased the conversation in a different direction.

He told her he'd spent most of his time organizing the FBI office. "Oh, a few interesting things have happened, but nothing comparable to catching and studying grizzly bears." It bothered him to say that. Anyone outside the Bureau and the other related agencies might think he had the dullest job imaginable. He'd nearly died today, but he wouldn't mention it to anyone on the outside as long as this case was open or the information didn't become public. So he talked mostly of home and school and told stories of his brothers and she laughed easily and met his eyes constantly. He liked those soft-brown eyes; they had depth and sparkled when she talked. He found himself getting a little lost in them.

"I'm leaving town this afternoon and I may not have any time off for several days, but I'd really like to see you again," he said. She seemed a little disappointed he'd be gone and it pleased him to see her reaction.

"We'll be in Mammoth till tomorrow afternoon, then in Bozeman for three days of seminars at Montana State, and then off to the next camp in Roosevelt. Dr. Kane does give us some personal time each week; maybe you could come down and visit one day."

He paid the bill, and as they walked out the entrance he told her he'd call her. Agent Dillard was on the sidewalk, pretending to look at a map. Win didn't expect it when she turned to him on the landing and spoke in a low voice.

"That guy in the gray jacket and blue cap. Something's not right. He watched everyone in the restaurant, ate lunch, but not really there for lunch, you know? He's standing over there now. You're not in some kind of trouble, are you?"

Win knew Agent Dillard hadn't been that obvious; this girl was sharp.

"No, no trouble. He works with me. We have lots of folks here. Didn't the Park Service say it was just drills?" He tried to smile a reassuring smile down at her. He avoided her probing eyes.

She still wasn't buying it, but her voice was gentle. "Thanks again for lunch. Look forward to seeing you again, Win."

They moved to the side of the small landing to let another couple enter the restaurant. She was standing close to him. Her hair smelled like flowers. Tory took his hand in hers. He really wasn't expecting that. He felt the warmth of her soft fingers. His breath caught in his throat and he went quiet and still. He'd spent years maintaining those solid walls that protected him from any woman except Shelby. For just a moment, as he stood there in the sunlight with her holding his hand, he sensed those walls beginning to crack. She squeezed his hand, turned, and skipped down the steps. Her scarf and her long hair were blowing in the breeze. *Whoa . . .*

CHAPTER SIXTEEN

Being in lockdown with the FBI SWAT Team was not what Win had in mind when Jim told him he'd stay on the case. One of the Denver SWAT Team members, who looked like he ate nails for breakfast, was standing guard over him in his office, while a second one lounged outside the closed door. This was not the loose protection detail he'd had before. These guys were dialed in. Security was so tight he felt suffocated.

He'd been back from lunch an hour now and had nearly completed the mind-numbing assignment of reviewing his previous cases from the Charlotte Field Office. He'd slogged through most of them this morning, before his early lunch with Tory. If he had enemies capable of murder in the mix, he hadn't found them. During the three years since the Academy, he'd worked numerous cases where criminals had gone to prison, where reputations had been ruined, where ill-gotten fortunes were lost, but he'd concluded nothing in those cases should warrant an attempt on his life. Nothing except the Brunson case. And he didn't even know where to begin on that one. He pushed back from the computer screen and closed his eyes.

The sheer volume of work was certainly helping force Win's attention away from the events of the morning, but beneath the surface nagging thoughts ran through his mind. *Who'd taken that shot? Why?* Probably someone with the Prophet's church, but what if . . . ? The fallout from the Brunson case was still happening—could someone see him as a loose end? In Congressman Brunson's office, or even in the Bureau? The Congressman had taken more than a million dollars in alleged bribes. People were killed for a lot less. He keyed back into the Sentinel system and began the systematic review of that case. *Am I grasping at straws here?*

The agent sitting in the corner laid his MP5 across his leg and adjusted his body armor. Win sighed. *I'm under house arrest.* The surreal nature of it nearly jogged his mind back to the present. Nearly, but not quite. His inner monologue continued to play. . . . *Maybe Luke had the answers. . . . Maybe Luke was the answer.* Murray's technical guys still had his personal phone. Maybe Luke had returned his early-morning call.

* * *

But Luke hadn't returned his call. Luke had checked the message and deleted it before the militia moved out of cell phone range. It was Win Tyler's voice, with a decidedly redneck slant. *Hey, buddy! It's 'bout seven ten in the morning. Great lookin' day! Ain't you loving it that Bama missed out on that strong-armed quarterback they were recruiting outa North Hills? Boy can throw the ball a mile. The Tigers may get him yet! Call back and let's talk some LSU football.*

It told him everything he needed to know. It had been a long-range rifle, fired from the hills north of Mammoth, the shooter had missed, and hadn't been caught. He felt a tremendous wave of relief, followed by hollowness in the pit of his stomach. *Damn—it's for real.*

He knew it had been the right thing to do, sending the text warning. But he still couldn't believe it'd really happened. He couldn't believe they'd actually tried to kill a man. Even after he'd overheard King's men last week talking about taking Tyler out, even after he'd warned the agent Friday night—still he couldn't believe they'd go through with it. The Prophet wouldn't be mixed up in killing, in murder. There'd been lots of angry talk—threats, even—but the Prophet wouldn't cross that line. Could Brother King have gone off on a wild hare of his own?

So for several minutes after he'd overheard the voices in the darkness this morning, he'd wrestled with it: *Sniper's taking Tyler out this morning.* He'd heard the words clearly, but he couldn't tell for sure who was talking. One of Brother King's new men, he thought. He should have walked up and confronted them—everyone was waiting for the militia muster right before dawn. But he didn't do a thing except stand in the cold and waller it over in his mind. He'd told himself he had to remember who his enemies were. Win Tyler was the enemy. The Prophet preached that the Feds were ruthless, attacking our families, stealing our lands, turning friend against friend. . . . Hell, they'd done it to me! The damn FBI had tried to ruin his good name—forced him into near-bankruptcy. They'd barely had money for the kids to have Christmas this year. If the church job hadn't come up, where would they be? He couldn't stand being a failure in Ellie's eyes, so here he was, earning better money than he had in years, but to do that—to earn her respect back—had he thrown in with the Devil? No, that can't be.

He'd tried to convince himself the boys were just being their usual blowhards, just posturing. There'd been plenty of that lately. They were preparing for the Prophet's declaration of a New America, getting ready if the Feds attacked them, but surely it wouldn't come to a shooting war. Then why'd he texted Tyler at dawn? *'Cause I was scared not to. . . . What if I was wrong?* He'd sent the text. He'd helped the enemy again. And if they traced the shooter back to someone in the church, a real war would be on.

* * *

Ms. Stuart convened a status meeting in the early afternoon, and it was clear they were no closer to finding the shooter than they'd been at seven o'clock that morning. He or she had seemingly vanished, and unfortunately so had several of Prophet Shepherd's scariest followers. Immediately after the shooting this morning, many of the surveillance agents had been recalled from the field. In that confusion, several of Ron Chandler's men had disappeared from their radar during the militia's training. To make matters worse, the ASAC's plane was delayed by bad weather in Denver. Wes Givens, the Evidence Response Team, and ten additional SWAT Team members wouldn't arrive before midnight. They were shorthanded, and Emily refused to give either the Park Service or the locals a greater role in the investigation. So as mid-afternoon approached, things were not going real well for the good guys.

Jim took Win aside as the brief meeting broke up. "The park's Special Response Team has been assigned to protect you till we get more boots on the ground. They want to get you off the grid—take you down in the park till midday tomorrow. Gus Jordon said they've got some hiker rescue thing going on. You're gonna tag along. A good idea, since it's very possible half the church's militiamen are milling around Mammoth right now. We had one hell of a security breach when Emily pulled the surveillance teams this morning."

"Off the grid? I've still got—"

Jim cut him off. "Hey, technically, you're supposed to be off duty for twenty-four hours after a shooting incident. I'm giving you a break here. You can keep your case agent status and we won't have Personnel coming down on us for breaking regulations."

"Doesn't sound like I have a choice."

"Nope. Besides, we need the rangers to watch your back. It frees up more of our folks to track down leads." An agent down the hallway was motioning for Jim's attention. He nodded to acknowledge her and put a hand on Win's arm as he turned to go. "Win, while you're on stand-down . . . chill a little, okay? Don't underestimate the trauma of a shooting—near miss or not."

* * *

Ten minutes later, disguised in a ranger's green coat and flat hat, Win was secreted out the back door of the office into a waiting Park Service SUV. The three law enforcement rangers in the Tahoe were clearly pleased to be on the road. Rescuing folks was definitely their gig, and while the rangers seemed excited about doing what they did, which was mostly helping people, they seemed much less excited about babysitting Win. They'd obviously been schooled on "Don't ask the FBI agent any questions about what's going on," as they had an amazing lack of curiosity about the morning's shooting. They stopped at Win's house just long enough for him to check on the cat and grab a few things. He made an effort not to look at the damage or the strips of yellow police tape encompassing his backyard. The entire episode still had a Twilight Zone feel.

The Tahoe's driver, Ranger Jimmy Martinez, filled him in on the mission. Two hikers, a father and his ten-year-old son from Wisconsin, were due back in Mammoth two days ago and had finally been reported missing late last night by a relative. There was confusion as to which trails they'd taken. They hadn't followed the park rules for filing an overnight camping plan, although they had signed for a backcountry use permit. More than likely they'd found their permitted trail still snow covered and had chosen an alternate route without notifying anyone. The Park Service's helicopter had been searching the area surrounding the hikers' planned route until it was called back to help with the shooting this morning. So far, no sign of the two. Best-case scenario: They were well prepared for cold-weather camping, had just wandered off the beaten trail, and were having a fabulous father-son adventure, all the while oblivious to the fact that a rescue effort was underway. Worst-case scenario didn't even have to be mentioned.

The twenty-five-mile drive, with its low speed limit, tourist traffic, and partial-gravel and snow-covered roads, took nearly an hour. They listened to Jimmy's country CDs, and Win stared out the side window at the cloudless azure sky and the constantly changing terrain. The brown plateaus and sagebrush vegetation around Mammoth had given way to steep, wooded mountains and narrow upland valleys. They stopped to let small herds of buffalo cross the road, and the rangers pointed out a black bear with three cubs near a tree line. The wildlife and beautiful scenery helped as Win tried to pull his attention away from the shooting, but his mind and emotions kept falling behind. *Anger? Confusion? Fear? Yeah, there's fear. Block it out . . . suck it up . . . deal with it later. . . . Face the issue in front of you.* He leaned his chin on his fist and tried to sharpen his sight out the window. His inward view was much more murky.

He'd been watching the map and the GPS to determine their location as they drove. They were half an hour in and they'd long since lost cell service. Win concluded they were officially in the middle of nowhere. Jimmy finally pulled off a sloppy gravel road by a set of stout log buildings and corrals that looked like an Old West postcard from the early 1900s.

The structures sat at the base of a tall, rounded mountain predominantly covered with bare trees, victims of the massive 1988 Yellowstone forest fire. Win had read that the historic inferno had wiped out over one-third of the park's woodlands. Thousands of towering blackened trees covered portions of the big mountain and stood as stark reminders that regeneration is often a slow, painful process. *Is it that way with people too?* Some scars heal in time, but for other wounds, the gray, gnarled stumps remain. He breathed a deep sigh. *Ease up, Win. You're letting it get to you.*

Win's escorts were gathering their gear and calling to colleagues who'd been waiting for their arrival. He could feel eyes on him as members of the group began sizing up the outsider. He grabbed his coat and backpack from the rear of the rangers' Tahoe and pulled his hat on. He had a feeling they weren't expecting much from him. Ranger Jimmy walked ahead to the ancient wooden corrals where a small group of men in gray and green had gathered to look over a map. They paused briefly for quick introductions and handshakes with Win. Friendly, but not overly so.

Jimmy was still in the lead. "Want you to meet our incident commander for this search. He's over there working his horse." On the opposite side of the large corral, Ranger Hechtner was going through reining exercises on a big bay horse, looking very much like he'd been born on one. *Ah, gee, not this guy again.*

Hechtner brought the tall gelding to a sliding stop in front of them, let him settle, then reined the horse toward them as they approached the graying rails of the enclosure. He pulled the bill of his Park Service ball cap up slightly and dropped condescending eyes directly onto Win.

"I warned you about the shot avenues from the hills behind your house," the ranger chastised him by way of greeting.

"Yeah, yeah, you got that right." Win wasn't in the mood to take any crap from this guy.

"One team went out hours ago. We didn't want to give them a late start. If you can't ride a horse, you can stay here at the station. If you stay here, I'll leave two men with you while the rest of us do the search. We'll be back no later than noon tomorrow." The haughty expression and the cold tone of voice—the other men had to notice. Win had the sense the man was counting on him not being able to ride. Hechtner wanted nothing to slow them down and as little as possible to do with Win.

"No problem. Where's my mount?" Win didn't even meet Hechtner's gaze. Jimmy raised his eyebrows, dropped the planned introduction, and moved ahead of Win through the gate.

"You think Domino?" Jimmy looked up at Trey for direction.

"Whatever. If he can handle him. Just get him set up. I'll be on the satellite phone for a few minutes. We leave at 1500 hours—in ten minutes—going up High Point Trail east of the warming cabin." He slid off the big bay and looped the reins around the top rail. He still hadn't met Win's eyes, and he brushed past him as he left the corral. Win thought they'd worked out a little understanding back in his office on Saturday. *Apparently not.*

"Huh. Real nice guy," Win said sarcastically as he turned to watch Hechtner's retreating back.

"Trey's actually a great guy." The slight Hispanic ranger shrugged and scanned the corral. "But he's got a burr under his saddle over something today, that's for sure. . . . Well, let's get you a horse!"

They walked across the muddy corral to a covered shed and approached a small, wiry man wearing a battered gray cowboy hat with his ranger uniform. He was at least twenty years older than the other rangers in the group, and his complexion was dark from long days in the sun.

"Hey, Sam, this is Agent Tyler of the FBI. He's riding with us today. What you got for him? Domino, maybe? He's really sure-footed."

The older man turned, wiped his weathered hands on his green pants and shook hands with Win. "Ranger Sam Morris, sir, good to meet you. Call me Sam." He cocked his head and looked past Win to the unsaddled horses. "Hmmm, don't know about Domino—might be having to rescue a couple of hikers and an FBI agent if he takes that silly horse." The best choices seemed to be Domino, a six-year-old spotted Appaloosa with perky ears and personality, or Chief, a tall, older blue-roan who looked as if he'd seen better days.

"Let's see about Domino—sure-footed sounds good," Win volunteered. The older man shook his head and sized Win up for a saddle. In just a few minutes the spotted horse stood ready, a little too ready, as he pranced from foot to foot, daring Win to climb aboard. Everyone had loaded their backpacks on the two packhorses, and the other guys were mounting up. Win checked the cinch on the saddle one last time, took a deep breath, and showed them how an Arkansas farm boy could ride. Domino decided to immediately test Win's mettle and reared several times. Win's right hand stayed firmly pressing down on his cream-colored mane. He whirled the horse in a complete circle to the left and then to the right before cantering him in tight figure eights to calm him down. One of the rangers was having his own issue with his cold-backed mount, but several of the other men stood or sat in silence and nodded their approval of Win's skill.

His riding ability certainly came in handy with the skittish little Appaloosa as the afternoon wore on. Domino took every opportunity to jump sideways or spook with any hint of unexpected motion on the trail. And there was plenty of unexpected motion, as Hechtner, Jimmy, Sam, Win, and two other rangers rode single file for miles through forests and across fire-scarred ridges above swollen creeks. Several small herds of elk and mule deer bounded away from the group as they traveled upward on the well-marked trail. Large pockets of snow were still evident in many areas, but the exposed rolling ridges and meadows were soft shades of green. It was beautiful country to see from the back of a horse. If their mission hadn't carried such an undercurrent of life-and-death urgency, Win would have thoroughly enjoyed the after-noon ride.

The older man, Sam, rode point and was seriously into tracking. About three miles into the ride, he found evidence that two people, one of whom could have been a child, had merged onto their trail from a game trail coming from the southwest. The rangers knew the miss-ing hikers had left their vehicle at Roosevelt and hitched a ride with at least one other hiking party to an area about ten miles to the south-west. It was assumed that they'd continued their hike in that area, but since the helicopter had turned up nothing, the riders had decided to concentrate their search along the benches of the mountain and its surrounding ridges and canyons.

They eventually stopped to rest the horses after a steep climb up the side of a rocky ridge. Win dropped off his sweating horse and stretched. When he was home, he often rode through the cattle just to relax. He'd even done that a few times when he was in Arkansas in early April, but his days of being in the saddle on a regular basis ended after high school. Football consumed too much of his time during college, then there was law school. . . . *Oh well.* He leaned into little Domino and scratched under his chin. The smells of the lathered horse and the saddle leather took him back to his childhood—it was a comforting feeling with the sun on his back. The men had all shed their coats and jackets in the warmth of the afternoon, and the group probably looked more like an armed posse than a rescue mission. Every man wore a handgun and all the rangers had assault rifles or shotguns in saddle scabbards. Not your typical Yellowstone rescue party, but then they were charged with protecting Win as well as finding the lost hikers.

While they rested the horses, Jimmy walked over and offered Win a PowerBar. Win wasn't hungry, but he appreciated the gesture and ate it. The small ranger then shimmied up a large boulder and began scanning the lower side of the ridge with binoculars. "Hey, hey, come up here and look," he called down to Win.

After securing Domino to a bush, Win grabbed his field glasses, climbed the rock, and looked toward the area where the ranger was pointing. At first he saw nothing, but then a huge dark-brown bear came into focus. "Whoa, yikes! Look at the size of that thing!"

Jimmy whistled for the others to look. The bear was moving in the new grass, between patches of snow, about five hundred feet below them. It had the large shoulder hump of a grizzly. Its massive head moved from side to side as it walked, smelling the area like a dog. Win guessed the bear was nearly twice as large as the mama bear he'd seen with the researchers last week. That would put it near eight hundred pounds and Lord only knows how tall. Win was thinking that having all of this heavy firepower with them was maybe not a bad thing—he'd had no idea the bears got that big.

"That boar is one of the largest grizzlies in this area of the park," Jimmy said. "We've seen him up here several times. This area will be closed to hikers until mid-June because of high bear activity. Early spring they're very active and hungry. Lots of sows with cubs up here too. . . . Not a great time to run into them. Sure hope that guy and his kid didn't wander off up here unprepared."

They watched the bear until it disappeared into the trees on the far side of the ridge. Sam pointed out a herd of pronghorn antelope frozen in fear as they stared toward the bear's last location. A group of elk trotted toward the woods in the other direction.

The tracker was conferring with Hechtner as they all mounted up again. It was nearly six o'clock and the sun was dropping lower in the sky. Win had been wondering why they hadn't run into other hikers, but Jimmy's explanation of the area being closed because of bears made sense. Sam was still following someone's tracks, and he seemed more confident that it was an adult and a child. It had to be the missing hikers; no one else was supposed to be up here. He asked Jimmy about that as they rode along the ridge.

The slender man stood up in his stirrups and turned in the saddle to face Win as he explained. "Nope, just because the area is closed doesn't mean there aren't people up here. We're constantly having folks get lost on the trails or just disregard the rules. It's a stiff fine if you get stopped in this closed area, but that doesn't seem to keep people from violating the rules. Two of the guys who've been killed by bears in the last few years were hiking alone; that's a terrible idea. Neither one had bear spray, and both were in high bear-activity areas. Some people just think they're bulletproof. Then again, sometimes it's just bad luck—can't predict wild animals." He clicked his tongue to move his horse along before he continued. "So the tracks we're following might be the man and boy we're looking for and they might not be, but at least they're fairly fresh, so we may know pretty soon. On a clear day like today, it won't be dark until nearly eight."

After another mile, the trail dropped down into a thick aspen grove and an area of evergreen regrowth from the fire. The dense stand of fifteen-foot-tall lodgepole pine trees crowded the trail, and the horses became skittish. The guy behind Hechtner started singing some old cowboy song and Jimmy got in on the second verse. Win asked Jimmy why they were singing, and he told him it was to avoid a surprise encounter with a bear in the thick trees and to calm the horses. Hechtner called out a George Strait song, and they all started in on "Amarillo by Morning." Win knew the words to that one. It seemed a little silly, but Win would have gladly harmonized on show tunes if that's what it took to avoid a sudden encounter with that monster bear.

CHAPTER SEVENTEEN

They were approaching an area above the tree line where the trail was very rocky and the ridge suddenly dropped off sharply, forming the side of a narrow canyon. The ride thus far had been relatively easy, but this area was dangerous, with three-hundred- to five-hundred-foot vertical drops on their right side and a steep bluff rising another couple hundred feet above the trail to the left. The rock-strewn trail was less than five feet wide. Bare sagebrush and a few scraggly dwarf trees were the only living things between the riders and the abyss. Win could hear a rushing stream somewhere far below them. A chill set in as they passed out of the sunlight into the shaded areas alongside the cliffs. Win's fear of heights kicked in, causing him to subconsciously lean to the left in his saddle, away from the edge.

Sam looked back down their line and told him to straighten up or he'd throw his horse off-balance. "Not to worry," he yelled, "Domino's as sure-footed as a goat!"

The other men seemed perfectly at ease, and Win tried to suck it up and not look down. He silently recited the Twenty-Third Psalm over and over to calm himself, hoping he didn't look as scared as he felt.

All afternoon, the group had been stopping and using their binoculars to scan the surrounding area for the missing hikers, but now the footing was so treacherous along the cliffs that they continued to slowly move along the trail without stopping. Win was reciting the Scripture for about the twentieth time when he thought he heard a faint cry.

The wind had been picking up as the sun sank lower, so he initially discounted the sound. *Just the wind in the trees below.* He didn't hear it again, but it nagged at him, and when they reached a wider spot, he called out to Trey that he might have heard something. Trey looked annoyed, but he pulled the big bay to the edge of the trail and let Jimmy and another guy ease on by. Trey hollered back to the man behind Win to ask if he'd heard anything. Win saw the tall ranger shake his head *no.* Sam offered to walk back with Win to the spot where he thought he heard the sound. Win stuck his sunglasses on his hat and gingerly dismounted into the loose gray shale on the uphill side of the trail. He ground-tied Domino by dropping the reins, and he and Sam walked back down the treacherous path.

"What'd it sound like?" the short man asked as they both shielded their eyes from the dust blowing up the trail.

"Sorta like . . . like the tail end of a call, a person. Uh, maybe more instinct than actually hearing it," Win said.

He thought the man would think he was a fool, but instead Sam nodded. "Yeah, a spirit call. . . . Sometimes in these canyons you have to be in exactly the right place to hear sounds."

Sam moved more quickly down toward a slight bend in the cliff's wall. A small piece of blue cloth was stuck on an old, twisted tree limb about ten feet below the trail's edge. It had been shielded from view when they first rode past it, but they could see it clearly now. *Maybe part of a shirt?* Win couldn't see beyond an overhang on the cliff, but he knew they were hundreds of feet above the trees and stream. Sam cupped his hands to his mouth and called down. *Nothing. Just the sounds of the stream and the wind in the trees.* Win sighed.

Sam moved a few feet farther along the trail and called down again. Immediately they heard a weak answer that the wind tried to blow away. Another faint cry came from far below. Someone was down there.

Sam raised his hand to signal Hechtner; he in turn signaled the three rangers who were farther up the trail with the packhorses. Sam walked down the trail to a spot where there was more stable footing and the trail was wide enough for two men to maneuver side by side.

Win leaned into the uphill bluff, marveling that the horses had navigated the tricky footing.

One of the rangers was moving all the horses up the trail to a more level area away from the cliffs, several hundred yards away. Jimmy appeared with nylon ropes and other rappelling equipment. A second ranger came toward them carrying more equipment bags and a collapsible metal litter. Win could see nothing to leverage or tie the ropes to on the narrow trail, but this evidently wasn't the rangers' first rodeo—they were moving fast and with purpose.

Trey was calmly orchestrating the action. "Jimmy, we've got no visual on him. Let's get you down to scout it out—we'll lower the litter down separately. If both of them are down there, Sam can swing down for the second patient with the other litter."

Jimmy was geared up in climbing harness, helmet, and medical bag, while the tall ranger finished tying off the climbing rope's anchors on two substantial rocks. The small ranger had finished his safety check, made sure he was on belay, and was over the edge of the cliff before Win knew what was happening. Once he began to rappel, progress came slowly as Jimmy tried to keep from dislodging any rocks from the cliff face. Win could hear him calling up instructions to his helper: "Down slow! Stop! Down slow!" Then, faintly, "Belay off!" He'd reached a stopping point. It occurred to Win that he was making absolutely no contribution to their efforts, so he at least sent up a few extra prayers for everyone's safety.

While Jimmy was carefully rappelling down the cliff with the assistance of the tall guy, Trey was giving instructions to Sam and the other ranger. "Let's assume we have at least one to come up. For one anchor point, rig the webbing over that boulder on the second ledge up. . . . Let's put two backup anchors on bolts in the granite directly behind us in the cliff wall." He moved along the upper wall beside the trail, looking for any possible anchor points. "Okay, got a deep crack in the rocks here—use a couple of chocks to hold that cordelette." Trey pointed out the narrow crevice where he wanted the metal anchoring device inserted. Sam began drilling and screwing steel bolts into the solid rock with a battery-powered hammer drill and wrenches.

"Okay, I want our focal point for the main hauling line right here."
Trey was still giving commands. "Agent Tyler? Rig the belay rope for
Sam with a wrap-three-pull-two and a Munter hitch on that little juni-
per, if it has enough load-bearing strength."

Uh-oh. Win just stood with his back glued to the wall of granite,
watching the ranger point toward a small twisted tree that was seemingly growing out of solid rock.

"What?" Trey didn't look understanding. "They didn't teach you to
rappel?"

"Well, no, not unless an agent is on a SWAT team or—"

The ranger cut him off; he had no time for explanations. "Then get
with Sam when he finishes setting the bolt anchors; he'll rig the belay
ropes for you. You're big enough to do some good."

Okay, then . . .

Trey suddenly turned and caught Win's eyes for a moment. Win
was hating it that the guy knew he was afraid. The ranger's glare softened just a touch and he moved closer and lowered his voice. "You in?"

Win pulled his hat down tighter and nodded. He met Trey's serious gray eyes. "All in."

"Alright, listen . . . it's not such a bad thing to be a little nervous up
here. Tight quarters. Near-vertical drop. High-angle rescue. Keep your
knees bent, go down on your knees or your butt if you get light-headed."
He saw Win glance at the drop-off. "Don't ever step backward without
knowing where you are on the top. The height doesn't matter—thirty
feet can kill you just as easily as three hundred. . . . Stay away from the
edge. Got to remember that gravity is always on."

Win nodded. It wasn't exactly a kumbaya moment with Trey, but it
was close enough to a pep talk that it moved Win's focus off the dizzy-
ing heights to the mission at hand. Sam was tying a safety rope around
him an instant later, and he was suddenly part of the team.

Jimmy radioed that he'd swung onto a ledge about seventy feet
below the trail. An adult male appeared to have severe back and leg
injuries, and a young boy had a broken leg and a compound fracture
of his left arm. Both had numerous lacerations, but neither had serious
external bleeding. They were conscious but exhibiting signs of shock.

The ledge they'd landed on was less than eight feet wide with at least a three-hundred-foot drop to the trees below. It was clear even to Win that a helicopter rescue in that location, with the wind picking up, would be extremely dangerous if not impossible.

As soon as he knew the hikers' conditions, Hechtner was on the satellite phone, calling for the rescue helicopter from Mammoth. He announced to the group still working on the rigging: "Helo's on a flight to the medical center in Idaho Falls with a visitor who had a heart attack. Won't be seeing it for at least two hours." He wiped the sweat from his face with a gray sleeve. "That would put it here around 1945 to 2015 hours—near twilight. Got to get them off that ledge to a level spot so the ship can operate in low-light conditions."

The four rangers on the trail completed their anchor systems for the main haul line, which would bring up the loaded litters, and for Sam, who would ascend back up the cliff alongside the first litter in order to keep it stable and the patient calm. Jimmy, the most experienced paramedic of the group, immobilized the little boy with a spine board and splints while the man was lifted. As senior medic, he was the boss for the arduous task of raising the loaded litters. Even with the intricate systems of ropes and pulleys, it was strenuous work getting the two-hundred-fifty-pound man up the stone face of the cliff.

When they finally got the large man above the edge of the cliff, Trey moved quickly to check his vital signs, all the time talking to him about how they were getting his son up next, how they would soon be on their way home. Constant words of encouragement. Despite the ranger's reserve and coolness toward him, Win was seeing another side of Trey Hechtner.

Sam took over the care of the hiker long enough for Trey to make another call on the status of the helicopter. Still well over an hour out. Raising the little boy took less than five minutes once Jimmy packaged him in the second litter. Within thirty minutes, both of the injured hikers lay safely in their aluminum litters on the trail.

When Jimmy and Trey were satisfied that their patients were as comfortable as possible, the group began the hard work of transporting the loaded litters up the trail to a level area on the ridge where the helicopter could land. Given the narrow, rock-strewn path, it was very slow going even with five of them carrying the litter holding the injured man. Win might not know their rescue lingo, but he was darn sure strong enough to make a big difference in hauling up the injured and transporting the loaded litters. He began to feel he was actually doing his share of the work.

It was nearly dark when they finally had both litters on top of the ridge and had set up camp lights for the helo—as the rangers kept calling the helicopter—to fix on. Trey was on the satellite phone with the copilot as he guided him in. In less than five minutes, they'd loaded the injured and the chopper lifted off into the fading light.

Win stood with the other men on the high, barren ridge, watching the red blinking lights of the helicopter disappear toward the mountains to the northwest. The sun had long since dipped below the far-distant range of mountains, and its orange glow sharply silhouetted dozens of purple peaks. The hue of the early evening's high clouds transitioned from blackish blue, to lilac, to orange, and finally to a fiery red. Even as the cold wind found them, they stood transfixed by the cascade of intense colors. Win glanced at his protectors as they marveled at the sky. Gus's words came back to him: *Best damn job in the world!* Was it possible he *was* in the wrong line of work?

* * *

He sat on a sloping gray boulder right near the edge of the cliff and watched the sun's final attempt to paint the high clouds and sky. It had been a brilliant sunset in a land of magnificent sunrises and sunsets. The beauty made his heart glad, and he reckoned if he ever needed some beauty to lift his spirits, it would be today. It had taken hours just to clear his mind of the morning's anxiety. He had to put it behind him; he had work to tend to. This morning he and his fifteen-man squad had held two hours of live-fire exercises with the other two squads before they'd even left the church property for the rugged terrain of the park and national forest. And it had been a long, hard day. They'd just eaten the evening ration and finished cleaning their weapons. Now his men were stretched out around him, utterly exhausted after the intense training deep in the wild country. Most were too tired to appreciate the beauty of a southwestern Montana sunset.

He pulled his camo field cap off and ran a hand through his thick black hair as he leaned back on the still-warm granite. His training contract with the church ended after today's extensive field exercise—all thirty-six of the church's militiamen were showcasing their skills in marksmanship, tactics, and maneuvers. They'd done amazingly well, considering some of the guys were well over forty and most hadn't been in the field in years. Several months of training for some, just a few hard weeks for others—they weren't a ragtag bunch of wannabes now, no sir! Even the three men King had brought in on Friday were working out well. King's other four guys had been working with the militia for a couple of weeks now and were operating as part of the team, but none of King's seven boys were the same breed of man as the blue-collar family men who made up the original church militia. All seven were ex-cons, and from the talk, they hadn't been in for penny-ante stuff. They had a violent side that wouldn't stay contained forever. Not men you'd mess with if you had any sense.

And now . . . now it was lookin' like Ellie'd been right. She'd said King's men were evil, and evil seemed to be playing its hand. *Thank God she and the kids are safe in Oklahoma! The Feds can't go after her now, can they?*

He'd been tipping Tyler off to the dangers he saw—he'd done it to spare Ellie any blame. After the events of today, those accounts should be settled, that's for damn sure! Ellie had let herself get sucked into talking to the Federals, to Win Tyler. He couldn't blame her for that—Tyler was likable. Luke pulled his rough hands into his tactical gloves. He paused for a long moment and stared off into the near-darkness. *Tyler ain't just likable, he's educated, he's handsome . . . he's a gentleman. More than once she'd mentioned how nice he was. . . .* He sighed. *Well, hell.* It wasn't often he felt threatened by a man, much less jealous, but after today he damn sure wasn't having anything more to do with Win Tyler. He needed to collect his pay from the Prophet tonight, go home and call Ellie, and figure out where he stood in this whole deal.

Four more miles and they'd be back in the comfort of the compound's cabins. They'd do that part with night-vision equipment, moving in through the Federals' surveillance lines—one last test for today. Would the Feds know they were there? Well, yeah, and for some weird reason, that was the plan. Plus they'd been sunning themselves on this high cliff in the Gallatin National Forest, far west of the church's land, for the last half hour. The drones and aircraft the Feds were flying out of that little airport east of Livingston couldn't help but spot them. They'd have to send up smoke signals to be any more conspicuous. Why? He didn't know. Those decisions were above his rank. He just took his orders; he didn't try to interpret them.

His ears picked up the raspy voice of Brother Bronte and the soft tone of the strange man that Brother King called Red. Those two men weren't the best troopers in the group, and he knew they were probably sneaking in some drinking at night, maybe something more, but they were both tough and hard fighters. Since all of Ron King's guys had moved out of his trailers and into Gardiner or to the church compound on Sunday, he wouldn't have to fret over them anymore, thank goodness. He was glad to have them gone from his land, even though he'd be making a little less cash. Ellie had been uneasy around them—that was reason enough for them to go elsewhere. It was even better it was Brother King's idea that his boys move closer to the church. Better to integrate with the brotherhood, he'd said.

The two men were slumped behind the big rock Luke was lying on. Either they didn't know he was there or they just didn't care, but their conversation suddenly chilled him to the bone. "Gonna be a bloodbath fore this is over." The redheaded man sounded pleased.

"The hit this morning's gonna stir up a hornet's nest—force them to move too quick. Force their hand," Bronte said.

"Why not just go in and do the job without all the damn drama? Why wave a damn red flag at a bull?"

"'Cause the Prophet don't do nothing the simple way; got to attract some national attention. He and Ron got influence all over the country—word gets out on this and we'll have hundreds of patriots coming to the cause," the small man, Bronte, responded.

The redhead laughed a high-pitched, scary laugh. "Hell, you're beginning to sound just like these backcountry fools. I ain't in this to save the country or start up a new one. You ain't in it for that. This here job is looking like the big payout we've been waiting for. Likely two down now. . . . If we have to waste two dozen more before we get the prize, I'm all for it. But tell you one thing, I'm getting real damn tired of this soldier shi—"

"Hey, you boys get your night-vision gear out. Gonna spend the night on that rock? We move out in five," the corporal interrupted them as he rousted the troops.

Luke drew a deep breath and held it as he tried to understand the implications of what he'd just overheard. Red and Bronte obviously knew about the planned hit on Win Tyler, but they didn't know the outcome. They appeared to assume he was dead. So what did Red mean "likely two down now"? Was someone else targeted? Had they killed someone else? What was the "prize" they referred to?

Then it occurred to him: The unusual training schedule Brother King had the militia follow today had a secret purpose. They'd been in full view of the Fed's surveillance agents on the fringe of the church's land from dawn until nearly mid-morning. They'd been watched by who knows how many planes and drones throughout the remainder of the day. They were seen so that everyone would be accounted for; none of these men could have been the shooter. The training today was an alibi. He remembered that Brother King and the Prophet had planned a 6:00 a.m. live video interview with some East Coast TV station about the government's iron-handed abuses of power. Another alibi. Leaves the Feds with no solid ground for raiding the church over the sniper attempt on Tyler. He sat up on the rock, slung his pack over one shoulder, picked up his rifle, and stood. *Someone else is involved and somethin' else is fixin' to happen. . . . Well, hell.*

* * *

Getting to the warming cabin was not as difficult as Win had assumed it would be in the dark. The rescue site was less than two miles from the cabin, and most of the trail's terrain was along rolling, open ridgelines. The ranger in front carried a high-beam light, and the horses followed along single file in the darkness with ease.

As soon as they arrived, they rubbed down, watered, and fed the horses. Everyone was exhausted, but the mood was upbeat. Win knew from their talk that these rescue missions weren't always successful. Win had done his part and for the time being, at least, he was treated as one of the team—he was enjoying the camaraderie.

There was a bit more to the "warming cabin" than Win had expected. The complex consisted of a sprawling log house, a wood-shed, a stable, and corrals, all constructed in 1930 as a permanent post for four to six rangers in the day of horse patrols. The rustic house contained a living area with a huge stone fireplace, a small kitchen, bunkrooms, and a couple of showers with solar-heated water. Coleman lanterns provided the light. Win volunteered with Jimmy in the kitchen, setting out sandwiches for supper, while most of the rangers hung out in the living area. A poker game was the norm after dinner, but Trey vetoed it since the men would be rotating guard duty. They opted instead for several serious games of darts, where Win was just happy not to embarrass himself. These rangers were competitive. He had the feeling they would bet dollars on a game of jacks if that were the only game at hand. After the chores and a shower, Win settled in front of the fireplace with an older John Grisham paperback and tried to chill, as Jim West had put it.

He read for a while, then found his bunk, but sleep wouldn't come. After tossing and turning for half an hour, Win gave up and decided some fresh air might help. He quietly pulled on his boots and his coat and stepped out onto the porch. As soon as his eyes adjusted to the darkness, he could see Sam Morris sitting on a bench with his assault rifle across his lap. He had on full military gear, including night-vision goggles. The getup surprised Win, and the intense cold surprised him even more.

"Didn't mean to bother you. . . . The stars are amazing! Whoa, it's cold!"

"No bother," Sam answered quietly. "Yes, the stars are nearly within reach in these mountains, and yes, it's about fifteen degrees and will get colder tonight." The older ranger paused a long time, then asked, "Is it like this: You close your eyes and you hear the gunshot?"

"I hear the explosion when the bullet destroyed the door. I hear it over and over when I close my eyes. How can I sleep?"

"I did two tours in Iraq with the military police. What you feel, what you hear, is common. It should get better as time goes by, but it will likely come and go. May be with you awhile. . . . It's a normal thing of war."

"I suppose that's what this is then, a war?"

"Someone is at war with you, Agent Tyler," Sam replied.

Win had to change the subject. "Uh, are you Indian, sorry, I mean Native—"

Sam laughed softly. "Indian is fine to call me. Yeah, I'm Osage, grew up in Oklahoma. I'm a permanent law enforcement ranger here and do a few of the Native American programs during the summer. Most rangers have double or triple duties."

"Seems like a rewarding job," Win said.

"Yeah, and it's a good group of people. You fit in real well with the guys today."

"Maybe . . . but I still feel like everyone's keepin' a little distance from me."

"Well, the FBI hasn't got the best reputation here. Oh, Agent Johnson's alright—just never makes any effort to reach out to us. But the agent who was here before you caused a world of heartache."

"What happened?"

"He was a mean-spirited young man. Trying to make a big case, trying to climb over people to get out of here, trying to move up in the FBI. That's what I think was going on. . . . There were trumped-up charges, intimidation, threats. It was real nasty business."

"That's why the rangers hold me at arm's length? Is that why Trey doesn't like me?"

"Trey lost his best friend in that mess. Folks didn't die or nothing, but it felt nearly as bad. Tremendous amount of distrust and bad blood still lingers. You won't be able to build that trust back overnight."

"You don't have the same feelings about it?"

"Ah, well, I'm a lot older than most of these boys—lived a little more life, I suppose. I've watched you for who you are, not for who you work for. Gus has a high regard for you. He's a person whose judgment I value."

Win stared up into the Milky Way's endless sea of stars. "I appreciate you telling me that."

"Try to sleep; it's not much past 10:30. One of the great benefits of this type duty is usually a good night's sleep. We'll be riding down the mountain to the station right after dawn, so go crawl back in your sleeping bag, Agent Tyler." Sam stood up, flipped down the night-vision goggles, and stepped off the porch to resume his patrol.

Hearing that the reserve the rangers exhibited toward him wasn't a personal thing somehow made it easier for Win. At some point, even amid the echoes of the gunshot in his mind, Win did drift off to a good night's sleep.

CHAPTER EIGHTEEN

Everyone was still in good spirits when they arrived at the back-country ranger station after their very early morning horseback ride from the warming cabin. Win was saying goodbye to his frisky little horse when they received the news that both of the rescued hikers were expected to survive the ordeal. The man was still in critical condition at Eastern Idaho Regional Medical Center in Idaho Falls, but the boy had been upgraded to good condition this morning. That news cheered the rangers even more.

Win briefly checked in with Jim West on the satellite phone—no progress on the hunt for the sniper, but the Bureau's revered Hostage Rescue Team had mobilized and would arrive late today. The HRT advance people would be in Mammoth by noon to plan a preemptive strike on the church compound. Everyone in the office was hyped up over that significant development. Win wasn't due back until one o'clock, and he was hoping to see more of the park. He wasn't, however, expecting Trey Hechtner to be the one who proposed the idea.

"I've got a place you might like to see on the way back toward Mammoth. I'll send the other boys on back and you can ride there with me," Trey offered.

"Okay, sure." It seemed a little unusual to be breaking up the protection detail, but Win thought this might be a good chance to improve his standing with the guy. Trey had been on and off the satellite phone all morning; maybe he'd gotten a report that changed his attitude for the better. Whatever it was, Win was glad the ranger had dropped the cold-shoulder routine with him.

They followed two SUVs of rangers on the road back to Mammoth, but Trey slowed several times, pointing out mountain ranges or buffalo bulls or other things of interest, and they soon fell far behind the others. They finally turned onto a snow-covered road running west from the highway. Trey stopped at a locked gate with a sign reading *Authorized Vehicles Only* and handed Win the gate key. They drove down the slushy, rough road into a spectacular upland valley filled with large evergreen trees, massive yellow sandstone boulders, and wispy waterfalls. Snowbanks still hugged the sides of shaded canyons. Trey explained that earthquake activity sixty years ago had made the surrounding cliffs unstable—the secluded paradise was closed to visitors decades ago, and funds were never available to reopen it.

He parked the Tahoe under a towering Engelmann spruce and they both pulled on heavier coats and clipped water bottles to their belts. Trey handed Win a ball cap and volunteered to carry the bear spray. Win could tell the area held some sentimental attraction for the ranger; he found himself thinking it was an awful shame this beautiful place wasn't developed for the public. They hiked through the old-growth woods on a moderately sloping trail for about a mile, then branched onto a faint path leading up a near-vertical hillside.

"This high ridge has always been one of my favorite spots. You can see forever. It's just off the beaten path. Nearly to the top. . . . Ice on the rocks here. . . ." Trey was moving up the steep side of the ridge like a mountain goat, talking all the time.

The guy is chatty all of a sudden, Win was thinking, as he clawed his way over a downed tree and tried to keep up. As they climbed higher, the deep forest gave way to scattered clusters of twisted trees, large boulders, and small, rocky bluffs.

"Last little climb. . . . It's slippery here. I'll give you a hand up—grab hold." The ranger reached down for him.

Win grabbed the extended hand and began pulling himself over the slick rocks jutting across the game trail. Hechtner pulled Win up over the last icy rock with a strong left hand and deftly lifted Win's

Glock from its holster with his right hand. The man quickly backed two steps away.

Win stood on the edge of the small bluff, winded and stunned. "What . . . what do you think . . . what do you think you're doing!" he gasped.

Trey kept the pistol pointed right between Win's feet—not directly at him, but damn close enough. His gray eyes were impossible to read. Both men stood there for a minute and caught their breath from the climb.

"Move on up the trail ahead of me." Trey motioned with the gun.

They were on top of a narrow, high ridge that seemed to overlook the entire world. At any other time, Win would have been awestruck by the scale of the view, but with the man who'd been entrusted to protect him now holding his own .40 caliber weapon on him, the view was the furthest thing from his mind. He was desperately trying to figure this one out.

Win stopped in a small clearing, just back from the edge of a cliff that fell off to who knows where. Hechtner motioned for Win to sit down on a rock and then did the same, about twenty feet away. The pistol hadn't moved, but Win could see the man's finger was on the trigger guard, not the trigger. That gave him a little relief but did nothing to clear the confusion.

"Now we wait a few minutes. . . . Might as well enjoy the view." Trey's voice gave no clue to his intent.

"Trey, I don't know what you've got in mind, but is it worth losing your job? Your career?"

"Just sit tight. Put your hands on your knees where I can see them," Trey replied. None of the hardness in those eyes had softened.

Less than a minute passed, and Win heard a soft whistle down the ridge. Hechtner's eyes darted to the right as he answered back with an identical whistle. Win took a deep breath and tried to steady himself for whoever was coming. He focused inward for a second; his heart was pounding, his mouth was dry, and his palms were sweaty. He forced himself to remain calm. His eyes swept the expanse of the view for a moment. Snowcapped mountains climbed into the crystal-blue sky far to the east; a long, narrow turquoise lake shimmered and sparkled hundreds of feet below; and rolling forests in shades of green marched up the slopes of the lower mountains across the lake. The colors were changing every second as the sun rose higher in the sky. *If I have to die today—*

He shook his head to clear that thought from his mind.

Luke Bordeaux appeared thirty feet from Trey as if by magic. Win had no idea who was coming up that slope, but Luke Bordeaux hadn't crossed his mind.

"He give you any trouble?" Luke casually asked Hechtner.

"Nope, but I thought he might be a bit jumpy considering everything, so I figured I'd hold onto his gun."

"Not a bad idea," Luke replied as he walked to the edge of the clearing and stood in the shadow of a boulder.

"You wanna tell me what's going on here?" Win's voice was harsh as he stood. He was quickly becoming more angry than puzzled or afraid.

Trey nodded to Luke and began to lower the pistol.

Luke raised his chin toward Win. "Got ourselves a problem, and Trey called this here powwow to see if we could sort it out. You gonna listen or not?"

Trey spoke up. "I wasn't sure we could trust you. But you nearly getting yourself killed yesterday morning did sorta rule you out as one of the bad guys."

"Luke, you sent me the warning yesterday." Win said it more as a statement than as a question. He saw surprise register on the ranger's face. Hechtner hadn't known about the warning.

"Yeah, I did."

"Were you the shooter?" Win had to ask the question.

"No, no . . ." Then Luke smiled broadly. "Heck, Win, if I'd been the shooter, you wouldn't be joining our little get-together here today."

Win was seeing none of the humor in that, but the man's confidence in his ability with a gun was sobering. He lowered his voice. "Alright, I'm listening."

Luke crossed his arms and locked eyes with Win. "Well, it's obvious somethin' big is fixin' to happen. I took a different way of lookin' at it since they took the shot at you. Before it was just folks exercising their rights in a free country to be who they wanted to be, but now . . . now they've moved beyond that. They've taken to killin'.

"And the FBI is running the show—or trying to. Somebody supposed to be shadowing me and here I am! Four miles south of Mammoth, and seven miles from where I lost 'em at dawn. How do you reckon I knew the surveillance rotation and dropped 'em this morning? How 'bout the shooter yesterday, Win? Knew your routine and the air coverage so well that, from what I hear, he came within inches of gettin' you."

"You accusing us of incompetence, or something else . . . someone on the inside?"

"Maybe a little of both." Luke looked off toward the far mountains. "That's why we're here this fine morning lookin' at the scenery." His dark eyes moved back to Win. "I think there's either someone on the inside or one helluva intel leak." He nodded toward the ranger. "Trey don't wanna see the park's image get damaged. I couldn't care less about that, but I don't wanna see good people get drug into a shootin' war with the Feds over a bunch of outlaws."

As he listened to Luke's explanation, Win was quickly trying to calculate what the two men might know. Trey wouldn't know about the deployment of the FBI's Hostage Rescue Team. He wouldn't know about the proposed takedown of the ex-cons at the church compound. He might know about the surveillance aircraft and drones, but Win wasn't sure. Trey was on the Joint Terrorism Task Force, but Ms. Stuart had refused to activate any non-Bureau JTTF officers. Win doubted if any case information had been shared with anyone below Gus's level at the Park Service. As for Luke, he wouldn't know about any of those plans or assets.

Luke was waiting for Win's response. The cold wind whipped through their little clearing as the sun found them and began its day's work of warming the high cliffs. Win stood facing the men. He didn't say anything.

Luke leaned back into the shadow of the rocks and spoke again. "Reckon if I's you, I might be thinkin' them boys is gonna trick me into telling the FBI's plan, then push me over that 1,500-foot cliff and nobody would be the wiser fer it. Is that it, Win Tyler?"

"Suppose that crossed my mind," Win answered.

"Well now, you ain't the only one of us havin' a hard time figuring out who to trust, and I sure as hell ain't excited 'bout being here, but Trey asked me to come . . . so I come." He squared his shoulders and looked hard at Win. "Occurs to me if a disaster is gonna be averted, we need to commit to the action, as they'd say in the Army."

Win hesitated. He had to be really careful here. Luke was only stating the obvious; that was the oldest trick in the book. What if these men were after information? What if they *were* the bad guys? They had his gun, that was one indicator. Without a word, Win walked to where Hechtner sat and held his hand out for the weapon. Trey stood and handed it back, grip first. Win met his eyes and saw a fleeting glimpse of fear dart through them. Trey knew if Win reported this, he wouldn't just lose his job. He could very well go to prison.

Win took his time checking the chamber and the magazine on the weapon. He was stalling and trying to gather his thoughts. His mind flew back to the conversation with his brother a few nights ago: *"I'm having trouble knowing who I can trust. Trouble trusting my judgment of people."* Test the spirits. That's what he'd told Ellie. *Test the spirits, Win.*

His eyes went back to Hechtner; he was standing close to the man. "So what do you have to gain in this, Trey? Hell of a lot to lose, I'd say, going around your bosses to get me off up here and lifting my gun. . . . What's in this for you?"

Trey drew in a long breath. "I asked Luke to meet 'cause things are getting outa hand, and the Park Service is totally out of the loop. This is my home—I'm raising my family here. Mammoth is starting to feel like an armed camp! We've got a missing informant, money on the street for intel, and then a sniper in the park . . . and I'm told to stand around and basically do nothing! I represent the law in Yellowstone—that's what my badge says—but I get relegated to traffic control and guarding you." He glanced toward Bordeaux. "Luke was the one who wanted you here. I called to warn him away from that church . . . and to see if he could help." Trey's eyes moved back to Win's face. "We're supposed to be on the same side here!"

But Win's anger hadn't passed, and as he holstered the Glock, he stepped even closer and glared into the man's eyes. "This isn't a difficult concept! There's the good guys and the bad guys! You say we're on the same side? Then what kinda dumbass move was that? Taking my gun! Lording it over me? And why? 'Cause you got some problem with the FBI over something I had nothing to do with." He was fuming. *Be smart . . . be cool. Don't let rage control you!* But he didn't want to be cool. He wanted to lash out, to prove he couldn't be defeated so easily. *Weakness.* He'd shown weakness.

Trey never backed up an inch. His voice was intense and threatening. "Back away from me, Tyler! You think you're in charge—why? 'Cause you work for some big-shot agency! This is my turf. This park is what I'm sworn to protect! And you cut us out, just 'cause of three initials after your name: F-B-I!"

Oddly enough, Luke stepped in as the voice of reason. "You young bucks wanna settle this with a duel, I'll call out the damn paces, but it occurs to me that we got more pressin' matters at hand than you two trying to prove who's the top rooster. Both of you dial it back and settle down! I didn't make a seven-mile hike to watch you bicker like schoolgirls."

Hechtner cut his eyes toward Luke, then raised his chin slightly and moved back half a step. Win acknowledged that with a small nod and blew out a breath. "We're not done yet, Trey . . . but he's right. This isn't the time or the place."

Luke called their little meeting to order. "Over here under the trees, just in case the drone pilot is paying attention. Even a blind hog finds an acorn once in a while."

Well, so much for subject awareness of that surveillance asset, Win thought as he sat down on a rock outcropping near Luke.

"The heavies are out of the compound—all of them by now. I was one of the last to go before dawn this morning," Luke began. "Brother

King's men took advantage of the scrambling your watchers did after the shooting to get out of Dodge yesterday and last night." He eased down on a log near the edge of the cliff. "The Prophet came back from his trip flush with cash and paid all the militia guys fer the time they've put in. He gave me the money he owed me last night."

"Where'd they go? Who left the church compound?" Trey asked.

"All seven of Ron King's guys are out. They also picked eight of my church militia guys to go. All eight of those men have been working with me for months and are hard-core followers. They were moving into prearranged places in Gardiner and the park. Some of the hide-outs I know, some I don't. Gonna lay low until you raid the church or their play goes down."

Win was watching Trey's face off and on while Luke spoke. He could tell the ranger was shocked by what he was hearing.

"So what's the play?" Win asked Luke.

"Don't know, 'cept your name's still on the list. After I got my pay last night, I hada feeling things was gonna get worse, so I managed to meet up with a couple of King's boys, the Thayer brothers, at a house in Gardiner. Took two bottles of Jack Daniel's over to celebrate our big training exercise. Those boys got real talkative."

Luke paused and looked down. His voice became more subdued. "Hit man is Richter, a pro. He was the shooter yesterday. Seems his connection with some of King's bunch may be through prison, white supremacy group, that's what it sounded like—but the boys I was with hadn't seen the guy lately, just heard he was in the area. They didn't know who put out the contract. They'd heard about the job . . . ahhh . . . they'd heard the job wasn't finished." He looked into Win's eyes. "Both of those men I was a drinkin' with . . . mean as snakes. Both of them scared to death of Richter."

Good Lord!

The mood was beyond sober. "Hear anything 'bout how he might come after me?"

"Naw, no idea. The warning I sent you was a fluke. Just heard talk right fore the militia's muster." Luke studied his boot. "I don't know the shooter's connection with the rest of the bunch, but I'd bet the Prophet ain't in on it."

Win nodded a couple of times and changed the topic. "Why would the Prophet think anyone would attack his compound?"

"'Cause your HRT has a raid planned fer dawn day after tomorrow, that's why."

Win had to fight to keep a straight face. *No way Luke has that information without someone on the inside.*

Luke went on to detail what he'd heard on the deployment of the FBI's Hostage Rescue Team and his knowledge of the various surveillance methods the Bureau was using. He knew about their continued JTTF and SWAT presence, right down to the number of agents and where everyone was staying. It was almost as if the guy was working in their offices. After a couple of minutes, he wrapped it up.

"Seems to me the church has been gettin' real good intel for 'bout ten days now. That oughta narrow it down some fer ya."

Trey had hardly spoken since they'd sat down, so Win asked him about his earlier comment that there was "money on the street for intel."

"I got word from another ranger several days ago that he'd heard someone was offering $10,000 for information on the FBI. We weren't really on the case, so I reported it to Gus and he got with your counterterrorism lady. Don't know where it went from there."

Win had an idea it went nowhere from there if Emily got intel from the group she kept referring to as "the Yellowstone police." Nothing on this had crossed his desk.

Trey went on, "I chalked it up to rumors until the shooting early yesterday. That's when I put out the word among our friends in Gardiner that I wanted to talk to Luke. Luke left me a coded message on the satellite phone from a burner phone after you arrived at the station yesterday afternoon. I got back with him on the sat phone before dawn this morning."

So that's how they set up this out-of-the-way get-together.

"Say . . . theoretically, what happens if law enforcement does raid the church compound to make fugitive arrests?" Win asked.

"Prophet's countin' on a raid, I think. Gonna video the whole deal and call in the press. CNN, Fox News, all those cable and network channels. The publicity won't hurt any—further the cause, you see." Luke paused and turned reflective. "Lots of comin' and goin' over the last few days, but I'd say at least fifty folks are stayin' at the church full-time right now. My militia guys who are still there are squeaky clean. Anything you Feds could get bent outa shape over is gone. It'd be mostly women and children terrorized by a raid—a violent violation of our right of free assembly. And I'm afraid your boys might go off half-cocked and someone might get hurt. The church folks are under orders not to fight back, but you never know what will happen in the heat of the thing."

Everyone sat there for a minute. Win couldn't help but notice Luke's references to "*our* right of free assembly" and "*my* militia guys." Trey was swinging his ball cap in his hand and staring off into the mountains. Luke's proprietary references hadn't been lost on him either, and he finally asked, "Who you with on this, Luke?"

Luke's eyes dropped, and he leaned forward with his elbows on his knees and rested his chin in his clasped hands. He stared off into the same horizon and suddenly seemed very sad.

"Would like to be on your side, Trey, but I reckon we both know that may not be possible—lot of water flowed under that bridge. I did the job I was contracted to do fer the church, and unless something changes I'm off the payroll there. Need to sort it out as to where I stand with the church. Ain't got no loyalty to King's boys, you kin see that, but the church . . . the Prophet, well, that's different."

Luke was becoming more uneasy, more wary, as their discussion turned in that direction. Luke leaned toward Trey, as if imploring him to understand. "I could see King's men were up to no good and I gave Win some information on them last week. I ain't askin' for nothing in return, 'cept for Win to take care of Ellie and the kids if things don't go good fer me when it all comes down."

Luke hesitated, and Trey turned and met his eyes. Win could clearly see the pain in both men. Win suddenly knew who Sam was referring to last night. Trey's "lost best friend" during the FBI poaching operation over a year ago was Luke Bordeaux. After a long moment Luke had had enough of it, as if he were afraid he might say something that shouldn't be said. He stood quickly and looked down at Win.

"Y'all need to be gettin' on back and figure this out." He turned to walk away.

Win stood and stopped him with a light hand on his arm. "I'm much obliged, Luke, both for the heads-up yesterday and for coming here today. If they come after you, our emergency case code is 'Roll Tide'. Call us with it and I'll send the cavalry."

Luke scoffed. "Who's more likely to need that code, boy? Me or you?"

He never looked toward Hechtner, but Trey stood and called to him after he'd taken a few steps down the ridge. "Hey, Luke, you've done the right thing here!" When Luke turned, Trey brought his right palm across his heart in some sort of salute. Luke stood silently looking back at him; the sadness hadn't left his face. Then he nodded slightly and returned the salute. Win was thinking these guys had watched a few too many gladiator movies, but he made a mental note to learn the meaning of some military hand signals.

CHAPTER NINETEEN

Trey and Win made it down the ridge to the truck about as fast as could be done without breaking any bones. Trey got the SUV started, reached into the center console, and pulled out Win's Bureau cell phone. Win hadn't even missed it.

"When did you—"

"Got it out of your heavy coat when you opened the gate for us coming in. Didn't want to take a chance on a locator. Sometimes there's cell service up there."

That didn't help his feelings toward the ranger any, but Win had much bigger issues to deal with at the moment. His mind was sorting through the information they'd just learned. Luke had dropped some bombshells, not the least of which was that someone still wanted him dead.

Win stuck to the case as Trey moved the Tahoe down the messy road toward the highway. "Got any idea who might be on the inside?" he asked the ranger.

"A hacker? Or a bug?"

"The FBI office and our Justice Center rooms are swept every morning and night. All Bureau radio and phone signals are high-level encrypted. The email traffic has both classified and nonclassified servers, but I don't know about that. Never was much of a tech guy."

"Since word was on the street, so to speak, offering money for intel, it may be a very low-tech problem—a paid snitch or even someone who's incredibly careless," Trey said.

Win mulled that over as they neared the highway and cell phone service. He didn't want to use the Bureau phones, so he called his supervisor's personal cell from Trey's satellite phone.

"Hey, Boss, this is Win. We've got a problem. I met with my source this morning. . . . Uh, long story, but there's a major information leak back to the bad guys from our end."

"What kind of leak? Surveillance? Tactical?" Win could tell his supervisor was sweating this.

"All of it. I'm thinking we need to get together and let me go over this with you and Ms. Stuart—maybe Johnson too if he's made it back." He glanced at his watch. It was after 11:30. "I'll be in Mammoth soon. How about meeting at the hotel's Map Room at one? Could make it look like everyone just went down for a late lunch. Keep it real quiet in the office and on communications."

"Yeah, okay. Okay. Yeah, Johnson came in today, and Mr. Givens has taken over since he arrived last night—I'll get with him. Still no leads on the sniper, and you know we have, ah . . . friends coming in today."

"Yes, sir, they'll be interested in what's said."

Jim West rushed off the phone. Win's boss was scrambling.

They rode the rest of the way in silence for the short drive to Mammoth. One of Trey's rangers waved from the porch as they pulled up to Win's house. After stopping the vehicle, Hechtner kept both hands on the steering wheel. He didn't turn toward Win when he spoke. "If you're going to have me arrested . . . I'd like . . . I'd like to have a few minutes to visit with my wife and daughter first."

Win took his hand off the door handle and turned back to the man. "Arrested and charged with kidnapping and assaulting a federal officer?"

Trey was facing Win now. There was no pleading in those gray eyes. "I knew the risks. I thought the risks were worth taking."

"Is it looking that way now?" Win kept all emotion out of his voice.

"Meeting Luke was the right thing to do. I had no reason to trust you and I didn't think you'd meet Luke any other way. I had no idea you knew each other."

Win sat back in the seat; he never dropped his eyes. Neither of them really trusted the other. Now Trey was obviously expecting him to take advantage of the information they'd gotten from Luke and then bring the hammer down on him as well. An effective way to get rid of the competition in a big-time federal case, Win supposed. Win had a sinking feeling this type of double cross had been effectively employed by the FBI agent who previously held his position.

Test the spirits, Win. The thought floated into his consciousness. The images that quickly ran through Win's mind were of Trey's care of the injured little boy and his father, of the heartache on his face as he watched Luke Bordeaux walk off that ridge, of the concern in his eyes as he asked Win on that cliff, "You in?" Win really wanted to believe Trey Hechtner was one of the good guys.

Win spoke slowly. "For the record, Trey, I didn't appreciate sitting up on that cliff wondering if I was gonna be murdered with my own gun. And I'm not so sure there wasn't somethin' else going on there . . . you trying to get back at the Bureau for some perceived affront by humiliating me. But I'm not gonna try to figure out where your head is on that." He paused. "I'm giving you the benefit of the doubt here. You had no way of knowing I'd already been getting information from Luke or how I'd react to him. Instead of having you arrested, how 'bout you call Chief Randall and Gus and invite them to the meeting. You get cleaned up, and y'all meet me at the hotel's Map Room. Chief Randall would know about your previous relationship with Luke, right?"

Trey nodded, then added, "He knows we knew each other, but not how well we knew each other."

"Okay then. As for this morning, after Luke reached back out to you and you told me about the contact, I insisted, since Luke is a confidential source for the FBI, that we meet with him and get the intel immediately. No time to plan anything else. Luke could've been spooked off if we both hadn't been there." Win shrugged with his eyebrows. "That sound to you about how it happened?"

"Seriously?"

"Yeah. But under no circumstances ever lie to an FBI agent—it's against the law." Win was smiling now. "Oh, I've wondered—is it against the law to lie to a park ranger?" His smile broadened. "You can answer that some other time." He stepped out of the vehicle. "See you at the hotel at one." He closed the truck door on the speechless ranger and walked to his front porch.

* * *

Win managed to get shaved, showered, and dressed in record time. He grabbed a blue blazer, downed a Coke and a handful of peanut butter crackers, and remembered to feed the cat at the last minute. Win and two plainclothes rangers made it to the hotel about twenty minutes before one, and he made sure the Map Room was reserved for their meeting. He'd just walked away from the front desk when he saw Tory exit the gift shop into the lobby.

Hello! Man, she looks good!

She spotted him at the same time and smiled that beautiful smile. He felt a flash of nervousness as he searched his suddenly blank mind for anything intelligent to say to her. He glanced over at one of his security guys. The ranger was dressed as a tourist, leaning against the lobby's staircase. He immediately gave Win a sharp *What do you think you're doing?* look as Win started to walk toward Tory.

"Hey, nice to see you again so soon. Buying souvenirs?" *Okay, good opening . . .*

"Had to get something to send my niece and nephew. What do you think?" She held up two little stuffed brown bears and two tiny T-shirts.

"Good choices unless they're teenagers," he offered. "Still enjoying your break from the woods?"

He was thinking she was every bit as pretty as yesterday, with her hair pulled back in a wide barrette and a hint of makeup. She was wearing a blue cowl-necked sweater, black jeans, and boots. Her voice was upbeat and she seemed glad to see him; that helped tamp his nerves down a bit.

"It's been so nice to have hot showers and sleep in a real bed! We leave for Bozeman in a half hour, so I've been packing. Thought you were out of town?"

"Drove in a few minutes ago. Got a meeting here at one."

"Oh, I have something for you. . . . If you have time, walk over to my cabin with me and I'll give it to you before we leave."

He remembered Luke's words: *Your name's still on the list.* He looked at his watch and casually scanned the lobby. Two rangers with him. Heck, let them do a little work. "Okay. I have to get back pretty quick."

"No worries, I'm in one of the cabins right behind the hotel." She led off toward the back entrance to the lobby and he followed, passing right by the second ranger, who was pretending to browse through the hotel's brochure display. The guy gave him a serious *Are you out of your mind?* look, but Win ignored him. Win was holding the back door of the lobby open for her when he bumped into a solid man who quickly turned down the hallway. The guy didn't speak, but a hint of apprehension swept over Win. The man seemed vaguely familiar. He shrugged it off as the rangers stepped in behind and followed them across the back lawn toward the small cabins.

He stood in the open doorway of her cabin and leaned against the doorframe as she went inside. Tory had all her gear out on the bed— obviously packing. She dug through a computer bag for whatever it was she had for him. She hadn't invited him inside—that was good and proper given what they knew of each other at this point, which was not much. She found an envelope and handed it to him. Inside were three copies of a really good photo of him holding up the grizzly bear cub. It was taken the moment he'd wished the little fella a good life. He looked really happy in the picture.

"One of the technicians took the photo and gave it to me and I had three copies made. Thought you might want to keep one, maybe send one to your mother . . . maybe one to a girlfriend back home?"

He smiled down at her. "No girlfriend back home."

"Was kinda hoping you'd say that."

"The photos are really thoughtful. Thank you."

They stood in the cool breeze on the cabin's porch and he told her about the huge bear he'd seen in the park yesterday. He figured the trip with the rangers wasn't case related, so no harm in talking about it. She said she wanted to hear every detail, and he promised he'd call her in the next couple of days. He stepped off the porch with only two minutes to spare before the meeting and wished her a good trip. The plainclothes ranger lounging over near the next cabin glared at Win as if he could kill him himself, and Win tried real hard not to smile.

*　*　*

The Mammoth Hotel's Map Room was a large, airy room adjoining the lobby. It had a small bar and was used for social activities. The park's 1920s wooden map of America took up most of one wall, hence the name of the room. Win got to the room's frosted-glass doors just as Trey, Gus, and Chief Randall walked through the hotel entrance. Win had never seen Trey in his dress uniform, and he was impressed. The guy looked sharp enough to be on a recruiting poster. All three rangers wore dark-green slacks, jackets, and ties with gray dress shirts and tan flat hats. The brass on their cordovan leather gun belts and badges flashed in the lobby's overhead lights. Chief Randall led the handsome group; his stern bearing conveyed the seriousness of the meeting.

Mr. Givens greeted the rangers and gave Win a questioning look as they all moved to a large table at the rear of the room. Jim West arrived a couple of minutes later with SSA Stuart, Johnson, and a slender, fortyish-looking guy with *military* written all over him. Emily Stuart sat down across from Win and he forced himself to nod and smile at her. He was determined to take Jim West's advice and build some rapport— think of her as Emily, call her by that name, lighten up a bit. But as the doors were being closed, Emily shocked him by asking Chief Randall to have Win's security detail of park rangers relieved. She told the Chief she'd have FBI agents resume that duty if she felt it was necessary. It was a quirky ploy of one-upmanship that implied to the Chief Ranger that his men weren't up to the task. Now no one was watching Win's back—he was completely at the mercy of one of Emily's whims.

As they settled around the table, the newcomer was introduced as Supervisory Special Agent Kirk Phillips, the on-scene commander of the Hostage Rescue Team, who'd arrived from Quantico minutes ago. He'd be in charge of the two nine-member HRT teams that would roll in later today.

The mood in the impromptu meeting was tense as Win and Trey recounted the morning's meeting with Luke Bordeaux. Both men avoided the lead-up to the rendezvous with Luke, and Trey's previous relationship with Bordeaux was downplayed. To say there was a serious intelligence leak within the federal operation was a vast understatement. The proposed raid of the compound, with the plan to arrest anyone in violation of anything more serious than a parking ticket, was clearly compromised. The church members were not only aware of the timing of the raid, they were actively preparing for it. No one wanted a repeat of the Waco tragedy, yet everyone wanted the criminal elements in the cult off the street. But raiding the compound would be pointless if Bordeaux's information was correct. Was it possible that the most dangerous subjects had eluded the Bureau's ring of watchers and were now roaming the park and surrounding community? Trey concluded their presentation with a report on the continued threat on Win's life. After Trey wrapped it up, everyone sat for a long moment in disbelief that so much sensitive information could have fallen into the wrong hands.

From that point on, the two-agency meeting became contentious. As the supervisor in charge of Denver's Domestic Counterterrorism Squad, Emily said she would moderate any further discussion of the case. Why Mr. Givens allowed her to run the show was beyond Win's grasp. Emily wasn't even willing to admit to the rangers that a preemptive assault on the compound had been planned or that the Bureau's Nightstalker airplane existed, much less concede that it was conducting electronic and heat-seeking surveillance every night over the subjects' known locations. As Win pointed out, if the bad guys knew about the proposed raid and the aircraft surveillance, then the Park Service's knowledge of it certainly couldn't jeopardize their case.

Emily's arrogant possessiveness of every aspect of the case was demoralizing even to Win. It was as if it were a game with her—as if she couldn't see the real bad guys because of her obsession with controlling the case, marginalizing every other agency's efforts to assist, and maintaining her own high profile in the Bureau.

They'd been meeting for over thirty minutes and Emily was belaboring some obscure jurisdictional issue. In an effort to stay alert, Win took the opportunity to shift his focus and size up the HRT guy, Commander Phillips. Other than a couple of one-hour lectures at the Academy, he'd never even seen anyone from HRT. He was expecting some hulking super-soldier, but Phillips wasn't a large man, maybe five eleven. He looked fit, but he wasn't someone you'd pick out of a crowd as a warrior type. Phillips was showing no signs of stress during the meeting, but Win knew he couldn't be happy with what he'd heard during the last half hour.

Mr. Givens finally got Emily back on point, and she immediately became openly critical of Win's "interview" process with the informant and began to cast doubts on the reliability of the information. Both Win and Trey had to admit they weren't sure if Bordeaux was a true follower of Prophet Shepherd or if he had some other agenda.

After forty minutes, Wes called a halt and sent Jim West and Johnson back to the office to hold down the fort there. Their bosses would try to reach agreement on a unified game plan to stop the intel leak and accommodate the Park Service's legitimate demands to be consulted on any ongoing or upcoming tactical operations within the park. Win and Trey were told to wait in the lobby until the meeting wrapped up.

* * *

Fifteen minutes later, Win was still killing time. The lobby of the Mammoth Hot Springs Hotel was not large, and it was full of guests checking in and out, along with half a dozen screaming children. Win sat down to lick his wounds from Emily's critical assessment of his handling of the source interview with Luke. Trey was standing on the far side of the lobby, talking with one of his female rangers. The higher-ups and the HRT guy were still in the Map Room.

Win watched a stooped, gray-headed man limp toward the lobby's front doors. He was using a cane and trying to hold on to a newspaper in the rising wind. Since the doorman was apparently otherwise occupied, Win jumped up and held the heavy doors open for the elderly man. The man brushed past him and averted his eyes. Win immediately felt uneasy. But he couldn't pinpoint any problem, so he nodded his usual greeting and reclaimed his comfortable chair near the fireplace. Within a minute the older gentleman sat down directly opposite Win, moved his wooden cane onto the adjoining empty chair, and settled the folded newspaper across his lap. Their eyes met and Win immediately knew—everything went icy cold.

"Don't even think about it," the man hissed softly as he shuffled the newspaper. He smiled and nodded to a woman who walked nearby. "You want these nice folks to get hurt?"

Win swallowed hard. "No, no I don't." He could see the nose of a silencer protruding from the newspaper.

"Good boy."

"You're Richter? Why me?"

"Yeah, I'm Richter and damned if I know. Fine young Aryan man like you . . . would rather be dealing with some Zionist scum. But that ain't my call, and so's you know, it ain't personal for me. You've been a little careless, but then this isn't your everyday occurrence. Convenient of your people to wave off your security guys a while ago—makes this almost too easy." He chuckled softly. "Hope you've enjoyed those extra hours. It ain't often I miss. Pretty little girlfriend you've got—"

"She isn't part of this!" Win shot back.

"Not to worry about that. I do my job, and as long as you cooperate, nobody else gets hurt. Just sit there for a minute."

Win's world was moving in slow motion. The adrenaline spiked as soon as he'd met the man's steel-gray eyes—as soon as he knew. He seemed to be watching everything unfold from somewhere outside of himself. And for some reason, he felt no fear. He was operating on a level just beyond the bounds of fear. He saw Hechtner still talking to the lady ranger, maybe forty-five feet away. A group of children were playing on the wooden banisters of the main stairs. There was a line at the register and people were milling around the gift shop. A large tour bus had pulled in moments after Win helped the man through the doors; its air brakes were still releasing. Win realized the assassin was waiting for the influx of people from the bus into the lobby. Dozens of Asian tourists were getting off the bus near the hotel's high wooden canopy. Sounds were running together. The steely eyes hadn't left his. They weren't hostile—they were indifferent. It seemed as if they'd been sitting there a long time, but Win knew it could only have been a few moments.

"What are they paying you for this?" *Stall! Stall the guy!*

"Well, that's my business. It ain't your business."

"Seems to me it is my business."

The man laughed a little. "Well, now I guess you're right. It's $35,000 to handle Special Agent Winston Tyler, the top FBI man here."

Win started to mention he wasn't really the top FBI man here, since Johnson was back from his leave, but it was probably a moot point at this juncture. The horde of tourists began streaming through the front doors of the lobby, and the noise level was rising with loud voices in what sounded like Chinese.

The man's face hardened. "My employer wanted me to give you a chance to make your peace. So I'd be doing that if I was you." He said it in such a conversational way, he could just as easily been talking about the weather.

Win had made his peace long before now. At this moment, he was desperately searching for options. Just then two brown-headed little boys ran behind him and one launched himself into the empty chair to Win's left.

"Not with the kids here. . . . That isn't right," Win began, as if killing him was okay as long as it wasn't in front of some eight-year-olds.

Richter leaned toward Win. "Then get rid of the kids." He said it tersely, just above a whisper.

The boy next to him was kneeling in the armchair, swatting at his partner, who was slapping back at him from behind the chair.

"Hey, hey, boys, I'm saving that seat. Need y'all to move on." No luck. Their battle continued. He changed tactics. "Boys, want to help me play a trick on someone?" He suddenly had their attention. "See that ranger over there in the Smokey the Bear hat? He's an Auburn fan from Alabama. Y'all run over there and yell 'Roll Tide!' real loud a couple of times. Will really rile him up."

"The forest ranger?" they repeated as one. They were grinning from ear to ear, clearly thrilled with a real mission in mischief. *Their parents should be proud,* Win thought.

"Yeah, the forest ranger—have at it!"

As they sprinted through the emerging crowd toward Trey, Richter unexpectedly stood and motioned Win up with his free hand.

"Hadn't counted on so many kids in here. Let's us take a little walk." As Win stood, the concealed pistol immediately lodged in his side. The man didn't even bother to take Win's gun; apparently this wasn't going to take too long.

The boldest of the boys made it to Hechtner and, having never been taught not to interrupt adults, made a loud announcement. "Hey, mister! The man over there says to tell you, 'Roll Tide!'"

"Roll Tide!" the smaller one chimed in.

Trey's eyes left them immediately. He scanned the waiting area where Win had been sitting, talking to an older gentleman. It was so crowded in the lobby it was hard to spot anyone. He felt rising panic as his eyes darted around the room. He ignored the youngsters and began moving toward the sitting area with his puzzled ranger following. He caught a glimpse of Win and the gray-headed man moving through the crowd toward the entrance doors. He'd watched Win open the doors for the man a few minutes earlier. Now Win and the old man were very close together and the older man was no longer stooped—he was also no longer limping. Trey did a double take and saw the cane lying across a chair. He charged toward the doors into the Chinese tourists and yelled, "Stop! Police!" at the top of his lungs.

Win had exited the heavy doors with Richter breathing down his neck. At Trey's first cry, Win felt the gun pull away for an instant as the gunman turned to grasp the situation. Win grabbed a stacked luggage cart and pulled it down hard with his left hand and dove to the right into the luggage that had been disgorged from the bus. He felt something catch his blazer as he fell. The tumbling luggage tripped Richter and he stumbled in front of Win into the covered driveway. He was still off-balance when he sent another round into the bags in front of Win, but Win's training had kicked in and the bullet from Win's Glock drove the man back three steps. Even after the deafening shot rang out, Richter was still on his feet, moving behind one of the hotel canopy's large columns.

Win was aware of people scattering in all directions. He saw Trey fighting his way out the doors amid a wave of panicked tourists. Trey was yelling "Get down! Police!" Win felt himself moving forward, his Glock held steady in a two-handed grip. But he didn't have another clear shot at Richter; the man had gotten behind the bus and was dragging a woman out of the driver's side of a red Jeep. Win kneeled beside the tour bus and hoped for a shot, but there were too many people on the sidewalk behind the Jeep. Within seconds the assassin sped away, weaving between cars and heading toward the highway leading south. Trey was hollering at some ranger to secure the scene. Richter's .22 caliber pistol with silencer was on the pavement in a puddle of blood. The Department of Interior couldn't wish this away—no imaginary drill this time—the bright-red blood was seared in Win's mind.

A Park Service Tahoe, with blue and red lights flashing, pulled up beside the tour bus from somewhere and Trey and Win both dove for the passenger doors. The HRT guy, Kirk Phillips, emerged from the crowd and piled in beside Win in the back seat.

"Go! Go!" Trey ordered. The driver knew what he was doing. He cut across a median, dodged a sign, and got them on the highway behind the Jeep in no time. Their vehicle raced past the two-story houses along Officer's Row, passed the Yellowstone Chapel, and dropped off the plateau into the expanse of the park.

Trey was calmly telling someone on the SUV's radio to block a bridge and also ordering the helicopter up for the pursuit. Win knew they were less than two miles from the deep gorge of the Gardner River, which separated the Mammoth area from the steeper, tree-covered mountains to the south and east. It was the same road he and Trey had driven up two hours ago.

Phillips asked the driver about the extra weaponry in the Tahoe. He was holding a .45 caliber Glock 38 in his left hand and hanging onto the SUV's handhold with his right. He didn't even turn to Win when he asked, "You hit?"

Win hadn't had time to think about that—the left side of his blazer had a shredded look, and when he touched it, his fingers came away covered in black powder. He wiped the gunpowder residue off his hand onto the jacket and saw the HRT commander raise his eyebrows and nod. "Close. Real close."

Richter's fast and erratic driving was evidenced by three carloads of tourists stuck in roadside ditches where they'd swerved to avoid the fleeing Jeep. The speeding Tahoe topped the final barren hill leading to the high steel bridge just in time for Win and the others to see a cloud of dust to the right of the bridge. The red Jeep rolled twice and disappeared over the side of the gorge. The two-hundred-foot drop to the Gardner River wasn't straight down, but it was plenty steep enough. A Park Service cruiser was sitting on the bridge with its police lights on. Trey's driver braked hard as they neared it.

"Until we get a body, we have to assume he jumped before it went over and is still a threat," the HRT guy said to no one in particular.

Two armed rangers came running from behind the patrol car as they stopped. They reported that the Jeep's driver was slumped over the wheel when the vehicle missed the bridge approach. The Jeep had never braked. It was upside down on the bottom of the ravine on their side of the river. Dust and wisps of smoke were rising from the wreck; two wheels were slowly turning. The only sound was the rushing river. For a long moment, everyone just stood on the concrete bridge approach, looking down.

Win finally snapped out of it, as it occurred to him that the FBI was technically in charge of matters like this and he was the FBI. He asked Trey to relay the situation to the Bureau office. A couple of minutes later, the yellow Park Service helicopter swooped in low and Trey sent it to the bottom of the ravine. Win watched as four Special Response Team rangers, with assault rifles aimed, jumped from the chopper, approached the wreck, and cautiously tried to find the driver.

A ranger from the helicopter radioed Trey that they'd found a deceased white male with what appeared to be a gunshot wound to the upper chest. He also had multiple traumatic injuries due to the crash—no idea which killed him. He was wearing a gray wig and had a .45 caliber handgun in his belt. No ID on him. No one else was in the Jeep, thank goodness. Reinforcements began arriving about that time, including the ASAC, Emily, Johnson, and a slew of other FBI folks.

Emily made the mistake of running from the Bureau SUV up to the bridge approach with gun drawn and announcing in a much-too-loud voice, "Pulling the security worked! Thug made his move," or something to that effect. It didn't set well with Win. *She used me as bait?*

He whirled and advanced on her. "You played your little catty control game, and now a man is dead! You don't get it! This isn't office politics—these are people's lives you're playing with. . . . This is life or death!"

Win was still advancing and Emily had gone pale. She was stepping back, gun in hand. Wes Givens moved in front of Win and placed a hand on his chest. The ASAC shook his head, and his eyes said, *That's enough.* Win angrily looked away from her and obeyed his boss's silent commands. It was indeed enough.

Wes told Emily to holster her weapon and go to their vehicle. He asked Johnson to take Win back to the office when he was ready to go, and to handle the preliminary on-scene steps in the shooting inquiry. He ordered another agent to reach out to all the Bureau folks who weren't on surveillance and get them down here or over to the hotel to begin securing the crime scenes. The ASAC squeezed Win's shoulder and shook his head sadly before he walked away to talk with Chief Randall, who'd arrived with another group of rangers.

Johnson rose to the occasion and even seemed to have a bit of sensitivity about him. He moved Win away from the bridge and out of the wind, alongside one of the rangers' SUVs. "This is so damned awful! It's a hard, hard thing. You want to go down to the Jeep? See him? Might help you close it out of your mind or might make it worse. I can't tell you what you'll feel, Win."

Win took a few deep breaths and squinted up into the whirling white clouds. "No . . . no, I don't want to see the body. . . . I don't need to. I wanna say a word to Trey, that's all, and then we can go, okay?"

"Sure. Sure, I'll wait on you here." Johnson leaned into the truck out of the cold wind.

Win walked back to the bridge where Trey was directing his rangers in the ravine by handheld radio. Win overheard enough to know the helicopter was lifting off to avoid the rising winds. The body would be brought up after the FBI had processed the crime scene. Trey finished the radio transmission and turned to Win. The ranger could see the shock of the shooting settling on him.

"Thank you," Win said softly.

Trey met his eyes and nodded. There wasn't any need for words. There wasn't anything that could be said that would make it any better.

CHAPTER TWENTY

He hadn't been in the stone chapel since the meeting with Ellie Bordeaux ten days ago. Everything looked the same except for a white vase with yellow flowers sitting beside the large open Bible on the altar. A nod to springtime in the park, he guessed. He walked down the center aisle and sat down in the second pew near the front. He took off his parka and stretched out his arms to the top of the smooth oak pew in front of him. It had been well over an hour since the shooting. He'd walked away from the near-frantic activity at the office and found himself here. The numbness he'd felt was wearing off, giving way to a sense of altered reality—as if he wasn't quite the same anymore. He leaned his head down on his outstretched arms and the quiet of the Holy Place embraced him. The only sounds were distant thunder and then the sound of rain on the slate tile roof. . . . It was starting to rain.

He tried to clear his head—easier to do than clear his heart. A second attempt on his life within two days. A second escape. Each time he'd survived only by the skin of his teeth, or as Mother would say, "only by the grace of God." And the second time was so different. He couldn't hold on to the detachment he'd forced into his mind after the bullet from the rifle missed him thirty-three hours earlier. This time he'd looked the killer in the eyes—he knew the man's name. This time a man had died. Death, even for the one who intended to kill him, left Win shaken.

There was an illogical self-blame going on in his thoughts. Had his lack of discipline put other lives at risk? Could he have averted the whole thing if he'd been more watchful? Or shot to wound the man instead of to kill? He couldn't lose the churning in his gut, the tightness in his throat. He formed his hands into fists and tried to force the trembling away. He finally leaned back in the pew and lowered his head. He tried to pray, but his prayers seemed to float to the wooden beams of the chapel ceiling and hang there. *Where has God gone?*

He heard the door open behind him, at the rear of the sanctuary. He heard boots move down the aisle toward him. He didn't turn. At this point, he didn't care. Trey put his flat hat and jacket in the pew in front of them and sat down beside him. He didn't say a word.

"I guess this means someone is still following me around," Win finally said.

"Yup, that isn't likely to stop just yet. You okay?"

"Yeah, just can't seem to . . . can't seem to get any peace about this." Win kept his focus straight ahead toward the flowers on the altar.

Trey cut his eyes toward him. "I can't even imagine what you're going through, but this is the right place to start looking for that peace." He took a worn black pew Bible and turned to the Twenty-Third Psalm.

He handed it to Win, who softly read it aloud: *"The Lord is my Shepherd, I shall not want. . . ."* Trey repeated all six verses along with him from memory. Then they took turns choosing a Scripture to read.

"Turn to Psalm 91," Trey said.

"Philippians 4:4–13," Win offered next.

"Turn to Romans 8:26–39."

The sound of rain on the roof had stopped and sunlight was streaming through the high opaque-glass windows of the old church when Trey closed the sacred book. Only hours ago they'd felt no trust for each other, but here in the Yellowstone Chapel they'd discovered a shared spiritual depth that grounded them both. The gut-wrenching roller coaster of emotions Win had experienced since the shooting began to subside.

"Where'd you learn so much Scripture?" he asked the ranger.

"Lutheran schools. All German Lutheran boys learn their Bible. You grew up in church." Trey stated the obvious.

"Southern Baptist. Was in church every time the door was open as a kid."

"And now?" Trey asked quietly.

Win dropped his eyes to his hands and shook his head slowly. "We'd call it backsliding in my church." He kept his eyes down and sucked in a breath. "The last couple of years I sorta drifted away from God. Did some things I'm not proud of . . . was deliberately sinful. It pulled me away from my family, my friends. . . . It eventually destroyed a relationship."

If Trey was taken aback by the unexpected confession, he didn't show it. "So where are you now?" Those gray eyes, so hard and angry back on the high ridge this morning, were compassionate now.

"I know God has forgiven me, I've asked Him to. . . . I just can't seem to forgive myself. I screwed up His plan, you know?"

"You were in a shoot-out—you're the one standing for a reason. There's still a plan." The ranger shifted in the pew. "None of us are ever gonna be good enough to work our way into Heaven, Win. We're all gonna fall short. Accept His grace."

In his mind, Win knew these truths, but he hadn't kept them lodged in his heart and soul for years. And now . . . now he'd killed a man.

"I've got to get back to the office. . . . You wanna talk about any of this, you call me. I mean that."

"You some sort of chaplain here?" Win asked.

He shook his head *no*. "Nope, just a park ranger. You want me to pray for you before I go?"

"Yeah, yeah. I'd appreciate that," Win answered in a whisper.

Trey stood up beside Win in the empty chapel and placed his right hand firmly on Win's shoulder. "Dear Lord, I lift up my brother, Win Tyler, to You. That You would not only give him Your protection, but give him wisdom, courage, and most of all Your peace. Your peace that is beyond comprehension, that will guard his heart, his mind, and his soul in Christ Jesus. Amen." His strong hand squeezed Win's shoulder.

Win repeated the *amen*, but kept his head bowed and his eyes closed as Trey collected his coat and hat and walked back up the aisle and out into the late-afternoon sunlight. For the first time since Shelby left him, Win was able to cry.

* * *

Win was focused on his computer when the HRT commander, Kirk Phillips, knocked softly on his office door later that afternoon. "Hey, sorry, I was a little deep in thought. Come in."

Phillips closed the door and made himself comfortable in one of the chairs across from Win's desk. "Didn't know if you were staying in town or shipping out. Got a minute?"

"Yes, sir. Staying, I hope. I've requested a delay on the shooting inquiry, but I haven't heard anything definitive from Mr. Givens. If Emily has anything to do with it, I'm sure they'll ship me out."

"That's not on you—Ms. Stuart will be lucky to keep her desk after her performance so far. I would hope she's smart enough to keep her best people around her at this point."

Win shrugged at that, but he appreciated the implied compliment. "Well, I got a little aggressive with her this afternoon. . . ."

"She deserved every bit of it and more. There's no place for—what did you call it?—*catty games,* when the stakes are this high. She's already heard that from plenty of others since the shooting went down." Phillips steepled his fingers. "I'm not here to argue with your decision to stay on the case, but there are good reasons to pull back for a few days after going through what you've experienced."

Win's silence told of his resolve to stay.

"I watched this afternoon's incident on the surveillance cameras," the commander said. "You handled the confrontation real well. Other people could have been hurt if you hadn't been smart."

"He still nearly killed me. Uh, there's video on that?"

"Nearly doesn't count. And yes, hotel security cameras—several angles—and I read lips so I know what was said between Richter and you. Lots of very good agents wouldn't have been able to improvise as well as you did under that type pressure. Provided some interesting insight on you and the subjects."

"What insight on the subjects?" Win wanted the spotlight off him.

"Well, everyone's been assuming the hit on the resident agent was just that—a hit on the Bureau's top man here. But I'm thinking it's a hit on you."

"Why? Even Richter said it was nothing personal."

Phillips leaned back in his chair and folded his arms. "What he said was it was not personal to him. He had nothing against you. But he also called you by name and gave you a direct message from his employer: Make your peace. The 'employer' is very likely Daniel Shepherd or one of his crew—unless you've found another angle."

"No, no I haven't developed any basis for it in my old cases. At least not yet."

"Well, think about it. The hit man was a professional killer, Win. There was no reason for him to take the risk of seeing you face-to-face unless he'd been told to make sure you got the message to make your peace with God. Without any security around, the guy could have easily taken you out with the silencer when the room got crowded and loud. You'd never know what hit you—then he'd disappear into the crowd. It's clear to me the attempt today was totally personal. The other attempt—long-range rifle?—totally impersonal."

The commander raised his eyebrows slightly and finished his thoughts. "It's not tracking for me. Is there anything in this screwy church's theology that would make that fit? Any way you could have crossed paths with Daniel Shepherd? Any way he would know you or about you?"

Everything Phillips was saying made sense. It *was* personal. Win could feel it. He just didn't know why. Phillips kept up his conversational tone. "If I were you, I'd lean pretty heavily on my instincts, and if you conclude it is personal, then I'd keep looking over my shoulder till we clean out this viper's nest."

He changed the subject quickly, almost as if to trick Win into a rushed response. "Ranger Hechtner wasn't totally truthful in the briefing right after lunch. There's more to his relationship with Bordeaux than he laid out."

It was Win's turn to lean back in his chair with his arms folded. He was thinking the Bureau probably didn't need polygraphs with this guy on the payroll. He decided not to respond. If Phillips thought Trey wasn't totally truthful in the meeting, Phillips likely suspected the same thing of him.

The HRT commander knew he'd made his point, which was "Don't even think about being less than completely honest with me." He shifted forward in his chair. "Your informant, Bordeaux—he may be the most dangerous one we're dealing with here. I've seen his military records; a real shame they forced him out. He has a lot of basis for anti-government sentiment right there, even if you don't consider the loss of his guide license up here. He fits our profile for a really serious domestic terrorist threat—fits it perfectly. Both you and Hechtner said he seemed to be struggling with where his loyalties lie. Lots of people waffle between coming down on the right side or the wrong side. You may not know how he will turn until it comes right down to it—he may not even know—but if you guess incorrectly, you could be the one paying for it."

He stood and picked his coat up off the other chair. "Want some unsolicited advice?" He didn't wait for Win to answer. "Knock it off here, it's nearly six. Go home, go see friends, do routine things to take your mind off the shooting. You'll be one hundred percent better tomorrow if you do. No one ever knows how a shooting's going to affect them. Besides, I'd like you to go over some intel with our teams in the morning if you stay in town. You'll need to be sharp." Win knew then he'd be staying on the case.

Johnson came to Win's door as Phillips was walking toward the stairs. "Boss says your request for a delay on the shooting inquiry was approved 'cause of your status with the confidential sources. So the Shooting Inquiry Team won't be here for at least a week. I've got to keep your weapon and jacket for evidence. Found this packet of photos in the blazer." He handed Win the envelope of photos Tory had given him. "Here's a brand-new Glock I've kept in the safe—keep it till you get your gun back. It's not a 19M, but it'll do."

Win took the handgun while the big man continued talking. "The rangers are going to continue their security detail for you since our SWAT folks are handling the initial evidence response workload. The ASAC's using your vehicle tonight. I'm heading out . . . wasn't expecting to get called back in the middle of my leave. Want me to drop you off at your place?"

Win started to say no. He hardly ever left the office before 8:15, but Phillips's advice was on his mind. He had no idea how he was going to deal with the shooting. *Maybe I oughta go home and crash for a few hours.* He took Johnson up on his offer.

Win grabbed his coat and as they walked down the stairs, Johnson made an offhand comment. "What the hell happened to the office while I was gone? You win some TV home improvement makeover contest or something?"

*   *   *

Since the threat on Win's life was assumed to have been diminished with the death of Richter, the rangers only assigned two guys to guard Win's house. They were, however, in full SWAT gear tonight—no one was pretending to be a tourist anymore.

For the first time since he'd come to Yellowstone, Win opened the fireplace flue in his den and made a fire. He'd enjoyed the warmth of the big fireplace at the rangers' cabin last night. *How could that have only been twenty-four hours ago?* He took Phillips's advice and turned on some music and set about doing the laundry he'd accumulated over the last two weeks. He wrote a note to his mother and enclosed one of the photos Tory had given him. He knew the picture would please her; he really looked happy holding that bear cub.

He sat down on the couch and let his mind wander. He'd driven into the park on April 8th. It would be May 8th tomorrow. He set his Coke down and looked back at the photo of himself. What had Tory said? *Maybe send one to a girlfriend back home.* Tomorrow, May 8th, was their anniversary. Shelby had always called it that. He'd never really known why—some girl thing, he supposed. Maybe it was when he'd first called her or maybe when they'd gone on their first date. How many years ago? Five years. It would have been five years tomorrow.

How long since she'd stormed out of his life? Since he'd talked to her? Nearly three months. *Why didn't I fight for the relationship?* He stared into the dancing flames in the fireplace. *What would she say about today?* He knew what he'd want her to say, what he'd want her to do. . . . But something had changed that last year in Charlotte. He'd gotten deeply involved in the Brunson case, and it had consumed so much of him, and she'd found a passion for clinical research, which dominated her time and energy. But he knew those things were only the symptoms of a much deeper problem. They'd drifted far apart, and all the little things their love was built on had slipped away.

She'd told him once, over a year ago, that he was leaving her. Was she right? Had the loss of their love actually happened long ago, had he been clinging to the comfortable, the secure—too much of a coward to end it? Had he left her? What did that old country song say? *"Nobody in his right mind would have left her—even my heart was smart enough to stay behind."* He had a bad feeling his heart had indeed stayed behind with Shelby.

He was letting the intense pain of his grief over the lost relationship seep back into him tonight, just as it had on so many lonely nights. How could he hope to move into a new relationship when he hadn't really left the old one? He listened to the crackling of the fire, knowing a far more weighty question lay just below the surface of his soul, where he didn't dare touch it yet—how to deal with his killing of another human being.

The clothes dryer buzzed, saving him from continuing to wallow in pity and pain. He forced himself off the couch to continue his laundry. He hadn't been through his mail in about three days, and among the bills and "current resident" flyers was a letter from his mother. He treasured those long letters she'd write him every few months. The first part of the letter was full of the usual news of home, but when he got to the second page, he sat down and read it closely. It was as if she'd written it for tonight.

You won't remember this, Win, but it's a picture stamped in my heart: you looking down at your boots, holding on to a young heifer's lead rope and halter at the county fair that first time you had shown a calf. It had not gone well and you had not won. You were barely six years old as I recall. Your little blond head was down and I remember thinking you needed a haircut, odd the things that stick in your mind. You were trying real hard not to cry and the heifer was licking at your ear. And you looked up at me with those beautiful blue eyes and declared through those tears that it wasn't fair. I remember telling you that life wasn't meant to be fair. God wants life to be cherished, and precious, and good, but until we're in Heaven there will be trials that test our souls and those trials will never feel fair.

It troubled me when you were here a few weeks ago—no longer my little towheaded boy, but a handsome man—who's been successful at everything he's ever done. I could see that you were feeling it wasn't fair that you'd been treated poorly by the FBI and by Shelby. You were letting those feelings of injustice defeat your spirit. But Sweetheart, I will say it again: Life wasn't meant to be fair. It isn't so much the circumstances that can tear us apart; it's how we deal with those circumstances.

God has put you in a new place, where I have no doubt you are already making a positive difference in the lives of so many, so don't dwell on your losses, move forward toward your next victories. I have prayed every day that God will put new people in your life who will reach out to you and encourage you. I know there are others who were just waiting for you to arrive so you could be an encouragement to them. The wonderful differences you can make in those lives are your victories. I pray every day that His angels will encircle you with their protection. Go looking for those victories, Win.

He reread the page three times. He thought of Ellie, who'd called him a "deliverer," and of Luke, who'd also pointed out—rather dramatically with his knife—that life wasn't fair. He thought of Trey, who'd prayed for him in the chapel; of Tory, who'd shown him an unexpected kindness; of Jason, who seemed to need a big brother; and Gus, whose life was a fascinating mess. He silently thanked God for giving him another chance to make a real difference in this world. Then he picked up his phone and called his mother. It was late at home, but he needed her to know how much he appreciated her wisdom and care.

*   *   *

Win was shocked that he'd actually slept well. His mother's letter and the long talk with both of his parents helped ease his pain. He was glad he'd called them, since the shooting had made the national news and they'd been trying to reach him on his personal phone all evening. The Bureau hadn't released the name of the FBI agent involved in the shooting, and he couldn't comment on it, but they knew it was him.

The weather had decided to take a turn for the worse during the pre-dawn hours, and the thunderstorms and rain had transitioned to sleet and snow. It reminded Win of that first frigid day when he'd driven into Yellowstone. Snow clouds were hanging only a few hundred feet above the buildings, and all the surrounding hills and mountains had disappeared into the swirling white. The Hostage Rescue Team members were not gonna be happy with their first full day in Yellowstone National Park.

One of the rangers drove him into the office and at 6:15 it was already buzzing with activity. Win hadn't spoken to Emily since confronting her yesterday at the bridge. He figured he might as well get that unpleasant task out of the way. He knocked on the open door and waited for her to look up from the computer screen. Her red hair was pulled back as tight as it would go into a fuzzy bun; her eyes were puffy under her wire-rim glasses. He doubted she'd slept. She didn't invite him into the office, so he spoke from the doorway.

"Ma'am, I owe you an apology for being so aggressive yesterday afternoon. I shouldn't have come toward you that way." He didn't apologize for his words, just his manner of delivering them.

She looked up over the computer monitor. "Whatever," was her only response.

Apparently she wasn't into accepting apologies or any other civility. As his granny would say, "Bless her heart, probably raised by wolves." He smiled at that thought and moved back downstairs to the conference room where Mr. Givens had set up his office.

"How're you doing?" the ASAC asked when he saw Win.

"Fine, sir. I'm sure it will hit me, but I'm glad it wasn't last night."

"Well, the press is all over this, but thankfully there's some big political crisis going on in Washington that has their attention. Hopefully it won't become a huge story. If anyone asks you about the shooting, refer them to our Denver office and our media relations agent will handle it." Wes took a sip of his coffee and nodded toward the window. "Can you believe it's snowing here? May 8th?"

"They say it snows here off and on until June."

"Wow, well, when this is finished, we'll get you back to a better climate in Denver." He waved Win in and shuffled through some papers on the conference table before looking up again.

"Kirk Phillips wants you to meet with some of his HRT guys at 7:30. They've already settled into the park's Annex Building. HRT wants to operate somewhat independently from our field office until the leak is stopped. I sometimes think the Bureau's Critical Incident Response Group doesn't appreciate the importance of case agents being in charge of these types of operations. In my experience, HRT has a tendency to try to run the show, even in the best of times." He smiled ruefully. "Not that anyone would call in HRT in the best of times!"

Win sat down across from him and grinned at the comment.

"Hmmm, well, Tom is flying in . . . if they can get through this weather to Bozeman this afternoon. Emily may be shipping out, we'll see. But then, there may be no time to realign. This may all go down in the next couple of days, if the lousy weather doesn't complicate things. You'll be answering directly to me till we get it sorted out. If HRT borrows you, you may be answering to them part of the time. Are you good with that?"

"Sure, whatever you need me to do, sir."

"You'll still have to keep up with the False Prophet case from this office. If it starts to overwhelm you, let me know and I'll pull someone in to help you and Deb. You'll get your personal phone back this morning. The technicians still don't know what caused the delay in alerting you to the warning text before the sniper hit. Everything seems a little harder here. Transmission delays—awful infrastructure. I guess being on the fringe of the wilderness has its attractions, but I couldn't handle it for long." He glanced out the window. "Look at that! It's snowing harder!" He shook his head in disbelief.

Win started to rise from the chair when the ASAC added one last comment. "Also, one of our surveillance teams saw Mrs. Bordeaux drive to their place yesterday afternoon. That's the first time she's been seen since May 3rd. Didn't look like the children were with her. You'll need to really monitor your personal phone in case she calls you again."

"Yes, sir." Win frowned at that bit of unwelcome news.

After the brief meeting, Win jogged back up the wooden staircase and closed the door to his office. There was something he had to tend to before activity overwhelmed the place. He spread out a cleaning cloth over his desk and set about his work. After he finished, he leaned back in his chair and stared into space. His thoughts wandered in random directions, then settled on his most recent task.

Daddy always said it was simply a tool. Just like any other tool, you could use it correctly and get something positive done or you could use it incorrectly and screw something up. But those tools from his youth were long guns: shotguns to chase blackbirds out of the cornfield, rifles to bring home dinner from time to time, precision guns used to compete in contests. In his more innocent past, they'd been tools, just like Daddy said. But not any longer. Now they were weapons. This new Glock was a .40 caliber—same as the one he gave up to Johnson at the bridge yesterday afternoon. Big difference between this new one and his gun. His gun had killed a man.

He'd finished cleaning the new Glock and the smell of Hoppe's gun oil had settled in the room. Win rammed the loaded magazine into the open grip, then racked the slide to chamber a round. The new weapon had the same comfortable feel in his hand. It was solid, balanced, and steady. Highly reliable. A familiar companion. Five thousand two hundred and twenty-six—that was how many rounds he'd fired a Glock handgun at Quantico. Two thousand eight hundred and eighty-one rounds during his quarterly firearms training sessions since the Academy. He'd kept count. The FBI didn't skimp on firearms training for its agents. He knew he was good with it—he'd won all the marksmanship awards in his class at Quantico. His name was on the marksmanship plaque back at the Academy.

But he'd never pulled it from its holster with the thought of using it until yesterday. He didn't remember reaching for it, or sighting, or pulling the trigger. He did remember the sharp report of the blast, the acrid smell of the discharge, the hard push of the recoil against the back of his hand, the man staggering backward. He remembered the bright-red blood pooling on the pavement. And when he allowed himself a moment to peer into his soul, he remembered a millisecond of intent. Not rage. Not anger. Just pure intent to kill. There was an unusual emptiness in his chest as he stared down at it now—the gun resting on his desk. A new gun, a new weapon . . . a new tool. He drew in a deep breath as his mind formed its conclusion. Daddy had been right. The gun was only the tool. The tool hadn't taken a life—Win Tyler had.

CHAPTER TWENTY-ONE

At 7:20 a.m. Win was leaning into an onslaught of freezing precip-itation as he walked down the icy sidewalk to the appropriated headquarters of the FBI's Hostage Rescue Team. Their two nine-member tactical teams, dozens of support staff, and on-scene com-mander, Kirk Phillips, had taken over a large two-story building that had been used for seventy-five years for park offices until federal bud-get cuts shuttered it recently. It was convenient and practical, and far enough out of the way to allow them to do their own thing. Win pulled the collar of his heavy coat up higher and pulled the brown felt hat down lower on his head. The wind and biting snow were unwelcome visitors after so many relatively nice days. His security guys were both dutifully skidding along behind him on the slick sidewalk, trying to appear inconspicuous.

Win ran into Kirk Phillips as he entered the old building. Phillips was on his way out, but he stood inside the entrance and greeted Win with a nod. The commander's tone was decidedly cooler than it had been yesterday afternoon. The awful weather had everyone in a foul mood. Phillips surprised Win with his first comments, "Thought maybe you and Ranger Hechtner could work on some of the local recon and intel for us. What do you think?"

"Yes, sir, Hechtner knows the area. He's got the tactical training—"

Phillips interrupted. "But we have a leak—a significant leak. You heard my opinion of Bordeaux's capabilities, and we both know

Hechtner has a lot more history with the man than he's letting on. Hechtner has top secret clearance . . . he could be the leak."

"You told me to trust my instincts. Well, they're telling me Trey Hechtner is a stand-up guy. He saved my life yesterday," Win said.

"Actually, your smarts saved your life yesterday; that, and maybe a lot of good karma. You used the ranger as a part of your play. True, he was paying attention, and that counts for something, but don't get all sentimental about it and lose sight of other possibilities." He started to turn for the door, but then stopped. "I don't trust him. But my job is to get our team into that compound and arrest the bad guys, so if I have to use someone I'm leery of, I'll do it under the right circumstances." His eyes focused even more sharply on Win. "Maybe he can explain what's gone on with Bordeaux. May not be as big a problem as I think. Maybe we can use him."

"Sir, I would hope we could work with Trey and his agency rather than use him."

The man raised his eyebrows slightly. "Point taken. Go get him. I'll be back." He was still talking as he walked away. "I want something set up within the hour." He pushed through the heavy doors, with two large men in tow, and disappeared into the snow squall.

Win walked one block back up the street to the park's Administration Building as the blowing snow transitioned to heavy sleet. Win had never been to Trey's office, but his security guys pointed him in the right direction as they huddled inside the front doors of the grand stone building and stomped their feet to get warm.

Trey was working on his computer, his back to the open door, when Win knocked. He stood when he saw Win and smiled easily. "Come in. . . . Have a seat. You alright today?" He noticed Win seemed rushed. "You shipping out?"

Given the time crunch, Win kept his coat on and skipped the usual pleasantries. He got right down to business. "Doing fine today—so far," he said as he arched his eyebrows. "And no, they're letting me stay." He eased into the metal chair across from the desk. "I don't trust the phones—came over here to see if you want to help HRT get a better handle on the terrain, trails, infrastructure. . . . Help us develop our ops plan."

"Sounds interesting, but why me?" Trey asked as he sat down.

"'Cause it's the quickest, smartest thing to do. You know the area and the people. . . . There is a catch."

Trey cocked his head to the side and leaned back in the chair. He motioned Win to close the office door. "What catch?"

"Commander Phillips didn't buy your story on your limited relationship with Luke yesterday. He wants to get a better feel about it before you start working for us."

"He wants to make sure I'm not the mole—that's what he wants and you know it."

Win shrugged. "Yeah, well, reckon he's got to start somewhere, but I also suggested you help us with the intel."

Trey took a deep breath and brought a hand across his eyes. Win leaned forward in his chair with his hat in his hands and lowered his voice. "You don't have to do it. But you were willing to take a huge risk yesterday in getting me to Luke. I would say this is a risk—especially if anything illegal went on with you and Luke when y'all were tight."

Hechtner seemed taken aback at Win's directness. "Nothing illegal"—his hand came to his chin, and he looked down—"but when it started falling apart for Luke over a year ago . . . there were lots of things . . . right on the line." He was staring down at his desk, focused inward on the past. He looked back up at Win. "Nothing I have a bad conscience over, that's for sure."

"Well, having a bad conscience and having the Bureau and the U.S. Attorney come down on you are two different things. You know what they say: 'You don't have to do anything wrong—they can find something to get you on if they want to badly enough.'"

"I saw that firsthand with Luke! You don't have to tell me how that works!" His usually calm voice held more than a hint of anger. "And why is it you're so quick to say 'they'? What badge are you wearing today?"

Win leaned back in his chair. "I've wondered if I'm carrying the right badge lately. But we're not here to discuss my job issues. I believe you want to get the bad guys as badly as I do. We're all taking risks. You'll have to decide if it's worth it to you. If you do come over, stay on your toes—Phillips is really sharp. Do not fudge on anything with him. He'll smell it out. He wants to meet within the hour."

"Alright, I'll think about it. I'll go get with Gus and Chief Randall. They'd have to approve it. I'll call you in a few minutes with a yes or a no."

"Do what you think is best."

Win rose slowly and scanned the office. He always thought you could tell a lot about a person by their office. Trey's was neat as a pin; he would have expected that. The large window behind the desk overlooked trees. There were framed Montana State diplomas on the wall, two or three framed professional designations—he could read *Advanced Emergency Medical Technician* on one from where he stood. A photo of an attractive blond woman and little girl on the desk—the wife and daughter Trey had mentioned. Books on everything from forestry to trauma medicine. The antique coat-tree held the ranger's flat hat, a Park Service field cap, and an assortment of dark-green coats, vests, and jackets to match the ever-changing weather conditions of Yellowstone. Two large professional-looking photographs of striking mountain landscapes hung on opposite walls—one looked very familiar. It was a sunrise photo from the spot where Win sat yesterday morning with Trey holding his gun on him. A lot had changed in twenty-four hours.

*   *   *

Win and his bodyguards slid back down the street into the improvised HRT headquarters. Even after the shooting yesterday afternoon, no one in the federal government was broadcasting the fact that an elite unit of the FBI was within the park. The cover for the operation was a company they were calling U.S. Seismology Testing Services. A nice sign to that effect was at the door's entrance, and several SUVs sitting outside had the company's name stenciled on their sides. The HRT guys were all in civilian clothes. The general public would think the large group was simply doing earthquake research at the park's thermal features.

The humorless agent, or operator as HRT called its members, who was guarding the front door, made an attempt to confiscate the side arms and phones from Win's protection detail. The two plainclothes rangers were protesting when another HRT operator appeared and explained to everyone in no uncertain terms that only FBI special agents could keep their weapons or phones in the building. Compared with Phillips, this guy was more in line with Win's imagined super-warrior—more than a little scary. Win negotiated some chairs and coffee for his rangers and tried to smooth over the obvious efforts at intimidation. He was getting more than a little tired of running positive PR for the Bureau with others in the law enforcement community.

After the five-minute delay at the front door, Win finally headed up the interior staircase with an escort. The operational center he saw was surprisingly functional considering it had been vacant office space less than twenty-four hours ago. The teams' forward operations staff had video, photo, and audio rooms, a mapping room, and a tactical operations center, or TOC, in place. They'd set up bunkrooms on the first floor and were using the second level for offices and the TOC. The old building smelled of mildew, disinfectant, and strong coffee. There were serious men and women everywhere he turned.

A few minutes later, Trey was escorted up the stairs by one of the more macho-looking operators, an African American guy who looked like a heavyweight wrestler. Trey was grousing to no avail about having his cell phone and handgun confiscated, especially since they weren't in an FBI-designated secure compartmented information facility, or SCIF, area. Apparently the Hostage Rescue Team had their own rules, and based on what he'd seen so far, Win didn't think they looked like a group you'd want to argue with if you were smart.

Commander Phillips's personal office wasn't large, and it was certainly Spartan in furnishings. They were apparently using any discarded office furniture they could find in the building. Trey took off his coat and hat, shook hands with Phillips, and took a seat in front of his desk. As soon as Trey sat down, two HRT guys entered the rear of the small office. Win wasn't liking the feel of this. Phillips introduced the newcomers as Supervisory Special Agents Stoddard and Smith, his two team leaders. No one moved to shake hands. Win assumed he wouldn't be a part of the meeting with Trey, and he moved toward the door. Agent Smith closed it. Trey glanced nervously toward Win. There was a decidedly tense feel to the air, and Win suddenly felt trapped. That was exactly what Phillips intended.

"Win, why don't you have a seat there beside Ranger Hechtner." Phillips's voice was smooth and cold.

As soon as Win complied, he continued, "We came across some interesting footage late last night after we took over the drone control from the folks who were attempting to handle it."

Uh-oh, this is going to get ugly. Win realized then that he'd led Trey into a trap—and it might well be a trap intended for both of them.

"I want you men to tell us about some photos that were taken yesterday morning, at 0957 hours. Wasn't that when you were meeting with your informant on the mountain south of here?"

Win was sitting a little behind Trey and couldn't see his eyes. He watched as the ranger straightened in the chair and swallowed hard. Win still had his weapon, which implied that Phillips didn't think he was a threat. That was the only positive Win could come up with, and with two armed HRT operators standing directly behind him, his weapon was almost irrelevant—the positive factor didn't count for much.

Phillips was half-sitting on the edge of his metal desk. He handed Win and Trey several remarkably clear eleven-by-seventeen black-and-white photos of a man holding a gun on another man. The first few photos showed the men walking up a trail on a ridge. Other photos showed the same men seated in a small clearing on large rocks—one man still holding the gun. There were close-ups of the Glock handgun, of the Park Service's arrowhead patch on the gunman's coat, and of the individuals. Win was guessing the series of photos were taken in a couple of slow passes by a high-altitude drone and the close-ups had been enhanced when the technicians found something interesting. Given Win's recollection of events yesterday morning, they'd been shot within a five-minute span. The last photos should have shown Luke—but Luke had stayed in the shadow of the rocks.

Win felt he had only two options here: either panic or turn this one around on Phillips. He went on offense. He leaned forward with the photos. "These are great! They support our report on Bordeaux's knowledge of our surveillance assets, and they clear Hechtner of any suspicion on the intel leaks!" Win sounded excited and pleased.

It was not the reaction Phillips or anyone else in the room, including Trey, was expecting.

"What?" Phillips was caught off guard. Trey turned halfway in his chair toward him, and Win heard the two HRT operators shift their stance behind him.

"Look carefully at the photos." Win continued his upbeat tone and went into his old courtroom mode, slowly standing, holding two of the photos side by side so everyone in the room could see them.

"I see Ranger Hechtner holding a weapon on someone who appears to be you, an FBI agent," Phillips commented dryly.

"Exactly! Hechtner had no way of knowing we had drone surveillance in the general area of Mammoth. If he'd known that, he would have had us under cover. I knew about the drone coverage, and I intentionally sat down in the clearing, hoping to be spotted. If Ranger Hechtner was the one funneling intel to the bad guys—who did know about the drones—he wouldn't have been sitting out in the open with a weapon in plain sight."

"And your proof the bad guys knew about the drones?"

"Who else is in this photo?" Win held up the last photo in the batch. It showed Win sitting with his hands on his knees, while Hechtner was still holding the gun; Trey was slightly turned to the right toward a large boulder. Win was praying some sign of Luke would show up in a more enhanced version of the photo. He confidently answered his own question. "You can't see anyone in this run of the photo, but Luke Bordeaux was standing in the shadow of a boulder the entire time. In fact, shortly after these photos were taken, Luke told us to move out of the clearing to avoid detection by the drones. Luke knew about the airplane and drone surveillance and stayed under cover, but Hechtner didn't know until Luke told him about it during our meeting."

The inquisition had gone in a totally different direction than Phillips had expected, but he was considering what Win had said. He handed the last photo to Agent Stoddard. "Get this shot to the photo lab ASAP and see if they can further enhance the shadowed areas." The man left the room and Win sat back down.

Phillips tried to get control of the meeting back from Win. "So, Ranger Hechtner, you haven't commented on the photos. Tell me what you see."

Trey took the "Don't answer the question directly" approach. "Sir, I wasn't aware of the aerial surveillance until Luke told us to get under cover."

Phillips was getting a little exasperated now. "Do either of you gentlemen see anything unusual with the Park Service's Special Response Team leader holding the FBI agent he was assigned to protect at gunpoint?"

Win looked down at his hands. *Oh boy.*

"Sir, I took Agent Tyler's gun from him before Luke Bordeaux joined us. I didn't know the extent of their informant relationship. Luke was coming to the meeting at my request, and I didn't want a confrontation between them. This all happened just over twenty-four hours after Agent Tyler was nearly killed by a sniper. He was a little edgy, and rightly so. I believed holding the gun was the safest course for everyone. I never pointed his weapon directly at him, and I returned it to him when he asked for it after Luke arrived." Trey calmly recited the event as if it were an everyday occurrence.

"Win?"

Win paused to meet Phillips's eyes squarely. The man could see a lie a mile away; Win wanted him to feel they were truthful, not just hear it. "That's exactly what happened, sir. It was a small thing. . . . It may have helped us get the information we needed from Bordeaux."

A light tap on the door and Agent Stoddard appeared with two photos and handed them to Phillips.

Win didn't breathe for the moments Phillips spent looking over both photos. He finally handed them to Win and nodded. The first photo was the original, close-range aerial showing nothing by the boulder. The second photo was blurred, but there was definitely a man standing within the shadow of the rocks. *Thank you, God*, Win whispered to himself.

Phillips moved to his chair behind the desk and ran his hand along his chin for a couple of seconds. Win knew they'd won round one.

"Ranger Hechtner, if you're going to assist in operational planning, I need to know the full extent of your relationship with Luke Bordeaux."

Trey let out a deep breath and leaned forward in his chair. "I met Luke shortly after I moved to Yellowstone a little over five years ago. He was starting a hunting-guide business and I'd transferred here from Zion National Park. Luke and I became good friends. We did things socially with our wives and children. About fourteen months ago he was indicted on poaching and conspiracy charges. In my opinion, those charges were fabricated by the FBI agent stationed here. The Park Service assisted the FBI in the prosecution of the case, and my contact with Luke ended then. I hadn't seen him in nearly a year until yesterday."

"How would you characterize your relationship before his trouble with the law?"

"He was my best friend. He was like a brother to me, sir."

All the men were quiet.

"Why'd you volunteer to work with us, Hechtner?" Phillips asked.

"This is my home and the place I'm sworn to protect. Candidly, sir, many of the other agencies, including some of the Denver FBI folks, are spending their energy and time infighting and jockeying for position on the case, while our agency is sidelined. I've been here a relatively long time. . . . I know the people and the park. I think I can contribute to your effort."

Phillips paused for only a second. "Smith, why don't you and Stoddard take Ranger Hechtner down the hall and get some coffee. Let me visit with Win for a minute."

Win stayed put while the others left. Phillips pivoted his chair and stared out at the snow through the dirty window as he spoke. "Well, you're even quicker on your feet than I gave you credit for. . . . Did you know Bordeaux was in the last photo, or make a wild guess?"

"Not a wild guess. Maybe an educated guess."

Phillips turned back and met Win's eyes. Win looked back and didn't blink. They sat there in silence for longer than most people would have. Win remembered his daddy always said silence could be the most productive part of a negotiation. Phillips had apparently gotten that message somewhere too.

The commander finally spoke. "If we believe your source, we have at least fifteen heavily armed, well-trained bad guys out there somewhere, another fifteen-plus still at the compound. We have several agencies more interested in their turf battles than in stopping a real attack, and we have an entourage of dignitaries who are determined to be here in five days. We have no aerial surveillance this morning because of the weather, we have little or no intel the bad guys aren't privy to, and we have a very capable man volunteering to help us who is emotionally tied to one of the more dangerous bad guys. What would you do?"

Win blinked and sat back when he heard the question. He answered slowly, "I'd have someone do some heavy leaning on all the agencies, including the Bureau, to get everyone on the same page, while I focused on finding the leak. I'd postpone any offensive action until the leak is sealed and I had a better feel for the overall situation. I'd have my folks do operational planning on various scenarios until the weather clears, and I'd keep all of my intel close to the vest. I'd also take advantage of Trey's local knowledge in finding the leak and on operational avenues for the dignitaries and the compound. Sir, I do trust him, but I suppose given the circumstances, I'd have someone watch him like a hawk."

"Not a bad overall analysis. Can you watch him like a hawk?"

"Yes, sir."

"Good. Then he won't have the opportunity to disarm you again." Phillips actually smiled slightly. "You can work the case matters out of your own office, but I want nothing on your computer, phones, or office chitchat relating to the HRT operation. This is unusual, but we're going to operate separately from most of the Bureau assets until we get this leak ferreted out. If Hechtner's agency agrees, he'll work out of this office under your direction. You'll both report to Matt Smith. He's my senior team leader. Got it?"

"Yes, sir."

He glanced at the window again, then back to Win. "I met with Mr. Givens earlier this morning and we've postponed any action against the compound for at least two days. Too many bad things could happen if we went in under these circumstances." He started to stand. "Oh, you may notice my men tend to be a little ramped up before an operation—don't let it bother you. We're all on the same team here. Welcome aboard, Win."

"Thank you, sir." Win smiled to himself. Not even 9:00 a.m., and they'd just won round two.

* * *

It would only be a few days now—all of the preparations had been made. Wasn't much else left to do; it would happen one way or the other. The rain was coming down sideways, and the heavy gray clouds had obscured the mountains. Supposed to turn to sleet, then snow before noon. The radio this morning said it was already nearly a whiteout at Mammoth and throughout the national park. It had been downright beautiful most of yesterday, and now winter was raising its ugly head. Spring had just been playing with them; it wasn't anywhere near ready to settle in. Winter was set to roar back. He flipped up the collar on his tan slicker and pulled down his Stetson as the wind whipped a sheet of cold rain onto the covered porch. It was that way in the West: best not get your hopes up for spring's fair weather—better to be on guard against winter's lingering hard hand. It gave no quarter to the unprepared. He reckoned he was the same way.

He was counting on the Federals overplaying their hand, so they'd lose either way they went. Raid the church compound and he'd have the press all over it—jack-booted Federal thugs infringing on their religious and civil liberties. A wonderful recruitment opportunity! If the Feds got cautious and chose to hang back, they'd just hit 'em with the original plan. They had the resources, they had the men, and Ron was chomping at the bit to go after the big score. He could go either way. . . . The Lord would show them His path.

He stood on the wide porch and watched his men troop back in from the firing range. They'd been at target practice in the awful weather since right after dawn. They had the look of soldiers, brothers-in-arms—slapping each other on the back, teasing, and laughing as they slogged through the mud back toward the assembly hall they'd set up in the big enclosed barn. It was nearly 9:00 a.m., time for him to lead the militiamen who remained at the compound in prayer. Most of the militiamen held regular jobs, but thankfully they'd all been able to take enough vacation time to work in the training and have a decent complement available to guard the compound at any given time. Dedication to the Lord aside, it hadn't hurt that he'd given each of them a generous payout in cash. Commitment to the cause was critical, but everyone still had to pay their bills.

The icy rain began to firm up and pellets of sleet bounced off the wet, wooden planks of the porch. The terrible weather should help Brother Ron and the fifteen men who'd left the compound move more freely into their assigned positions. Initial reports were that at least nine, maybe ten of their men were completely clear of the oppressors' surveillance. They needed to shake the other boys loose, but there was still time for that. The Federals couldn't use airplane or drone surveillance in the high winds and thick, low clouds predicted for tomorrow, much less in what was shaping up to be a blizzard today. Just another sign that the Lord stood behind their cause.

The Federals had been a little slower in responding to the militia threat than either he or Brother Ron had predicted. He needed them to focus on that activity. He didn't think it would even hurt if there were more confrontations—might bring in the national press a little quicker. Brother Ron didn't agree with the strategy of continued confrontations at this stage of the game, but then, they didn't have to agree. He was the Prophet. Yesterday's shooting of the man, Richter, by the Feds hadn't generated as much press coverage as he would have expected, but the turn in the weather and events in other parts of the country were factors in that, he supposed. He still needed to give prayer and thought to the botched assassination, but today it was important to focus on other issues.

This afternoon they'd launch their updated website. Two of the younger guys were internet wizards. Their new recruitment piece showed their peaceful church, their smiling schoolchildren, their trained militia, and the oppressors looking down on them from the surrounding hills and ravines. Brother Luke had taken great video footage of the Feds in their various surveillance outposts, not quite infringing on the church, but darn close. He'd even gotten night-vision shots of the military drones and airplanes the Feds were flying out of Livingston. The man was truly amazing at getting in close and getting the shots—just wait till he went after them with more than a camera! The video would generate indignation and anger from God-fearing people across the land. Once the uprising began, there would be no lack of enthusiastic patriots ready to step in and support the New America.

He pulled the heavy front doors open as one of the ladies made a dash from her car to the building. She stomped her rubber boots and grinned at him as she balanced two large pans. "Thank you, Prophet. Tell the men there'll be homemade cinnamon rolls in the dining room after they finish. I'll put more coffee on."

"Bless you, Sister Aubrey! That'll motivate me to move a little quicker!"

He hadn't made it two steps before Sister Bethany yanked the heavy door open and rushed outside. She was hugging her jacket to her and shooing a little boy in front of her with one hand. Her long blue skirt and her brown hair were blowing wild in the wind. The child had his head and his eyes down. "You wanted to see Colby, Prophet. . . . He's been a little terror this morning already!" Sister Bethany had apparently lost all patience with the youngster.

He smiled a quick smile at her. "Sister, the weather has worsened—get back inside and Colby and I'll have a man-to-man talk about this. I'll have him right in."

He went down on one knee on the wooden planks between the six-year-old and the cold rain. His back blocked the frigid wind off the child.

He gently raised the boy's chin up to face him. "Your daddy's off on a mission for the Lord, Colby. What would he think if he heard these reports I'm hearing about your bad behavior?"

A single tear slid down the face of Corporal Jeffery's little son. "I didn't mean to . . . she was hittin' at me . . . didn't mean to make her cry . . ."

"Look here, son." He met the boy's eyes. "Men of the Lord don't hit girls. Men of the Lord are kind and gentle to their sisters—and all girls are your sisters. Men of the Lord set the example for other men. Isn't that what God teaches us?"

"Un-huh . . . uh, yes, sir." Colby sniffed back a sob.

"We have people watching us, Colby. Some evil, some just lost, but they're looking for reasons to keep us down. We have to be shining examples of God's love to the world. Are you doing that?"

"Nuhh-uh. . . But she hit me first!"

"What?" He had to stifle a grin at the boy's indignation.

"No, sir. Sorry. Sorry I hit her."

"Then you go tell your sister that, and your teacher, and your class. And you tell them from here on out you're going to be a real man of the Lord. Can you do that, Colby?"

"Yes, sir." He nodded and dropped his head again. He was dying to run for the door.

"I saw your marks in reading and writing last week. Good work! I'm really proud of you, and I know your mom and dad are too."

The child's eyes shot up. They sparkled at the praise.

"Go on back to Sister Bethany. I know I'll be hearing only good reports!"

The little boy ran toward the double front doors just as the Prophet's phone buzzed.

"Yello!" He called into the phone and stood as another gust of liquid ice hit the back of his slicker.

"Hey, after watching the stars last night, I've decided to come on back to the church this morning. No reason not to!" He laughed that sinister laugh of his. "I thought you'd want to know, on account of the fine weather, Legion won't be a factor for a couple of days, but Malachi will be with us soon. It's happening. Malachi is coming." His voice got tighter. "If you're still set on it, we can buy a couple of ponies in the lowlands. We can make the purchase within the next ten days. I have Two on it. Whatever you say." He waited.

"Ah, look forward to seeing you—you can tell me all about it! On the purchase . . . no, no, not with the weather this helpful. Not really any need today. Take care." He slipped the phone into his pocket and smiled as he stepped off the porch directly into the sleet for the short walk to the big barn. He was going to be a few minutes late for prayers.

The code with Brother Ron on the brief cell phone call was a keyword code: simple and effective. He decoded it again as he walked. One of their sources in law enforcement, or *stars*, had told Ron that the Feds had Ron back under visual surveillance, so there was no point in Ron staying out. Having him tagged was no great loss, since he was scheduled to come back to the compound tonight anyway if the Fed's Hostage Rescue Team, or *Legion*, wasn't set to attack tomorrow. The coded message told him the HRT raid had been postponed for at least two days due to the bad weather. And the purchase of two ponies? His smile widened. He'd just vetoed Brother Clay's planned killing of two FBI surveillance agents, within the next ten minutes, somewhere in the park. The militia's sniper, Clay Ferguson, or *Two*, would be disappointed, but no need to stir the pot today with Malachi on the way!

Now about those prayers . . .

CHAPTER TWENTY-TWO

By ten o'clock that wintery morning, Win was trying his best to project some degree of competence while surrounded by the Hostage Rescue Team's high-octane juggernaut.

Supervisory Special Agent Matt Smith, who was called an operator supervisor in HRT parlance, was a tall guy from Georgia in his late thirties who looked like he could play linebacker for any NFL team. He had a friendly, down-to-earth manner that contradicted his penetrating eyes. He assigned Win the job of developing suspects related to the information leak. Trey was to assist Win and would also serve as HRT's main resource to get a feel for the park's terrain, including the small patch of real estate twenty-four miles southwest of Mammoth where the dedication of the Cohn Monument would take place in five days, on May 12th.

Win set up shop in an empty space down the hall from Phillips's office. While the support staff got him plugged into the FBI computer systems and set up a landline, Win pulled out a yellow legal pad and began work the old-fashioned way, writing down the known time line of the intelligence leaks. He'd been at it for well over three hours before Trey stuck his head in the makeshift office.

"The team's breaking for lunch, so I'm free. What've you got?"

Win stood up and stretched, glad for the interruption. "Trying to pinpoint the time line of the leaks. Praying it's a hacker—would make life simpler. Denver's got a team of technical folks working on that end.

I'm just looking at on-site personnel, and I'll need your help with that; you know lots of these folks." He motioned Trey into the office. "Drag over a chair. They been treating you alright?"

Trey dusted the chair off and closed the door before he sat down. "Yeah, sharp bunch, real professional. They understand the difficulties of working in remote locations, and they're accustomed to doing a job under less than optimal circumstances. They're not, however, accustomed to having dozens of curious tourists milling around." He glanced down at the tan ranger hat he was holding. "Are we supposed to be pretending we're seismologists, like these guys? Wearing civilian clothes?"

"Naw, since we're gonna be out spy catching, we probably need to look like we do normally—otherwise it would be a tip-off. Don't you think?" Win replied.

"Yup, guess so, but I'm gonna go with my field uniform and lose the tie. . . . On another subject, what do you suppose the odds were of that drone spotting us up on that ridge yesterday morning?" the ranger asked.

"I sure wouldn't think too high." Win shrugged and sat back down. "Got a little tense in there this morning, huh?"

"When those two guys came in behind me and Phillips pulled out those aerials . . . I thought . . ." Trey looked to the side and paused for a long moment.

Win finished the sentence for him. "You thought I'd double-crossed you. You know, Trey, if we're gonna work together, it would be real nice if we could trust each other." *Never mind that I'm charged with keeping an eye on you.* He ignored his internal moral dilemma and didn't miss a beat. "I won't ever forget the time you spent with me in the chapel after I shot Richter. We oughta be able to build some trust off that." *Uh-huh, that's all true.* Win was having a hard time reconciling his little lecture on trust with the reality of his mission to make sure Trey wasn't the mole.

"Takes time to build trust, Win." Trey was quiet, then he nodded and smiled. "You bailed us both out today. After watching you this morning with Phillips and his boys, well, if you do decide to leave the

FBI, you'd make one hell of a lawyer. How'd you know Luke was in that last photo?"

"Didn't for sure. Had to play a wild card. Now we have the chance to work with the A-team and make a difference in the outcome here. Oh, meant to tell you—Ellie Bordeaux was spotted coming back into their place yesterday afternoon. No kids with her. I'll bet Luke didn't know she was coming home. . . . That is not good news."

"That's for sure." Trey looked down at his hat again. "I even sent my wife, daughter, and dog to my sister's in Bozeman for a few days. They left before the weather turned. I'm not comfortable with what's going on here, plus it doesn't look like I'll be spending much time at home for a while anyway. At least I won't be constantly worrying about them." A pause. "No way to warn Ellie off?"

"You know there isn't. . . . Luke Bordeaux has enough sense to send her away again. He just needs to tell her to stay gone till this is over."

"Just like that! Tell her to stay gone!" Trey shook his head and grinned at Win. "It's sure sounding like you've never been married."

* * *

While the team took their late lunch break, Trey made it back to his office to nail a few things down and Win did the same. Win logged on to his computer and scrolled though Murray's updated report on the Bureau's considerable efforts to track down the source of the contract hit on his life. While the Arm of the Lord Church was still the prime suspect, with the exception of Luke's conversation with the Thayer brothers, there was no concrete evidence Richter had met with or talked to anyone in the church group. The Violent Crime Squad was nearly twenty-four hours out from the shooting and coming up empty.

The fingerprint results had come back on Richter. Win thought long and hard before he clicked on the section of the report detailing the life of the man he'd killed. He skimmed it while he fought off the sick feeling in his gut. It didn't help to know Richter had killed several men who were suspected turncoats in the white supremacy movement two years ago. Richter had gone to ground after that massacre, but he was strongly suspected in several murders since that time. He'd been a professional killer in the shadowy world of racial hatred, anti-Semitism, and anti-government extremism. In Bureau lingo, Richter was a real bad actor.

Until yesterday, Win didn't think he'd met any truly evil people in his twenty-eight years on this earth. As he thought back to those flat gray eyes—Richter's eyes—he decided he'd met his first evil man. But he wasn't sure it made any difference. *I still killed a man.* He fought down the bile rising in his throat. . . . He clicked off the screen and forced his mind to shift to other matters.

He'd nearly finished the bulk of the documentation for Luke and Ellie's confidential human source files, but his near-death experience with Richter spurred him to complete the voluminous paperwork. He couldn't carry out his commitment to Bordeaux if he ended up dead before the requests were approved. Neither Luke nor Ellie had asked for money, but in the workings of government, a cash payment was the cleanest route to go. He could figure out a way to get Ellie and the kids out of Montana later, if it came to that, but he reasoned they deserved a financial reward as well. The Bureau routinely paid six figures to their informants in terrorism cases, often for information far less valuable than what he'd received from Luke and Ellie. Luke was too proud and stubborn to accept any money, so he sent a request for $100,000 for the information provided by Ellie and an additional $100,000 to be held in trust for the children. The money would be transferred to Ellie Bordeaux upon the indictment of any of the numerous suspects in this case. Convictions, which could take forever, weren't necessary.

He also drew up ironclad protections from prosecution for Ellie and Luke on any aspect of the case, DOJ commitments to drop all pending charges against Luke, and authorization to reinstate his hunting-guide license on federal lands. There were provisions for the government to provide medical care and attorneys' fees on any matter related to the False Prophet case. Win leaned back in his chair and scanned his work one more time to ensure that no one could determine the real identities of his sources from the online forms. All human sources were given code numbers, and all source reports went into a separate Bureau online file system; someone reading these materials should not be able to determine the identity of the informant. Fulfilling his commitment to Luke was both gratifying and humbling. Without Ellie's help, they might not have a case, and without Luke's warnings, he might not have his life.

*　*　*

He'd just hit the send key on the computer when his personal cell rang. He knew the number that popped up on his phone better than he knew his own. No name appeared—he'd removed the name weeks ago. He held the phone in his left hand and stared at it with a mixture of apprehension and hope. Just seeing the number caused his breathing to stop. On the fourth ring, he slid the lock off to answer. He wasn't even sure he could speak, but he found himself saying hello in a questioning tone, as if someone else could have been on the call.

Less than twenty-four hours ago he'd faced a man intent on killing him—he'd killed that man. Hearing her soft voice now hit him harder emotionally. He felt deeply ashamed of that.

They talked for only a couple of minutes—she had to go to her surgery rounds. She told him she'd heard about the Yellowstone shooting from a friend; he knew she never watched the news. She said she knew in her spirit it was him, and he didn't deny it. She wanted him to know she was praying for him. Wanted him to know she was concerned. She said all the right things except for the thing he wanted so desperately to hear: that she wanted him back in her life. She didn't say that, and it took every ounce of will he possessed not to plead with her to come back to him. He kept his composure, thanked her for calling, told her it was good to hear her voice, great to hear she was doing well, told her goodbye, and punched END. He sat staring at the red button on the phone and started falling apart.

"You okay?" When there was no response, Deb asked, "Win, you okay?" She was standing in his open doorway with her coat and notebook in her hands. He managed to look up for a moment. He knew he was blinking tears away. He bit down on his lower lip and knew he couldn't say anything. *No, I'm not okay. Will I ever be okay?* He turned his eyes away and covered his face with his hands. She slid in the office and closed the door, calling over her shoulder to someone that she'd meet them at the Justice Center.

He fought to control his emotions. *C'mon, Win! A real man doesn't break down in tears in the office, for Pete's sake!* He'd always thought of himself as a strong, roll-with-the-punches, suck-it-up type guy. The breakup with Shelby was proving him wrong—big-time wrong.

Deb dropped her coat onto one of the guest chairs and leaned forward on the back of the other chair across from his desk. "Win, I think you've underestimated how emotionally devastating a shooting incident can be, and you've had two within two days. And the outcome . . . the man's death. And something else is going on? The phone call?" Deb honestly didn't get the concept of privacy, but at that moment, Win didn't have the strength to ask for any.

He found his voice, but it was barely a whisper. "That was the girl I was engaged to. . . . First time, uh, first time we've talked in a long time—she'd heard about the shooting." He pulled in a deep breath and tried again to get it together. "Uhmmm, we dated for five years—broke it off three months ago." He stared down at the desk. "I can't seem to move on. Just when I think I'm getting better . . ." He quit talking and closed his eyes again.

"Five years! Ohmygosh! . . . Healing isn't a straight-line progression, Win, it's one step forward, two steps back. Sometimes for a long, long time. Three months is nothing! And with everything else you're dealing with—oh, man!" Deb rocked back on her heels and he could tell from her voice she was fixing to launch into action. "You wanna talk about it some? Might help?"

He shook his head *no*, which she somehow took as *yes*, and she gently starting talking about how life often throws us punches. He'd never seen her go thirty seconds without checking her phone, but she somehow managed to give him her undivided attention for more than fifteen minutes. He didn't tell her all the details, didn't tell her all the things he'd done wrong or didn't do right. Instead, he let her coax out his feelings of loss and abandonment—they never even touched on his equally consuming emotions of guilt and regret. But for a first step, as she put it, it was enough. Enough to put his feet back on the ground, enough to pull his focus back to the present . . . enough to realize the world hadn't ended quite yet. *Not quite yet.*

* * *

The two-block walk back to the HRT building was even tougher after lunch than it'd been this morning. The weather was as bad as Win had seen it at Mammoth, with high winds and heavy, blowing snow. He'd switched into his insulated hiking boots and warmer parka. He could barely catch a glimpse of the American flag on the fifty-foot flagpole standing between the FBI office and the park's Visitor Center. The sharp clanging of the flag's hardware against the silver pole was the only sound as the snow and wind tore all other noise away. When they finally entered the HRT building, he and his rangers shook themselves off like dogs shaking off water.

A few minutes earlier, the FBI's surveillance supervisor had given Win her assessment of the day's situation: "Surveillance has gone to hell. Aerial assets can't get up, most of our planted GPS trackers are sending faulty readings because of atmospheric interference from the storm, and our folks on the ground can't see a damn thing!" The Bureau's operational capability was going nowhere fast. Win figured the HRT boys were gonna be stressed. But Win's supposition of anxious HRT operators was incorrect. The eighteen men on the two tactical teams were sleeping on cots, listening to music on headsets, or quietly playing cards. They were apparently accustomed to the "hurry up and wait" routine. Their numerous support personnel were scurrying around doing dozens of critical tasks, but the warriors were patiently waiting for the war.

Trey and a couple of their intelligence analysts were going over aerial maps of the area surrounding the church compound, and Win started back through reams of personnel time sheets for the forty-something folks who could have had relatively easy access to the compromised intel. The only positive in his tedious job was its requirement for complete focus—he didn't have the chance to let his mind wander back to the conversation with Shelby.

"Win Tyler!"

"Sir!"

"With me! Now!" Matt Smith sang out as he strode down the hallway past Win's open door. Win lunged out of his little office and swung into the HRT's makeshift operations center, four steps behind Smith. They both stopped and stared up at an overhead screen showing a bright digital readout of what appeared to be a conversation between two people, with one part of the text in blue and the second part in red.

Smith didn't glance at him as he spoke. "This came in from Ron Chandler's, a.k.a. Ron King's, cell phone to Daniel Shepherd's cell phone at 9:02 this morning. Our guys in the Justice Center screwed around with it for six hours before sending it over to us. . . . That kind of delay is not gonna happen again!"

Ken Stoddard and two of HRT's intelligence analysts joined them in the middle of the room, while a thin, techie-looking analyst filled them in on what they had so far.

"We call this a schoolboy code—real simple and, unfortunately, real hard to break. Works great with groups who know each other well. It's a favorite among drug dealers, illicit lovers, and junior high school boys. The folks over in the Justice Center haven't gotten anywhere with it. It wasn't sent up to the Bureau's Cryptanalysis Unit until about mid-morning. No word back yet on their analysis. We've matched a little of it up based on earlier conversations between Chandler and Shepherd that Agent Tyler's source reported on." He touched his electronic tablet to highlight several words. "We believe *stars* is a reference to whoever they've got on the inside in law enforcement . . . but *Legion?* Don't know. . . . The reference to a delay of two days because of the 'fine' weather? Could very well refer to our postponement of the raid on the church compound due to the snowstorm. Purchasing ponies?" He shook his head. "No idea."

Smith jumped in there. "The decision to delay the raid was reached at 0745 hours, 7:45 this morning. How could they have that information that quickly? By nine o'clock! Win, how many names on your list right now? Cross-check your list with this new time line. Can't be that many potential suspects out there on this."

He didn't wait for Win to answer. "Our guys will get you the tapes on this call, and other bits we've picked up that appear to be in code. Phillips says you're up on this Bible stuff." He motioned for the tech guy to highlight one section of the screen. "See here . . . this Malachi thing is obviously a game changer for them. Chandler says 'Malachi will be with us soon. It's happening. Malachi is coming.' Who or what is Malachi?"

"Uh, the book of the Bible? The Jewish prophet?" Win was trying to figure out which of Smith's questions to answer first. The others were all waiting for him to say something else. He mentally regrouped. "Okay, if they're using words from Scripture or common usage as symbols for other things . . . they may have a pattern. What's their pattern? If *star*—like a sheriff's badge—is a lawman, then *legion* . . . uh, maybe like five thousand, a Roman legion. No, no, they're using it more like a name. . . . Legion was the name of the demon Jesus cast out of a man near the Sea of Galilee. The demon's name was Legion because he was comprised of many demons in one host. That could be a reference to us—to their many enemies, all within the federal government. Are they using *Malachi* as a thing rather than a name? It's not one of those books of the Bible that you hear about much. Old Testament. Malachi was one of the Minor Prophets—an Israelite prophet."

Smith cocked his head and raised his eyebrows. "Why would these guys use Jewish references in their code? Don't they hate the Jews?"

"Their theology isn't exactly consistent—that's for sure." Win shrugged. "Could be a code name for one of the Jewish dignitaries who are coming here . . . maybe the Ambassador?"

"I'm sure we have someone who's up on this religious terminology at the Cryptanalysis Unit, but since no one has broken the code yet, how 'bout you give it a try." Smith was staring at the screen, but his order was directed at Win.

Surely the guy is kidding. "Does this take precedence over my work on the intel leak?" Win asked.

Smith glanced at him, perplexed. "'Course not! Weather is supposed to be nearly this bad tomorrow. Just get on it."

"Yes, sir. I'm on it!" He hoped his attempt at enthusiasm would
cancel out his initial hesitation.

Smith paused as he started down the hallway. "Oh, I expect you
and Hechtner to be sharp, so get with our logistics folks and eat dinner
with the teams. They're bringing in real food tonight. You'll need some
sleep too."

Uh-huh . . . and how many hours are in your days? Win gave an
affirmative nod. *Oh well, rather be held to high expectations than low
ones.*

* * *

Win didn't make it back to his office in the FBI building that day, but
he and Trey made good progress on eliminating potential suspects on
the leak. Every time Win came up for breath from the mounds of paper
and computer-generated personnel forms, he prayed that the tech guys
would conclude that some hacker had gained access to their systems.
But so far, no luck there.

His security detail had been reassigned for the afternoon to rescue
snow-stranded tourists after Chief Randall decided that if Win wasn't
safe among the FBI's most elite tactical group, he wouldn't be safe anywhere. The blizzard eased back a little as the afternoon turned to evening. Win could make out a small herd of elk wandering down the
snow-covered street outside his office's filthy window.

He and Trey were both growing more comfortable with the HRT
team members, although *comfortable* wasn't exactly the right word.
The HRT operators were members of an incredibly exclusive and very
dangerous club—and they knew it. Anyone else, no matter their status, was just not on their level. Win wasn't sure if the HRT culture
encouraged that underlying aura of superiority, but it was evident,
even when they tried to dial it back to be more welcoming. Thankfully,
football was a common interest, and they shared a steak dinner in
their thrown-together dining room while hashing out every big game

of the last several seasons. He wasn't surprised that some of the men knew of Arkansas wide receiver Win Tyler. As they ate, several of them recounted games and pivotal plays from years ago. Win smiled to himself as he reflected on that. Shelby had always been confounded that he could remember what she considered completely irrelevant facts and statistics about college football and other players, even from decades past, but he could never seem to remember a grocery list with more than three items.

Long after dinner, as Trey was headed downstairs to work with the teams on possible intrusion points in the compound's terrain, Win caught up with him.

"Hey, hey . . . I'm gonna be leaving directly, maybe eleven or so. How 'bout you stay at my place for a couple nights while we get this leak worked out. We can't stay down here and work all night, and if you were there we could bounce ideas off each other without picking up the phone. I'm still not sure I trust the phones." Trey seemed to be considering his offer, so Win kept up the persuasion. "Your family's out of town, and two of your rangers will be outside, guarding my house. Just give it some thought."

He was hoping Trey would agree; otherwise, he'd have no way of keeping up with the guy. It was unrealistic to think he could actually watch the ranger 24/7, but having a little sleepover at his house sure would help.

CHAPTER TWENTY-THREE

Dark was still holding on as Win finished fixing ham and cheese omelets and Trey took coffee out to the near-frozen rangers who were guarding Win's house in the continuing awful weather. The snow was only coming down in tiny, crusty flakes this morning, but the wind was howling straight out of the North Pole, the clouds were at treetop level, and most of the roads were sheets of ice. The two rangers were holed up in the small frame garage located at the rear of Win's backyard. The little yellow building was actually a 1910 carriage shed, or so the historical brochure said, but it hadn't been used for anything except storage for many years. The shed was certainly serving a practical purpose in the lousy weather by keeping some really good rangers from freezing to death.

Trey stomped his boots off in the mudroom and threw his cap and coat across the washer. "I see they got everything fixed after the shooting," he casually remarked as he slid into one of the dining room chairs and dove into his food.

"Yeah, looks good as new—could almost pretend nothing happened." Win didn't want to let his mind go there this morning.

They ate, then drank an extra cup of coffee and outlined the day's schedule, which Win knew would probably change the minute they hit the office. He and Trey had gotten nowhere in their biblical research of Ron Chandler's reference to Malachi, but they'd eliminated four more potential suspects as they continued to whittle down the list of possible moles. Not bad for an impromptu sleepover.

"Hey, babe!" The ranger's countenance changed as he answered his phone. He smiled at something his wife said. Then, "Hate to tell you, but this FBI fella is in the running for tastiest ham and cheese omelet in town. Told him you were the best cook in the park. Can't wait for you to get home and defend your title!" He laughed into the phone at her reply. "Yup, everything's going fine. Tell me how you and . . ."

Win finished putting their plates in the dishwasher and left the room to give the guy some privacy. He heard the ranger laugh at something else she said, and sadness found him. He absently wondered if Shelby had found some guy to tease and laugh with over breakfast, someone to help her ease into the day.

* * *

Fifteen minutes later, the protection detail dropped Trey off at HRT's building and slid their Tahoe to a stop on the ice next to Win's office. Win was giving himself two hours this cold Friday morning to catch up on case-related matters before he joined Trey for more work on the leak. After the lengthy round of case meetings and calls, he looked up to see Deb and Ramona leaning into his open doorway. He signaled them in as he wrapped up a call with Denver. Since dinner Monday night, Ramona had been friendly but professional. He sure hoped she kept it that way, but darn, she was wearing those swaying silver earrings again. He forced his attention off that distraction and onto her words.

"I'm reviewing the background research on Daniel Shepherd, and I've run across something you need to give a look-see. I ran it by Emily late yesterday afternoon and she waved me off, but you should at least see it. . . . May be nothing. . . ."

"Sure, what've you got?" Win hoped he didn't sound too impatient. He was standing now and anxious to get back to the leak investigation.

Ramona and Deb stood over his desk, and Ramona laid out several eight-by-ten-inch black-and-white photos on top of it.

"Where'd you get these? What's this about?" Win was puzzled and frustrated; he had no time to fool around. The photos were of him.

Ramona was totally noncommittal, and Deb seemed to be intrigued.

"These seven photos either came out of your personnel file, or off an internet search for Winston R. Tyler, or from some other internal Bureau file. Look them over. See anything unusual?" Ramona asked.

He glanced through the photos quickly: a photo of him in a Razorback football uniform; another lower-quality shot at football practice; one of him with a rifle, probably at a marksmanship tournament; two candid shots of him in workout clothes; and two photos taken indoors. None of the pictures was recent; they were all several years old. He flipped them back down on the desk and shrugged. He really didn't have time for this.

"What about these two?" Ramona dropped the additional photos on his desk. The first was attached to a press clipping from the *Livingston Enterprise*, the Gardiner-Yellowstone area's only daily newspaper. The article was dated March 25th, and it announced Win's appointment as the new resident special agent for Yellowstone National Park. It gave brief background information on him and included his Bureau file photograph. It was the standard press release for any agent receiving a new posting in a small town.

The second photo was a grainy blowup from a news article published in the *Rapid City Tribune*. It accompanied a lengthy article entitled "Separatist's Son Shot by FBI in Robbery Attempt." It was dated four years ago. Win did a double take at the two photos from the newspaper articles and slowly sat down in his chair. He didn't know what to say.

Ramona tossed three of the other photos Win had assumed were of him on top of the photo from South Dakota. "These three came out of Dennison Shepherd's file at Headquarters. Dennie at his junior-college football practice, a photo taken during one of his many trials—that one for assault—and a surveillance shot."

Ramona crossed her arms. "Daniel Shepherd's youngest son died the day of the bank robbery. He wounded the bank guard and two customers. Four years ago, you'd have passed for brothers, maybe even twin brothers just based on photographs. His features were rougher than yours and he was two inches shorter. I photoshopped tats off his neck and an arm. But if Daniel Shepherd saw the Bureau's announcement in the newspaper with your picture . . . it had to have brought back some memories." She let it hang there.

But Win knew. He'd felt it since he and Phillips talked after he shot Richter. He'd felt the attacks were personal. Now he knew why. He scanned the South Dakota news article. Dennison Shepherd, a.k.a. "Dennie," began a life of crime at a young age, killed at the age of twenty-six by the FBI during a pursuit after a violent bank robbery. This was deeply personal. This was about revenge. And it wasn't over yet.

* * *

Later that morning, Win was mulling over the ramifications of Ramona's photo investigation as he walked down the hall in HRT's building to get a third cup of coffee. From Win's perspective, the unfortunate consequence of the probable connection between the attempts on his life and Daniel Shepherd meant that it was only a matter of time before Mr. Givens pulled him off the case and out of danger. He and Deb had agreed to forward Ramona's research and their conclusions to the ASAC, bypassing Emily, and let the chips fall where they may. It would be irresponsible to stay in Mammoth if some personal vendetta had fueled the attacks. A personal motive made it much more likely Shepherd would strike again—and much more likely someone else would get hurt. He'd hate to pull back, to leave, but he knew it was the right thing to do. He couldn't afford to put anyone else in danger because he wanted to stay in the game. After all, what was it he'd yelled at Emily on the bridge? *It's not a game—it's life or death.*

* * *

The rest of Win's day consisted of nose-to-the-grindstone reviews of personnel files, time sheets, and video surveillance footage from the

Justice Center. By late afternoon, he and Trey had narrowed down their focus on the leaks to that building. Based on the time line they'd developed, almost everything that had been compromised had originated there, especially the specifics that Luke gave them on agent numbers, surveillance rotations, and aerial-asset scheduling. Their list of "possibles" had spanned the gamut—everyone from the cleaning people to Park Service employees, even little Jason was scrutinized— but the names on their lists were dwindling.

Evening rolled around and Win was puzzled no one had called him about the Daniel Shepherd connection to the attempts on his life. Maybe Mr. Givens had agreed with Emily that the evidence of motive was too flimsy, or just as likely, events on the case were moving so rapidly that his bosses had other, more pressing matters to deal with. He knew the surveillance efforts were going as badly today as yesterday. He also knew the Park Service and Secret Service honchos were now pushing for the Israeli contingent to enter the park through West Yellowstone rather than Mammoth. That was a logical decision, since many of the roads in the western part of the park were now open. It wouldn't eliminate the potential threat from the Arm of the Lord Church, but it would certainly move the Israelis and the other VIPs beyond the church's immediate vicinity. West Yellowstone was typically a two-hour drive from Mammoth, and from the current location of most, if not all, of the bad guys.

It was nearly 9:00 p.m. and Win was getting cross-eyed reading through the enigmatic Book of Malachi for the third time in less than two days. No one in the Bureau had broken the church's code, and so far he had nothing to contribute. He was closing the Scripture when Trey stuck his head in Win's tiny office.

"They're still looking at a possible preemptive strike on the compound day after tomorrow, or maybe a redeploy to West Yellowstone." Trey shook his head. "It's all up in the air. I'm finished with the logistical stuff tonight. You wanna call it a night and maybe do a prowl-through of a couple of our suspects' offices real early morning? Might turn up something."

"Alrighty. . . . We've gotten 'em whittled down. I've got emergency requests in for financial and phone records on seven potential suspects." Win watched Trey lean into the doorframe. He sure wasn't gonna mention that one of the seven was Trey Hechtner. No red flags on the ranger yet. But he wasn't finding smoking guns on any of their other suspects either—it was a slow, methodical process.

"Any hits?" Trey asked.

"Nope, not yet." Win averted his eyes, but kept talking. "Let me shut down. I'm starving—I'll fix us a late supper at my place. Meet you at the door in ten."

Win wasn't feeling real good about spying on Trey while Trey was supposedly helping him catch the spy. He was actually beginning to like the guy; they'd worked like partners these last two days. But every FBI agent had the espionage tale of Special Agent Robert Hanssen drilled into them at Quantico. For years the FBI agent in charge of catching an internal mole, a man who did incredible harm to the country and cost several lives, was Agent Hanssen himself. The ultimate example of the fox guarding the henhouse. Win watched Trey move away from the door. *Still doesn't make me feel any better about it.*

* * *

He and Trey were wolfing down grilled cheese sandwiches with Cokes and going back and forth on possible leak scenarios when the local TV news came on at ten o'clock. The first story showed a Bozeman reporter standing in the wind and snow in front of the Mammoth Hot Springs Hotel, giving an update on the shoot-out that occurred outside the lobby three days ago. Thankfully, details were still scarce, and the park's pert, outdoorsy public affairs lady said that federal law enforcement groups were taking part in drills in the Yellowstone area and that the deceased man, who had a long criminal history, had stumbled into an FBI group. Names were still not being released and the FBI would not comment. Yellowstone is perfectly safe now and all is well—that was the impression given in the reporter's wrap-up. Win wished that were true.

Win was lying on the couch and Trey was stretched out on the rug in front of the TV as they watched the rest of the news broadcast. The weather was forecast to improve in the next few days, and Montana State had just landed a three-star recruit for next year's basketball team. Trey wasn't a big talker, but Win took the opportunity to probe a little.

"Why'd you go to Montana State? You're from Idaho, right?"

"Football and basketball scholarships got me to Montana State. They had a good football team, and my folks didn't really want me to go to the Northwest or down into Utah."

"What about Boise State?"

"Just didn't seem like a good fit, and they wanted me to play a single sport. Plus I'm a rancher. Montana State had the ranch-management program I wanted."

"What'd you play?"

"Played quarterback. . . . We had some good years."

No kidding, Win thought. He knew Trey Hechtner had been the quarterback for a team that had won two Big Sky Conference championships. He'd also started in basketball his last two years at the university. The guy was a ballplayer. Win hadn't had to pull Jason's trick and google Trey to find those facts. Instead he'd requested an FBI profile of Trey from an intelligence analyst two days ago. He knew everything—from the ranger's 4-H awards in high school, to his four speeding tickets in college, to the timing of his car payments. There wasn't any public record or article the Bureau couldn't pull up quickly. Private matters were a lot trickier to uncover without a subpoena—short of that, he needed to get the guy talking. He was making a stab at that tonight.

"Said you were a rancher. . . . Planned to go back to the ranch after school?"

"Nope, not out of college. I've wanted to be a park ranger in Yellowstone since I came here for the first time as a seven-year-old. I got a seasonal position here during the summers of my master's program. This is my dream job, you know. It's my calling. After I retire, we might go back to Idaho, maybe start our own horse farm. My brother-in-law works with my dad on the ranch." He stretched, reached behind the chair, and rubbed Gruff's ears.

Win couldn't believe the cat was letting the guy touch him. For some stupid reason it annoyed him that his cat, who he fed and cleaned up after—every single day—had taken up with a complete stranger. It got his focus off track. He needed to be asking the ranger questions he already knew the answers to.

Win tried to ease back into his low-key interrogation. "That's a blessing to know what you always wanted to do. I was never sure, just knew I didn't want to go back to farming. I loved so much of it, but a farmer has no control over his life. . . . I guess I needed that control."

Trey snorted a little as he continued to pet the cat. "Hate to break it to you, Win, but we're never really in control. Remember what the Bible says, 'The mind of man plans his way, but the Lord directs his steps.' Just when you think you've got it nailed—when you're totally on track, when you're getting cocky about it—then God lets life step in and teaches you a little humility."

He looked into Win's eyes. "How'd you end up in the FBI?" Win felt the mood shift. *Uh-oh, he's turning this around on me.*

"Uh, went to law school since I couldn't think of anything else to do . . . didn't really like it . . ."

"But let me guess, you made all As and were editor of the *Law Review*." Trey sat up and pulled his arms around his knees.

"What's with the sarcasm? I wanna have a good working relationship with you."

"Is that so? Wouldn't ever take up poker if I was you, Win."

"Why? Why's that?" Win shifted on the couch and looked down at the man.

"You might not be too good at it. Not too good at covering your intent or your thoughts. You watch everyone's eyes—and I'll grant you, yours are hard to read. Yet every once in a while I see through you. I'm pretty good at poker, Win, and what I've seen in your eyes from time to time yesterday and today is not that trust you keep talking about. More goin' on here than you just inviting me over for a bunking party, some guy talk, and working on the case. You've got a separate agenda and I don't know what it is."

Well, dangit! I screwed that up. Win's instincts told him this guy was solid. If they were going to be a team, there had to be complete honesty; their lives could depend on it. He knew he'd been a fool to handle it this way. Orders or no orders, he could have handled it differently. Win took a deep breath and slouched back on the couch.

Trey leaned back against the front of the chair. "You want to tell me what's really going on?"

"Yes, I do. . . . I haven't been totally honest with you and I'm sorry for that. You're right. It's not my nature to hide things, to not be up-front . . . to mislead anyone. So here it is. Phillips knows how capable you are, and how valuable your assistance is to HRT and the Bureau in setting up the raid on the compound and protecting the folks who're coming in from Israel. But he's nervous about your relationship with Luke. He considers Bordeaux to be one of the most dangerous guys we're dealing with, and he warned me that there's no telling which side Luke will come down on when push comes to shove. I told Phillips you could help us tremendously in bringing down the bad guys, but under the circumstances—you being so close to Luke—you should be watched. Phillips asked me to work with you *and* keep an eye on you, to make sure Luke doesn't come back into the picture in a bad way."

Trey took that all in and finally dropped his eyes to stare down at the rug. He didn't make any comment.

"Put yourself in Phillips's place. . . . Put yourself in my place. What would you do? It comes across pretty clear you feel you let Luke down in some significant way in the past. It's possible he might pressure you to make it right now that y'all have reconnected." Win knew his efforts at reasoning were going nowhere.

Trey glanced at his watch and moved off the floor. He sat in the chair and pulled his boots on. "I'll, ahhh, go outside to check on my men. Then I'll sleep on it. Will let you know if I'm still on this assignment in the morning. Don't bother with breakfast. We're out of here at 5:30."

* * *

Win was eating a piece of toast in his kitchen when Trey came downstairs at 5:15 the next morning. Win poured them both coffee, then leaned back against the counter and waited for him to speak.

"Our goal is to stop the bad guys. We don't necessarily have to like each other to do that, but we do have to trust each other—if we don't, someone could get hurt. In order to have that trust, we have to be honest with each other. There is no partnership without that as the base. You and I are both Christians, and you were right the other day when you implied that our faith should be a strong foundation for that trust. But you didn't trust me to tell you if Luke makes an appearance, and that was wrong of you. That said . . . well, last night I thought about how you must have felt up on the ridge, with me holding your gun. I shouldn't have treated you like that. So we've both made mistakes here. Do you see it that way?"

"Yeah, I do," Win answered.

"If you still want me as a part of this operation, I'll be there beside you. But no more games."

"No more games." They shook hands on that and Win felt tremendous relief. He needed this guy. He needed a teammate. He needed a partner.

CHAPTER TWENTY-FOUR

Susan Hapsburg was on his radar. Not that he wanted it that way. She was funny and friendly and she seemed to have made it one of her goals in life to make him smile every time he saw her. She and her husband had moved to Mammoth three years ago, and she was in the process of transitioning out of her earlier career as a Park Service law enforcement ranger. Susan was smart, ambitious, and seriously conflicted about her dual roles as a police analyst and the mother of two-year-old twin daughters. Win figured that she'd taken the clerical Park Service position because it was low-key and predictable compared to a ranger's hectic schedule. One of her duties consisted of serving as the administrative officer of the area's annex unit of the FBI Joint Terrorism Task Force. She was the coordinator for JTTF training and information dissemination for a five-county area of Montana and Wyoming, as well as Yellowstone National Park. For the time being, Trey, Gus, four sheriff's deputies, and a couple of Montana game wardens were the only JTTF officers in their unit who weren't in the FBI. It wasn't what Congress had envisioned when the number of JTTFs dramatically expanded after the 9/11 attacks.

The JTTF concept was great: have all local and federal law enforcement agencies contribute men and women to a working group that would have top secret clearance to share both local and national tips and leads on potential terrorism activities. It was an effort by the FBI to coordinate resources and intelligence assets with local law enforcement. In reality, a lack of manpower in many rural areas, not to mention the lack of any impending terrorism threat in most regions, led to the disbanding or scaling back of many of the JTTF units across rural America. Johnson had done little to nothing to keep the local JTTF unit alive during the last several years, and Win saw an opening to contribute something, at least, to local law enforcement. It wasn't like he had much else to do during those first few days in Mammoth. Even before the False Prophet case gained momentum, he'd already held two meetings with Susan in the hope that they'd be able to recruit a few new JTTF members and get the local program back on track.

Susan's JTTF credentials gave her the FBI clearances to know much of the information that seemed to be falling into the wrong hands. Her office was in the Justice Center, down the hall from the break room. She was in a good position to either access or overhear plenty of sensitive information. And, unfortunately, she had a motive—she'd mentioned to Win more than once how tight her family's finances had become since the twins were born.

It was nearly 7:00 a.m., and Susan always got to the office early, even when she worked on Saturdays. Win knew that was so she could leave to pick up her girls at day care in Gardiner before 4:30. He had her schedule for the last ten days memorized. He was leaning back in a metal chair in her office, admiring her latest phone photos of the twins at play in yesterday's snow. She dumped her satchel on her desk in front of him and turned to get coffee from down the hall.

"Need to be taking sugar in your coffee, Win. Wouldn't hurt to sweeten up that smile a bit. . . . You've been frowning way too much lately—gonna break all the girls' hearts."

"No sugar . . . no thanks . . . but no way not to smile lookin' at these babies in the snow!" He grinned and winked at her and handed over her phone as she passed his chair on her way out the door.

She'd only been gone a moment when Trey appeared in the doorway, moved toward her desk, and began scanning every scrap of paper that was visible. "We'd need a warrant to look in her purse. . . . Win, I haven't got the nerve to even dig through my wife's purse! I'd feel like a thief looking through her desk. . . . She cannot be involved in this mess.

Just can't be." The ranger stood staring down at the huge handbag and the cluttered desk.

"Won't be going through anything else—not right now. And the desk is federal property. I got a passkey to the locks and went through it this morning before she got here. Found nothing. Guess you checked those two contractors' offices we talked about? They're still scheduled to come in over the weekend?"

Trey nodded and raised an eyebrow. "Yeah, they're both working today. Felt like a cat burglar, rummaging through peoples' desks. Do you think I don't know it's federal property!" He was scowling.

"Hey, you're not hating this any more than I am. Let's see if we can get her talking a little. She thinks we're here to plan JTTF training. Try to keep your emotions out of it."

Trey cut Win off. "And how're you doin' with that?"

"Not much better than you, but it has to happen. I filed to get access to her bank accounts and phone records yesterday, might get something there. Got to go through the process—process of elimination."

Trey slumped into the other metal guest chair as Susan entered the room with her coffee and a big stack of chocolate doughnuts balanced on a paper plate. "Not gonna help me get rid of this extra thirty pounds of baby fat, but what the hay! Breakfast, boys!"

They were all leaning forward in their chairs, about to start in on the doughnuts, when Trey looked down at his phone and flinched. The text said very little: **L, bronte help scared**. It had been sent from Ellie Bordeaux's phone less than a minute ago.

Trey called an abrupt halt to their pig-out. "Ahhh, excuse me, Susan, but something came in that we may have to deal with." He slid his phone down the desktop toward Win. "It's Ellie, she just forwarded me a text she sent to Luke. Who's Bronte?"

Win stopped with the pastry touching his lips and shot Trey a warning look before glancing at the screen. His breath caught in his throat. "Susan, we'll get with you later—sorry about this. We've gotta go. Urgent!" He stood, grabbed his coat and hat, and quickly moved out the door.

Trey was right beside Win in the hall as he whispered, "Bronte is one of the original four guys who were staying in Luke's trailers. One of Ron Chandler's men." Win felt the adrenaline hit his system as he said the words.

"Ah—Good Lord!"

Win was reaching for his Bureau phone when it rang. He took the call as they trotted down the hall and across the small lobby past Bill Wilson, an FBI guard, and through the building's entrance doors. It was the Denver Field Office telling him Mrs. Bordeaux had called in the emergency code thirty seconds earlier. She was alone and someone was trying to break into the house.

"My rig!" Trey called as they raced down the granite steps, which thankfully someone had salted to clear the ice and snow. Win was clutching his phone and holding his hat in the frigid wind. He wrestled open the passenger door of the ranger's Tahoe. He was on the phone to the FBI's SWAT team leader within seconds as Trey made a quick U-turn in front of the Mammoth Post Office and headed toward Ellie's house. Trey hit a button in the vehicle's console, activating the flashing lights and siren. He was driving with his left hand and pulling on his seat belt with his right. "Get your belt on!" he ordered as he passed two snow-covered RVs lumbering in front of the park's medical clinic.

Win knew they were running only sporadic surveillance on Bordeaux's entrance road. Most of their manpower was spread out elsewhere. For the last two days of near-blizzard conditions, the surveillance teams had concentrated on locating the men who'd reportedly left the church compound. Win was praying someone from one of their teams was nearby. He knew there was no hope for a helicopter with the low-hanging clouds and high winds.

"Do we call the locals in? Call in my folks?" Trey asked as he whipped down the first of several switchbacks leading down the mountain.

"Whoa! Let's get there in one piece! No—no locals. No rangers. Not till we know what we have. Got our SWAT boys comin'. Ellie's an informant. We've got to be careful with this!" Win closed his eyes for a split second as Trey passed another slow-moving vehicle. Either the guy had spent his entire youth playing *Grand Theft Auto* or he'd actually run from the law. Trey braked sharply and came down another switch-back in the wrong lane. Win dropped the phone on his lap, gripped the handhold, and pulled his seat belt on.

Win was trying to focus on something other than Trey's driving and the horrible things that could be happening to Ellie. He had to raise his voice above the wailing of the siren to finish his calls. It occurred to him that he'd only been in a police vehicle with the lights and siren on during an actual emergency once—the short chase to catch Richter. Except for that day, the Tactical Emergency Operations Center prac-tice track at Quantico was as close as he'd come—and as the reality of the danger hit him, he realized his training couldn't compare with the actual experience. Self-doubt was raising its head.

"You ever done a dynamic entry against armed subjects?" Win asked through gritted teeth.

"No. . . . No, have you?"

"No, but I've been told it's speed and violence of action—uh, sheeees! Watch the road!"

"You've been told! Well, I've had SWAT training, ah, maybe not up to *your* high and mighty standards, but you haven't had any tactical training! I know the layout at Luke's place!"

"Okay, okay, let's stop competing with each other. Too much at stake here and you know it! So tell me about the layout, I've only been in the front."

Trey took a deep breath and calmly walked him though the house, room by room, as they continued to speed down the highway toward the gravel entrance road to Luke's house. As they dropped in elevation, the snow depth receded. The highway was plowed, and thanks to Trey's skill with the Tahoe, not to mention a good dose of angelic protec-tion, they were making amazing time. Win was notified by phone that the nearest surveillance agents were almost three miles from Luke's entrance road—he and Trey would get there first.

"How are you with your weapons?" Win asked.

The ranger grimaced a bit and kept his eyes glued to the oncoming tourist traffic. "Pretty good . . . better with a long rifle."

"Then I'm the lead on this."

Hechtner shot him a sharp glance and spat out his reply. "Because you're FBI?"

"No, because I'm real good with the guns. All of them. So I'm the lead." It wasn't bragging; it was a fact. He was eyeing the ranger's Colt M4LE, law enforcement's equivalent of an AR-15. The rifle and a shotgun were locked between them against the Tahoe's center console.

Win closed his eyes tight as Trey made a NASCAR-worthy pass around a minivan. He kept his negative internal narrative to himself. His mind alternated between praying and replaying forced-entry methods he'd learned in training.

"Keep the siren on? Tip them?" Trey asked nervously as he slowed to negotiate the barely plowed, slushy gravel road that led from the highway to the house.

"Pluses and minuses . . . I'm thinking yes, leave it on till we're almost there. Might slow down whatever's going on." He didn't want to dwell on what might be going on.

Trey whipped to the side of the gravel road before the brow of the hill where the house sat, and they both jumped from the vehicle into the deep woods. No need to drive right up to the house and into an ambush. Win took the short-barrel Remington 870 shotgun and Trey grabbed the rifle. They moved quickly through the snow-filled woods on opposite sides of the road. Win could make out a muddy red Chevy pickup parked beside Ellie's Toyota in the drive. The front door of the house was wide open. The wind was whipping the curtains on the windows inside. He spotted no movement in the house. Trey was hugging a huge evergreen on the right side of the yard. The ranger motioned him to move up.

So much for being the lead! Neither one of us is real sure of what we're doing. Win crouched low and held the shotgun at the ready as he ran from the tree line toward a small well house or shed about fifty yards to the left of the main house. He was halfway across the snow-covered yard before he remembered to click the shotgun's safety to the off position. *Good Lord, Win!* As he neared the shed, he saw two figures moving toward the woods far behind the house.

At the FBI Academy, new agents work through various armed-entry scenarios in a mock-up town called Hogan's Alley. Win remembered thinking how stressful and realistic it had felt with paintballs peppering around him during simulated attacks. He'd thought at the time it couldn't get more intense in a live-fire situation—he was very wrong. As soon as the bullets from Bronte's AR-15 began clipping the weathered boards of Luke's well house, Win's adrenaline hit a new level. He dove into the back wall of the little frame shed and clutched the shotgun with both hands. He knew he had no chance for a shot with the shotgun or his handgun—the shooter was at least three hundred yards away. The distance was probably the only thing that saved him. He was at the far end of the accurate range of the assault rifle unless the guy was a real marksman. A second long burst hit the little building, and Win yanked his hat down tighter, as if it would somehow protect him. His heart felt like a drum in his chest and he knew his hands were shaking slightly on the shotgun. This was very different from the shoot-out with Richter—that shooting had happened so quickly, he'd had only seconds to react. Out here, huddled in the snow against Luke's well house, he was facing the opposite situation. He was overthinking his responses rather than letting his training dictate his moves.

Trey whistled to get his attention, then sprinted from the trees to the red pickup. He glanced inside the cab, keeping his assault rifle tucked close to his body, and quickly moved on. He jumped the front steps of the porch and flattened his back against the house beside the open door. Win thought about trying to run toward the house to back up Trey's entrance, but the gunman changed his mind with another volley of automatic rifle fire. Win squeezed his eyes shut and ducked lower behind the well house as several rounds thudded into the snow between him and the porch.

When he looked back up, he realized Trey had made his entry. He was too exposed to change his position and help Trey clear the house. He hazarded a quick peek around the corner of the shed and saw no one in the distance. He'd hold his ground unless Trey called for help.

Where's our backup? He checked both his phones for cell service: none, zero, zilch. *Damn!*

In less than two minutes Trey reappeared on the front porch with a long gun in each hand. Crouching low, he zigzagged across the yard to Win and dropped down on one knee next to him. No gunfire came from the far woods.

"House is clean—rear door open. I was watching him from the back window. He had Ellie by the arm, half-dragging her down the trail. I didn't see anyone else. Looks like just one guy. No way we're gonna get a shot at him until we can get some separation. Can't risk hitting her."

"Hope it's only one guy—we're totally in the open if we follow the trail they're on." Win was taking quick glances around the shed's corner at the wide expanse of sagebrush the trail meandered through toward the far tree line. "I can't get a call out, but agents should be here anytime."

"Cell service is iffy here, comes and goes. Luke has a cell booster in the house—won't work in the yard. But I've got a plan. He's headed for the river. There's a shortcut. Maybe we can get around them." Trey slung a deer rifle over his back and started moving down a lightly used path at a low crouch, the assault rifle at the ready.

"Why the river?" Win called after him.

"Luke has a cable crossing on it, but the guy won't be able to cross it in the spring flood. We'll have him trapped."

Trey's idea to outflank the bad guy nearly worked. The faint path was mostly an indention in the snow. They alternated between jogging and sliding along it through the dense woods for nearly a quarter mile. Win and the ranger got to the brink of the sixty-foot bluff above the river just as Bronte was dragging Ellie up onto the wooden platform that Bordeaux had built for the cable crossing.

Win was shocked at the sight of the violently churning river. Even standing hundreds of feet away, he could feel the thundering power of the water roaring through the narrow ravine flanked by yellow-gray slate cliffs. The two wooden platforms supporting the cables were about fifteen feet tall, standing on opposite sides of the stream, right at the edge of the swirling water and less than a hundred feet from the base of the cliffs.

The bad guy was up on the platform now, pushing Ellie ahead of him toward the cables. Bronte hit the release bar and sent the three cables to their lower horizontal positions above the river. In low-water conditions this would work—you could merely tightrope across the bottom cable to the opposite platform while holding on to the two higher cables. At high river levels, however, the bottom cable was nearly touching the seething surface of the water. Each whitecap wave or piece of debris that slammed against it forced it to jump up and down like a bucking horse. And instead of a seventy-foot-wide placid stream, the Yellowstone River was a hundred-fifty-foot-wide muddy, raging torrent.

"Whata you got?" Win gasped as he tried to catch his breath from the sliding run. They were still over three hundred feet from the couple on a level area atop the bluff. Trey was pulling the breech back to load a cartridge into the long gun.

"Luke's .30-06 . . . deer rifle . . . gonna try to get a shot. He can't hit us from here. . . . Just gotta have a little separation from Ellie."

Bronte proved him wrong by sending two quick bursts of automatic rifle fire toward them a second later. Rounds thumped into the yellow shale at their feet and ricocheted off the rocks to the right. Trey dodged to his left as Win retreated behind the nearest boulder.

"Damn! Little help here! Little help!" Trey's voice didn't sound panicked, but Win turned and saw that the ranger had slipped and gone down on the edge of the bluff. Gravel and loose rocks clattered down the jagged rock face. Trey lost the rifle and was halfway over the lip when Win dropped his weapon, lunged forward, grabbed the ranger's left arm, and threw himself flat to anchor them there. Bronte's next burst was wild and rounds zinged high overhead. Win held tight to Trey's arm as the man struggled to find a foothold on the cliff face.

Win stared over Trey's short blond hair at the scene unfolding below them at the river's edge. Bronte had given up on the assault rifle. He'd pulled a pistol and was holding the high cable with his free hand and pushing Ellie along the cable with the handgun. *We have to get to her!* Trey's boot found a toehold; he pushed himself up a few inches. Win reached for the back of Trey's gun belt with his right hand and pulled him over the lip of the cliff and behind a boulder.

The ranger's fair complexion was a few shades lighter, but otherwise he didn't seem fazed. "Gotta get down there!" He was reaching for the assault rifle as he caught his breath.

"How?"

"A path . . . down the cliff . . . twenty-five yards to the right. I'll cover you." As Win grabbed the shotgun and turned to run, he heard Trey cut loose with what he'd consider warning shots from the assault rifle. Maybe that would at least give the bad guy pause—someone was shooting back.

Win sprinted through the snow and sagebrush along the top of the bluff to the steep trail leading to the river. He paused long enough at the trail's high point to see Bronte pushing Ellie farther along the cable. A dark, frothy wave rose up toward the cable and pulled at it, sending both Ellie and Bronte into a wall of angry water. Win held his breath and prayed that Ellie's grip on the thin metal wire would hold. *Please don't let her fall! Please don't!*

As soon as he dropped below the lip of cliff, the sound of the rushing river became all-consuming. It was like a living thing, roaring a dare at anyone foolish enough to approach. He maneuvered among the icy boulders and down the trail's slick switchbacks, grabbing at scrub brush and handholds, with the shotgun in a death grip. He was unsteady on his feet as he neared the foot of the cliff and the riverbank—as he neared a point where he could see them again.

Win glimpsed the couple just as a log and a second huge wave swept toward them. Bronte still held the pistol, but he had pulled it away from Ellie. His other hand was still gripping the higher wire, and his heavy camouflage coat was blowing open in the wind. The pistol waved wildly. *Is he giving up or balancing?* Win wasn't sure. Win was closing in on them now, nearly within range. But he had no idea what pattern the ranger's shotgun would throw—he'd likely kill them both if he fired it. He dropped the shotgun in the snow and found himself aiming his Glock with one hand as he ran toward the platform across the mixture of snow, sand, and mud. He was shouting for the man to drop the gun, for Ellie to hold on, but they couldn't hear him above the water's roar.

Suddenly the small man seemed to freeze—then he crumpled backward into the white-capping brown river and disappeared into the swirling torrent. It happened so fast that Win wasn't even sure what he'd seen. Had he fired? No. Had someone else? He caught sight of other men in civilian clothes on the cliff behind him—the good guys had arrived. *Sure hope it's the good guys!*

He stopped at the foot of the dripping platform, disoriented for a moment as he scanned the water. Ellie? *Where is Ellie?*

CHAPTER TWENTY-FIVE

For a second, as Win scrambled up the ladder to the platform, he thought she was gone. But when the swirling wave moved past, he saw she'd fallen to the lower cable, wrapped her legs and arms around it, and was clinging to it with her back partially in the river. Her face was a mask of panic—if she was screaming, he couldn't hear it over the roar of the water. He threw his hat and parka off. His Glock went down on top of the coat and he turned and faced the river. Pure fear caused him to pause for a moment before his hands caught the cold steel of the upper cables and he pulled himself up to try to make contact with the lower wire. He caught another glimpse of Ellie's blue shirt through the chocolate-colored water maybe fifty feet in front of him. *She's still hanging on, thank God!* His boots found the top of the bouncing cable just as two strong hands grasped his waist and pulled him back onto the platform. Trey wrestled him back two steps and was out on the cable before he could react.

The man had done this before. Trey moved with confidence and was nearly to Ellie before a wave drove the foot cable into the churning river. Win saw Trey's boots lose contact with the lower wire. He pulled himself upright out of the water and righted himself on the lower cable just as it took another dive. Giving up on the two guidance cables, Trey swung down onto the lower cable, turned his chest into it and let the rapid current crush him against it, then lunged forward and grabbed Ellie's arm. He inched back up the cable, pulling her behind him with every pause in the torrent. Instead of fighting the river, he was letting the ebb and flow of the stream work to his advantage as he slowly brought them both closer to shore. The SWAT Team leader appeared beside Win on the platform just as Trey and Ellie outlasted another huge wave. Win felt totally helpless standing there out of reach and unable to help. *Dear God, please let them make it.* After what felt like forever, Trey and Ellie reached the less violent part of the river near the platform. The agent and Win pulled the two to safety and helped them down the wooden ladder.

Trey was holding a sobbing, drenched Ellie tight as Win put his mostly dry coat over her shoulders and moved them both toward the yellow cliff base. He was walking back toward the platform to collect the discarded weapons when one of the four SWAT agents who'd made it down the cliff's path grabbed Win's arm and pointed. A lone figure in the same camouflage pattern Bronte had been wearing was coming down the bluff on the opposite side of the river, rifle in hand. The SWAT guys immediately went into alert mode, with guns drawn and aimed.

The noise next to the river was deafening—no one could hear anything. Win moved ahead of the other agents so they could see him. He raised his hand high to Luke Bordeaux. The man slowed and returned the wave. Luke slipped the assault rifle onto his back and climbed onto the cable platform on the far side of the stream. As Win watched him, he remembered thinking how much Luke reminded him of a big cat: completely at ease in motion, deliberate and balanced. He was fixin' to cross the river on that cable—he didn't even hesitate.

The SWAT Team leader moved next to Win and shouted over the thundering sound of the water, "He's with us?"

Win wished he knew. He spread his hands and shrugged his shoulders and shouted back to the man, "Not sure. He's with me—but stay clear of him!"

The agent was watching Luke handle the cables like an acrobat. "No problem!" He clearly wanted nothing to do with anyone capable of making that walk across the river look easy. He motioned his guys back a few yards to the base of the cliff. They kept their guns at the ready.

Luke paused near the cable's low point and waited for a breaking wave to hit it. Win was watching Luke's gloved hands; he never saw them leave the two guidance cables, even when the heavier foot cable kicked upward with the waves and he had to kneel to keep contact with it. Within seconds Luke was on their side of the flooded stream and down the platform ladder. He hadn't even gotten his boots wet.

But Win would've bet money Bronte's blood was on Luke's right glove where he'd gripped the cable. He didn't think the man simply lost his hold and fell into the river. No way to hear a shot with the crashing of the water, but Win was just as sure there was one less cartridge in Luke's scoped rifle. Bronte's hand on the guidance cable would have been the most stable object, the surest shot, and the point farthest from Ellie. *That's the shot I would have taken.*

Ellie buried her face in Luke's chest and they stood holding each other for a long minute. Someone loaned Trey a dry coat as Win tried to find a spot where he could be heard on the SWAT guy's satellite phone to call for a stand-down. He sent word to the operations center that they needed to start searching the riverbank for the subject—or more likely, for his body. Two of the SWAT agents began that search and worked to retrieve the hunting rifle Trey had dropped off the bluff. One of the agents had hot-wired one of Luke's four-wheelers; Luke commandeered it and drove Ellie back to the house to keep her from developing hypothermia. Win, Trey, and two of the other plainclothes SWAT guys walked the nearly quarter-mile trail back to the house in the cold wind.

"Did she say anything to you? She okay?" Win finally asked Trey as they trudged along through the melting snow and swaying trees.

"Says she is . . . said he hit her once and dragged her around, but nothing worse. She thinks he was on something. She said he was convinced they could cross the river. Said Bronte told her he was going to walk to Gardiner and steal a car, then carry her off to South Dakota."

"Sounds like he was on something. Why not just drive out the way you drove in?" Win shifted Bronte's AR-15 to his other shoulder.

"Don't know. Maybe he knew she'd texted Luke, maybe he heard the siren when we came up," Trey said.

"So this looks like an abduction by a lone wolf. Not a move against her by Shepherd's group?" Win asked.

"That's how it's looking right now. Still want to talk to her and make sure we're getting the full story. She was coming apart back there." Win noticed the ranger was beginning to shiver from the cold.

When they got back to the house, there were six more SWAT agents there, all heavily armed, all in civilian clothes. Luke had gotten their attention as he drove in with Ellie on the four-wheeler, but they were staying out of his way, as Win had instructed. Win had a bad feeling that as the case agent he was technically in charge now. He had no idea what to do. One thing was clear, however, the more agents at the house, the greater the possibility the bad guys would suspect the Bordeaux were informants.

Luke was standing in the middle of the kitchen, fully armed, with a barely contained look of rage about him. One of the agents was gently washing the side of Ellie's bruised face with antiseptic while the others fingered their weapons and cast concerned glances toward her lethal-looking husband. *Time to create a little space.*

"Hey, Luke, leave the rifle in here, it's, uh . . . making everyone nervous." *That and the two handguns and knife on your belt.* "You take Ellie in back and I'll send some of these folks on their way." Win couldn't believe Luke was letting him boss him around in his own house, but the guy obviously had other things on his mind. Luke obediently leaned the rifle in the corner of the kitchen and shepherded Ellie toward their master bedroom.

Helicopters and drones couldn't get up in the weather, so there was no way to search for Bronte except on foot or by four-wheeler. Win sent two additional men to join those who were already combing the riverbank. He sent the other agents back to their surveillance duties. Only Trey and Win remained in the house with Luke and Ellie; that seemed more manageable.

As soon as the agents left the house, Win walked to the kitchen and picked up Luke's rifle. He slipped the magazine out and counted twenty-seven cartridges and one in the chamber—two missing. It'd been far too long for the barrel to still be warm, but he smelled the discharge from the rifle as soon as he opened the breech. Luke walked in with a stack of clothes in his hands just as Win slid the magazine back into the weapon. Their eyes met for a second.

"Where's your gloves, Luke?"

"Probably ruined 'em comin' across that cable. They won't be much use to me now. No tellin' where they are." Luke sounded indifferent.

"Real nice weapon," Win said, balancing the Recon Tactical Rifle in his hands.

"It was a gift from a client. We 'bout done here?" Luke's eyes were narrowing.

"You always load two cartridges short?"

"Keeps the cartridge flow from jamming iffen you pack 'em a little short, so I usually load a magazine one or two rounds light. . . . By the way, it ain't a real good idea to fool with a man's gun, Win." The dark eyes were evasive.

"Not likely to find a body in the river the way it's rolling, but you never know." Win lowered the rifle to its spot in the corner, but he kept his eyes on Bordeaux.

Luke shrugged at the last comment and moved past Win to take the dry clothes to Trey. The ranger was wrapped in a blanket in the den, watching Luke and Win's exchange but saying nothing. He was shivering even in the heated room.

Luke turned his attention to Trey. "Ellie said to tell you to get a hot shower and put these on 'fore you freeze to death. I'm gonna start the fire and make coffee. She's cleanin' up—she'll be out directly. Said y'all wanted to talk to her."

Win glanced down the hall to make sure they weren't overheard. "Luke, is she alright? He didn't hurt her?"

Luke looked down at the hunting clothes he was holding and closed his eyes tight. When he opened them, he drew a sharp breath. "He didn't hurt her bad, no, but if y'all hadn't got here when you did . . ." His voice trailed off.

Trey leaned his head back in the chair and closed his eyes. "Thank God."

"I seen it from the other side of the river. After Bronte dropped off . . . wasn't nothin' I could do 'cept stand there and pray. I figure Ellie and me got God and you both to thank." Luke stoked the fire in the big fireplace and shook his head, as if willing the horrible thoughts of what could have happened to leave his mind. Then he settled back onto practical things. "Win, make yourself useful and fix the coffee. I'm gonna work on the door where he kicked the bolt in."

While Trey took a shower at the other end of the house and Luke worked on the front door, Win got the coffee going and decided he'd better try out Luke's cell phone booster and check in with his bosses. He wasn't real sure how to handle this. An attempted abduction on private land would normally be handled by the locals, but Luke's land was within the boundaries of the park, so the rangers could be the lead agency. A man had gone into the river and there should be some rescue or recovery attempt beyond what the agents were doing. Mr. Givens told Win he'd reach out to Chief Randall; the Park Service would probably end up calling in the locals. Win's next call was to Matt Smith, to let him know where he and Trey were. They were supposed to be working on the leak for HRT this morning. Win was surprised when Smith told him he and Phillips would be dropping by in a couple of minutes. They were a mile up Luke's entrance road. "Let's not mention that to Bordeaux," Smith said.

Luke had taken Ellie hot coffee and was back on the porch, working on the front door, when the HRT guys pulled in beside the various vehicles lining Luke's front yard. The two men exited a muddy blue SUV with *U.S. Seismology Testing Services* stenciled on the side. Luke stood up, wiped his hands on his camo pants, and watched the two newcomers approach. Win took his cup of coffee out to the porch to meet them. He let the men introduce themselves, since he had no idea if they'd use their real names. He was actually surprised when they did. Phillips and Smith both shook hands with Luke and nodded to Win.

"I see y'all know each other, so I'm guessing y'all ain't doing earthquake studies out here," Luke remarked.

Phillips nodded. "Win and Trey work with me. I know you and your wife have had a scare, but I'd appreciate it if we could visit with you."

Luke considered that for a few seconds. Win could see that Luke and Phillips were sizing each other up—like fighters before a bout. Luke was totally focused on Phillips; he hadn't even glanced at the much more formidable-looking Matt Smith after the initial handshake.

He finally agreed. "Sure. C'mon in. Win made the coffee. Y'all make yourselves at home."

As they were getting seated with their coffee, Trey appeared from down the hall in Luke's hunting clothes and sock feet. He was trying to dry his short hair with a hand towel and obviously didn't know they had company.

"Luke, I got your .30-06 out of the gun safe and I've got to go find— ahhh." He pulled up short when he spotted the new arrivals in the den. Trey glanced at Win and rolled his eyes just enough to let him know he wished he could become invisible.

Well, that should do wonders to convince Phillips that Trey isn't too tight with Luke, Win thought. Phillips and Smith both nodded to the embarrassed ranger and turned their attention back to Luke.

"I understand your wife wasn't harmed. We're glad for that. She's still here?" Phillips asked.

"Yeah, in a hot bath tryin' to get warm. She and Trey were both soaked from the river. These boys hadn't gotten here when they did, it could've been real bad."

Phillips took a sip of the coffee. He had a conversational tone. "And her attacker?"

"Went in the river; Win's got guys out lookin' fer him. Why am I telling you things you already know? Ain't no need to dillydally, let's get on with your purpose fer bein' here." Luke was upping the ante, but his voice remained cordial.

"You know who we are?"

"Special ops of some sort, probably HRT."

Phillips sat back on the couch and raised his eyebrows. "That obvious?"

Luke shrugged and cradled his coffee cup in both hands. "Make my livin' watching things, animals and such; you make yours watching people. Y'all are here fer one reason: to size up the competition fer tomorrow."

Phillips leaned forward and considered that before answering. "Yes, that's true, so how is it going to go tomorrow?"

"Wouldn't know, since I ain't planning on being there, but no reason fer anybody to get hurt since y'all don't exactly have the element of surprise. And why go in on a Sunday, of all days to raid a church? Why go in at all and give the Prophet what he wants? Some FBI rule? Fly out West—hit a target—fly back East . . ."

Luke's cell phone rang. He fished it out of his jacket pocket with his free hand, glanced down at it, and looked genuinely surprised. "Excuse me—need to take this call." He put the phone to his ear and dropped his head. "This is Luke."

"Brother Luke, is Sister Ellie all right? Such awful news within the fellowship! I'm so sorry it happened." They could all clearly hear the caller's midwestern accent. Luke made no move to walk away or turn down the cell's volume.

"You're kind to call, Prophet, she's gonna be fine. Just really shook up."

Phillips traded a sharp glance with Smith, and Win and Trey both perked up considerably. Win looked at his watch. It had been less than two and a half hours since Ellie first sent that text to Trey, and already the bad guys had the word.

"Ah, I hear it was Bronte. Brother King sent him away yesterday— no discipline in his soul. He was no longer a part of the church, but I can't imagine why he'd do such a reckless and evil act. What happened? Did the police arrest him?" The man's voice sounded earnest and concerned.

"Ellie texted me and an old ranger friend of ours when Bronte pulled up at the house early this mornin'. She began to feel threatened by him and locked herself in before he busted open the door. Thank goodness, the ranger showed up with a Fed. That put him on the run. . . . I showed up when he was tryin' to cross the river with Ellie. Bronte never made it across that river. Dangerous to cross on a cable this time of year."

"So the hand of God brought him low!"

"Yes, sir, you could say that." Luke's voice was hard and direct.

"Well, some of the sisters can come be with her, if you think it would help, or we could bring a meal. Whatever we can do for you."

"Appreciate it, sir, but we'll probably just hole up here and let her rest."

"Of course . . . of course." It was quiet for a moment, then, "Remember my offers, Brother Luke, there's glory to be achieved in the coming days."

"I'll be praying on it. And I'll tell Ellie you called. It'll cheer her."

The call ended and everyone just sat there staring at their coffee mugs. Win was thinking this was the first real-time conversation where he'd heard the voice of the man who likely wanted him dead. Then Phillips asked the question the lawmen were all wondering.

"Not that I'd want to be listening in on your private conversation, but what did he mean when he said there's glory to be achieved in the coming days?"

Luke smiled at the man. "You listened to my private conversation 'cause I ain't got no reason to hide anything from any of y'all. I'm also thinkin' you've got my phone tapped, so what the hell. I haven't broken any laws, so you've got nothin' on me."

Win was thinking that might be true unless you counted him shooting Bronte off the cable an hour ago. As if that thought had suddenly occurred to him, Luke turned slightly toward Win to see if he'd bring it up. Win just glanced back at him and raised his eyebrows slightly. Some things were best left unsaid in present company.

Luke paused for a long moment. "Welp, y'all are apparently all workin' together, and I told Trey and Win what needed to be said up on that ridge the other day. Don't get trigger-happy and the raid will go down just like the Prophet hopes." He gave Phillips a dismissive look that said the little visit was over and stood up.

The SWAT Team leader showed up at the door with the missing deer rifle and warily handed it off to Luke as everyone was leaving.

The man gave his two cents' worth on the chances of finding Bronte, "No way anyone survives that river. Body could be twenty miles downstream by now." Win asked him to continue to search as far down as the highway and told him the locals were supposedly on the way to relieve them.

The SWAT guy hitched up his collar and headed back toward the river. The rest of them stood on the porch in the biting wind as melting snow dripped from every surface. Phillips had a parting word for Luke.

"I understand you've finished your contract training Shepherd's militia, but you're still working with them—you're still involved. You nearly lost your wife. You can see where this is getting you," Phillips said as he pulled on his cap.

"Last I looked it was still a free country," Luke replied softly as he rested the rifle across his arm.

As the HRT men moved down the steps, Win was remembering Phillips's words from three days ago, *He fits our profile for a really serious domestic terrorist threat—fits it perfectly.* Luke certainly looked the part: camouflage field clothes, military hiking boots with gaiters, high-powered scoped rifle, tactical belt with weapons, brown fleece face mask scrunched down around his neck. His black hair was windswept; his dark eyes were emotionless. He looked completely at ease and decidedly dangerous. If Trey Hechtner could be the poster boy of a spit-and-polish park ranger, this guy could just as easily be the epitome of an anti-government, right-wing militiaman. They both looked their parts. Win wondered for a second how others saw him. Sort of a silly question, when he wasn't even sure how he saw himself.

＊　＊　＊

Phillips and Smith didn't waste any time heading for their vehicle, and Luke went back inside the house. Phillips beckoned to Win, who walked over and leaned next to the SUV's open window. "The bad guys had the intel on this within what, three hours of Mrs. Bordeaux's call to the emergency desk?" Phillips asked.

"More like two and a half hours by my watch. As soon as the locals get here, we'll get back on it. Based on this situation, it doesn't look to me as if it's an electronic compromise. Far as I know nothing went out on our side by phone, text, or radio that would have identified the perpetrator as Bronte, yet Daniel Shepherd knew it was Bronte. It looks like someone on the inside is actually passing the information. We're gonna run a sting on our principal suspects this afternoon. Should narrow it down further. . . . Hoping it breaks the case."

"Well, get back on it as soon as you can," Phillips said.

"Your impression of Luke change after meeting him?" Win asked.

"If anything, I'm more concerned—a very intelligent guy, very confident. And he's certainly not on our side. Don't let his good ole boy act fool you, Win. That guy speaks four languages fluently. I would guess redneck English isn't even one of them."

Win raised his eyebrows in shock. The commander smiled a thin smile. "I've seen Bordeaux's military black file—it's above your clearance level."

Smith was leaning his large frame back against the passenger-side door. "How's it working with the ranger?" he asked.

Win looked past Phillips toward him. "We're trying to work as partners. He's helped tremendously on the leak analysis. He risked his life to save Luke's wife. Trey's a good man." Smith took that in and nodded slightly.

Phillips started the truck, and Win moved away from the window. As he turned to go back to the house, Phillips's voice followed him. "What actually happened to the bad guy?"

Win returned to the open truck window and met Phillips's probing eyes. "I saw him fall off the cable into the river. Never saw him resurface."

"Bordeaux shot him off the cable?"

"Probably—can't prove it without a body."

"And you're thinking he had it coming. Thug is trying to kill the man's wife. But was he trying to surrender, or was he still a threat? You don't get to decide if it was justified or not. You're not the judge and jury here. Keep that in mind, Win."

"Yes, sir," Win answered.

"Find me that leak . . ." Phillips put the SUV in reverse and Win stepped back from the vehicle. The wind was howling through the tops of the big spruce trees. It had started to spit snow again. Win suddenly felt very cold.

* * *

Ellie had waited until the HRT guys left to come out into the den—which was probably a good thing, Win was thinking as she went straight to Trey, buried her head in his borrowed hunting shirt, and tearfully thanked him. She kept her composure for only a few seconds in Trey's embrace and then she began crying. Trey appeared to be good at this—comforting crying women. Win was guessing it went with his job of rescuing folks and all.

Luke was standing in the kitchen, making another pot of coffee, and Win stood in the den, wishing he were somewhere else. Shelby had never been one to cry, and Win knew he wouldn't be any good with sobbing women. When Ellie moved to him a minute later, he internally scrambled for something helpful to say or do. It hurt him to see the red welt on the side of her face where Bronte had hit her, but words didn't seem adequate. He figured the best route was to hold her real tight, pat her on the back, and tell her it was okay. Luke walked in with his coffee, shook his head, then smiled at him.

"It's obvious you don't have sisters or a wife, Win Tyler." He sat the coffee down and gently pulled her away from Win to his chest. "If you hold them too tight, they just cry harder. . . . They sob like this when they're happy with you or mad at you or sometimes for no reason at all. It's one of God's great mysteries." He tipped her chin up to his face and smiled down at her and she started to laugh through her tears at his teasing. Then Luke pulled her down on the couch next to him and kissed her on the top of the head.

Win was saved from further embarrassment by a car pulling up in front. Trey looked out the window and announced that the locals had finally arrived. Win noticed then that the weapons had all disappeared.

Luke had changed shirts and had removed the camo jacket, gun belt, and gaiters. He now had more the look of a guy just back from squirrel hunting than a domestic terrorist.

The two deputy sheriffs who got out of the cruiser were gray-headed, older men who actually seemed concerned for Ellie. They checked out the red pickup Bronte had driven and found it had been reported stolen in Gardiner yesterday afternoon. They also found two grams of crystal meth in a plastic bag in the glove compartment—that went a long way toward explaining why Bronte thought he could cross that river on the cable.

Ellie went back to the bedroom to rest, and the deputies let Trey and Win give their statements first since they needed to get back to work. Win was careful to concisely answer the questions the officers asked. He didn't want to get dragged into working a crime scene. It was fortunate that Trey's text message from Ellie was their tip-off to trouble at the house. Trey's long-standing friendship with Luke and Ellie helped deflect suspicions that the Bordeaux had any relationship with the FBI. As far as the deputies were concerned, Win was working with Trey today and just came along for the ride. He'd called in more FBI help when it became apparent Mrs. Bordeaux had been abducted and was in imminent danger.

Win didn't volunteer his suspicions on the cause of Bronte's fall from the cable. If a body turned up with a gunshot wound, well, he'd deal with it then. He told the officers the other FBI agents who'd witnessed any aspect of the incident would be able to give statements within twenty-four hours.

No one thought there was any chance of the man surviving a fall into the river at flood stage, but the deputies said they'd conduct a search below the highway and an aerial search whenever the weather cleared. Given the circumstances, Win didn't volunteer any next of kin information on the man—whose real name wasn't Bronte, and whose lengthy criminal and military records were neatly stacked within files on his desk back at the office. That could wait until the situation with Prophet Shepherd and his flock wound down a bit.

The deputies finished the initial interviews and sat in their cruiser, calling in a crime scene technician and extra help from Gardiner. Luke walked Trey and Win down the road to Trey's vehicle.

"Hadn't had time to really process all this, but you boys can't imagine how much I owe you both." Luke was looking at Trey when he said it. He continued, "Meant to tell you, Win, I heard what happened with Richter. God was with you that day. Hope you're alright. . . . Ain't an easy thing."

"No, no it's not. . . . And how about you today?" Win responded.

Luke met his eyes squarely. There was no remorse. "Some things are easier done than others." The dark eyes flicked back to Trey. "I'm gonna get Ellie out of here. Told her to stay in Oklahoma, but she wouldn't."

"Why not have her call Cindy. She and McKenna went to my sister's in Bozeman a few days ago. They'd love to have her up there for a visit. Be like old times for them."

"Yeah, like old times . . . well, yeah, I'll talk to her 'bout it after the cops get outa here." Luke took a step toward the house, then turned and spoke. "Some free advice. Looks like you boys are runnin' with the big dogs. Be careful. Special ops commanders typically don't care too much who gets trampled underfoot as long as they accomplish their mission."

Win had already figured that part out.

CHAPTER TWENTY-SIX

They drove from Luke's house back down the wooded hill and across the sagebrush flats to the highway in silence. The low, whitish-gray clouds and freezing fog continued to hug the tops of the higher ridges, and it was still snowing lightly. There would be no aerial search for the bad guy's body this morning, that was for sure. Win had already called the SWAT Team leader and asked that the FBI search team take Luke's four-wheeler back to his house and turn the search, if there was to be one, over to the locals.

It was only 10:35 a.m. when Trey turned the Tahoe onto the highway, but Win felt as if the day had gone on forever. He'd been having lots of those days lately. "Feel as if I'm on a roller coaster these last few weeks. I was led to believe nothing ever happened in Yellowstone National Park."

"That why you got sent out here? Banishment to the middle of nowhere, where they hoped you'd get bored and quit?"

Well, Trey is certainly direct this morning. Win stared straight ahead at the nearly-empty gray highway with its thin white waves of blowing snow. The bad weather was thinning out the tourists. "*Banishment . . .* well, I suppose that's as good a word as any for it."

"Hasn't turned out that way for them, has it? You've even got my bosses in Washington and HRT impressed with your work, not to mention your Denver people. They'll have you out of here as soon as this case with the Prophet winds down."

"You tryin' to make me feel better about something?"

"Oh, just noticed you seem awfully subdued. We both oughta be feeling really blessed this morning. Some guys our age haven't even had their second cup of coffee at work yet and we've already had the privilege of saving someone's life. You were goin' on that cable to get Ellie before I came up behind you—"

"I hesitated."

"You hesitated 'cause it looked impossible and you were scared, but you were still going. I had to pull you back. You were smart to let me go. I'm the one with the rescue training, and even with that, it's a miracle Ellie or I didn't go down the river."

"Appreciate you saying that. I don't know. . . . Maybe I'm down 'cause I've seen two people die in less than a week and it's not something I'm used to."

"Don't ever want to get used to that. Every life is precious to God." Trey stared ahead at the road. "Did Luke shoot Bronte off the cable?"

"Yeah, I think so. I think he shot the guy's hand where he was gripping the cable. Won't know without a body. The man may have been giving up—just not sure. You watched me question Luke in the house. It would be what, second-degree murder, manslaughter, justifiable homicide, needed killing, or some obscure western law y'all have out here?"

"Don't know, but I would have shot him off the cable myself if I'd had a clear shot and hadn't slipped on the bluff." Win thought Trey seemed to be considering telling him something, but instead the ranger moved the conversation in another direction. "By the way, I appreciate you grabbing ahold of me. You nearly lost your new partner early on."

"Glad I didn't. . . . Now if you can teach me how to properly hold a crying woman."

Trey glanced over at him and grinned. "Lot more fun to hold a laughing woman. And speaking of which, two of my guys told me you had a sweet little rendezvous the other day. Real pretty brown-haired girl, they said."

Win felt his ears go red. "Well, I . . . I saw her at the hotel. Didn't even go in her room. But that was stupid of me, I'll admit. It could have put her in danger."

"She the girl you met out with the bears?"

"How'd you know about that?"

"Gus was telling me you suddenly had a real strong interest in the Interagency Grizzly Bear Research Project and that one of their researchers was a girl from somewhere down South—really good lookin'."

"Is there no privacy here?" Win shot back in mock alarm.

"Naw, not much." Trey smiled back at Win. "And that might actually help us catch our spy this afternoon."

Trey had radioed for the two rangers assigned to protect Win to meet them at the Justice Center. When they reached Mammoth, Trey pulled in beside the rangers' Tahoe. He left the truck running while they sat and tried to plan their next move on the intel leak investigation.

Trey frowned down at the steering wheel. "Well, given what happened this morning, we oughta be able to narrow down this leak pretty fast. I hate to think this, but it has to be a personnel leak, and there weren't that many folks around at 7:00 a.m. when that text from Ellie came in. That should eliminate two or three folks still on our lists."

"Yeah, I'm thinking the same thing. I'll touch base one more time with the folks who are doing the communications sweeps. See if they've hit on anything. Need to know if Bronte's name went out over any of our radios, computers, or phones early this morning."

"While you're at that, I'm gonna run to my office, get out of Luke's clothes, and figure out how I'm gonna write up my report on those warning shots—we're not allowed to fire warning shots." Trey gave Win an *Oh, well* look. "My guys will watch your back while I'm gone. Meet you at your office in forty-five minutes?" He reached behind the seat for his gun belt and the trash bag containing his wet clothes and opened the driver's door before Win could respond.

Saying no would tell Trey he wasn't trusted, while letting him go alone would violate his instructions from Phillips. He opted to go with his gut on this one. "Yeah, okay, see you at the office. I'm gonna sit in your truck and make a few calls." The ranger stepped out into the light snow, and Win waved to his two guards in the adjoining vehicle.

He hated having people follow him around all the time. He couldn't do the same thing to Trey. He'd promised no more games.

And speaking of promises, he'd told Tory he would call her within a couple of days—it was Saturday morning. *Geez, I saw her on Wednesday.* He was losing track of time, too much happening too quickly. He punched in her number, figuring she was probably in one of her Montana State seminars, but at least she'd see he'd made the effort to call. He was pleased when she answered the phone.

"Hey, it's Win Tyler, my getting you at a bad time?"

"No, it's fine—we're finished till noon." Her voice was cheerful. A good sign.

"Wanted to call you last night, but we've been working late and it's likely to go that way for a few more nights. Been pretty stressful down here since you left town."

"We heard there'd been a shooting at the hotel. That was the afternoon I saw you. Did you see it happen?" she asked.

"Yeah, I did. Can't really talk about it now. Bureau policy. But I'll tell you about it someday. Tell me what y'all are doing."

They spent the next several minutes taking those little steps getting to know someone requires, the give and takes of likes and dislikes, and he found himself laughing at things she said and thinking he felt good when he talked to her. He knew his phone was monitored and some Bureau technician was bored to death listening in on his flirting with her, but he really didn't care. The nice thing was, she was flirting back with him.

He'd been on the phone for almost fifteen minutes and he knew he had to get back to work, so he started winding down the call. "Not real sure where I'll be next week, but I'd like to come see you while you're at Roosevelt if that's good for you. Hopefully things will slow down by then."

"I'd like that." She paused for a long moment. "I hope I'm not being too forward here, but I've got a feeling you're in some trouble or having some problem or well, whatever. . . . I don't need to know what it is—God knows. I just wanted you to know I've been praying for you and I'll keep that up if you're okay with it."

"I'm more than okay with it. Thank you. I'm embarrassed I haven't told you how important my faith is to me. Maybe I thought . . ." He struggled for the right words, and she finished his sentence.

"Maybe you thought I'd think you were too straightlaced or something?"

"Well . . . maybe."

"You do seem pretty straightlaced," she said with a soft laugh, "in a good sort of way. You're a gentleman, and I like that a lot—and just so you know, my faith is central to my life too. So I'll keep praying for you, and I'll see you when you get free."

They said their goodbyes, and he sat in the cold truck, staring at his phone for a minute. Tory Madison was obviously one of those people his mother was talking about in her letter. She was God's encouragement to him when he needed it. The relationship might go nowhere, but for this moment, which was all he had, she'd made his heart glad.

*　*　*

It was a short list. After two and a half days of analyzing time lines, conducting mind-numbing reviews of dozens of personnel records and schedules, and running seemingly endless scenarios, it was a very short list. Win kept hoping it was someone on the outside—maybe a computer hacker affiliated with the Prophet's church had broken the Bureau's encryption or accessed internal communications—but after the event with Bronte and Ellie this morning, he knew it wasn't that. It was an individual or individuals who'd traded information for personal enrichment. Money for lives. And it was someone who worked for their team—it had to be one of the good guys.

It was 1:45 now, and Trey was sitting across from Win's desk with his head down, deep in his notes. The door was closed, and they were both working on their respective final lists. They'd decided to rank their suspects in classes. Anyone falling within the top three or four on either list was highly suspect. Win had finished his ranking. He watched Hechtner mentally work through his names one more time. A little sunlight was peeking through the drawn blinds in Win's office. The weather was finally trying to clear, and the snow outside was continuing to melt.

He leaned back in his desk chair with his hands behind his head and watched the ranger work. Trey had changed clothes; his tan flat hat and heavy green coat were hanging on Win's antique coat-tree. Win had taken to keeping a clean set of clothes at the office as well—the way this day was shaping up, he might be wishing his whole wardrobe were here. He watched as Trey ran his hand through his short blond hair several times and pinched the skin between his eyes. Everyone on both of their final lists was likely to be a Park Service employee. Win knew the ranger was having a hard time dealing with the real possibility that the traitor was within his own agency.

Trey finally raised his head. "Ahhh, you got yours ready?" He said it absently, as though he would rather be anywhere else in the world.

Win shuffled his written list. "I've got three names that are serious contenders—maybe a fourth."

"Okay."

Win called them off, "I've got Park Service Clerk Susan Hapsburg, Ranger Bill Wilson, and William McGinnis, Park Service technical contractor."

Trey stared down at his notes, then read off his names as if it were physically painful for him. "I've also got Susan, McGinnis, and another contractor, Jim Dallas. Bill Wilson is on my list too, but fifteen years here—can't see it. Actually, I can't see it in any of these folks. I've known all of them for years except Jim Dallas. Susan's the only one with top secret clearance." He looked up. "You said you had a fourth name?"

"That would be you," Win said and studied Trey's reaction.

Trey leaned back, raised his chin a little, and narrowed his eyes before he responded. There was more than a little anger in his reply. "Oh, come on! You even told Phillips you eliminated me from consideration after I didn't know about the drones. . . . Don't be screwing around with this. It's serious!"

"That's the point. It not just serious, it's deadly serious. Heck, I even had to investigate Jason—a seventeen-year-old kid! We have to look at every possibility and come up with defensible reasons to eliminate names. You may not have known about the drones or you may have just been careless that morning. You had access to most, if not all, of the other information we think has been compromised. I have to consider the possibility there could be more than one person involved in the leak. Would a reasonable investigator put Trey Hechtner on the short list? Ask yourself that."

"What about this morning? I was with you the entire time after we got the text from Ellie!" Trey was a little hot.

"Actually, you weren't with me the entire time—you did the house entry and were out of my sight for a few minutes. You coulda made a call." *This isn't goin' well.* "Hey, I'm just saying . . ."

Trey had apparently had enough. He blew out a long breath, shook his head angrily, and stood up. "Time for a break! I'm getting more coffee." Just as he opened the office door, his phone buzzed. Trey walked out of the office and away from Win as he answered. Whoever was calling, it was clear the ranger didn't want Win overhearing the conversation.

Win hit his office intercom for Deb. It was time to round up the troops, call in their bosses, and implement the sting he and Trey had designed yesterday afternoon. They had decided to run disinformation by their top three suspects and see if anyone took the bait. Nothing promising had come back on the financial records check, but bad guys didn't always deposit their ill-gotten gains in the bank. There wasn't enough probable cause on any of the suspects to obtain phone taps, and there was too little time to do any type of protracted surveillance. Given the circumstances, Mr. Givens and Phillips had both agreed that a quick takedown was required. The leak couldn't remain in place while HRT geared up to hit the church compound tomorrow. The raid had already been postponed once because of the snowstorm; putting it off again was not gonna make Win's bosses happy.

Trey showed up with his coffee and a cup for Win about the time Win finished filling Deb in on their top suspects. She had developed the disinformation that was to be fed to the suspects, and she was ready to call in the surveillance teams she had on standby for the effort.

"We only have six teams on standby, Win. You've got four suspects, and we need two teams per suspect. If we call in two more teams from Billings, that means we'll have to wait until tonight to move on this," she said. "They wouldn't be able to get here before five o'clock at the earliest."

"No, we don't need the delay of waiting for other teams, but call them in for backup support. Trey and I can handle feeding the intel to Bill Wilson. He's our least likely suspect. Wilson is used to seeing us over at the Justice Center constantly, he's scheduled to be on duty today until six o'clock. You and Ramona can help us with that surveillance. If nothing goes down before he goes off duty, we can turn the surveillance on him over to the Billings teams. The information on Ellie Bordeaux's abduction got to Daniel Shepherd really fast this morning. I think it's likely whoever's selling us out will move quickly."

"Ten-four, I'll buzz you when I have everybody lined up to meet in the conference room. Give me ten minutes. Wes will have to decide what to do about calling Chief Randall—he's not going to be pleased. These folks are all his."

"I know. I know." Win sighed and took the coffee from Trey. He sat back down in his chair and motioned Trey to close the door behind him.

"Thanks for the coffee. I didn't tell Deb I had you as my number four. I guess we can revisit that possibility if none of these others pans out." Trey's gray eyes were still narrowed. *Need to do a little damage control.* "Hey, you *know* I don't think you're dirty. But we have to justify all of our decisions on this deal." Trey continued to glare at him over his coffee cup. Win was thinking maybe he should have kept his fourth pick to himself, but he kept talking. "Since we're goin' to go with all four of the suspects on your list, you okay with you and me handling Bill Wilson? Didn't want to wait for surveillance teams to come in from Billings. You okay with that?"

Trey snorted a little, but then got down to business. "Yup, whatever. Our job shouldn't be too hard, since I can't imagine Bill being involved in something like this. The guy is sixty-one years old and maybe six months away from retirement. It's not like I know him well or anything, but he's always had exceptional reviews. His work history has been mostly traffic control and security for the courthouse, even when it was here in this old building. Typical police-type work; he's never done the traditional ranger duties. I've always just thought of him as a nice, friendly guy."

"Yeah, I'm thinking we may be barking up the wrong tree there, but his work schedule sure did hit the time lines when the information went out. But then so did the others'—especially Susan's. This whole thing just makes me feel sorta sick, you know. . . . Whoever leaked this information nearly got me killed. And it could get worse. Who knows what those yahoos have planned." They both sat there frowning and sipping coffee.

Trey was tapping his finger against his cup. He cleared his throat and began to speak. "Ah, I need to talk to you about—"

Win's desk intercom buzzed with Deb's call, interrupting Trey's request. They both grabbed their hats and coats and quickly moved downstairs to the conference room for the final operational briefing on the sting.

At exactly 2:45 p.m., all four of the suspects would receive different pieces of disinformation from various agents. All the fabricated intel would appear to be time-sensitive for the bad guys, and every bit of information was very different in nature. If it showed up in the hands of the Prophet's people, there would be no doubt which suspect had passed it along. Other case-related information could be conveyed as long as it was already in the hands of Shepherd's group. Two surveillance teams of two agents each were assigned to each suspect, and extra electronic monitoring from both aircraft and ground sites was focused on every member of the Prophet's group for which they had wiretap approval. The weather had cleared enough to deploy the plane and two electronic-sensing drones. HRT was assisting with the surveillance on some of Ron Chandler's guys who'd left the church compound. The tension in the conference room was palpable as the four agents who would deliver the disinformation reviewed their assignments.

Win memorized the two sentences of false info Deb handed him, and he passed it down to Trey. He could improvise any way he chose, but those two sentences had to get to the suspect. One of the agents from Denver was studying the lines she would deliver to Susan Hapsburg. Win really hoped the mole wasn't Susan. The pictures of her darling little girls playing in the fresh snow flashed through his mind. Her finances were tight and the bad guys were apparently throwing around big money for information. He sighed again and stared down at the polished wood of the conference table. He hoped it was one of the two guys he'd never met; he hated the thought that it could be Susan or Bill, folks he spoke to several times a week. He didn't really focus on the possibility that they could have a dry run—that all their targeted suspects were guilty of nothing worse than unfortunate coincidences within their work schedules. That would put them back at square one. Or worse yet, that the mole was among the suspects, but didn't take the bait today for whatever reason. That would take them back beyond square one. Win wouldn't let his mind consider failure, not yet anyway.

Mr. Givens and Emily were running the sting's operations center out of the old FBI building's conference room. Win hadn't felt good about setting it up at the Justice Center—too much of the intel had gone missing from there. Phillips had several heavily armed HRT guys ready in the back offices if they were needed to assist in an arrest. The agents were carrying small recording devices to capture the conversations with the subjects. Win was too leery of the Bureau's main communication center to even authorize traditional wires. Internal communications with the other teams were also problematic. The surveillance teams were going with rental cars, since the suspects could be familiar with the local FBI vehicles. They would have to use hand-held radios on a seldom-used frequency, since it was very possible the spy had access to the same encrypted radios as the agents. There was no reason to think the mole would be surfing the radio channels while the operation was underway, but it was just one more thing that could go wrong. At 2:35 p.m., Trey and Win walked out of the conference room and through the heavy wooden front doors of the old building.

Game on.

CHAPTER TWENTY-SEVEN

Both men held their hats to their heads as they walked the 180 yards down the street to the Justice Center in the blustery north wind. They climbed the granite steps and entered as an FBI agent buzzed the inner doors open. Trey and Win both greeted the Bureau guard and moved toward the elevator, passing Bill Wilson's small security office. The older ranger stuck his head out of his office immediately. Win was struck by his quick smile and eager expression. He reminded Win of Shep, their cattle dog back home—mostly at rest, but ready to spring up at any sign of activity, needed or not. Bill Wilson would have been a pistol in his younger days.

"What's happening this afternoon, boys? Any action?" Bill was holding a piece of beef jerky in one hand and a Styrofoam cup of coffee in the other as he leaned against the doorframe of his office. If he had any regard for Trey's higher rank, he didn't show it, but Win was thinking that wasn't unusual with the rangers. They seemed uniformly friendly to everybody.

Win started talking. "Hate this weather, Bill, it's May 10th, there should be flowers blooming. It's spit snow all morning—wind is cold as ice!"

"Just a little nuisance, be pretty before you know it. You boys had a busy morning!" Win wasn't surprised he knew about the incident with Bronte and Ellie; even the locals were all over that by now.

Win asked about Bill's wife, Maddy, and Bill said she'd gone to visit relatives in Reno for several days. What passed for spring in Yellowstone wasn't her favorite time of year, and she'd spend the rainy, snowy, icy days with the grandkids.

Trey stood there looking bored at their conversation. He took off his hat and slapped it against his pants leg a couple of times before telling Win they needed to get up to the operations center and make their report ASAP. Win snapped back that they'd been working 24/7 and he'd stop and visit with Bill if he wanted to. Win moved toward Bill's office, out of the hearing of the front-door guard. Trey hit the elevator button and told Win again that they needed to get upstairs now. Win waved him away and asked Bill if he had an extra cup of coffee. As Trey entered the elevator, Win stood inside Bill's small office, unzipped his heavy coat, and leaned against the wall. He took off his felt hat and dropped it in the metal chair, rubbed his face with both hands, then ran a hand through his thick, dark hair. It occurred to him that he needed a haircut.

"Man, I'm beat, Bill. Been a tough few days. . . ." *Here we go.*

"Heard you were involved in the shooting the other day. Hard thing for anyone to handle. . . . Had to deal with that sort of thing more when I was a state trooper. You've got something big going on now?" He handed Win the last of the coffee from a small pot in the office's corner and sat down on the front of his cluttered metal desk.

Win realized his palms were sweaty as he took the Styrofoam cup. He felt his heart beating hard in his chest. He held his breath for a few seconds and tried to settle down before he answered. "Oh, yeah, yeah . . . this case is never-ending, and I'm so tired I can hardly stand. Hechtner keeps pushing. . . ." Win took a sip of the bitter coffee.

Bill nodded sympathetically. "Know how that is. Spent many a damn week out on assignments that never went anywhere. Trey's a good guy, but our Special Response Team folks can get a little full of themselves—intense as hell. You know it's hard for me to just sit here, watching you come and go. Wish I was more a part of it. . . . What's going on now?"

Being from the South, Win was accustomed to nosy folks, but Bill Wilson had asked him twice about an operation they both knew was closed to personnel without top secret clearance. Maybe they weren't barking up the wrong tree after all.

"Well . . ." Win glanced over his shoulder at the door guard. He took another sip of the awful coffee and lowered his voice. "You mighta heard we had the Hostage Rescue Team come in earlier this week? They're here helping run surveillance on some folks affiliated with the Arm of the Lord Church. Well, they've been ordered back to the East Coast tonight for some crisis that's going down back there. What a screwed-up mess! After all the effort we've put into keeping tight surveillance on that bunch of yahoos at the church compound—all for nothing! So I've gotta go in and tell JTTF and SWAT to realign."

"You mean HRT is pulling out tonight?"

"Yeah, can you believe that? Bad guys could scatter like quail and do Lord knows what all if they knew our surveillance was going down! We won't have a solid surveillance perimeter for at least ten hours after eight o'clock tonight." Win's shoulders slumped and he sighed again. "Hey, thanks for the coffee and for letting me blow off a little steam. I'm just fed up with the whole deal."

"No problem . . . no problem. Take care of yourself, Win." The older ranger seemed distracted.

"Tell Maddy hey for me—looking forward to more of her good cooking." Win said that and he meant that. He was praying Bill Wilson wasn't the mole. But deep in his spirit he wasn't sure anymore; that prayer might have come a little late. He hit the elevator button and met Trey in the hallway on the second floor. No one in the operations center knew the play was on to take down the mole. Everything was strictly *need to know*. He and Trey nodded to each other and stood there silently, checking their phones for five minutes. Then they took the elevator back down to the lobby. Win waved to Bill as they walked across the gray slate floor, past the guard, and out the front doors.

Deb and Ramona were sitting in a white rental car across the street from the building, pretending to look at Yellowstone brochures. Win and Trey walked by without acknowledging them. The girls would cover the front entrance and Win and Trey would cover the back. Thankfully, the morning's bad weather had discouraged most of the tourists, and the area was not as crowded as it could have been in early May. The fewer people to get in the way, the better. It was one of those rare times when Win wasn't in the mood to be friendly.

They climbed into the small rented SUV that was parked behind Win's office, and he drove it to a gravel parking lot overlooking the rear of the Justice Center. He turned off the vehicle, called in their position, and played the recording of his meeting with Wilson for Trey. The ranger's face was locked in a deep scowl. His eyes moved back and forth between the back doors of the Justice Center to Bill Wilson's personal truck throughout the short recording.

"Nice job of subterfuge, Win. Maybe I have you pegged wrong. You might have a future in poker after all."

"I wouldn't bet on it. I kept my eyes down almost the whole time—played hangdog. I remembered what you'd said about my eyes giving me away. Just hate misleading anyone . . . even for the sake of a just cause."

"Ah, he asked you twice about the operation."

"Yeah, yeah, he did, but maybe that's just him feeling left out. You know, feeling over the hill. Just standing around can't be a good place to be for someone who was in the trenches in law enforcement most of his life." Win moved the seat back as far as it would go and tried to stretch out his legs under the steering wheel. They obviously made these little SUVs for short people. He could feel air coming through the seal around the window. It was gonna get cold in here in a hurry.

He and Trey were settling in for what Win hoped would be a long, uneventful wait for Bill Wilson to do nothing. Given the communications issues, the agents stayed off the radio except to call in their status and positions. All the disinformation plants had gone more or less according to schedule. Win had helped with numerous low-level surveillance assignments in Charlotte, but the Bureau had specially trained surveillance teams in every office. Those people were the pros. He was glad those teams were on three of the targets; he tried again to tell himself Bill Wilson was their least likely suspect.

Trey dropped his field glasses to his lap after ten minutes and asked Win to take the "eye" for the next ten. They were into it for thirty minutes with no talking other than to switch off. Win remembered how tedious and mentally exhausting visual surveillance could be. He was hoping one of the other teams would get a hit soon. It was now good and cold in the vehicle, but that kept him somewhat alert and Trey didn't seem to mind. Win was glad Trey wasn't big on idle conversation; he just wanted to focus on the distasteful matter at hand. The ranger seemed introspective and pensive. Win figured spying on someone in his agency had to be pulling him down.

"Win, I need to talk with you about something. I've been—"

They both jumped when Win's radio suddenly came to life.

"Delta One to Delta Two, subject moving to the rear. Copy?"

Trey stared straight ahead and slammed his fist down hard on the dashboard. "Dammit, Bill!" Then he took a deep breath, turned his head, hit the button, and calmly reported into the handheld radio, "Delta Two, copy that, subject moving to the rear."

The planted HRT operator guarding the Justice Center's front door had just reported to everyone that Bill Wilson was on the move and was heading for the rear of the building toward their position. Bill Wilson was the fourth suspect in the group—subject D, or Delta. They were designated as Delta team. Delta team was now in play.

They both watched him with binoculars from 190 yards away. Win started their vehicle and tried to focus on Wilson's demeanor as he exited one of the gray metal doors at the rear of the Justice Center. The man had to grab his flat hat to keep it from sailing off in the wind. His dark-green uniform jacket was blowing open. Win couldn't help but notice the bright-gold embroidered Park Service law enforcement shield on the coat. He saw Wilson's handgun as the coat blew back again. The man's face looked flushed, his mouth was set in a hard line, and his movements were hurried. He fumbled with his keys before he was able to get his older Chevy pickup started.

As soon as Win could tell which direction Wilson was moving in the gravel parking lot, he dropped the field glasses and hit the radio call button: "Delta Two to Delta Three, subject in a light-blue Chevrolet pickup, extended cab, silver toolbox . . ." Trey held up notepaper with the license number. "Wyoming license: Serra—Charlie—Alpha—one—three—zero. Moving onto Highway 89 North out of rear parking lot. Copy?"

"Copy that, Delta Three," Deb responded quickly. No one else was on the radio. They were a little over thirty minutes into the sting and they were the only game in town. Bill Wilson turned out of the parking lot onto Highway 89 headed down the mountain toward Gardiner. Win watched two carloads of tourists pass, then Deb and Ramona's white rental car. He and Trey took the second position behind more tourists another hundred yards back.

"May be nothing, Trey. . . . Maybe he needs a little fresh air." But Win knew better now; he had a terrible feeling about it. It was about five miles to Gardiner. Wilson was scheduled to work until six o'clock tonight. Win was thinking the guy had to be going somewhere close so he could get back to work before his typical fifteen-minute afternoon break was over. *Where is he going?*

That got answered pretty quickly. "Zulu Three to Delta Three, Bearcats Four and Six are southbound on 89 in a silver Trailblazer, cleared park entrance at Gardiner. Zulu Three following. Copy?"

Trey swore softly and covered his eyes with a hand. Win pulled a faded Razorback ball cap down lower on his face and glanced at Trey. Zulu was the call sign for the HRT operators who were surveilling a few of Prophet Shepherd's most dangerous guys during the sting. Two of their subjects were in a Trailblazer coming this way from Gardiner—it was looking like Wilson had a little meeting planned.

Bill Wilson pulled his vehicle into the Boiling River parking lot at the bottom of a barren mountain about two miles north of Mammoth. Deb radioed that they were pulling in as well. Win doubted that two women dressed like tourists in a rental car would grab much attention from Wilson or the bad guys. There were four other carloads of tourists in the lot as Win passed it by. He watched Trey from the corner of his eye and saw him pull his coat over his uniform jacket and an old cowboy hat down over his face. They met the bad guys' Trailblazer just as they turned on their signal light to enter the lot. Trey set his jaw and drew a deep breath as Win drove past the lot's entrance. There wasn't any doubt now.

Deb and Ramona were good. The HRT guys were good. They all got plenty of photos and video of Law Enforcement Park Ranger Bill Wilson welcoming two domestic terrorism suspects into the passenger seats of his blue Chevy truck. Win turned down a service road another mile closer to Gardiner. He drove over a low ridge, out of sight of the highway, turned around, and waited. Neither he nor Trey said a word. The clandestine meeting took less than three minutes. Wilson and the subjects headed back the way they came. The FBI electronic surveillance plane flying overhead picked up a phone call from the guys in the Trailblazer to Ron Chandler within seconds. It always helped when someone got a little careless, and they were careless that day. The Bureau now had a recording of a cell phone transmission from one of the bad guys that said in part, "the boys from Virginia will be leaving tonight. . . . It's wide open after eight," before Chandler cut him off.

* * *

Win watched it all unfold as if he were in an audience at a play; none of it felt real. Wes Givens gave Chief Randall the option of arresting his own man, and he chose to do just that. As the case agent, Win was technically in charge of the arrest and the interrogation, so he watched from camera monitors in the Justice Center's second-floor security room as rangers discreetly sealed off the building. It was imperative the Arm of the Lord group not know Bill Wilson was being arrested. Less than twenty minutes after Wilson walked back into his little office, just as he was making himself another pot of coffee, the HRT guy guarding the front door pretended to trip and fall outside Bill's office. When Wilson came out to assist the man, Trey and two of his guys were on him. Win watched Trey pull Wilson's Sig Sauer handgun free with the same finesse he'd used to disarm him up on the ridge. Win winced as he remembered that moment of helplessness. The three rangers pushed Wilson back into his office, cuffed his hands behind his back, and frisked him. His back pocket held $3,000 in crisp new bills. The money went into an evidence bag—the bad guy's fingerprints on those bills would be one more nail in the coffin.

But Win's focus was on Wilson's face. Bill Wilson had folded even before his Miranda rights were recited. He was ghostly pale and his eyes were flat, as if he were suddenly relieved to have it over. Four of the HRT guys, in their blue-collar civilian clothes, rushed Wilson out of his office and up the back stairs to the U.S. Marshals' interrogation room. This was a high-level counterterrorism case; a law enforcement officer had betrayed them and everyone was angry. In spite of the anger, there was no lack of professionalism in the arrest. Win felt a little pride in that, but it still couldn't take away the sick feeling in his stomach.

Win turned his attention back to the monitor's view of Wilson's office. The other rangers were filing out. Trey was still standing with pistol drawn, looking down at Bill's desk. Trey took off his hat and wiped his sleeve across his face. His eyes came up and Win caught the fire in them. Win could feel the man's fury even through the video feed. He made a mental note not to get on the wrong side of Trey Hechtner.

* * *

Win's ASAC stepped in front of him as he moved down the hall toward the interrogation room. "You're a little close to this—he may have put your life at risk."

Win raised his chin and his deep-blue eyes locked on Mr. Givens. "Just me in there. . . . I've got this, sir." There was no hesitation, no timidity. It'd been ten minutes since the arrest—things were moving fast and he was on go.

He saw Jim West, Deb, and Phillips farther down the hallway. He knew Chief Randall and Gus were already in the security room, watching the video feed of Bill Wilson sitting with his head in his cuffed hands in the interrogation room with two less than friendly HRT operators standing over him.

Win lacked confidence in many areas of Bureau work, but suspect interrogation wasn't one of them. He'd done this job dozens of times in his Bureau career—long, difficult interrogations during the Brunson case. He was good at it and he knew it.

Wes Givens seemed to consider him for a moment longer, then he moved aside and nodded for Win to pass.

Win handed off his Glock and his jacket to his supervisor as one of the operators opened the heavy metal door. He entered the small, windowless room with a leather-bound notebook in his hand. He liked to have something in his hands, made it easier to steady them if need be. He asked the HRT guy standing over Wilson to uncuff him from the stationary table. The operator gave him a momentary questioning look—not standard procedure in a terrorism case, but the man did as Win asked. He took off the metal shackles and both operators left the room.

They were alone. Or as alone as one can be with six video cameras focused on every angle, digital audio feed, and a troop of onlookers in the security room next door. Win leaned back against the stark gray wall and looked down at Law Enforcement Ranger Bill Wilson. The man hadn't raised his head. Wilson's gold badge was reflecting the fluorescent light down onto the smooth metal table. Win wondered at the psychology behind the design of these spaces. Everything had been thought out: very clean, very sterile, very quiet. All outside stimuli, all distractions had been stripped away. That's what Win wanted too; that's what he demanded. All insulating excuses or blame stripped away. The truth laid bare.

He sat down directly across the table from Wilson in one of the metal chairs that were bolted to the floor. He began in a low, soft tone of voice—no emotion, no intensity. "You've been in law enforcement almost forty years, Bill, so you know the drill better than I do. The only good deal is the deal you're gonna make with me right now. Agent Deborah Mills says you've signed a copy of your Miranda rights, you've waived an attorney, you're freely talking to me. So talk to me."

Wilson suddenly stood and leaned forward over the desk. His right hand slapped the metal top. His face was crimson, and the veins bulged in his thick neck. "You played me down there! Damn you! You set me up!" he yelled into Win's face.

Win didn't flinch. "Uh-huh, and you provided intel to someone who took a shot at me with a high-powered rifle. Wanna call it even and get on with our business here?"

Win's statement took the wind out of the man's sails; his jaw went slack and he slumped back into the stationary chair. His shaking hands came back up to cover bloodshot eyes, and Win saw him bite down on his quivering lower lip.

"Wanna tell me what's been happening, Bill?" Win's tone had never changed. "This isn't like you. . . . How'd you get sucked in?"

"Didn't think it could come to this."

They never do.

"It was just harmless stuff at first—how many agents in town, what your schedule was, who was under surveillance . . . harmless stuff. I, uh . . . I've got a money problem. Didn't want Maddy to know." Wilson's voice was trembling now.

Win raised an eyebrow and nodded.

"Got into the internet gambling thing two years ago. Then every trip to the grandkids in Reno, I'd hit the casino. Retirement coming up and I'm down over a hundred grand, and . . . hell, I didn't mean for it to get out of hand." Sweat was beading on his forehead and his hands were shaking badly. "I heard talk about someone paying for information . . . approached one of the church members, a big guy named Billy Thayer at the Zippy Mart in Gardiner. He put me in touch with Ron King." He caught a sob in his throat and buried his face in his hands again.

Win waited a moment, then spoke. "Walk me through it, Bill. Cooperation is the key here. You're gonna help me on this. . . . You want to make it right." Win's calm demeanor and quiet voice hid an underlying intensity and focus he knew Bill Wilson couldn't see. He forced himself to compartmentalize the process—to target his goal: Find the truth. Tromp through all the excess, let the man work through his fears and pain, patiently sift through the rights and the wrongs. Only then would the truth come out. Only then could justice be served.

Compartmentalization had another convenient benefit. Win's own sins could remain shut away, his fear of his own untruths hidden. Did he want to face the truth or lack of it within himself? Did he want

to face deserved justice? *No way!* Did he want the truth and its result-
ing justice for Bill Wilson? *Hell yes!* It was an agonizing paradox in his
own moral code that unfortunately tried to slide into his soul every so
often during his work. He blinked and dropped a mental curtain on
his own feelings of infidelity. He casually leaned forward in the chair,
silenced his soul, and began to verbally take poor Bill Wilson apart.

At the end of the lengthy, gut-wrenching process, Win stood up
and told Wilson he wanted his badge. There were tears in the man's
eyes and his hands were still unsteady as he slowly unpinned the gold
shield from his gray shirt. The sorrow and regret in those tearful eyes
were real. Win closed his hand over the badge and knocked on the
door. Two HRT operators entered to handcuff Wilson, and Win moved
to face the group of officers who'd entered the hall. He handed Chief
Randall the dishonored badge with a mumbled word of condolence.
Gus Jordon still had the stricken look in his eyes Win had seen earlier
in the afternoon. Win managed a sad nod toward the man.

Wes Givens called a ten-minute break before operational strategy
meetings were to commence and everyone began to drift away. The
ASAC patted Win's shoulder and whispered, "Good job," as he moved
past him down the hall. Phillips just nodded and seemed to be apprais-
ing him; Win had seen that look from NFL scouts back in his football
days. He knew the successful interrogation had raised his stock. He
knew he should feel good about it. What he actually felt was a nearly
overwhelming desire to throw up. Instead, he walked down the hall,
smiled a strained smile at Deb, and got a cup of stale coffee.

*   *   *

Twenty-five minutes later, Win moved into the Justice Center's big
conference room and listened as an ambulance with siren wailing
pulled up to the front steps outside. He looked down from the second-
story window as four green-clad EMTs maneuvered a stretcher up
the steps and in the front door. A small crowd of tourists and curious
workers were gathering outside in the cold wind. A few minutes later
a bundled patient was carried out on the stretcher to the waiting Park

Service ambulance. Its red lights continued to flash and the siren sounded, calling even more attention to the spectacle at the Justice Center. Word would get around fast.

Ranger Bill Wilson, beloved keeper of the courthouse, had been stricken with a heart attack and was being rushed to the hospital in Bozeman. Win glanced across the street to the park's medical clinic, where four real park ranger EMTs were probably wondering why they'd been sworn to secrecy and what the hell was going on. The siren was fading in the distance. The Bureau folks would have the traitor on lockdown at the hospital, and the Prophet's guys would just chalk it up to bad luck—relying on a snitch who was an old guy with a bad heart. *A bad heart? Well, maybe they'd be right about that.*

Win let out a deep sigh. The nausea hadn't totally subsided after the two-and-a-half-hour interrogation. In less time than that, Bill Wilson would find himself held captive in a hospital room in Bozeman until the thugs were taken down. His sweet wife, Maddy, would go through the horror of thinking he was actually in critical condition in coronary care only to discover all too soon that the truth was maybe worse.

The interrogation had gone well. Real well. Bill Wilson had taken a total of $23,500 in eight separate cash payments. He didn't know any of the group's plans, but he knew enough names and identified enough mug shots to start the wheels turning on some heavy-duty conspiracy and bribery indictments for at least six of Shepherd's men, including Ron Chandler, a.k.a. Ron King. Not as weighty as terrorism charges, but it would do to get those guys off the street.

The only big surprise for Win had been Wilson's main method for obtaining the information he'd sold. Wilson had guarded the old courthouse while the new one was being built. He knew the unfinished portion of the Justice Center's second story, where the FBI contingent had set up shop, had a partially completed intercom system hidden away in the framing. He discovered he could use it as an audio feed to overhear anything that was said in that area. Wilson had to be careful when he listened in—if there was too much foot traffic at the building's entrance, or if the FBI guard was lurking too near his office door, he couldn't risk tapping into the intercom from his security office on the first floor. Even with those limitations, he'd managed to sell out the good guys on everything from agent numbers, surveillance schedules, and air assets to HRT's deployment.

The information on Bronte's attack on Ellie this morning had been gathered the old-fashioned way. Wilson had helped himself to some of Susan's doughnuts and asked her where the fire was after Win and Trey went running from her office at 7:05 a.m. Modern technology aside, the old World War II slogan was still true: "Loose lips sink ships."

Bill Wilson swore he had no advance knowledge of the attempted hits on Win's life. The man certainly had plenty of incentive not to admit to providing information tying him directly to a conspiracy involving attempted capital murder of a federal agent—a big no-no with a likely twenty-five-years-to-life sentence in a federal penitentiary. But Win's intuition told him Wilson was being honest on that point and was clueless about the attempts to kill him. Wilson did confirm the information Bordeaux had provided on the ridge three days ago. Most if not all of Ron Chandler's seven men, plus the eight chosen militiamen, were out of the church compound and scattered in Gardiner or within the park. The Bureau only had eyes on five of them, and Wilson knew nothing about the whereabouts of the others. Big problem.

CHAPTER TWENTY-EIGHT

Win leaned his head back against the top of the grungy couch in the thrown-together break room. There were stacks of empty pizza boxes on both tables—these guys did occasionally eat, but they sure weren't tidy. It had to be creeping up on 11:30, but he didn't have the energy to even look at his watch. For most of the day he'd run on pure adrenaline. Now he was starting to crash. Trey had been asleep on the couch at the other end of the room for more than an hour while Win continued the debrief with the HRT guys on Bill Wilson's arrest and interrogation. He still felt a little nauseous when he thought back over it. He kept remembering Maddy, Bill's cheerful wife, bringing him coffee and muffins that first cold morning after he'd arrived in Yellowstone. He brought a hand over his eyes and tried to push the thoughts away. He realized someone else had entered the room, but he didn't look up.

"Hey, y'all had a big day." It was Matt Smith's slow Georgia drawl. Win opened his eyes to see him glance over at Trey and pour himself a cup of coffee. Smith surprised him when he pulled up a metal chair, straddled it, and sat down across from him. His voice was low since the ranger was sleeping. "You and your partner have done good work on this one. . . . Let me see, y'all rescued a woman in distress, caught and turned a mole in a domestic terrorism case. . . . What you got goin' for the rest of the night?" Win forced a grin and sat up a little straighter.

The big man was leaning toward him over the back of the chair with the coffee cup cradled in both hands. He looked relaxed and at ease—reminded Win way too much of his cat, just before the cat was getting ready to pounce on something. Win responded with a quizzical smile. "Why am I thinkin' you're not gonna suggest we just take tomorrow off and get some much-needed rest? Why am I thinkin' the next shoe is fixin' to drop?"

Smith laughed softly. "You're an interesting one, Tyler. Phillips is really high on you and he isn't easily impressed. You turned his little drone surveillance shakedown completely back on him the other day. Gutsy, I'll give you that. Sniffing out the leak and the takedown was good work—heard the ranger's interrogation was a crowd-pleaser too. Your marksmanship and aptitude scores are out of sight. You've got what it takes, Win. Why don't you apply for HRT when this mess clears?"

"Yeah, right. You know the Bureau threw me to the wolves out here—you know why I was sent here. You've obviously seen my file." He had to fight to keep the emotion out of his voice, and he wasn't real sure it was working with Smith.

"Yeah, yeah . . . the loss of effectiveness transfer. . . . You caught a real bad break, but that's not the way it works everywhere in the Bureau. At HRT we actually value loyalty to teammates. You're winning enough points in this case to squash that crap—doesn't have to stay in your file forever. Think about HRT when this case is over."

Smith sipped the coffee and switched gears. "Given the current intel, we may go with bringing in as many of the subjects as possible—preemptive move. See if we can't get several of them off the street." He cocked his head. "Bordeaux is leaning their way. That's how I read him today. You could see it. Luke Bordeaux is real smart and real dangerous—a bad combination if he's not one hundred percent on your side. He's way too close to Trey, so we have to cut Trey loose on this operation—and the fact that the mole came out of his agency didn't help matters any. I don't want you thinking for a second we haven't gained a lot by having his help. And you're right, Trey's a good man, but even the best men can be put in compromising situations if they aren't awfully careful. We can't take a chance on it."

"Then tell Trey that." Win nodded toward the sleeping ranger. "He came into this to bring down the bad guys and he's done an excellent job. If you have to cut us both loose, that's your decision. But just so you know, I think Luke is still conflicted, but when it comes down to the lick-log he's one of the good guys—I can feel that in my heart. And even if he doesn't eventually come to our side, as you put it, I don't think Trey would cave to Luke."

"Well, I wouldn't bet my life on it, and that's what it comes down to in some of these deals. Wouldn't worry about you getting cut loose till it's over; looks like you'll be helping our liaison with your ASAC and the rest of the Bureau. Since the intel leak has been handled, we'll operate in a more traditional vein, with SAC Strickland as the official on-scene commander as of 0700 hours. I assume you've already heard we're not going to hit the church compound tomorrow, not after Wilson confirmed everything Bordeaux told you about the main players being gone. Our revised operational plan needs to be developed tomorrow morning, so go get some sleep and be back here at seven."

"Trey comes with me in the morning?"

"No, his agency will handle some of the logistics for the dignitaries' visit. He'll probably be glad to be rid of the obligation to work with us. You'll talk with him?"

"Or you could just tell me now." It was Trey.

"Playing possum?" Smith stood up and turned his attention to the ranger. "That was careless of me. How much did you hear?"

"All of it," Trey responded as he sat up on the other couch.

"Then you know how much we appreciate your help and that you've made a real contribution to this operation. You also know why we feel the relationship needs to end tonight. I've enjoyed working with you, and if this mess doesn't get resolved soon, we could all be working together again, but for now, you go back to the Park Service tomorrow."

"Understood. Glad I could be of some help. We out of here, Win?"

To his credit, when Trey stood up to go, Smith walked over to him and shook his hand. "I'll have a couple of my guys walk you over to your vehicle so you won't have to call anyone to come down. With those thugs roaming the park, Win still needs to stay on guard."

The two HRT guys Smith had called out were downstairs waiting near the ever-present guy guarding the door. They had their civilian winter garb on, with equipment pouches, and had black H&K submachine guns tucked under their arms. The Hostage Rescue Team's compact MP5s fired 10mm rounds—they were lethal-looking little suckers.

As they exited the building, Win suggested one of them move ahead to Trey's SUV in the park's Administration Building lot and the second one follow as flanker. Trey and Win quickly walked the two blocks to the rear of the big stone building and through the row of Park Service vehicles. The wind had finally died down, and it wasn't nearly as cold as it had been the last several nights, but with the temperature hovering around twenty-eight degrees, it wasn't exactly balmy. They thanked the HRT operator who was standing next to Trey's Tahoe and Trey started the engine. Win scribbled on the notepad stuck to the truck's console, then turned on his cell phone light to illuminate his written warning: BUGGED??? CAREFUL!

Trey gave him a startled look and Win started talking. "Well then, you get to go back to rangering tomorrow! Bet you're glad about that. Your stuff's at my place and it's so late—just crash over there again tonight." As he said it, he was nodding his head *yes*.

Win and Trey managed to come up with vague, generalized statements about nothing for the two minutes it took to drive to the rear of his house. Trey called on his radio to the lead ranger in Win's protection detail. There were two of them at the house tonight and nothing out of the ordinary was happening.

Trey pulled into the rear parking area, and the ranger acknowledged his boss's arrival with a quick wave before Trey killed the headlights. Trey didn't even grab his hat off the dashboard as he stepped out of the Tahoe and approached the man. "Did anyone have access to the house today? Anyone?"

"We did an interior sweep at seven o'clock tonight when our shifts changed. No one has been inside since then. No one," the man replied.

"Okay, call whoever was on the earlier shift and ask them. I want to know ASAP."

Win was standing outside the ranger's SUV. He pulled his parka tighter around him, moved into the deeper shadows at the side of the small garage, and waited for Trey to join him.

"Are you kidding me!" Trey was still calm, but just barely.

"Maybe I'm paranoid, but how did the HRT operator know which of five identical Park Service Tahoes parked in that lot was yours? He walked right to it. Plus, didn't you think it was odd those two HRT guys were already in winter garb with night-vision equipment, like they were waiting around for us—and this just a couple of minutes after Smith's off-the-cuff mention of having agents walk us to the vehicle. They're probably watching us right now! As for Matt being careless and talking to me in that break room with you in there . . . the man didn't get to be a senior team leader in the FBI's Hostage Rescue Team by being that careless. I'm not buying it!"

"Man, I hope you're being paranoid—what do you think's going on?"

"I'm guessing they decided to tail you after the meeting at Luke's house this morning. I was a little concerned about that, and not only for you. Luke was treating me like a long-lost cousin as well."

"You think they suspect you're somehow involved with Luke? Naw, that's a stretch," the ranger said.

"They don't make their living trusting rookie agents or anyone else, for that matter. They've probably seen plenty of good people go bad. Heck, look at Bill Wilson! There's a sickening example. Good folks make horrible mistakes! I don't blame anyone at HRT—they're trying to do their jobs. I figure there's also a good chance they've got your personal phone tapped, probably since this morning, but it could have been earlier than that."

"So why would they waste their time keeping up with us?"

Win stared into the darkness toward the parade grounds—from where he was sure someone else was watching them. The wind was picking up, but neither man was bothered by the cold night air or the late hour at this point.

"I got to thinking. How did Phillips and Smith even know we were at Luke's place early this morning? They were halfway up his road when I called to tell them where we were. HRT isn't directly connected to the SWAT Team's communications. They've kept HRT's communications system separate because of the leak. And how did Phillips know Bronte might have been trying to surrender? I never mentioned that—I'm not even sure of that. They may have watched the whole thing develop on a low-level drone feed. HRT has one of those specialized drones here. They can fly it under weather conditions that wouldn't work for more traditional, high-altitude drones. If they got good video footage, they may have enough to charge Luke with something during the incident with Bronte. That would mean Luke would be part of the subject take-down Smith was talking about. A charge of second-degree murder wouldn't likely stand, but it would be enough for them to arrest him. They'd be able to hold him at least temporarily."

Win paused as he brought his hand to his chin. "But why string it out in front of us tonight?" His eyes shifted back to Trey. "And what if you *had* been asleep. Why string it out in front of me? What's to be gained there? Looks to me as if they want to see if there's anyone else who can be caught up in the trap with Luke. You're definitely in their sights, and I may be too."

"Why you?"

"You haven't seen my file. Phillips and Smith have. I worked on a really messy political corruption case in North Carolina that fell apart because of pressure out of Washington. Some senior agents lost their jobs. Real good men. I got shipped out here and kept my job, but there are some in the Bureau, in high places, who'd like nothing more than to see me leave the FBI. I know too much. Phillips and Smith could score big points with some higher-ups by tripping me up on something out here. Some of the bad guys were in the Bureau in that deal."

"It's feeling to me like some of the bad guys are in the Bureau in this deal."

"Lordy, I hope not, but I think we both have to assume HRT has our phones, vehicles, and houses bugged and the surveillance is on us as well as the bad guys. This is a high-level domestic terrorism case; they could get emergency authority to wiretap almost anyone under these conditions and it could be arranged through the Washington office. It's possible no one here except my SAC and HRT would even know about it." Win paused, then asked, "Anybody go in my house today?"

"Jimmy's checking. . . . Not since seven o'clock tonight."

Well, Win thought, *might as well lay it out.* "Do you know where Luke is?" There was silence. Win tensed when the ranger shifted in the darkness. *Don't lie to me. . . . Don't lie . . . don't do it.*

Trey finally gave his answer. "Yes." He took a deep breath before he continued. "After the sheriff's deputies left this morning, Ellie took Luke to get his truck on the other side of the river, then she drove on to stay with my family in Bozeman. Luke needed to get clear of King's men in Gardiner, so he switched vehicles with another friend of ours and came into Mammoth around mid-afternoon. He's been at my house since then, as far as I know." Those facts hung heavy in the cold air.

Before Win could absorb all that, Ranger Jimmy walked up and made his report. "Earlier shift said no one went in the house except for a plumber, who was doing some routine pressure tests on park housing, hmmm . . . kitchen and bathroom lines. They said the guy had all the correct IDs and papers. One of our guys went in with him and he was only in there for a few minutes. He left at 6:17 this evening."

Win was really glad the rangers couldn't see his face. Some of the hard questions were starting to get answered. A skilled communications tech could plant wireless bugs throughout a house within minutes, even with someone shadowing him. He'd had experience in that type of electronic bug placement on white-collar cases in Charlotte. Win was really beginning to feel Trey wasn't the only one on HRT's radar.

Jimmy walked back to his post, and the two men stood there in the cold darkness. The blackness of the night seemed to envelope them like a shroud.

"Well, hell," Trey finally offered.

"No kidding! They probably would've hit your house about the same time. Likely decided to go that route after the interrogation of

Wilson this afternoon. They may not think he was the only source of intel the bad guys had, or maybe they're just casting a wide net. Could Luke have dodged them at your house?"

"Yup, there's a hideout in the attic. He and I built it for the kids to play in, but the wives nixed that idea early on—you'd have to know it was there. He could've hidden if he spotted them ahead of time. I'd be shocked if Luke got caught flat-footed."

Win was still stunned from Trey's earlier answer as to Luke's whereabouts, but he figured he needed to cover all the bases. "Anything on your phone today?"

"The call with Ellie, setting her up with Cindy. Ah, that was around noon. No problem there." He paused for way too long, then, "Luke called me from a throwaway early afternoon when I was in your office. I was not on my phone. He'd put two burner phones in the pocket of the hunting clothes I changed into this morning at his house. There was a note in the code we used back when things weren't good for him with the FBI last year. Said he'd try to get to my place. . . . Hey, I know this isn't sounding too good."

"You think?" Win was furious. He had to fight to control his anger when he spoke again. "Let's stand in the shed for a minute." Win really needed to see Trey's eyes.

He pushed open the old wooden door and pulled the string cord on the single light bulb. The small shed smelled of oil paint, mildew, and dust. They stood on the dirty concrete floor in the circle of dim light, facing each other with their arms crossed. Trey's gray eyes told Win nothing. He remembered Trey's comments about being a good poker player. He asked himself if he was blind to Trey's actions because he wanted so badly to have a partner, a teammate again. *Have I been betrayed?*

Win finally spoke. "Seriously? Are you telling me you took untraceable phones and a coded note, invited Luke to stay at your house, and didn't bother to tell me!" It was no longer a question. "Are you working with him, Trey? If not, well, if this guy was a true friend of yours he wouldn't have put you in this type of bind! And since I'm the one standing up for you with HRT, it's put me under the same suspicion!"

Trey wasn't backing down. "If you'll recall, I tried twice to fill you in this afternoon, but things got a little busy. Remember that? We can't undo what's happened, but they're wrong about Luke and you know it! You said it to Smith tonight—you said you felt it in your heart. I think Luke got himself in too deep with some folks he initially thought were just playing soldier, and he's looking for an honorable way out. We need to give him that way out. Yeah, and he may have been a little caught up in the Prophet's rhetoric for a while, but after Bronte attacked Ellie this morning, I think it shocked him back to reality. If they arrest him there will be no way he'll cooperate, and someone could get hurt. We have to appeal to his better angels."

"Well, we sure need to do something fast, 'cause if they have warrants and Luke is discovered at your place, or if they're able to somehow trace that call he made to you, then either way, you've got major problems. A new warrant on Luke plus those federal charges he's out on bail for, that would make it harboring a fugitive for you—real big problems!" Win let that sink in for a few moments before he continued. "Can you text him in your code and see if he's there? No way to call. If the house is bugged, it will pick up the sound."

Trey quickly texted a message on the small throwaway phone and a response came in seconds. "Yup, he's there. House was bugged at 6:45 and it's being watched. One, maybe two guys outside."

Win stood there and stared at the light playing on the dirty floor, dust flecks drifting up through the yellow hue. The simplest and least risky course for him was to give up Trey and Luke to HRT and hope to come out of it unscathed. But nothing about that option felt right.

It was like Trey was reading his mind. The ranger let out a deep breath that rose in the cold air. He spoke quietly. "You're holdin' all the cards here, Win. I can see that. I went with my heart instead of thinking it through. I think Luke's finished with the Prophet's people, but I didn't expect HRT to come after him like this . . . to come after us like this. I won't blame you if you call them now. I'll go back over there with you and turn myself in, if that's what you want."

"After you text Luke to clear out?" Win actually felt himself smiling.

"Yup, you know it." If Trey was sweating this, his calm voice didn't give him away.

Win pushed the felt hat back on his head and stared into Trey's eyes. There wasn't time to do a lot of analysis here; he had to go with his instincts. He thought back to the Brunson case. He'd risked his career and nearly lost it. He'd refused to turn on his friends then—he *knew* what that felt like. It was time to fish or cut bait with Trey.

Win looked down and ran his hand along his chin. "I'd probably do the same thing if he was my friend. I'd like to think I would. . . . Maybe there's another way out of this." He studied the concrete floor for a minute longer. "I say we try to get Luke to meet with Phillips and Smith tonight. Set it up as our last effort as partners to move Luke toward a working relationship with the good guys. He probably has a healthy respect for HRT or any special ops group—that's what he's used to. He has no great respect for the FBI as a whole. I can't see him talking to Emily or Wes."

Trey nodded his agreement as Win finished his thoughts. "HRT could have warrants in hand for arrests if our legal folks in D.C. started working on them late this afternoon. More'n likely they're looking at tomorrow morning, but you've seen those operators work. I don't want to chance waiting. If we miscalculate and they move on Luke at your house tonight . . . all bets are off."

CHAPTER TWENTY-NINE

As plans go, it wasn't much. Trey pulled his tactical duffel bag, which included his night-vision equipment, out of his Tahoe and they quickly walked through the house, turning on both TVs and trying to make chitchat that would convince any listeners they were settling in for the night. A few minutes later, Trey appeared in his dark-green SWAT overalls and body armor just as Win emerged from his bedroom in his darkest version of hunting clothes and boots. His body armor was in his Bureau vehicle back at the office; he'd have to do without. They checked their handguns, pulled on heavy parkas, gloves, and ball caps, and nodded silently to each other. Both men held up their various cell phones to confirm they were powered down. Trey made an offhand comment to the walls that he needed to check outside with Jimmy one last time before they turned in. Win cracked the blinds and watched Trey call out to the rear guard and then walk quickly across the small yard to Ranger Jimmy.

Win glanced at his watch and hit the timer: *Exactly one minute till all hell breaks loose.* There were all sorts of ways this could go sideways—the Bureau's tendency to plan things to death was beginning to look more and more reasonable. He wiped a layer of sweat off his forehead with a gloved hand. As Trey came back across the yard toward the back steps, Win crouched in the mudroom beside the rear door. The back of the house was very dark. The front area wasn't much brighter; the ornamental light pole out near the front parking lot had long since been disconnected so the security detail could better utilize their night-vision equipment during their evening house patrols. But anyone turning from the highway into the parking lot would illuminate the front of the house; they couldn't take the chance on being seen. They'd go out the back way, away from HRT's surveillance team.

Win and Trey would use Win's personal vehicle for their getaway. It had been parked in the visitor's lot near the Lower Terrace boardwalk since security had been tightened around his house. Win couldn't imagine HRT going to the trouble of bugging that truck. He hardly ever drove it. HRT might not even know about the Explorer. It still had its North Carolina plates.

He glanced down at his stopwatch and swallowed hard. They'd make a break for it right . . . *now!* He leaped out the back door as the beeper on his watch sounded and he heard the shout from Ranger Jimmy in the backyard: *"Police! Show yourself! Police! Hands up now!"* The guard in the front was also raising the loud warning that two intruders had been spotted northeast of the house. Win felt more than saw Trey jogging along beside him in the darkness as they ran in the opposite direction from the rapidly developing confrontation. They jumped the little stream and raced down the well-worn trail toward the boardwalk and away from the shouting rangers. There was more yelling now from the east side of the house. He couldn't make out the words, but the anger and intensity in the voices was unmistakable. *Please don't start shooting!*

He hadn't been in the old Explorer in days. He prayed that it would start in the high-country air. The engine came to life without a hitch. He eased the truck out of the parking spot without headlights and made a quick turn off the highway onto a restricted side road that looped back toward Officer's Row and the chapel. They hadn't driven two hundred yards before they heard sirens blaring. *Commit to the action!* Those were Luke Bordeaux's words. Win drew in a deep breath. *Well, we're damn well committed—God help us!*

Trey's calm voice eased his fears just a bit. "Saw them with my night-vision optics. It was two of them, just like you thought. Told Jimmy to radio Brent in front and call in the troops—told him it might be HRT out training, not to get trigger-happy. . . ." He let his voice trail off.

Win turned on the headlights. It took them less than a minute to swing past the Yellowstone Chapel and enter the modern employee-housing development called Lower Mammoth. Two carloads of tourists and a large RV passed by on the main highway from Roosevelt. Win was hoping the late-night traffic would help them move away from his house unnoticed.

"You get ahold of Luke?"

"Yup, he knows we're comin'. How long before HRT traces the texts?"

"Not sure. Infrastructure is terrible out here, but they can do it. If nothing else they can get a location on Luke—probably based on the call he made to you this afternoon. Your texts tonight will just confirm that location. Let's hope we get there before they get into position to make a raid on your house."

Win pulled to the side of a dark, empty street and Trey gave him a quick rundown of the subdivision's layout. They were two streets over from Trey's house.

Win couldn't make out any of Trey's facial features in the dark vehicle, but he felt as if he needed to say something, some word of encouragement to show a little leadership.

"Uh, you okay?" It was a weak attempt.

"What could go wrong?" the ranger deadpanned. Win could see his white teeth flash a quick smile. *Hell of a lot!*

"Well then . . . let's do it." He leaned over the steering wheel and manually disconnected the SUV's interior lights. He heard the passenger door open, and Trey was gone into the night.

Win slumped lower into his seat and tried to melt into the darkness. His heart was pounding and he felt sweaty, even in the cold. Hugging himself with his arms generated very little warmth. He jumped when two elk calmly walked across the street to graze on somebody's lawn. Blue and red police lights were reflecting off low clouds in the vicinity of his house, less than a mile away. The rangers were all over the HRT guys, or vice versa. The confrontation should at least stall any planned assault on Trey's house.

While Trey scouted out the situation in the neighborhood, Win killed time by trying to rationalize his actions. Luke was Win's confidential source; Win was charged with protecting him. They needed a diversion to get Luke out of Trey's house. He reasoned that he had no *actual* knowledge of a legal warrant for Luke's arrest. So as far as he *knew*, HRT had no right to come after Luke, and no authorization to stake out Win's house. HRT knew the rangers were charged with guarding it—the rangers had to assume the intruders were affiliated with the bad guys. His mental outline of excuses felt way too much like those times in high school when his stern father had questioned him over some infraction he'd later concede just seemed like a good idea at the time. He sighed and glanced at his watch again. All rationalization aside, someone was gonna catch hell over this deal and he hoped it wouldn't be him.

He could see the occasional car headlights on the main highway leading into Mammoth, but the neighborhood was quiet and most of the houses were dark. The subdivision of sixty-two modest rental homes for park employees had no streetlights, in keeping with the wilderness feel of Yellowstone. He flinched as two more sirens wailed from the direction of his house, setting him further on edge. He jumped again when Trey softly knocked on the passenger-side window, slid the door open, and flipped up his night-vision goggles.

The ranger was breathing heavily, but his whispered voice was steady. "We've got one guy in the empty lot north of the house. He's kinda up on the hill. Normally there'd be another one in the rear, but either I can't find him or they're just covering the front of the house. The truck Luke came in is in our driveway. If you can create enough of a diversion in the front—any light will make his night vision worthless—I can get Luke out the back door. We'll meet you here. That's assuming there isn't anyone on surveillance in the rear."

"HRT uses their snipers for protracted ground surveillance," Win offered.

"Well, that's a comforting thought—just gotta hope there isn't someone back there. We'll need about ten minutes. Give me five to the house, then five in and back." He glanced down at his watch. "Set . . . go!" He was gone.

Win's stopwatch hit five minutes after what seemed an eternity. He turned on his lights and drove slowly up Trey's street, calling out his open window, "Here, Shep! Here, Shep! Here, boy!" He used his high-beam flashlight to scan all of the surrounding brush and the neighboring yards. Trey had said the HRT guy was across the street from his house, so that's where Win's "dog hunting" got most intense; he circled the area three times, shining the flashlight into every bush. When his stopwatch hit five minutes for the second time, he turned the old SUV down the street and continued his dog hunt in a somewhat lower voice. No reason to wake up the whole neighborhood.

He circled a cul-de-sac right behind a herd of elk. Luke and Trey appeared out of the rear of the herd and climbed into the back seats so quietly that he wasn't even sure they were there. They both kept their heads down as he drove to the other side of the subdivision and parked on the street in the blackness of an overhanging tree.

"Okaaay, boys, do you think we're clear?"

Luke spoke first. "Lookin' that way. Downright creative, Win. Learn that in your FBI school?"

"Nope, made that one up. No time for small talk, let's decide what we're gonna do here. Trey and I both know you never had any intention of getting mixed up with bad guys like these, Luke. We're afraid innocent folks are fixin' to get hurt—we need your help to stop this deal. We need your help badly." Win shifted to face the back seat. "The Bureau will be moving to arrest as many of the Prophet's men as possible to keep something awful from happening during the next few days. They still consider you to be one of the Prophet's men, Luke. They could have a new warrant out on you tonight, early tomorrow for sure."

"Fer what? They don't have nothin' on me!"

"They may have drone footage of you shooting Bronte off the cable. They'll probably claim he was in the process of surrendering. Likely enough probable cause to get a warrant, even if charges have to be dropped later. Enough for an arrest—you don't want that." Win noticed Luke didn't jump in and deny shooting Bronte. He forged on. "The truth is, we don't know what Shepherd is planning and you may not know either, but we need some help."

Trey spoke up quietly from beside Bordeaux. "Those guys are not your friends, Luke—not the men King, or Chandler, or whatever his name is, brought in. Look what happened with Ellie. Will you at least talk to the HRT guys tonight? If we wait till tomorrow, the traditional FBI folks will be handling this end of it, and I know you have little regard for them."

Win held his breath waiting for Luke to respond. When he did, his voice was low and measured. "After the house got bugged, it occurred to me I'd put Trey in a bad position by hidin' out there. I got outa my place 'cause a couple of Bronte's buddies, King's men, were still in the area. Had no desire to end up dead in my own bed. Shoulda handled it better than I did. I ain't been using real good judgment here lately. That's not who I am, you know that, Trey."

Win heard Bordeaux take a deep breath. "I ain't gonna turn against my militiamen. They're just followin' our church, but Ron King and his boys are outlaws. I don't need no more convincing there. Any talkin' I do with HRT is only gonna deal with Brother King and his guys."

Not exactly what he wanted, but Win would take it. "I suppose that's the honorable thing to do. So you'll meet with Phillips and Smith if I set it up?"

"Yeah."

Thank God! Win glanced at his watch, 12:18 a.m. He was shocked it wasn't later. Trey handed him one of the throwaway phones. He powered it up and dialed the number. Matt Smith answered on the third ring. "Hey, this is Win. Sorry if I woke you, Matt."

"Not in bed yet. . . . Why are you calling from this number? Where are you?" The man's tone was sharp and accusatory.

Win was trying real hard to remember he was in the same agency with this guy. His voice took on an edge. "Look, Matt, I didn't buy your efforts at carelessness earlier tonight. I don't like having my house bugged or my partner's house and vehicle bugged. I liked the stakeouts at those places even less. So you tell me now what team I'm on and we'll go from there."

Win heard the team leader clear his throat. "Is Trey with you?"

Luke and Trey were both leaning in, listening to every word of the phone conversation, as Win angrily replied, "That's immaterial! I want to know why you're playing us!" He couldn't believe he'd just challenged the senior agent, but he'd noticed Smith hadn't answered his question either.

Smith hesitated for a long moment then responded, "Okay, listen . . . we got real nervous about Trey's relationship with Bordeaux, especially after he nearly got himself killed saving the man's wife this morning. And it looks like Bordeaux did shoot the guy off the cable—or at least tried to—that's a bit sketchier. Got that incident on live feeds off our low-altitude drone, as I'm sure you suspected by now."

Win shifted in his seat as Smith kept talking. "Bill Wilson is probably just trying to save his own skin, but all the way to Bozeman, he kept saying there were others in the Park Service involved in the leak. It would take time to run it all down, but Trey was the most obvious name on the list. Neither Phillips nor I believe that, but it made Washington even more anxious about the guy. So you got watched 'cause we were watching him."

Win tried to make a comment, but Smith cut him off. "I'm not finished here. It got worse for Hechtner this afternoon, when he took a call on a burner phone from Bordeaux. Part of the conversation was in some code—maybe a Native American language, we're not sure—but there were definitely plans to meet. Bordeaux lost his Bureau surveillance team five minutes later, and we didn't know where he was until we got locational hits from that phone again tonight. Win, did you know about that call?"

"Yeah, I knew about the call." *Technically true.* "We're trying to develop intel here, Matt. That's part of our job, as I understand it. I'm the case agent for False Prophet, for Pete's sake! What am I supposed to be doing? Luke is my source, you know that. I have every right to contact him and so does my partner." *Probably not correct, but sounds plausible.* He paused. "Does HRT still have the operational authority to help develop the intel on this case?"

"Yes, until SAC Strickland signs on in the morning."

"Do you want help on that?"

"What? How?"

"Luke will provide us with information on the current locations of some of Chandler's men in Gardiner. But I have to have HRT's assurance there'll be no warrant on Luke Bordeaux. He is under my supervision." *I wish!* "If there is a new warrant, I want it pulled."

"Kirk is standing here beside me, listening in on this. Let him give you HRT's assurance."

Phillips came on the call. "Win, I don't know what you've got—but you are the case agent. I can give you HRT assurance we won't enforce a warrant for Luke Bordeaux on any matter we have to date, *if* he's willing to provide the Bureau with credible intel leading to arrests." Phillips's voice was as cold as the night air.

Let's try to put the best possible light on this. . . . "Thank you, sir. Luke will be glad to help you get Ron Chandler's men off the street." Win wasn't feeling real trusting; taking Luke to HRT headquarters didn't feel real smart. He needed a neutral site. He wrapped it up with Phillips. "Meet us in the Yellowstone Chapel sanctuary. We'll be waiting."

Win pulled the Explorer into the south parking lot of the chapel within seconds, and as soon as he turned off the engine, he froze at the sound of a pistol slide being racked directly behind him.

"Not to worry, just unloading my weapon. I can't have a loaded gun in the park, you know. Leaving it and my knife in your truck. Let's move." Now Luke seemed to be in charge.

It took Luke all of ten seconds to jimmy the lock and get them inside the front door of the chapel. Win flipped on several lights, and all three men walked down the center aisle toward the front altar. Win mentally ran through his goals for this little meeting: save Luke from a potential arrest and a shoot-out with the good guys, save Trey from arrest for harboring Luke, and hopefully get some information that would help them put an end to this seemingly endless series of crises.

Luke abruptly turned to Trey and Win as they walked down the aisle. It was as if he were on an internal countdown to HRT's arrival. His eyes had a steely focus Win had never seen before. An emotion just short of fear settled over him as Luke spoke.

"Listen to me, both of you! HRT may try to intimidate, to cower us. They may come in here like the Hounds of Hell! Do not, and I mean do not, give them any reason to see you as a threat. Take your caps and coats off now. Keep your hands away from your body. If they want your weapons, let them take them—do not move, do not talk back, do not resist them. If the lights go out, raise your hands behind your head. Do not hesitate! Have you got that?" The dark eyes were intense and the tone was quiet and direct. There was no Louisiana drawl, no hick accent. The voice was military precise. As Luke's piercing eyes locked on Win's, a cold chill went through him. He suddenly understood why Smith and Phillips kept calling Luke Bordeaux the most dangerous one.

Win had just dropped his cap and coat onto a pew when the lights went out. All three men immediately raised their hands behind their heads as operators swarmed the room from both entrances, shouting commands and flashing lights. It was meant to be frightening, and it worked on Win. He closed his eyes, tried to remember to breathe, and prayed that some good would come in this Holy Place from his effort to do the right thing. He obeyed Luke's command to stand perfectly still as his Glock was lifted and rough gloves patted him down. A moment later there was a sharp call and the lights came on. Win and Trey were standing where they'd been when the lights were killed, four gunmen around them. Luke was on his knees near the altar, his hands behind his head. Three operators surrounded Luke, and one stood at each entrance. That meant an entire nine-man team was at the chapel, and they'd obviously been outfitted before Win's phone call minutes ago to Smith—chances were good they were already geared up to go after Luke in that hideout.

All the operators were in their olive-green tactical gear with helmets, night-vision devices flipped up, and balaclava face masks. Every man's MP5 was trained on a target. The black FBI lettering across their armored vests gave Win no comfort, since he was clearly one of those targets. These were the same great guys he'd been working with, joking with, and eating with for the last several days. Now they were terrifying.

They stood there for only a few seconds before Phillips walked in from the front foyer. He was dressed in civilian clothes and orchestrated much of what happened with simple hand signals. *Like you would with hunting dogs,* Win was thinking. Phillips asked one of the men to dim the lights slightly and he moved to face Trey and Win.

"Well, boys, you're sure full of surprises." He didn't sound amused. "You may stand down." They both dropped their arms, but the HRT guys didn't lower their sub guns. No one moved to return their handguns. Win had about had it with the intimidation, although he had to admit it was working on him. He was equally certain it was not going to work on Luke Bordeaux.

Win took a breath and addressed Phillips formally. "Sir, I called this meeting to have a confidential discussion of matters that are critical to the False Prophet case."

"Alright, let's do just that." More hand signals and they had Luke on his feet, then in a chair someone had pulled from the small choir loft. Win was watching him closely. Luke kept his hands behind his head with his fingers locked together. He seemed to be staring straight ahead. He didn't meet any of the men's eyes—as if that might provoke them—but he never dropped his eyes either. He was dressed in black cargo pants, hunting boots, and a gray wool shirt. He didn't look like a terrorist or a criminal; he looked like a regular guy. Win wondered where Luke had stashed his assault rifle, fatigues, and other militia garb. He had a feeling Trey's house was fixing to have uninvited visitors again—if they weren't there already.

Matt Smith, in full tactical gear, appeared from the front of the chapel and moved toward Phillips. He gave Win and Trey a glance that could kill as he and Phillips conferred for a moment. Someone on their internal communication system was apparently reporting something to them that they weren't particularly happy about. Win was feeling way out of his league here.

Then another hand signal and the four operators on Win and Trey lowered their weapons and moved toward the front door. Win took a deep breath and swallowed hard. It was time to get his game face on.

* * *

Win, Trey, and Luke walked toward the back of the church sanctuary about fifteen minutes later. Several of the operators had vanished five minutes after Luke began his "interview," as Win liked to think of it. It wasn't really an interrogation, yet it had an adversarial feel. The operators kept their helmets and masks in place; everyone's weapon was visible. It was clear from Bordeaux's demeanor that he wasn't thrilled with the position he found himself in, and Kirk Phillips knew better than to play hardball with the guy. Luke Bordeaux clearly had respect for the operators, but just as clearly he had no fear of them. Luke reported the whereabouts of four of Chandler's thugs to Phillips as if he were reporting to his commanding officer. He didn't give up any useful intel on the men he viewed as "militiamen" or on *his* prophet, as he called Daniel Shepherd, no matter how cleverly Phillips couched his questions. Once Luke started stonewalling, it was obvious to everyone that they could talk till kingdom come and no more helpful information would be forthcoming. Time was at a premium. They needed to go with what Luke had given them.

They'd wrapped it up with him just moments ago.

"So we're finished here?" Phillips's hands had gone to his knees as he started to stand.

"I've kept my agreement with Trey and Win," Luke had replied. And with that they were done. Phillips's sharp eyes had left Bordeaux for the first time and had settled on Smith. They'd shared a quick nod and moved seamlessly into their tactical mode. Phillips stood and turned away. He immediately began communicating with someone on their com system. Trey had motioned Luke up the aisle behind the departing operators. It had gotten very quiet in the little church.

As they moved to go through the foyer doors, Matt Smith removed his helmet and pulled Win aside from the group. He was standing too close to Win to be friendly when he spoke. "Not sure how I want to take all this yet—we'll see where the tips lead. Two of the bad guys he ratted out were already under surveillance. The other two? We'll see if they're where he says they are." A pause, then, "How'd you know we were planning to come down on Bordeaux at Hechtner's house?"

"Figured y'all could track the throwaway phone calls and texts somehow—even with the poor communications setup out here. So I figured Trey was compromised this afternoon, and I knew we'd be tagged when we texted Luke a while ago. Matt, if you had gone in there after him with guns blazing—"

"Yeah, yeah, we all knew that was a big risk given who we were dealing with. Maybe your stunt prevented someone from getting hurt, but I *did not* like having my plan disrupted or my guys set on by the rangers at your house." The imposing man was leaning in toward Win. His voice was harsh.

Win stood his ground. "You didn't trust me to be on your team, Matt, so I went with the team I had. And *our* team needed a diversion to get Luke out of that house. I'm not making any apologies to you for protecting my source."

"You know as well as I do he's not telling us everything he knows."

"Maybe he feels as if he needs to hold some things back for insurance, or—"

Smith interrupted. "Or ever hear of a double agent, Win? Playing it both ways? Has that occurred to you? Think about the lives that could be lost if Luke Bordeaux *is* one of the bad guys! You're going to let the guy walk out of here, scot-free! Is that what you want to do?"

As tired as Win was, that thought had run through his mind more than once tonight. He remembered his gut reaction to Luke's steely eyes when they'd entered the chapel—the same reaction he had the first time he walked away from Luke and Chief Randall weeks ago, when Luke called after him, "See ya around, Win Tyler!" Win had felt that same cold chill earlier tonight. It was almost as if Bordeaux had two different personalities. Deep down Win wasn't one hundred percent sure who was getting intel on whom. He knew Smith could tell he was waffling, but he stuck to his guns on this one.

"No, Matt, he's lived up to his end of the bargain as far as I'm concerned—as far as the Bureau's concerned. He goes free. If something changes tomorrow we can deal with it then."

* * *

Win finally pulled himself into the driver's seat of his Explorer and started the truck. He was sure glad he didn't really drink, 'cause if he did, he was afraid he'd tie one on tonight. He sat back in the cold seat and watched while Trey and Luke continued to talk beneath the flickering antique streetlight outside the church's entrance. The HRT operators had all melted into the darkness. They were already moving to arrest some of Ron Chandler's men tonight. Scenarios of that sort had been drawn up and rehearsed dozens of times since HRT had been in Mammoth—they'd only been waiting for confirmed suspect locations and the go-ahead. Now they had both. As the case agent, Win knew he could insist on being a part of any arrest, but he also knew he didn't have to be there, since Deb was on call. He'd opted out. One more thing was too much tonight. The operators and Deb might get the luxury of sleeping some tomorrow. He knew he would not.

He sat in the truck and filled his supervisor in on the evening's highlights. In typical FBI fashion, Jim West appeared to be fully awake the moment he answered the phone. West hardly asked any questions. Win knew his judgment on the night's events would receive a complete review at the appropriate time—and 12:57 a.m. on the night of subject arrests was not the appropriate time. Win was saved from further questioning when Wes Givens called in on Jim's phone. Phillips had reached out to the ASAC on the impending arrests, per Bureau protocol. Win pocketed the phone as Trey opened the door and slumped into the passenger seat. Luke eased into the back.

"Where to, boys, I'm driving!" Win made a lame attempt to appear upbeat.

Trey sounded tired and frustrated. "I gotta go back into the office and make a report on the near shoot-'em-up between our folks and the

HRT boys over at your house. Gus is furious, so things may not go real smoothly there. . . . My rig is at your house, just take me there."

"Luke? You're welcome to stay at my place tonight. Got extra bedrooms and a bath upstairs. You can head out tomorrow, or whenever you want."

"Me and Trey talked it over, and I'll stay over at his place tonight. I ain't too happy with your kind, and I damn sure ain't feeling too good 'bout me right now. I know exactly what you're thinkin', Win—thinkin' that fool Cajun done got himself into this mess and he'd be right smart to thank me fer saving his hide tonight. But just so's you know, I ain't feelin' too grateful at the moment. I aim to drop out of sight fer a few days till this deal is over, so don't come lookin' fer me! You got that?"

Win could hear Luke reloading the handgun directly behind him, and he could tell from his tone that he was conflicted and angry about placing himself in a position where he had to "snitch," as he saw it, on a bunch of criminals he shouldn't have been involved with in the first place. Win didn't want to get on the wrong side of Luke's anger, especially when Luke had a loaded pistol behind him.

"Okay, okay, I got it! Uh, why don't you leave the gun with me? You aren't allowed to carry in the park," Win said.

"You gonna push that tonight, boy?" The low voice sounded deadly.

Win quickly weighed the pros and cons of keeping his informant on the right side of the law. There was one serious problem with pushing the matter: Luke Bordeaux might be angry enough to kill him.

Trey saved them from a confrontation neither man wanted. "Why don't I hold the weapons till we get over to my place. Probably just leave 'em on the kitchen table. Where they end up after that . . ." The ranger shrugged.

After Luke handed over his knife and Beretta to Trey, there wasn't any more conversation on the short drive back to Win's house. The old stone dwelling was lit up like a Christmas tree, and as they drove up, Win could see several rangers milling about in the yard. It was the aftermath of the run-in with the HRT guys, which had happened only fifty-five minutes earlier—events had been unfolding at a frantic pace.

An odd sense of detachment settled on Win for a moment as his headlights swept over the five Park Service vehicles surrounding his house. His mind went to the *Federal Operational Threat Assessment* that had come in from Headquarters earlier this evening. In less than forty-eight hours, the Israeli delegation would have been here and gone. Many honchos in the Department of Justice, the National Park Service, and to a lesser degree the Secret Service still thought that the Arm of the Lord Church cult and their sketchy followers were using the dedication of the Jewish monument purely for recruitment propaganda. All bluster, no credible threat. Those attached to that way of thinking considered the two attacks on Win to be totally unrelated to the church group. Win was an FBI agent, they reasoned; agents often made enemies.

The FBI, especially the agents on the ground, certainly weren't thinking along those lines—not on either issue. But Win knew the consensus of the higher-ups in three federal agencies was that there was an eighty percent statistical probability that nothing bad would happen during the next two days in Yellowstone National Park. Win pulled the Explorer to a stop beside Trey's Tahoe and frowned into the night. *That leaves a twenty percent probability that it will.*

CHAPTER THIRTY

It was just too quiet in the house. Nearly 10:30 on Sunday morning and no squealing little girl, no list of honey-dos, no big slobbering dog. He hadn't even managed to go to church this morning; he'd slept late instead. The birds were hard at it outside the curtained window, singing their cheerful songs, trying to hurry spring along. But inside the house it was just too quiet. His second cup of coffee and over six hours of much-needed sleep had finally cleared most of the cobwebs from his mind, but he was still having a hard time sorting through his thoughts. *Had last night really happened?* He wasn't even sure Cindy could comprehend all the convoluted activity, much less his conflicting emotions. He'd called her with the CliffsNotes version of events when he'd first awakened. As he recalled, she kept saying, "Oh my . . . Trey, oh my . . ." At least McKenna had cooed "Love you, Daddy!" to him a half dozen times before she ran from the phone to continue her princess games. He drew in a long breath—it was Mother's Day, and he missed his girls so badly it hurt.

He gently brushed a dirty spot off his tan felt hat. He was holding it under the bright light above their small breakfast table, trying to make sure every speck of dirt and grime was gone. It was May 11th—hat rotation day at Yellowstone National Park. All rangers switched as one from the tan felt Stetson to the summer's straw version of the flat hat. It didn't matter that it was still hovering near freezing outside; summer season in the park had officially begun. He'd worn the hat for nine years now—the first time as a summer seasonal ranger back in graduate school, and seven years now as a permanent law enforcement ranger. It had a tooled leather hatband intricately carved with oak leaves and pinecones. The peaked crown was designed in the 1920s to shed water and snow. Folks called it a Smokey the Bear hat. To some rangers it was a hassle to carry around and deal with, but to Trey, it represented his life's calling. It was a powerful symbol of what he'd always wanted to be.

Late last night that had all been called into question. Gus Jordon had handed him his butt—the man was livid. Gus didn't exactly say his promotion to Mammoth District Ranger had been ill-advised, but he sure did imply it. He'd sat in Gus's office and gone through the situation, as they were calling it, between his two Special Response Team rangers and the two HRT guys who were spying on Win Tyler's house. Then there was the fact he'd let Luke Bordeaux move into his place yesterday afternoon. Gus hadn't been subtle.

"What was going through your mind?" Gus's face was red—the man almost never got red-faced. "Thank God it ended with four men just cussing each other, but in the dark, with all four heavily armed . . . someone could have gotten killed! And we turned out six more units because of the perceived threat! Two FBI agents in handcuffs! Do you have any idea how ticked off everyone in their agency is tonight?"

Trey had tried to respond. "Our team was charged with protecting Tyler. Two men with night-vision equipment sneaking up on his house. Yeah, I thought they were HRT, but I didn't think it was advisable to walk over and ask them—hell, Gus, you know they don't have any regard for our tactical ability. To them, we're the junior varsity!"

"Well, there's damn good reason for that! Compared with them, we are the junior varsity! How much SWAT training does our team actually get? Twelve days a year? And that's if everyone's able to show up! And them? Hell, even their Denver SWAT Team trains four days a month. HRT trains constantly. They train with Delta Force and the Navy Seals—constantly. And you send Jimmy and Brent after two of their guys? What were you thinking!"

Trey crawfished a little. "They could've been the bad guys. . . ."

"You didn't really think that."

True. "No, no I didn't. . . . Tyler and I hatched a plan to spring Bordeaux from my house, and we needed a distraction. We were both pretty sure it was HRT watching us."

"Yeah, well, lucky for you, Win called me right before you walked in and made a pitch to fall on his sword for you on this deal. He pointed out that technically you were still working for him and he was calling the shots. He said it was his decision to tag the HRT guys and move Bordeaux out of your house."

Well now, that's a bit of a welcome surprise. Trey raised his eyebrows at that revelation and shrugged.

"That still doesn't explain why my Special Response Team leader lets a man who's out on federal bond—a man who took shots at Chief Randall just over a month ago, a man who is obviously mixed up with this Arm of the Lord cult—why he lets that man stay in his home!"

"He was my best friend for a lot of years, Gus. Back before you got to the park. He was my best friend. You know Luke is Tyler's informant. And he has a temper. We were trying to avert a shootout between Luke and HRT."

"So you nearly created one between our guys and HRT!" Trey kept his eyes on the Park Service ball cap in his hands. And Gus kept talking. "So now what am I gonna do with you? Hell, I may have to give you a Valor Award for saving Ellie Bordeaux's life on the river yesterday—but what I feel like doing is shipping you to Gates of the Arctic for the rest of the year! Let you freeze your ass off in the middle of nowhere in a park where you can't possibly screw things up too badly!"

Trey's boss took a deep breath and leaned back in his chair. Trey mustered the courage to meet his angry eyes. He was praying Gus's fury was nearly spent.

Gus was still glaring at him, but he blew out the anger with a long breath. The brown eyes said, *We're not done with this yet,* but his tone softened as he turned his attention to their larger mission. "Looks as if the FBI and Secret Service are finally going to take our advice and bring the Israeli delegation in through West Yellowstone's airport.

They're gonna deploy to the Interagency Fire Center at the airport sometime tomorrow—but, hell, it's already tomorrow! Randall and I will be going down there to help them set up a command center. You'll stay in Mammoth with part of your team in case we need a medical response or the FBI needs some form of backup. Which is not likely, given their current mood."

Okay, so he's not replacing me as team leader just yet.

"Randall will want a recap on the Bill Wilson situation—maybe early afternoon, but don't put anything on paper about his arrest yet. The FBI still wants the story out there that Wilson has heart trouble. They've got him in Bozeman at the hospital. I had to call his wife late yesterday. . . ." Gus's voice wavered as he reflected on that painful event. He took another deep breath and kept talking.

"Alright, damn it . . . get back over there and calm the folks down at Tyler's house. I've got four extra rangers there now. Everybody's too hyped up and gung ho. And you haven't had any time off in days— go home and get some sleep. Don't get in here before noon tomorrow unless I call you in. I mean it!"

Trey remembered easing out of Gus's office when the man dismissed him with a wave as another call came in on his landline. Calls at 1:30 a.m. were never good news—there'd been a lot of bad news lately.

He wiped a small amount of cordovan polish onto a cloth and worked it into the leather hatband. He grimaced a little when he thought about Gus's threat of a TDA, or temporary duty assignment, to Gates of the Arctic National Park. Banishment to the frozen tundra above the Arctic Circle, with no real towns for hundreds of miles. Surely his boss wasn't serious. *Banishment.* That's what he'd called Win Tyler's assignment here at Yellowstone. He placed the pristine felt hat into its summer storage box and wondered how Win was making out with his bosses this morning.

*   *   *

That question got answered when Trey's phone rang about five minutes later and he heard Win Tyler's southern accent.

"Hey, man. You still working for the Park Service?"

"At the moment . . . but I'm hanging by a thread. You?"

"Coulda been worse. I managed to get five hours of sleep and avoid the topic with the brass this morning. Everyone's a little preoccupied—most of our people are leaving soon to finish setting up a tactical operations center in West Yellowstone. Did you hear that HRT got two of Ron King's, uh, Ron Chandler's men last night?"

"Naw, haven't heard—I haven't gone in yet. Any resistance?" Trey asked.

"No, thank goodness. Caught them sleeping in a sleazy motel on the outskirts of Gardiner, where Luke said they'd be. It was two of the guys Chandler had recently brought in. They're tight-lipped; my folks are telling me they haven't said a word. The Bureau is trying to keep the arrests under wraps until the Israelis are out of town tomorrow. We're holding them under the Federal Rules of Criminal Procedure related to the Terrorism Act, so we've got several more hours before we have to provide them with lawyers. HRT could have collared a couple more based on Luke's tips, but Headquarters called them back in to realign down to West Yellowstone around 4:00 a.m. Sure woulda been nice to have more of those thugs behind bars, but it wasn't my call. You and I may not catch too much heat over our adventure last night since the intel Luke gave us proved so valuable." Win paused. "Luke still at your place?"

"He was gone when I got up around 9:30 this morning. He left the vehicle he came in, so I suppose he'll be back in a day or two."

"He doing okay?"

"We talked awhile after I got home last night. He's really conflicted over the Prophet's church. Really struggling. He doesn't believe any of the anti-Semitic, white supremacy crap, but he wants so badly to belong. . . . I feel awful for not reaching out to him sooner. He was so isolated after the FBI drug him through those trumped-up charges last year. If I'd been there for him as a friend, it might not have come to this."

Win grunted a response. He really didn't know what to say. He had his own regrets about a failed relationship weighing on his shoulders.

So in characteristic fashion, he avoided the emotionally charged topic and switched to more comfortable ground.

"I'll bring the gear you left at my house over to your office this afternoon. I'll be staying in Mammoth today and tonight while everything gets reorganized for the Israeli visit. After the ceremony, I'm shippin' out to Jackson Hole till this death threat issue gets a bit more resolution. If Daniel Shepherd doesn't get indicted and locked up soon, I could be down there awhile. There's some evidence he coulda ordered the hits on me as revenge for the death of his son in an FBI shootout years ago. Nothing concrete on it, it's all circumstantial, but Mr. Givens doesn't want to take any more chances with me stationed this close to their church compound."

"Kinda hate to hear that. I was lookin' forward to showing you more of the park when things settle down. Anything you need done while you're gone?"

"Not that I can think of right now. Jason Price came over early this morning; he's keeping my cat till I get back. Tia's gonna keep dusting the house . . . so I'm good." He hesitated. "Nope, wait—I told Tory Madison, uh, that girl I met out here, that I'd come down to Roosevelt and see her next week. No cell service where they're camped. Is there a post office?"

"Not any general mail service, but no problem. I can get a note down to her if you want, but then again I could make some points by letting Gus deliver it for you. . . ."

"No way! Gus might be on the prowl! Since you're married, I'm thinkin' you'd be a better delivery boy on this errand."

Win could feel Trey smiling through the phone. "Gus has the reputation of *always* being on the prowl, but that may just be talk. No problem, I'll handle it."

They ended the call and Win leaned back in his office chair and stared at the far wall, which was dominated by the remarkable painting of the bear. He'd been accomplishing one thing after another with a determined pace this morning. In between meetings with the HRT liaison, he'd called his dad and texted his brothers and several friends. When he couldn't reach his mother on her special day, he settled for a text. His original plan had been to send flowers, but those good intentions got misplaced during the chaotic week. He wrote Tory a brief note of apology and checked one more thing off his mental to-do list. He wondered absently if he'd see her again. . . . No telling how long they'd keep him at the Jackson Hole RA, and Mr. Givens had mentioned a possible transfer to Denver. Then there was the job offer from Tucker. . . . He breathed out a deep sigh. He might not even come back to Mammoth for more than a day or so, just enough time to completely pack up. *I may never see her again. She made me smile. . . .*

He blinked rapidly and sat straight up in his chair. *Why am I thinking in the past tense? Why am I thinking this way?* It was as if he was being spurred on to tie up loose ends for a purpose that went beyond just leaving town for a few days. The strange feeling of detachment emerged again. Did his soul sense something in his future that he couldn't yet see?

* * *

He promptly forgot those uneasy sensations as he dove back into the vast amount of work required to coordinate between HRT and his ASAC, or the more traditional Bureau, as he liked to think of it. Each Hostage Rescue Team deployment included two HRT liaison agents who made sure everything ran smoothly between the requesting office for the mission—Denver, in this case—and HRT personnel. Win had met both liaison agents, but he'd never worked with them until this morning. After the events of last night, Win was shocked that Kirk Phillips was still using him as the coordinator between HRT and the Denver Field Office.

Shelia, the attractive, studious-looking agent who served as HRT's lead operations liaison, had been quick to tell Win the reason he was still on board. "Don't let them fool you, Win. Kirk and Matt actually loved it that you took the initiative, and took significant risks, in successfully getting your informant clear last night." She lowered the dark glasses on her nose and peered at him over them. "Well, I won't repeat word for word what they were saying," she said, blushing, "but the whole HRT culture is based on traits like courage, risk-taking, and loyalty—all for a successful mission. They even admire that in their adversaries." She shook her pretty, long blond hair. "Best of all, your actions led directly to successful arrests on our part—a win-win!"

Okay, then . . .

But she hadn't finished. "Kirk also saw the run-in with the rangers as a positive thing. He'd been concerned that Blue Unit's operators were getting complacent sitting here for days on end in this crappy weather in this middle-of-nowhere tourist trap." Her eyes took on a predatory look. "At HRT we don't reward failure. That altercation with the park rangers will cause the boys to be a lot sharper tomorrow, when it counts."

He nodded. *Shelia won't likely be writing a positive review for Yellowstone on TripAdvisor, but the girl knows her job—success seems to be the theme here.* He wondered what had happened to the poor operators who got nabbed by the rangers last night. Her words: "We don't reward failure." *Yikes!* They may be wishing the rangers had kept them.

He got a break from Shelia when Deb called from Billings at noon to report that both of Chandler's guys who'd been arrested last night would have federal complaints filed against them for a whole slew of big-time charges as soon as the Israeli delegation's plane lifted off from West Yellowstone tomorrow afternoon. Deb, Ramona, and Murray had driven to Billings to meet with the U.S. Attorney for Montana since the arrests had been made across the state line, in Gardiner. Everyone was trying to keep a very low profile on the takedown. No need to tip the other bad guys to the arrests until the Cohn Monument dedication was over.

After he got off the phone with Deb, he hit the send button on the confidential human source report he'd written on HRT's interview with Luke last night. He noticed with satisfaction that Washington had approved the required documentation for the Bordeaux's informant payments. The federal charges against Ron Chandler's two guys tomorrow would trigger confidential source payments to Ellie Bordeaux and to a trust fund for their children. It was a done deal. He'd kept his word to Luke—he'd taken care of his family, just not exactly in the way Luke had in mind. The fact that neither Luke nor Ellie knew they'd receive government checks totaling $200,000 in the mail next week had to be addressed. He smiled to himself. *I'll call Ellie on that one tomorrow.*

Denver's surveillance supervisor unleashed her frustrations directly on Win as they nearly collided in the hall a few minutes later.

"Headquarters just ordered a complete realignment of resources— our entire SWAT Team is being pulled out, going to West Yellowstone with the HRT guys. Do you know what that does to our surveillance containment?" The short woman's tone was incredulous.

"Uh, for real?" Win dodged back against the wall as she tromped down the hall to the communications room. He stood there a moment and digested that unwelcome news. If all their tactical forces were hitting the road, Shepherd would have nearly free rein to operate in Gardiner and Mammoth.

Win leaned into the communications room to confirm the new orders. Evidently the Prophet's latest video campaign, which launched online earlier in the week, was creating quite a splash among the country's anti-government, separatist, and white supremacy elements. Someone well placed in the Justice Department panicked and ordered the FBI Director to redeploy all of Denver's SWAT agents to West Yellowstone and secure a firm perimeter around the Jewish monument dedication site. With HRT and most of the other FBI contingent already pulling out of Mammoth, that move would eviscerate the Bureau's surveillance efforts at the church compound and on the few hard-core bad guys they still had eyes on.

The Bureau had been raising the alarm about the threat from Daniel Shepherd's cult for over three weeks, yet someone way up the ladder at DOJ was reacting as if they'd just heard about it today. Worse yet, they were trying to second-guess the Bureau managers on the ground. A good, well-thought-out containment plan was already in place—and suddenly the higher-ups at DOJ wanted a new plan. Win was almost glad he was leaving town tomorrow. If common sense didn't prevail, this whole situation could go off the rails for the good guys in a hurry.

By mid-afternoon, the small FBI office and the Bureau's work spaces in the Justice Center were nearly empty. All of Win's bosses, as well as Denver's entire SWAT contingent, the JTTF agents, and parts of the Violent Crime and Domestic Terrorism Squads were either on the fifty-five-mile drive to the West Yellowstone Interagency Fire Center or already there. The Fire Center was active during the summer and fall months for forest fire suppression, but the site was largely deserted this time of year. The main attraction for the Feds was the 8,400-foot asphalt runway and wide taxiways used as staging areas for the nation's smoke jumpers and the large air tankers used for fighting wildfires. The Israeli Ambassador's contingent could land their Boeing 767 there and be completely shielded from the public—and hopefully from Daniel Shepherd's hooligans.

* * *

While most everyone else was making the slow drive through the park to the new operations center, Win and Shelia made a final walk through of the former HRT building at Mammoth. It was only 3:00 p.m. He'd been in the building a few hours earlier and it'd been the hub of activity for more than seventy folks. Now there was literally no sign HRT had ever been there. The place was cleaner than it was before they'd arrived, and every shred of evidence that an elite federal tactical force had spent five days there was gone. Even the trash cans were empty. Win was in awe—those guys were good. Shelia tossed Win the keys to the old building as she deftly jumped onto the running board of the last large utility truck idling in the parking lot.

He walked a little closer to the truck. "So you'll be set up down there tonight?"

She laughed. "We've been set up for hours! Got a C-5 flying in at 1700 hours with Charlie and Echo Teams from our Gold Unit for backup. That's eighteen more operators."

"That's amazing!"

"No, that's HRT! Your tax dollars at work!" Shelia slid into the cab and rolled down her window as the driver shifted into gear. She spoke loudly over the rumble of the big engine. "Don't be a stranger, Win, when you get back to Washington!" She glanced back at him one more time as the truck began to move and called out, "I know my way around!" She winked at him and he felt his ears go red.

Yeah, I'll bet you do.

* * *

An hour later, Win walked out of the park's Administration Building after finding it almost vacant. Gus, Chief Randall, Trey, and most everyone else were twenty-four miles southwest, helping organize the security perimeter at the Cohn Monument site. Win had dropped off Trey's tactical bag and Tory's card in Trey's empty office and scribbled him a short note.

> Partner, Thanks for taking this to Tory. Been an honor being on your team these last few days. Catch you later.
> Win

Trey Hechtner would likely be back in his element after the ceremony tomorrow: protecting the wildlife from the tourists, protecting the tourists from the wildlife, protecting the tourists from the tourists, and so on. Win remembered again what Gus Jordan had told him . . . *park ranger—best damn job in the world*! He watched a tiny elk calf try out its long legs in playful leaps around its frantic mother on the new grass near the flagpole. At the moment, his security detail was far more concerned about the photo-hound tourists surrounding the elk family than about protecting him. He could see the excitement in the rangers' eyes as they watched the newborn calf's antics. Win was a little envious. . . . He'd felt that way about his job not so long ago.

They made the five-minute walk from the office to his house for a very late lunch at five o'clock. His security guys visited with the two rangers who'd been stuck guarding the outside of the house all day, while Win scrounged up a ham and cheese sandwich and Coke, then made his first stab at packing for the trip to Jackson. The park's roads were still blocked by snow south of Old Faithful, so he'd take the longer, seven-hour route to Jackson through West Yellowstone and down through Idaho. He changed into more casual clothes and wondered if he'd ever have the opportunity to wear a short-sleeved shirt again. It was May 11th, and at best it was only in the mid-thirties at night.

After he changed, he stood beside the desk in his bedroom and found himself at a loss. The feeling of detachment emerged again. *This is strange.* For some reason he couldn't quite grasp, he wasn't sure what to plan for, what to take, what to do. He felt indifferent to the task, as if it didn't matter. *Something is wrong here.* Maybe the emotions surrounding the shootings were catching up with him—maybe it was the pent-up fear of being someone's target, maybe the weight of the responsibility of the job. *Something is very wrong.*

His hand found his study Bible on the corner of the desk. It opened on a familiar page. His eyes fell on Psalm 31:14–15, Scripture he'd underlined years ago and knew by heart.

"But as for me, I trust in You, O Lord; I say, 'You are my God.' My times are in Your hand; Deliver me from the hand of my enemies, and from those who persecute me."

He said a simple prayer of thanks.

His unsettled mood began to lift with the prayer, but he still found no motivation for the job at hand. Maybe he was pushing too hard, struggling too desperately to prove to the Bureau he didn't belong in this dead-end place. *Maybe I'm actually trying to prove that to myself.* He shut out those thoughts; there'd be more than enough time for reflection with seven hours on the road tomorrow. He'd return to his comfort zone—the office. There were still things to attend to there before he left. Packing and thinking could wait until tonight.

* * *

The skeleton crew the Bureau left behind in Mammoth that evening included Johnson, Emily, Win, a surveillance supervisor, and a few technicians. There were still two five-agent teams running the scaled-back surveillance of the church compound, but several more of the Prophet's militiamen had slipped surveillance. It was looking as if the FBI wasn't the only group repositioning during the last several hours.

He and Johnson would be riding down to the dedication site together tomorrow. The weather was predicted to be awful tonight, but tomorrow was supposed to be at least tolerable—cool and windy with thunderstorms. Win had watched the SAC and ASAC leave the Justice Center late in the afternoon. His bosses' expressions of worry were obvious—no one had any idea what Daniel Shepherd's group would do. Shepherd had perfect targets: the Israeli Ambassador, the U.S. Ambassador to Israel, and a host of other Jewish dignitaries, right in his backyard. At the very least, Win expected some form of confrontation at the monument site; he was just praying it wouldn't be violent. Following the afternoon ceremony, Win would drive his Bureau vehicle on to Jackson, and Johnson would hitch a ride back to Mammoth. Tomorrow was shaping up to be a very, very long day. He decided to call it a night. Nothing to do at the office now but sit around and hope everything was in place.

Win had managed to avoid Emily ever since Mr. Givens benched her after Richter was shot, but his luck ran out as he was leaving his office at 8:30. She was leaning against the hallway wall, watching him like a hawk watches a field mouse. Her frizzy red hair was pulled back tight; her metal glasses were low on her nose. She was wearing an expensive version of a safari jacket with a green scarf. Her eyes matched the scarf, but they were flinty. It wasn't one of her better looks. She didn't even pretend to be consolatory.

"Think you've clawed your way out of this hole, Tyler? I heard you might be transferred to Denver." She shook her head knowingly. "Samuel Cushing is a very powerful man. He's a powerful friend." She lowered her voice and dropped her chin. "A very *dear* friend of mine. Mr. Strickland, Wes, all the supervisors are aware of that. Do you think *any* of them will be willing to stick their necks out to help you move along in your career? At the expense of jeopardizing their own careers? I know better. You know better. Not gonna happen."

Win just stood there with his hat and his Gore-Tex jacket in his hands.

"You've had a little success with this case—things have fallen into your lap—but if you think for a minute it'll go smoothly for you in

Denver, think again!" With that she wheeled and disappeared down the hall into the communications room.

Win was blindsided. He had no idea how to respond to her, but then, he knew she didn't want a response. She simply wanted to bully him. Samuel Cushing was using her to force him out of the Bureau. The Deputy Assistant Director was still out to destroy Win's career, and he'd found a very willing and effective ally in Emily. Win slowly let his breath out and tried to quench the smoldering rage he felt. How to fight back? When to fight back? He drew in a deep breath before he started down the stairs. *My career in the Bureau . . . my career as an agent?* He blinked away the emotions flooding over him. *This fight might already be lost.*

* * *

"Hey, bud!" Tucker's voice was breaking up as Win waved away his ranger escort and pulled into the narrow gravel driveway leading to the rear of his house. He stopped the SUV to try to let the phone connection take hold. As his headlights flashed across the ranger guarding the front of the house, the guy shifted his rifle and gave Win a weak wave.

"Can you hear me?" Win asked loudly.

"Yeah, yeah! Got it, saw your text on Jackson—you're going there tomorrow. My aunt has a condo there. Happenin' little town, by the way. Major step up from the boonies you're stuck in now!"

Win tried to focus on Tucker's words, which were fading in and out. He hoped his answer was going through. "Should get there late evening," he said. "Be good to see you. . . . Can you hear me now?" The low cloud cover was impacting the cell coverage again. *Oh, well, back to civilization tomorrow.*

"Terrible connection!" Tucker shot back. "Hey, if you can hear this, I'll fly to Jackson later this week and we'll talk about the job. Maybe finalize it. Damn shame the FBI didn't appreciate your talents! I'm off!"

The connection dropped. *Yeah, real damn shame.* His stomach had an empty, hollow feel. He hadn't completely recovered from the anger he'd felt earlier. After the run-in with Emily a few minutes ago, he'd come to the painful conclusion that it might be time to cut his losses and move on. At the very least, it was time to seriously start looking at other options. He'd texted Tucker about the job less than five minutes ago, and Tucker, enthusiastic as ever, had insisted on a road trip out West to hash it out in person. Of course to Tucker, a road trip just meant a three-hour flight to Jackson in his daddy's private jet.

As Win pulled into his parking area, he refocused on the preparations for his trip. He'd squared everything away at the office—he'd be able to pick up the False Prophet case on the Bureau's Sentinel system from Jackson without missing a beat. His written notes and printouts were organized in the numerous working files he'd boxed to take with him tomorrow. He'd also made an extensive packing list so as not to have a repeat of this afternoon's packing paralysis. *Need to get it done and get more sleep tonight.*

The dark silhouette of the ranger at the rear of the house waved to him as he killed the SUV's headlights. He wasn't sure who was on duty tonight, but he needed to thank his night guards. Since this could be the park rangers' last night for guard duty, he wasn't likely to see them again. He was sure those men were much sicker of it than he was.

He turned off the ignition and stepped off the running board. The gravel crunched under his boots, and the north wind stung his face as he pushed the door shut and locked it. He waved to the guy. *Might as well get the goodbyes over with.* Light drizzle was beginning to fall, making the surroundings even darker. He saw the other ranger out of the corner of his eye. *Why is the guy at the front coming my way?* Win stopped mid-stride. The ranger at the rear had just saluted the one approaching from the front—it was the same palm-across-the-heart salute Luke had given Trey on the ridge several days ago. A cold chill hit Win's spine, and he suddenly felt light-headed.

He hadn't seen it coming.

CHAPTER THIRTY-ONE

The big man hit him from behind with as much force as any SEC linebacker. Win's chest went hard into the hood of the SUV, knocking the breath out of him. His hat and keys were flung to the gravel. He was too stunned and disoriented to grab for his gun. There was a gloved hand over his mouth, someone twisting his right wrist backward, and extreme pressure on his back.

"Not a word!" an intense voice growled. The man behind him pushed him even harder against the hood and pulled his Glock free from its holster. Win felt the cold metal of a gun barrel on the back of his head. He was gasping for breath through the gloved hand.

"Hands behind your head! Now!" The urgent commands were low and quiet. Win struggled to pull his hands to his head—to comply. The man who had Win pinned was huge and powerful. He jerked Win away from the truck by his collar and steered him through the darkness toward the old garage. The pistol's muzzle never left the back of his head. Someone opened the wooden door and called for lights—the single bulb dimly illuminated the interior of the small, windowless shed. Win blinked to adjust to the light and realized if they hadn't killed him yet, there might still be a chance.

"On your knees!" The big man still had him by the back of his collar. His strong arm forced Win down on the concrete floor. He found himself staring directly into the faces of two park rangers who'd been stripped of their tactical coveralls, helmets, and weapons and were

sitting bound and gagged against the far wall. He had the same floating sensation he'd felt in the Richter shooting—everything seemed to
move in slow motion, every sense was crystal clear.

Almost immediately his rational self began to compartmentalize,
to filter the evidence, to collect the data—all within his own crime
scene. He instinctively knew it was a defense mechanism to hold the
fear at bay. For a few moments, at least, it was working, as he began to
assess his predicament. The two men who'd been dressed as rangers
were apparently still on guard duty outside the house. There were six
others in the shed, all in masks; three were holding assault rifles, the
night-vision optics on their helmets flipped up. A deadly-looking M40
sniper rifle leaned against the wall. It had to belong to one of the two
men kneeling beside him. So there were at least eight of them—they'd
come in force. The large man at his back had to be the church's militia
sergeant. Win remembered his name as Jon Eriksson from the surveillance files.

As the seconds ticked away, Win's breath was coming back, but his
heart was racing and his ears were ringing. He felt sweat trickle down
his chest. Someone pulled his hands down and forced them behind his
back. Win knew the bitter taste in his mouth was fear; he kept fighting
to keep it from overwhelming him. He drew a shallow breath and tried
to focus on the thin man in military camouflage kneeling beside him.

"Please . . . don't take that," he quietly asked the man, who was
systematically going through his pockets. The militiaman had already
confiscated his phones, wallet, pocketknife, handcuffs, and Bureau credentials. It was just a tiny book bound in brown leather and wrapped
in plastic.

The man peered out from his mask with a questioning look. "I don't
reckon you get to keep your stuff. You ain't in charge no more, Fed." His
voice was slightly muffled by the brown fleece mask.

The big man was watching another militiaman adjust a set of zip
ties on Win's wrists. He glanced down in the dim light at the small
package. The single bulb was swinging slightly, throwing yellow stabs
of shifting light into the dark corners of the old garage. "What is it?"
the big man asked. His deep voice was in keeping with his size.

Win figured the question was aimed at him, so he answered, "Bible . . . had it since, uh, since fifth grade. Always have it with me when anything big is happening. . . ." Win's voice trailed off as he realized how silly that must sound to these hard men.

The big man reached for it and removed the plastic cover. "New Testament . . . all right, Agent Tyler, can't imagine anything bigger happening to you than what you'll face in the next few hours." He handed it back to the militiaman who was now squatting beside Win. "Put it back in his pocket."

"Thank you, sir," Win whispered as the man replaced it in his cargo pants. The guy behind him pulled the plastic zip ties tighter on his wrists. *The next few hours. He said, "The next few hours . . ."* Win's heart clung to Eriksson's words with hope. *They're not gonna kill me right now. . . . There's still a chance!* For a few more seconds no one spoke. The two men who'd been kneeling beside Win moved away and took up their rifles. It puzzled Win that none of them seemed to be in any hurry. When the big man spoke again, he realized they'd been waiting for the rangers' check-in with dispatch. His guards did one-hour check-ins with their dispatcher before 9:00 p.m., or 2100 hours, and every two hours thereafter until the next morning.

"Time to call in the all clear, boy." The younger of the two rangers' eyes widened. Win recognized him as one of his escorts on the road trip down to the area where they'd rescued the hikers. His name was Maddox. The other rangers had been teasing him about adjusting to fatherhood; the kid had a two-month-old baby. One of the armed men stepped to the ranger's side, bent down, and yanked the duct tape from his mouth. The poor guy gasped in pain. The militiaman pulled the ranger's head back by his hair and produced a black commando knife from its sheath.

The big man was still doing all the talking. "Alright, same as last time, I know exactly what has to be reported. It's the nine o'clock report. Your man is here—you deviate one word and your throat's slit. You hear me?" The low intensity in the man's deep voice was nearly as frightening as the knife the other guy held.

The young ranger whispered yes. The thug let go of the guy's hair and hit the button on the ranger's handheld radio. Maddox cleared his throat best he could with the serrated blade still touching it. "This . . . this is YP12 to base, it's 2100 hours, Tyler's house. All clear. Tyler . . . Tyler is here. Do you copy?"

The radio crackled and a clear, cheerful voice came back, "Roger that. YP12 at Tyler's house; Tyler in. All clear. Supposed to rain tonight. Stay dry, boys! Base out." It would be two more hours before anyone checked on the house again. Win's heart sank. The masked man with the knife stepped back and the young ranger dropped his head. He seemed ashamed to look Win in the eyes. The exchange between the men told Win the bad guys had been here since before eight o'clock, around twilight, not even completely dark on this gloomy night. The younger ranger had obviously called in for them earlier. Win's eyes scanned the little shed and found discarded hikers' backpacks, civilian clothes, and utility bags. They'd probably shown up as contractors or tourists and lured the rangers into the shed right before dark.

"Alright, gag him, we've got to get to the vehicles. Let's move," the big man began.

"We're not leaving those two to report anything." It was the masked man who was farthest from the captives. The militiaman standing above the rangers froze with the duct tape in his hand. He quickly looked toward Win's captor.

Win felt the big guy shift toward the man who'd spoken. "The Prophet's orders are to bring Tyler to him. We have no orders to harm the others if they cooperate."

"Well, I've got a different way of thinkin' and we're leaving this my way. Two fewer Feds to deal with later! You boys don't have to do a thing, just move outa my way and turn your damn heads if you ain't got the stomach for it." As he talked, he slung his AR-15 over his shoulder and drew a sheathed knife. He'd taken two steps toward the younger ranger when Win found his voice.

"You can't let him do this! It's against Scripture! God demands at least two witnesses to a successful mission—you have your two witnesses! It's in Deuteronomy 19:15!" Win was talking loud and fast and hoping these men weren't Bible scholars. "Listen to me! You've got a chance to glorify God through an act of mercy—letting them live! It's in Matthew and Luke, uh, Luke 6! You can't let him nullify that!" he pleaded. "What would your prophet say?"

The huge man still had his hand on Win's collar, and Win twisted to try to look up at him. The masked man who stood over the captives seemed unsure, conflicted. But the aggressive one now had Maddox's hair in his left hand. The ranger tried to scoot away on the concrete. The aggressive one was ignoring Win. He was taking his time—he seemed to be enjoying the horror of it. Win heard the ranger quietly plead, "Please no, please . . . ," just before the giant who was holding Win stepped around him and grabbed the arm of the man with the knife.

"I'm in charge here! We're the Arm of the Lord! We won't kill just to be killing. There's glory for God here, like the Fed says." Then softly, "Put up the knife or you'll be the one dying here." He still had a huge hand on the man's arm. Win could see sullen anger in the thug's eyes, but he slowly lowered the weapon.

The confrontation ended as quickly as it began, and the younger ranger slumped back against the dusty wall. One of the militiamen finished the task of re-taping his gag. They quickly had Win on his feet. He locked eyes with the older ranger for just a second and saw those eyes register thanks. He nodded slightly to acknowledge that and tried hard to swallow. The large man pulled the string on the light and the room was plunged into darkness.

The big man moved Win outside the door and gently closed it behind him. The blackness of night had become dense, with fog setting in and drizzle falling. Eriksson steered Win behind the shed and stood close, facing him. The guy had to be six nine or ten. Win couldn't see much, but he could smell, and he didn't expect the man's uniform to smell clean. He picked up the normal scents of a hunter: musty canvas, leather, and gun oil. *They're the hunters . . . I'm the prey. Please help me, God.* That plea had weaved through his mind a hundred times in the last few minutes.

The big man quietly spoke down to Win. "It's not my job to end your life, unless you slow us down or cause us trouble. It's my job to deliver you alive, but it's really up to you if you live or die on this trip. No gag so you can breathe on the climbs, but if you call out to someone or try to escape, you die—and it may cost innocent lives. You hear me?"

Win stammered a reply, "Yes, sir."

"Used NVD before?"

Win knew he was referring to the night-vision equipment. "No. No, sir."

"You'll have to adapt your depth perception to negotiate the trails; using binocular goggles makes it easier. Agent Tyler, you better catch on fast." Win felt him turn slightly.

"Two!" The big man called out in a low tone, and the tall, thin man with the sniper rifle appeared at his side.

"Sir!"

"Get a helmet and twin goggles on him. Hold on to his collar till he gets used to the goggles and can manage alone. He's got hiking boots on, that'll do for the trail."

Win had to try to reason with them. "You men . . . you men don't want to get any deeper in this. It doesn't have to come to—"

The big man closed his massive hand around the front of Win's throat and squeezed just a little. It got his attention. He growled down at him in a whisper, "Did I say it was up to you? Follow orders and you may come out of this fine, otherwise . . ." He didn't have to finish the sentence.

* * *

The six men in camouflage, along with their captive, moved in single file up the trail behind the shed, alongside the hot springs' thermal features. The bright-green glow of the night-vision goggles created an otherworldly experience for Win. The fog, combined with the whirling steam from the hot springs terraces, made it look as if he'd been dropped into some menacing, green version of Hell. He'd only worn night-vision goggles for a few minutes at the Academy's brief introductory course.

He'd marveled then that anyone could move quickly or effectively with those things attached to their head. Thankfully, they were taking him up the well-worn hiking trail that snaked behind his house, a familiar path where he'd run several times. The rangers had long since closed the trail as part of the security measures for him. They wouldn't meet anyone for miles.

The goggles were taking some getting used to. Win nearly fell on both of the narrow wooden bridges crossing the small stream uphill from his house. "Two" steadied him and eased him forward. Win kept his head down, concentrating on the obstacles just in front of him. As they hiked up the hillside, the dense fog stayed in the lower elevations, giving the goggles more ambient light to filter. Win's visibility began to improve. He forced his mind to stay on simple tasks: Master the goggles and pray for rescue. First, master the goggles. If that wasn't accomplished quickly, he knew he might not live long enough for his prayers to bear fruit.

Less than an hour into the forced hike, the thin man pulled Win to a halt and then onto a rock next to the trail. Win had overheard enough whispered conversations to know they were waiting for the two men who'd been impersonating the rangers to catch up. When they stopped, he realized how heavily he was sweating and how chilled he'd become. He tried to calm his breathing and keep himself from shivering in the cold. He couldn't feel his hands now. The pain from the zip ties had been horrible for the first fifteen minutes or so, and then his hands had gone numb. While he couldn't feel anything below his wrists, his arms were cramping from the unnatural position. He had to force himself not to groan out loud as he shifted his weight on the damp rock.

The big man approached and flipped Win's goggles up. Win blinked to see in the sudden blackness. "Two says it looks like the zip ties might be too tight," the deep voice said. He bent low behind Win to examine the bindings. "Uh-huh. Going to clip them off. It'll hurt like hell until the blood flow returns. Work your fingers and wrists when I get 'em off. Can damage the nerves if they're too tight. Open your mouth. . . ."

Bite down on this." He reached down for something and forced a small stick into Win's mouth.

When the man cut the plastic bindings, the pain in Win's hands and arms was so intense it took his breath away. His arms hung limp from his shoulders. He doubled over on the rock and blinked back tears as he slowly tried to massage some feeling back into his fingers. There was sticky blood in narrow grooves where the ties had cut his wrists. As the anguish gradually subsided, he was thankful for the gritty stick in his mouth; he'd managed not to cry out—he hadn't shown weakness. *One little victory.* The thin guy stood at his side, but the other men gave him a wide berth and let him suffer through the pain alone. It took all of five minutes for any feeling, other than the stabbing, needle-like pain, to return to his hands.

He still couldn't see worth a darn, but he heard someone say the men they were waiting for were coming up the last switchback behind them. The tall, thin guy rustled Win off the rock and offered him a canteen. Win spit the dirt and wood splinters from his mouth and drank. The man retied Win's hands behind him—much looser, thank goodness—then adjusted his helmet and dropped his goggles into place. His world became bright green again.

As they started back out on the trail, one of the other men brushed up against Win's shoulder and spoke in a low voice. "I mighta got those ties a little tight . . . mighta been too ramped up, is all. Never done this before. No harm intended." The guy moved on up the trail.

Win wasn't real sure what to make of the apology. Except for one man, these guys weren't acting like a bunch of cold-blooded killers. But he remembered what the young militiaman had yelled at Marniski and him one afternoon: *You work for the oppressors!* They saw him as one of the pro-Zionist Federals their prophet kept vilifying, the enemy—their enemy. Win had enough sense to know that folks who were normally good, decent people could be manipulated into murder by a charismatic madman. It had been happening since the beginning of time.

They'd split off the original trail awhile back and were hiking northwest on the Sepulcher Mountain Trail. He'd seen the signs and knew from studying topographical maps that the trail led to one of the highest points above Mammoth Hot Springs. He also knew the Arm of the Lord Church compound was only five miles, by trail, north of that mountain. The church had to be their destination. At the pace they were going, once they topped Sepulcher Mountain, they could be at the compound well before daybreak. As they approached the mountain, the trail became rougher and steeper, but Win had mastered the night-vision goggles to the point where he was able to focus on other things besides his next step forward. There was a downside to that.

His anxious heart fought to override his rational mind. His thoughts alternated between frantic prayers for rescue, crushing stabs of regret, and reckless thoughts of escape. His tendency for rational thinking wasn't much help either. He knew they'd been hiking for over two hours, but even with the limited visibility his goggles afforded, he could tell the scattered fog and low clouds were persisting. His guys couldn't get search helicopters up in this weather—not in these mountains—and the Bureau's drones were too far south in West Yellowstone to be of any help. Not only that, but the kidnappers had specifically mentioned, in front of the captive rangers, that they needed to get to their vehicles—a ruse to throw off any pursuit. His guys wouldn't know where to begin searching. His mind kept coming back to the same, very logical conclusion: *They probably won't find me in time.*

His heart kept going back to his family. His folks must have been disappointed. He'd given up the pursuit of pro football or a successful law career for *this*? His father once thought he might come back to the farm—might take over the land, keep the legacy alive. But now Blake had filled that role. Blake had provided the grandkids his folks had dreamed of, all while he was in North Carolina living in sin, with a lifestyle that hadn't really included family—at least not *his* family. He'd pulled back from them because of selfishness and shame. He'd spent most of his leave time in Martha's Vineyard or Boca Raton with Shelby and her family. That's where she'd wanted to be. Her folks were modern thinkers, she'd said: "They couldn't care less if we live together." He wasn't so sure that was true either, but Shelby was much better at lying to herself than he was. . . . Was he blaming her for his sins? *Yes,*

I often did. That unfortunate trait of men had started with Adam and Eve—he'd just kept up a very long and damaging tradition.

He and Shelby hadn't really formed a family; she'd just moved in with him. He'd seen it, at least in the beginning, as reasonable, cost-effective, even practical—never mind that it broke every tenet he believed about a man and woman's journey in life together. It might not have been sin for someone else, for someone without his strict interpretation of Scripture, but for him it was sin, and he knew it, and he did it anyway for two solid years. *And it really screwed up my life.* He'd put on the face of a hypocrite and he'd worked hard at living a lie. He'd been unfaithful to his God. Now, in this dark forest in Yellowstone, he knew he was gonna pay for it. Here he was, bound up like a prize hog, trudging through the mountains in a cold drizzle to his well-deserved fate. Justice. *We reap what we sow, damn it.*

CHAPTER THIRTY-TWO

Trey had just turned off his bedside lamp at 11:04 p.m. when he got the call from dispatch. He was standing within the dim light of Win's old carriage house thirteen minutes later. His most experienced men were hours away in West Yellowstone or within the areas of the park where the dignitaries would soon converge. He'd put in a call to Chief Randall and the FBI office on the frantic drive over. He'd been told Agent Johnson was the point man for the FBI in Mammoth.

Trey's heart was still in his throat as he stepped around the dangling light bulb inside the old building where he and Win had stood facing each other twenty-four hours earlier. Maddox and Gentry were both wrapped in blankets and leaning into the wall. A paramedic had already checked them out, and other than the pain inflicted from the removal of the duct tape, both men were unharmed. Maddox was still shaking from the trauma of the attack, but Gentry seemed to have his wits about him. Five other Park Service folks were standing in the shed, but the rangers' numbers were so thin that three of the rangers facing Trey weren't even in law enforcement.

Gentry had already given Trey and the group a brief run-through of the incident. The attackers who'd nabbed his rangers had arrived in a white electrical company van and lured them into the shed with a report of faulty wiring. Other than a good description of the driver and two of the fake utility guys, they had little to go on—the license plate came back as stolen and the company name was fictitious. Gentry reported that he'd heard the van pull away early on, but with dozens of white utility vans in the park, it would be nearly impossible to find. They had barely enough information to put out a BOLO, or "be on the lookout," to law enforcement. After Gentry and Maddox were disarmed by the "repairmen," the other bad guys had slipped into the shed dressed as hikers and backpackers. They would have easily blended into the early-evening visitors near the Lower Terraces. They'd donned their masks and camo as two of their group outfitted themselves with the Special Response Team members' uniforms and weapons. They were on guard duty outside the house within minutes. The kidnappers' leader mentioned going to the vehicles as they left the shed, but that gave them no firm leads.

Win's small backyard was illuminated by a dozen headlights, but Trey had ordered no Code 3, or lights and siren response, until they figured out where they were in this. And that wasn't happening nearly fast enough. He had a man stringing yellow tape around the yard and buildings, trying not to further contaminate the crime scene. Jimmy Martinez was checking for tracks with a high-powered light. The helicopter crew was on standby in case the weather cleared enough to get the ship up. A thousand details were running through his mind, competing for his attention.

He turned that attention back to Gentry. "Okay, think. Anything else you noticed . . . car keys, maps, anything else?" He had to work at keeping his voice and manner calm and steady. *This is not the time to panic.*

Gentry wrapped himself tighter in the olive-green blanket and stared down. "Well, their leader was a giant, he'd be easy to spot. And when they left out, they all had night-vision equipment . . . all dressed in military fatigues. All with backpacks. Fully armed. If they were going toward the parking lot—to vehicles—they'd have been a lot less conspicuous in civilian clothes. There'd be no need for night-vision gear. No vehicle pulled in behind the house. We'd have heard it." He looked at Trey. "Could they have hiked out?"

"That's what I'm thinking—Jimmy's checking," Trey said. "But they could have moved Tyler into a vehicle and then the larger party walked out. They could have split up any number of ways. The Beaver Ponds Trail is the most logical route. We've had it closed for several days now. . . . Doubtful they'd meet any late hikers going north from here."

"Trey, who are those guys?" one of the rangers asked.

Trey drew a deep breath. It was general knowledge that the Arm of the Lord Church was under some form of FBI surveillance due to the Prophet's constant anti-Semitic rhetoric and the upcoming dedication of the Cohn Monument. His Special Response Team and a few other folks knew the FBI's Hostage Rescue Team was in the park, but most of the other Park Service personnel had no idea of the scope of the federal operation. The attempted hits on Agent Tyler were rumored to relate to some case Tyler had been part of back East, in his previous posting. Trey hated keeping his folks in the dark, but those orders had trickled down directly from Washington. Even after the shooting at the hotel, their Department of Interior bosses were still hoping the problem would disappear. But Daniel Shepherd had played his cards tonight. He'd sent a team to kidnap Win, and his men had flat-out said who they were working for. Two rangers had been left alive to report it. Prophet Shepherd's war was on.

As Trey started to answer the ranger's question, the room went darker. Johnson's large frame filled the doorway as he barged into the shed. "Whata we got?"

Trey knew Johnson had driven from his home in Gardiner. The man looked like he'd been rushed out of bed, but his eyes were sharp and his jaw was set. Trey moved to his side and gave him a hurried run-through of the facts. As they were talking, Ranger Jimmy stuck his head in the door.

"We've got several pairs of boots going north up Beaver Ponds Trail. I went up as far as the second bridge—there's mud on the bridges. A group went that way since this rain started tonight," he reported.

"It's not even seven miles to that damn church compound as the crow flies. How many miles by trail from here?" Johnson asked.

Trey knew the trails by heart. "It's 12.2 miles to the church over Sepulcher Mountain. That's a difficult trail, 7.2 miles to the summit— an elevation change of more than 3,400-feet from here. Quite a climb.

It would be really slow going in the dark. If they're well trained, they could reach the church in seven, maybe seven and a half hours taking that route. . . . They've got more than a two-hour lead. They could get there before dawn."

"They have night-vision equipment?" Johnson asked.

"Yup, I assume Win would know how to use it?"

"No idea. He's never done SWAT training, so maybe, maybe not. He could get motivated to learn it pretty fast with someone holding an AR-15 on him. Our surveillance perimeter at their compound has been down to bare bones since most of our folks were repositioned today. They could probably drive a damn tank through our lines and no one would notice! If they get him to that compound, we could have a drawn-out hostage situation."

Johnson stretched his back and stared up at the cobwebbed ceiling. "I see you're getting the scene secured. . . . We can't get tunnel vision here. They could have him in a vehicle. We'll call the locals and set up roadblocks outside the park near Gardiner and Cooke City. You have some folks do drive-arounds, look for anything hinky here in Mammoth—might get lucky. Can you get a tracker in here quick? I'm gonna reach out to my bosses again and see who's on the way. Visibility is near zero at West Yellowstone—they can't get anything in the air. Still no chance of getting a chopper up here?"

"No, ceiling's way too low, but it's supposed to clear some later tonight. Our best tracker is camped down near the monument site. I'll get him up here. Will be at least two hours ETA in this fog. We'll get some folks driving the roads and the parking lots. Let me know what you need."

A half hour later, after about a dozen phone calls and urgent, hurried conversations, Trey walked over to the front of Win's Expedition. The Park Service's crime scene photographer had finished her work outside and was moving into the carriage house. Trey saw Win's brown felt hat lying crown-down in the wet gravel. He bent over and picked up the damp hat as he swallowed a rising rush of emotion. He'd started to respect the guy, even like him . . . and now, now Win's life might be in his hands. He fingered the hatband and pulled in a breath. He'd been running on autopilot. It embarrassed him that he'd forgotten to pause and pray. His hands gripped the hat's soft brim tighter and he closed his eyes for a moment as he tried to find the right words. *Heavenly Father, please . . .* The words wouldn't come, but he knew he had another phone call to make.

* * *

They'd hiked for what seemed like hours on a very difficult stretch of the trail through volcanic rock fields and alongside ridges of deep snow on 9,652-foot Sepulcher Mountain. Win had heard that one could see the Teton Range, eighty-five miles to the south, from here on a clear day. He was sure the hike would have been spectacular on a warm, sunny morning. After midnight, in night-vision goggles, with drizzle, low clouds, and the temperature hovering around thirty-three, he wouldn't recommend it.

Visibility had become much poorer since they entered the clouds on the high mountain. The footing near the summit and its immediate side slopes was rocky chert and flat granite slick from the light rain. At least the trail was mostly free of snow and ice, but the cold had set in with a vengeance. They must have hit the crest somewhere along the way in the dense clouds, but Win's total concentration was on his tenuous footing and he hadn't noticed.

He let his mind drop back into thoughts of remorse as the group slowly moved down the switchbacks on the north side of the mountain. His preoccupation caused him to stumble badly on a stone in the rocky trail. Two broke his fall just before he slammed into the ground, and that brought everyone to a halt. The near-disaster snapped Win back into the present. Two had steered him another hundred feet down the steep trail when there was a faint whistle from far down the slope. "We're getting here right on time," he heard someone say.

"Get him on the rocks over there." Eriksson was giving orders. "We're just above the spot . . ." Win couldn't hear what else was said. Two and another guy moved Win off the trail and sat him on a rock behind several jagged boulders. He could still see glimpses of the six men standing on the trail. Then movement below—someone was coming up the path.

"Keep your mouth shut or I'll tape it," the guy beside him whispered.

He kept his mouth shut.

There were five men in winter hiking clothes making their way up the nearest switchback. He saw them grab the hands and slap the shoulders of his kidnappers. The newcomers *looked* like typical backcountry hikers, except for the fancy monocular and twin night-vision devices and the assault rifles slung across their chests. *Lordy, more militiamen!* Win began to catch fragments of their conversations. "Cabin ten was martyred for the cause!" There was laughter. "No problem getting through their surveillance lines." "Feds can't fly . . ."

He noticed the new guys were dropping their backpacks and stacking their weapons. He glimpsed one of them pull a camping shovel from his pack, then another shovel appeared. They were mostly out of his sight, moving below him in the scattered boulder field, which was strewn with pockets of snow. Then he heard the sounds of digging, of shovels scraping rock. His tall, thin bodyguard stood up and moved back toward the trail. The other man still had Win's arm locked in his. Win turned his head slightly to get a better view of the activity thirty yards below him. He immediately forgot about the frigid air and the aching in his arms and legs. *All five of them are digging. Oh, no . . .* He swallowed hard. Maybe they weren't taking him to the compound after all.

"You want a Snickers bar?" The whispered voice again.

"What?"

"Got a sack of those itty-bitty Snickers bars here. Best invention since sliced bread! Want some? Got water here too."

Chocolate wasn't real high on Win's list of concerns right then. "What's goin' on down there? It isn't right not to tell me, if . . . if . . ." Win's voice caught in his throat.

The guy craned his neck to see the diggers below them. "You thought . . . ? Oh, hell . . . hell no. That ain't it." His smile looked weird in the green glow. The man shook his head. "Some of the brothers are switching out of their uniforms. They're digging up the cache—regular clothes, hiking gear, and such. They'll swap out clothes and stuff, then rebury the cache boxes with the military gear. We're splitting up and they're going back to the church. You're going with our team. We don't want those five boys to know you're here. . . . *Need-to-know* mission, you understand."

Win closed his eyes tight for a moment and swallowed hard again. "Yeah . . . yeah, a candy bar and water sounds real good."

* * *

Win couldn't hear Eriksson's instructions to the group of men who headed down the trail to the north several minutes later, but all nine of them were dressed in hiking garb and every man was armed except for one, a guy about his size. That man had his hands loosely tied in front of him and was taking some good-natured teasing over being the "hostage" for what five of the group thought was a routine training mission. Win knew exactly what they were doing. He could do the math. Anyone tracking the kidnappers from his house would follow nine men in combat or hiking boots north over Sepulcher Mountain directly toward the Arm of the Lord Church. Unless the tracker was really on his toes or just got lucky, he would never notice that five men had hiked off trail on the flat rocks to the southwest. Any Bureau flyover or ground surveillance with thermal imaging would show eight armed men and one unarmed man, who appeared to be bound, moving toward the church's land. The good guys would assume Win was being smuggled back through the Bureau's surveillance lines into the church compound. That would certainly draw more law enforcement resources back to the compound and away from both the Cohn Monument site and Win's actual location. His heart sank again. *Where are they taking me?*

The hike became significantly more difficult as Win's group of five carefully inched their way off the back side of the mountain through the exposed-rock and boulder fields above the tree line. They followed a faint high-altitude trail serpentining through vast snowfields. Any slip here could send a man tumbling hundreds of feet off the exposed-rock walls and cliffs. It occurred to Win that he could easily fall to his death from the damp granite. His confidence in his ability to maneuver with the night-vision goggles dropped in direct proportion to his increasing stress level. One advantage, though: He had such poor depth perception with the goggles that he wouldn't know how far he'd fallen till he hit bottom. It wasn't much of an advantage.

Win was guessing it had been well over an hour since they'd split from the other group of nine. His legs were trembling from fatigue after the long, difficult descent off the mountain. The terrain finally began to moderate and roll, and they hiked through open meadows, sagebrush flats, and dense forests. When Eriksson called a halt in a thick stand of budding aspens, the other men, including Win, collapsed exhausted against the trees, sliding down to rest on the wet ground.

Eriksson seemed to have superhuman energy. He checked on each man, then moved over to Win, flipped his goggles up, and knelt down in front of him. "We're past the four-hour point, so we'll see how quickly your people respond. We're going to rest here for about fifteen minutes." Eriksson held a canteen up to Win's lips. "Drink this. It's Gatorade with butter and caffeine mixed in—it'll give you energy." Win drank several swallows of the awful-tasting mixture. "I'm going to clip those ties off while we rest," Eriksson said. "You drink water, eat, and tend to any business. Two will be watching you. Don't be stupid."

Win just nodded. He didn't have the strength to speak. He closed his eyes against the unnatural blackness—he was blind as a bat for a few moments. Some of the other men wore single-lens night-vision devices because of the temporary lack of vision that occurs when the twin goggles are removed. With the single-tube optics, they could at least see out of their "free" eye when the device was flipped up or turned off. The downside was the difficulty in adjusting to the monocular devices—couldn't master those on a one-night hike. Win finished off Eriksson's gift of water and protein bars while he waited for his vision to improve.

There were fewer of them now, and Win's thoughts turned to escape, but he saw no sign of complacency in any of his four captors. The one he'd come to think of as Candyman was friendly, but watchful. The man they called Two seemed to have eyes in the back of his head and super-quick reflexes. Eriksson was, well, professional, as kidnappers go, Win supposed; the huge guy was also terrifying. The fourth man was harder to read. He was having more trouble with the physical demands of the forced hike than Win or any of the others. He was the man who'd wanted to kill the rangers. He was likely one of Ron Chandler's thugs, and Win was guessing, based on his size and demeanor, that he was either Billy or Bobby Thayer. He'd never been able to tell them apart in the Bureau's surveillance photographs. He remembered Luke saying the Thayer brothers were mean as snakes. *Yep, he got that right.* Whoever the guy was, based on his earlier actions, he'd be the one quickest to kill him.

He knew he needed to snap out of the cycle of morbid thoughts clogging his mind and come up with a plan. He needed to become more of an observer, to start looking harder for openings, for options. One thing he had noticed was that all the men had lowered their masks since they'd split from the larger group. They no longer cared that their captive could clearly see their faces, could make positive identifications. Win was thinking that really wasn't a good sign.

The game trail they set back out on wasn't nearly as dangerous as hiking Sepulcher Mountain, but it was far from easy. But knowing the Bureau should be in response mode by now gave Win hope and more energy—he was thinking the souped-up Gatorade probably wasn't hurting any either. They spooked a herd of elk that had bedded down near a meadow, and the commotion of the wildly running animals in the dark forest seemed to throw Chandler's guy into a bit of a frenzy. He'd whirled and aimed his assault rifle—only the quick action of the big guy kept him from firing off a few rounds. While Eriksson chewed out the Thayer brother, Win took in the sky for a moment and caught glimpses of stars through fast-moving clouds. The weather was clearing! The helicopters could get up, the drones could fly . . . *they can find me!*

CHAPTER THIRTY-THREE

"Can we find him?" His SAC's question was telling. The Bureau was not given to tentative, faltering uncertainty, even during an unplanned phone call at 1:30 in the morning. They were, after all, *The FBI*—they always got their man. Wasn't that the motto of some FBI detective show from fifty years ago? Or maybe the Canadian Mounties' unofficial motto? Or was it both? He was too tired to remember. It might have been fluff created for TV audiences, an image the Bureau worked hard to project, but Wes Givens also knew it was damn well true. They got their man—and right at this moment, *their man* was in the hands of the bad guys, somewhere deep within a wilderness nearly as large as a small state.

Wes Givens measured his words carefully as he answered his boss. "We're pulling out all the stops, Tom, but I'll be honest, this weather is killing us. Visibility is just now inching up above zero. No way to get anything in the air. We can't even fly agents from other offices into Bozeman—that airport is closed. We've got SWAT teams from Seattle and Salt Lake City sitting on runways waiting to fly into Bozeman when they reopen the airport. I've got fifteen of our SWAT agents and several park rangers moving up the road from the Cohn dedication site toward Mammoth. That's only twenty-four miles, and it's been nearly two hours since we called them out. Got a satellite call a minute ago from their convoy. They're still nearly an hour out of Mammoth, inching along in the fog and having to shoo bison off the highway to get through." Wes closed his eyes as he tried to comprehend that bizarre mental image.

Wes was having problems visualizing the bison roadblocks, but he could clearly see Mr. Strickland in his mind. His SAC would have his hand to his broad forehead and his eyes focused squarely on his large desk as he methodically reviewed each possible option given their circumstances. The Bureau had every imaginable law enforcement asset at its disposal; no other agency in the world could be better prepared for an event like this. But they were at the mercy of Yellowstone's fickle spring weather, just as surely as Win was at the mercy of a madman named Daniel Shepherd.

Mr. Strickland recited what they had: "Locals are assisting with roadblocks, rangers are canvassing the Mammoth area. The Park County sheriff said there was a small-building fire at the church compound earlier tonight. The area's volunteer fire department showed up—all sorts of confusion. Shepherd, Chandler, and who knows who all could be in the wind." He sighed. "Our surveillance teams are real thin near the church. No way we can prevent them from reentering that compound. . . . Right now, the kidnappers are actually better armed than our folks on the ground up there."

Wes's voice rose in anger. "We knew it was a mistake when Headquarters ordered us to reposition our entire SWAT Team! Without them . . ." He worked to curb his frustration. "The militiamen are all former military and you're right, we're outgunned at the church. Our surveillance teams wouldn't stand a chance trying to engage them tonight. In fact, we've got so few folks on the ground up there, we may not even get a good thermal or visual hit on the group as they hike back into the compound."

"You've got HRT set to go to the church compound?" Strickland asked.

"Yes, sir. Two teams from the Blue Tactical Unit. They trained for a compound raid for days in Mammoth. HRT's Gold Unit has operators taking their places at the Cohn Monument site as we speak. I've got eighteen operators sitting in a hangar here at the airport, ready to go surround that church." Wes hesitated for a moment. "They're predicting the fog will clear out of here before dawn, but that . . ."

Mr. Strickland finished the halting sentence. "May be too late." He paused. "God only knows what that maniac Shepherd will do if he gets Win into that compound. Some type of spectacle to draw in the press, for sure."

"Is the Critical Incident Response Group sending their hostage negotiators from Headquarters?" Wes asked.

"They're already in the air. Where they'll land, who knows. I've talked to the Director twice tonight already." The SAC cleared his throat and proceeded more slowly. "Wes, it's now clear Shepherd was behind the attempted hits on Win. He's tried to kill him twice. . . . The militiamen who went into Mammoth tonight could have been a hit squad, regardless of what they said in front of those rangers. Win could already be dead. . . . I know that's not for general consumption, and I know we have to operate under the assumption he's still alive, but what's your gut feeling? What's your level of certainty this is Shepherd's plan—taking Win back to the church?"

Wes stared into space and took a deep breath before he answered. "I'd say there's a pretty high level of certainty the church is where they're headed . . . with Win as a hostage. It's the scenario that makes the most sense if Shepherd is after national publicity. We'll have overwhelming force surrounding the Cohn Monument site. Looks as if Shepherd has decided to upstage the dedication rather than make some foolhardy attack on the actual event. He can use Win to do just that. Killing him ahead of time makes no sense."

"If only we were dealing with someone who made the logical choices—who had some sense!" Mr. Strickland responded.

"We're trying our best to verify that Win's still with the kidnappers. The Park Service has four of their rangers reconning the trail behind Win's house. They're reporting back every fifteen minutes by satellite phone. So far they've tracked nine men moving for almost four miles to the north of the incident point—that's the eight bad guys and Win. It's three more miles on that trail before the rangers reach the top of some mountain . . . let's see, ah, Sepulcher Mountain. The church compound is about five miles by trail northwest of that mountain. The kidnappers seem to be making a straight shot for it."

"And we still haven't picked up any unusual activity near the dedication site? Nothing on aerial or drones in the last few days?"

"It's not foolproof in these mountains, but there's been no sign that any of Shepherd's militiamen have been within twenty miles of the monument site since those sightings way back in mid-April."

Mr. Strickland's voice was subdued. "Wes, we've got to try to stay positive here. I'm flying in to you as soon as they clear us to land there. Sounds like very early morning, from what you're telling me. Go ahead and reach out to our surveillance people at the church and to the park folks. Let's keep trying to determine if Win is still a hostage—thermal imaging or visual, if we can get in close enough. But *do not* engage them. When our SWAT Team gets to Mammoth, we may change that strategy, but if we try to stop them from reentering the compound without adequate manpower, things could quickly go from bad to worse."

As Wes Givens hung up, he glanced out the window of their makeshift operations center in West Yellowstone. The fog was so thick he couldn't even see vehicles parked under the streetlight thirty feet away. He resisted the urge to blame himself for not shipping Win out of Mammoth when Deb brought him evidence that the attacks on the agent could be a personal vendetta. This wasn't the time for self-recrimination. He thought back over his boss's final comment: *Things could quickly go from bad to worse.* No, things were already beyond bad—they could quickly go from worse to much, much worse.

*　*　*

Trey was trying to catch his breath as he rested behind a smooth boulder jutting into the trail. They'd left Win's carriage house nearly an hour ago—they hadn't waited for Sam Morris, their best tracker, to arrive. The kidnappers already had a significant lead; standing around, waiting for reinforcements, was no longer an option.

They'd used headlamps instead of their night-vision equipment to try to make better time—at many points they were actually jogging up the path. All four rangers knew it was risky. If the bad guys hadn't continued on—if they'd stopped for some reason—they'd see the rangers coming for a mile. They could be ambushed by a force twice their size packing plenty of firepower. But there were well-used trails forking off both the Beaver Ponds and Sepulcher Mountain Trails, and there were backcountry campers in this area. The rangers were tasked not only with pursuing the kidnappers, but also with protecting the park's visitors. No one questioned the urgent push toward the mountain.

Two of the rangers huddled behind trees in the damp woods while Jimmy shined his Maglite at the base of a large rock to illuminate something that had caught his attention. The light picked up short links of white plastic cord—the remains of zip ties. Trey stared down at the ties and drew in a sharp breath. He pulled his phone from his pocket and took two photos, then quickly placed the ties into a clear bag. He shined his headlamp into the plastic baggie for a closer inspection as Jimmy searched around the rock for more evidence.

"Trey, there's a little blood here . . . a couple of places on the rock."

"Yup, it's on the ties too. Get a couple of pictures, write down the coordinates from GPS for the exact location. I'll call it in."

Trey killed his light and pulled the heavier satellite phone out of its pouch; he took it off standby and placed the call to Chief Randall. The phone surprised him by connecting in seconds.

"Chief, we're at 4.1 miles from the point of the incident on the Sepulcher Mountain Trail," Trey reported. "We've got a clipped set of zip ties with blood on them, also a small amount of blood on a rock along the trail—looks like a stopping point for them. We've got nine sets of boots to this point. They've already passed the other trails that split off. They're going straight for the mountain. We're good to proceed."

Trey could tell by the tone his boss was irritated. "The FBI wants you to hold your position. Do not advance any further. They don't want any chance of engagement."

"We're the only ones following them, sir. We know these trails. We're the *only* pursuit!"

"We're working with the FBI to coordinate containment, Trey. We're not calling the shots. We need to make sure no visitors are between Mammoth and the Sepulcher Mountain area. Looks like we've got four groups of backcountry campers permitted for the primitive campground at Clematis Creek, all adults. Dispatch is telling me no one has been permitted to camp at either of the other two campsites in that area, but we need to double-check those sites. Roust those campers out tonight. Escort them down to the trailhead ASAP."

Trey swallowed his objections. "Roger that. I'll send Maddox and Gentry to Clematis Creek campground; they can check the two other primitive camps on the way."

"Ten-four. Our folks with the FBI's SWAT convoy from the monument site are still at least forty-five minutes out of Mammoth. Sam Morris is with that group and can assist with tracking if the FBI chooses to send a team up Sepulcher Mountain."

Trey's boss paused for several seconds. "Move a little further up the trail. . . . Make sure you're still tracking nine men. Check around your immediate position. They may have been changing out the zip ties or . . ." He paused again. Trey knew the Chief Ranger was working through the possibilities. "Yeah, well, if you're confident you've still got nine men on the trail, you and Jimmy come back down and wait for the convoy to arrive. Weather reports out of Gardiner and Mammoth are showing some improvement. We might be able to get a ship in the air from Mammoth within an hour or two. We're still totally socked in here in West Yellowstone. You'll be the incident commander for our part of this deal in Mammoth. Get back down to the office and get set up."

Trey put the sat phone on standby and called his small team over. "Jimmy, move up the trail a bit, let's verify how many we're tracking." The small man moved off into the darkness and clicked on the light strapped to his helmet. Trey turned to the other two men crouching beside him. He normally wouldn't have thought of bringing Maddox and Gentry along for this ride after the trauma they'd just experienced, but both men had been adamant about taking part in any rescue attempt. Maddox had stood in the carriage house with a blanket wrapped around him and reminded everyone that Win Tyler had pleaded for their lives, not for his own. "Trey, I get to go home to my wife and baby cause of that man. I'm not sitting this one out!" Trey couldn't argue with that, not to mention the fact that, except for Jimmy, he had no other Special Response Team members in Mammoth.

While they waited to hear back from Jimmy, Trey stood on the trail and explained the mission to clear out the primitive camping sites. "And since they cut off his cuffs, let's do a quick, narrow grid search here—to make sure we're not missing, ah, something." He didn't want to say—he refused to say—"a body."

* * *

The steady *thump thump thump* of a helicopter could be heard in the distance and immediately the men moved off the trail into the surrounding forest. Win's guard dragged him into the trees and pushed him down beside a car-size boulder. The chopper was definitely coming closer, and Win could hear the other men taking cover. It had the high whine of a medevac or search-and-rescue copter, not the heavy, pulsing sound of a military Black Hawk. It had to be the rangers looking for him. The militiaman pulled a lightweight tarp over the top of them and flipped up Win's night-vision goggles. Everything went dark, but he could sense the man sitting close beside him against the cold rock. Win's sudden movements against the boulder caused his arms to spasm with pain. He gritted his teeth to keep from crying out. The thermal blanket that was blocking their location to any heat-sensing equipment on the helicopter was claustrophobic.

The man's raspy voice was low and hard. "You need to know that if they land or if there's any rescue attempt, I have orders to kill you. Some of the other boys don't know, but this isn't a hostage deal. This is us takin' you to someone else who'll kill you tomorrow at first light." The words hung in the closed space between them, and Win suddenly felt a wave of overwhelming heaviness and despair. He'd fought it off successfully for hours—actually for days—but within the blackness of the stifling blanket, he felt himself drowning in it. He recognized his pent-up emotions were from the sniper shot, from his killing Richter, from all the days of looking over his shoulder, all the little moments of fear. The raw emotions were suddenly pressing down on him like a dam fixing to burst, and he had no idea how to deal with it. The sound of the helicopter had given him hope, but after the man's words, it only added to his crushing sense of dread.

The sound of the rotors began to fade away. Win could no longer hear it clearly. He strained to hear it, and he involuntary groaned when he realized he couldn't. He felt a firm hand rest on his shoulder and move him back into the boulder. "Easy . . . easy . . ." Two was talking to him as if he were a dog or some animal to be calmed. "We'll stay here for a few minutes, breathe shallow—not a lot of air under this blanket. If the copter doesn't have heat-seeking equipment, sometimes a heat-seeking drone is trailing."

Win was surprised to feel hot tears on his cheeks. Even in the complete darkness, he turned his head so the man wouldn't see. He fought to control his emotions; he was shivering from either the cold or, more likely, the stress.

The man dug around for something in his pack and moved even closer to Win. "You need a heavier coat. . . . You're cold, that's all. I got some coffee in here somewhere . . . might still be hot." It occurred to Win that the man was attempting to show compassion. Maybe he'd realized how hard his matter-of-fact comments about killing him had been. "This here little thermos keeps coffee warm for nearly a day, it seems. Here we go."

Win wasn't sure how the guy was seeing well enough to get the coffee to his lips, but it was warm and strangely comforting. He drank some and swallowed, and for a moment it pulled him away from the cliff of despair he'd nearly gone off.

The man pulled the thermos back and rested it on Win's chest. He could feel the warmth of it radiate through his jacket. The words were whispered, and because of the closed darkness they seemed to float in the air. "This is a hard thing, but you're making it harder on yourself. You're looking back, ain't you? You don't have any peace with yourself."

Win's retort was angry. "What's it to you?" But then he folded. "Okay, so I've done some things I'm ashamed of."

"Like what?"

Why am I letting this criminal quiz me on my sins? But he answered anyway. "I, uh, lived with my fiancée." He drew a shallow breath after the confession and hoped he could keep it together.

There was silence from the other side of the blanket. Finally, "And?" The man snorted in disbelief. "That's it?"

"What? We're gonna one-up each other on our sins?"

"You didn't beat her, steal her money, or cheat on her?"

"'Course not!" Win couldn't believe he was having this conversation.

"You loved her?" the man asked in a softer tone.

"Yes. I loved her."

"Well, Tyler, as sins go, I'm thinkin' I may have you beat there. Know why they call me Two?"

"No."

"'Cause I've been Ron Chandler's number two man for goin' on eleven years. The boys here don't know that." He laughed softly. "You Feds don't know that either, now do you? Ron and me, we go way back. . . . Let's see, you heard of the Stockmen's First National Bank, the Warrenton Bank, the Falls City Bank, then there was that Wells Fargo armored car and a few other smaller bank heists you may not have tied to us. I like to call 'em heists—sounds kinda classy, and a man's gotta do somethin' to supplement a military pension. Not to mention it's kept the Prophet's church rolling in cash all these many years. It's hard to make a decent living raisin' a few cows out here, but it sure as hell is a great place not to get noticed. You boys never noticed me, never noticed ole' Clay Ferguson, retired U.S. Marine Corps sniper. . . . I moved here years ago, but me and Ron never lost touch. We had us a real lucrative business arrangement."

"You're the one who brought Shepherd and Chandler here? To Gardiner?"

"Yessir! It's workin' out real well for 'em, too. But back to our talk on sins . . . I been around lots of sinners, Tyler, and somethin' tells me shacking up with your woman was just the tip of it—sorta like one of them icebergs. Bet you were raised strict, bet you needed to break out, to rebel! Hell, maybe your real sin was being too much of a coward to pull out of a relationship you didn't have no business in, see if you could make it without God for a while. Wanted to live on the wild side, but couldn't quite make yourself get there."

"You don't know!" Win was horrified this stranger was striking so close to the truth.

"That's the damn point. You don't know either. Only God knows why you pulled away from Him."

Two was quiet for a few moments, and then the voice in the darkness took on a gentle tone, like you might use with a child. "You're gonna die in a few hours, Agent Tyler, and there's only one real question you need to answer. Is Lord Jesus gonna take your hand in the light when you go over? If you can answer *yes*, then there ain't no need to be looking back—you can't undo anything that's behind you. Just trust Him and lean forward, son."

Trust Him. The clarity of the man's simple message brought Win almost immediate calm. *Trust Him. How odd*, he thought, *to be reminded of my core faith by someone who robs banks for a living.*

The man spoke again after a few seconds. "The end of your trail won't be a lonely one. . . . I'll be going over with you tomorrow, probably several of us will, so you won't be alone in this."

"What?" Win stammered. He was shocked at what the man was implying.

Two cleared his throat, as if emotion had suddenly taken hold. "Not much time left. Maybe that's why I'm so talkative. I ain't usually a talker, you see. That's probably why I've stayed below the cops' radar all these years—I ain't a talker. But I don't have many more hours here than you do." Win didn't know how to respond. The man blew out a breath. "For me, it's a good thing. . . . I'm ready, been ready for a long while. I'll see my family—had a daughter who'd be nearly your age, she'd be mid-twenties. My fault they're not here . . . drunk when I went off that road. I know God has forgiven me, but I still suffer with it nearly every day. Forgiveness and forgetting ain't the same thing."

Win could hear the pain in the man's voice. Then, a more hopeful tone. "The Federals will take notice of me tomorrow! Prophet says we'll be martyrs for the cause. I can end my suffering, strike out at the Zionists, and see my family again. Can come into Glory! You're a believer; could see it in your eyes back in that shed when I was holding your little Bible."

"Yes, I'm a believer . . . I'm a Christian." Win was afraid to say more. It was some sort of suicide mission. *How has their faith become so twisted?*

Win had to try to convince the man to help him, but it was becoming hard to breathe under the Kevlar blanket. He struggled to form his argument. "You don't have to go through with this. . . . It doesn't have to go down this way—" A whistle from the woods interrupted him.

The cold air hit Win in the face as Ferguson quickly threw the blanket off, took Win's arm, and pulled him to his feet. As he stuffed the thermos and blanket back into his pack, he leaned toward Win and got in the last word. "Remember what I said, son. I'll see you on the other side tomorrow and neither one of us will ever have to look back in sadness again."

The man steered him back onto the trail, and for the next two hours he hardly took his firm hand off Win's jacket. Escape wasn't looking promising. But after having teetered on the edge of emotional breakdown, Win spent a good deal of those two hours preparing himself for what was to come. He turned his focus inward, and instead of the regret and fear that had dominated his thoughts most of the night, he found himself reflecting on the people and places he loved. He once again had the detached feeling of floating above it all, but this time it wasn't the anxious, frightened sensation he'd felt earlier—this time there was peacefulness to it, as if an invisible hand were gently holding him there. There was a deep assurance that even in his failures, God would create some good.

CHAPTER THIRTY-FOUR

He recited the Scripture again softly under his breath, and prayed once more for God's hand to move against the Zionists and their pawns. He raised his head and leaned back against the frame of his heavy backpack. It was less than an hour before dawn, and so dark in the cave that he couldn't even see his breath as it rose in the cold air. The cavern smelled of damp canvas, sweat, and gun oil—and something else. What was it? Ah, the sweet, putty smell of the Semtex. Twenty pounds of it resting against his back.

Brother Luke had shown them this place. Far off the public trail system, in what the Park Service had designated a bear management area, a 50,000-acre restricted zone that made it easy for them to operate without the fear of stumbling onto a bunch of hiking tourists. They'd been using the cave as a staging point since early April and had brought supplies in gradually. Within its thick walls they were invisible to the enemy's heat-seeking drones and aircraft. Rock overhangs at the entrance and alongside the adjoining granite cliffs allowed the men to get some fresh air and to watch the heavily used game trail that snaked through a small clearing just a hundred feet below the cave's mouth. A spring provided fresh water to the shelter. No one had to leave the hidden sanctuary; it was self-contained. There was no cell service for miles, but that wasn't critical. They were less than seven miles northwest of the site where the Zionists and the Feds would dedicate a monument to a Jew in less than twelve hours. He was thinking what a disgrace that was for our once-great nation.

Two or three of his men were snoring, and more than one was tossing in the night. He and this team of ten men had hiked to the cave in separate small groups over the last few days. Most should be well rested. One of his men hadn't been able to shake his FBI surveillance team near Gardiner; he'd returned to the compound yesterday—he couldn't take a chance on being followed inside the park. Everyone else had arrived at the cave on time, except for two of Ron's newer recruits. Apparently those boys had decided this outing wasn't for them. Even three men short, they had more than enough men and weapons to carry out the mission. The Lord knew the men he needed. Didn't the Scripture say in the Book of Judges that God trimmed Gideon's army of ten thousand down to three hundred men to defeat the Midianites? He smiled to himself at the thought of that miracle.

The men bringing Tyler should be within two miles by now. They'd taken a much longer route in order to meet the other brothers on Sepulcher Mountain and confuse the Feds. And the FBI should be convinced that Agent Tyler was tucked away at the church. He smiled when he thought about how shocked the enemy would be when their man wasn't to be found. He was hoping for a direct raid by the Federals on the church this morning, hoping for the greatest amount of violence and its accompanying publicity. A terrible shame that some of the innocent sisters and children living at the church might be harmed, but the nation's press would not respond in numbers unless blood was spilled. The more blood spilled, the greater the media coverage, and the greater the media coverage, the sooner the battle would be won. There were patriots across the country who would rally to their cause, who were just waiting for a bold Christian leader to emerge. Collateral damage—the deaths of innocents—was just an unfortunate part of revolution. He would pray for those innocent martyrs to have their rewards in Heaven.

The sentry had reported a helicopter several miles to the northeast nearly two hours ago. But there was no reason for concern; God's strong staff was guiding them. Tyler would be brought to him at dawn, and he'd do what he should have done in the first place. He'd made a mistake and obviously displeased the Lord by hiring a pagan to kill the FBI agent. Richter had been a godless man whose only interest in the thing was the money. Daniel Shepherd would not dishonor God again. He would handle it according to God's leading.

He sighed a little as thoughts of Ruth suddenly filled his mind. He felt the familiar emptiness in his chest as the pain stabbed at his heart. It had been nearly three years since she'd passed—nearly four since Dennie was shot by the Feds. The grief had never lessened. The government hadn't just taken his son, they'd taken her as well; she was never the same after the shooting. Their youngest son gone—he knew she'd died of a broken heart.

And he'd known it was a sign from God the moment he saw Winston Tyler's picture in the newspaper back in late March. The resemblance between the FBI agent and their boy was uncanny. The Fed had been sent here to ease his suffering, to restore God's order—an eye for an eye. Ruth would approve of this, of his taking another young man's life from the oppressors to atone for their taking Dennie's life. He wanted to please her, and he prayed it would ease his aching soul. For many long years, nothing else had.

He sat up and turned on a tiny green glow light. He rose on aching knees and carefully made his way among the prone figures littering the floor of the cave. The eerie green light bounced off the rock walls. As he stepped over the small stream that originated somewhere in the depths of the place, he twisted the tiny light off and moved near the man standing guard at the entrance.

"Brother Jeffery . . ." He said it in a whisper from ten feet behind the sentry, so as not to startle him. Even in the dark night, he could make out the armed man silhouetted against the opening of the cave.

"Prophet? Is something wrong?" the young man answered with concern.

"No, no . . . just finished early prayers and wanted to stretch a bit. You know we're standing on the edge of glory! I'm just rejoicing in the day. It'll be daylight soon. How are you doing, brother?"

"Fine. I'm fine." The guard sounded strained; he didn't sound fine. "Sir, you know, I haven't had the combat experience of most of the brothers. I only drove trucks over in Afghanistan."

"Ah yes, but you served. Never forget the significance of that—so tragic for our nation, for our government to be run now by the Jews, by internationalists who have created a puppet state. You couldn't have known that when you joined the Army. The Federals are well practiced at deceit! Masters at evil! But we'll take it back. We'll take America back," he whispered urgently. "We take the first step today toward taking it back! Think of how proud your wife and son will be of you." He sensed the young man pulling himself up straighter. "Your son, Colby, he's a precious little man. So spirited! Think of how proud he'll be when you see him. And aren't you and Sister Hannah expecting another little one? When?"

"In October." The young man was smiling in the darkness.

The Prophet reached out and touched the man's arm. "Let me pray for you, Brother Jeffery, for you and your family—a special blessing for you that the Lord is putting on my heart . . ."

After a time, the Prophet followed the faint green glow back to his sleeping bag near the rear of the large cavern. He lowered himself and felt his right knee give a little. *Ah, I'm getting too old for this.*

"Can't sleep?" The man beside him moved in the darkness.

The Prophet drew in a deep breath of cold air. "Ah, you know I'm always restless before a mission."

"Worried that they didn't get the agent?" Chandler asked.

"No, no, Eriksson's a good man. They'll bring him. Something's nagging at me, though. I'll have to give Tyler the chance to claim the Lord's salvation before he dies. . . . If he accepts or is already a believer, it could unsettle the men if I kill him outright."

His friend shifted beside him and quietly replied, "You know for the longest I didn't think killing that FBI agent was a good idea, not with the mission going on. But it's turned out to be downright helpful. Caused them to scatter in lots of directions. It's been a major distraction to the enemy—lots of positives there." Chandler paused for a moment. "If you get the least concerned that the blood doesn't need to be directly on your hands, I'll take care of it for you."

Even in the pitch blackness, the Prophet knew Ron Chandler was grinning an evil grin as he continued talking. "You know, that might actually work to our advantage tomorrow. We need the boys to see you as living above the fray, full of compassion and mercy. We need them seeing me as the damn wrath of God!"

*	*	*

It was thinking about gettin' light. His whole life he'd gotten up before sunrise. Often he'd been so preoccupied with thoughts of school or work that he'd miss the changeover from darkness to light. He'd miss the dawn. That wasn't happening this morning.

It got light early in Yellowstone, and the sun stayed longer during the early evening. The park was so far north that it got nearly an extra hour a day of spring sunlight compared to the southern places Win was accustomed to. He wasn't used to the quick transition to daylight at 5:30 in the morning in mid-May.

Two had taken the night-vision goggles and helmet from him as the first hint of yellow hit the tops of the mountains to the east. They'd stopped at a sharp whistle from somewhere up ahead, and Candyman had moved forward to meet the camp's sentry. Win could smell coffee and hear muffled voices in the distance. It was still too dark to make out anyone's features, but Win could sense a change in Eriksson's demeanor. There was a different intensity, maybe anticipation or an underlying anxiety.

The big man towered over Win on the trail. "The brothers are at prayer so we're gonna wait before we move into camp. Drink a little water?"

Win swallowed some of the offered water and tried to reason with the man again. "You know this isn't right. You can't tell me you don't know that."

"This is between you and the Prophet, Agent Tyler. I've got nothing against you, but you're on the wrong side in a war. We're taking back

America, or at least our piece of America. The government has failed us. It's our right—hell, it's our duty—to take it back."

"We *vote* to change our government. We don't wage war. We're both Americans! C'mon, you're not a criminal—look at what you're doing!"

The deep voice was threatening. "You bring it up with Prophet Shepherd! Say another word to me and I'll gag you! You hear me?"

Win turned his head away from the man and shifted his attention to the new day's arrival. The trail was on a high bench on a mountainside, and he could see the sharp outline of the mountains forming to the east. He watched the far horizon through the trees as color returned to the world. He could see his breath in the air; he knew it was cold, but other things had pushed that discomfort away. A bird was calling somewhere in the forest. Win tried to place it, but this western bird's call was new to him. He made a mental note to research it, then smiled to himself at his foolishness. It wasn't lookin' like he'd be in this place long enough to learn its birds.

He shifted from one foot to the other and tried the bindings again. He'd tried with all his strength to break them, but these men hadn't skimped, they'd bought the heavy plastic flex cuffs rated to withstand six hundred pounds of pressure. His wrists and hands were sticky again with blood. It wasn't working. Dawn was breaking and he now knew with certainty there was no escape.

CHAPTER THIRTY-FIVE

They hiked in just as the prayer meeting was breaking up. The group was gathered under several large spruce trees at the uphill edge of a small clearing below the black, gaping mouth of a cave. The men appeared as dark shadows as they rose to their feet under the gloom of the overhanging trees. The early light was too dim for Win to clearly make out any details, but he heard the distinct clatter of long guns being shifted as they stood. This was Prophet Shepherd's army.

The man Win assumed was Shepherd was bareheaded, dressed in a heavy coat, and carrying a thick book. He stood a little apart from the others, and although he wasn't a tall man, his bearing conveyed his distinction as their leader. He and a stocky man, who Win guessed was Chandler, walked away from the group and along the slope to meet Eriksson. They both gave him approving nods and handshakes. They traded words Win couldn't hear, then the Prophet walked through the short grass on the slight slope toward Win with an expectant, purposeful stride—he was coming to him. The other men followed Shepherd at a respectful distance and formed a loose circle around Win. He sensed as much curiosity as hostility in their manner.

"Do you know why you're here?" Daniel Shepherd stood just above him on the slope near the trail. The faint light was falling on his features, and Win could see a mixture of satisfaction and mania there. His eyes were too hooded in the early light to read, but Win had no doubt he'd see fanatical madness in them—this man was crazy in a distinctly dangerous way. There would be no reasoning with Daniel Shepherd. Win would have to appeal to the others.

"Why don't you tell me? You've broken the law by bringing me here."

"We don't recognize the laws of the United States any longer, Agent Tyler. Our revolution begins today, and you have the distinction of being the oppressor's first casualty of that war!" He said it loudly and with authority. There was a shifting and a slight murmur within the group of men. Most of them hadn't expected this.

Shepherd raised the book, a large black Bible, over his head for effect. "God's Word in Deuteronomy 19:21 tells us to not show pity, to take a life for a life, and an eye for an eye! My youngest son, Dennie Shepherd, died at the hands of the FBI four years ago! God has brought this man, this agent of the FBI, here so that I can avenge that death—to bring balance and order to His Kingdom and to bring justice to me and my family!"

Win wasn't gonna go down without a fight—at least a verbal fight. His voice was loud enough for them all to hear. "I'm sorry Dennie Shepherd died. But he was killed robbing a bank—after he'd shot innocent bystanders! He chose the wrong path! What does Christ say in the Book of Matthew about your 'eye for an eye' quote? He tells us to turn the other cheek—not to repay evil for evil. We have laws for that . . . for justice." Win took a breath. He couldn't believe Shepherd was letting him have his say, but his voice was strong as he finished his plea. "You're trying to justify a murder—these men know that! I'm a Christian and you're going to murder me? You're tying all these men to your evil plans by making them accessories to murder—to this crime! You're turning them into criminals and you're twisting our faith! You're a false prophet! Nothing but a false prophet!"

That didn't go over so well. Ron Chandler stepped toward Win and backhanded him hard across the face with his gloved hand. The strike snapped Win's head back. He tried to dodge to avoid another blow, but the two men behind him held him firmly in place.

Shepherd quickly stepped down to the trail and grabbed Chandler's arm. "Brother King, we have many steps to take toward victory today, let's finish this first task now." Chandler clearly wanted to get in another lick or two, but Shepherd tugged at his arm and they moved a couple of steps back up the slope. Win shook his head to clear the bright spangles that were still flashing in front of his eyes from the blow. Shepherd turned his attention from Win and addressed his troops.

"Brothers! This man claims to be a believer! Only God knows his heart and in Glory, God can correct his mistaken thoughts." Shepherd spoke to the group along those lines for a minute or two, quoting Scripture and raising that Bible . . . trying to ramp himself back up for the ugly task at hand.

But Win wasn't really there. He was in that floating state again. *He's staging this show for his men,* Win thought, as his mind drifted. He knew in his heart he couldn't reason with them. Individually, maybe he could have, but when men form a pack, and their leader chooses the wrong path, it's nearly impossible to turn the group—the pack—back to the right. He knew that. The pack mentality allows mobs to form, riots to occur—rational thinking rarely prevails and truth is generally trampled. Win held no illusions that his arguments would free him. He'd said what he needed to say. The peace was settling back in.

When Shepherd's short speech ended, Win focused back on the present. Some of the militiamen were easing back toward the trees, and Win sensed one of the men behind him moving. A hand squeezed his right shoulder and he caught a glimpse of Two sliding away from him. The surroundings were becoming lighter, and he could make out individual faces and expressions better. He scanned them again for anyone who would step out and be an ally. He found none. *It must be time.*

Win didn't want anyone to be able to tell his daddy he hadn't died like a man. He raised his chin and squared his shoulders as he watched Ron Chandler unzip his heavy camouflage coat. He watched the man's right hand go to the checkered grip of a holstered .357 revolver in slow motion. His left hand pulled an eight-inch silver cylinder from a pocket, a Liberty suppressor or silencer. Chandler had come prepared. The man's eyes under the camo field cap were flat and icy. Win's world collapsed into the six feet between them. He drew in a breath. He had control of his emotions. He was ready.

But Win was wrong about those emotions. As soon as he heard the voice behind him, a cold chill ran down his spine, his knees went weak, he closed his eyes tight in disbelief.

"I'll handle this fer you, Prophet. This man was too familiar toward my wife. . . . This Fed dies by my hand and we both have our revenge." The voice was direct and firm.

The horrible realization of the betrayal hit Win full force. How could he have been so wrong? Before he opened his eyes, Win heard Matt Smith's warning to him as clearly as if the man were standing there: *Think about the lives that could be lost if Luke Bordeaux is one of the bad guys!* He'd gone with his instincts and made a terrible error. Ron Chandler smiled a devilish smile, put the big silver .357 Magnum back in the holster, and shrugged.

Prophet Shepherd nodded slowly, as if trying to decide whether Luke's statement was a request or a command. "As you want, Brother Luke. I just need to see him die—I need to do it for my Dennie, you understand?"

"Alright, I'm moving him off the trail. We don't need blood there. We'll need the elk to confuse our tracks when they move through here today. They won't walk through blood. Step down below the trail and we'll finish this."

Win wasn't sure he could even will his legs to move, but Luke's strong hands had him by the back of his jacket and his shoulder. Luke pulled him along as he stumbled backward to a more open, grassy area on a slight slope. The break in the execution had given several more of the militiamen an excuse to move back toward their small camp stoves in the cave. Most of them would rather have another cup of coffee than see the Prophet's revenge play out with a man killed in cold blood.

When they stopped moving backward, Win's fear mixed with anger and he twisted to look into Luke's face. Everything had been said, but he wasn't about to let the man kill him without seeing his eyes. Luke's tan face was within inches of his—the eyes looked nearly black. Win hoped the man saw his anger when they locked eyes, but he knew at that moment Luke could also see his fear—he just hadn't expected to see that same emotion in Bordeaux's eyes. But those black eyes showed no sign of regret or guilt, and the fear, if it had been there at all, was quickly replaced by the hard, steely stare Win had seen in the chapel the night before last. Luke was *in the zone,* as he'd once put it. Luke was fixing to tend to business.

"Damn you, Luke!" Win spat the words at him and hoped God would understand. Luke responded by knocking Win's feet out from under him with one move of his leg. He caught the back of Win's jacket and took him to his knees. Then he kicked him facedown into the grassy slope.

Win's first reaction was to close his eyes tightly, but he didn't want his last memories of this world to be darkness, and he opened them to focus on the new spring grass taking hold on the mountainside. He could hear the sounds of a stream a few yards to the south. It was a nice sound. A bird was singing a welcome to the dawn somewhere nearby in the forest. Despite the fury he'd felt a moment before, a calm was returning to his soul. Time was suspended. For a few more seconds he was a spectator floating above the small clearing as the world awoke from the night.

Then a heavy knee was on his back, forcing him harder into the ground. He heard Luke's voice tell the others he was wrapping the gun to stifle the sound, he heard the metal slide move backward then forward on Luke's Beretta as he chambered a round, then he felt the cold steel of the gun's muzzle against the side of his head. Win gritted his teeth, closed his eyes, and silently asked God to take him home.

"Take care of Ellie and my babies. Don't move!" Whispered words from above his left ear, then much louder and harsher, *"La Porte Battante!"*

And then the deafening roar and sharp pain from the pistol's concussion—the shattering blow to the side of his head. Intense pain in his left ear, warm liquid on his head and neck. He kept his eyes closed. He didn't breathe. He'd expected to see light, but there was no light. *Did Luke somehow miss?* The whispered words confused him. *Why ask me to care for his family if I'm gonna die here?* He took a shallow breath and held his breath again. He willed his body to lie still in the damp grass. He smelled the metallic smoke from the handgun's discharge. He could taste blood as it reached his lips. He fought the strong urge to be physically sick. He heard them above him, but the roar in his ears was too loud to understand words. *What are they saying?* He could only catch pieces of it at first.

"Just a Cajun war cry.... Never killed a man like that ... blood all over my hands.... Need to wash this off ..." That was Luke speaking.

Another voice above him: "You've done a good service for me, Brother Luke. An eye for an eye." The man's voice changed, got softer and sad. "Somehow I thought watching him die might ease my feelings for Dennie more. He looked so much like my boy." A long pause. "Ah, maybe in time ..." The Prophet's voice trailed off. "Yes, maybe in time." No one else spoke, and the voice rose a notch as the Prophet shifted back to their mission. "Brother Luke, it's good you've come back to us today—we're a few men short. Will you go with Brother King's team? He can use your skills."

"Yes, Prophet, wherever you want me to serve," Luke answered.

"What about the body? Want some of the men to move it down the ridge?" Chandler's voice, a little shaky. He'd lost some of the swagger with a dead FBI agent four feet away.

All three of them must be standing nearly on top of him, Win realized, just above him near the trail. He continued to hold his breath; his heart was beating wildly and the intense ringing in his ears hadn't let up. As the pain at the side of his head grew, it was starting to sink in that he was still very much alive.

Luke's voice again. "No need to move the body. It's gettin' full light now, and the wolves and bears will be drawn to the blood. They'll drag it off—won't be much to find by mid-morning." Luke's voice shifted to the clipped, military inflection Win had heard him use before. "This is done. We've got ground to cover before three."

They were walking away, up the slope toward the militiamen. He sensed activity somewhere above the trail; they were moving out. His head was pounding and his mouth was filling with blood. He kept fighting the urge to gag on it.

He didn't move for what seemed like forever. He knew Luke had placed him in the open intentionally. The drones or helicopters could spot him if they were flying in this area. He couldn't see it, but he felt the sun break over the mountains. It warmed his back and lit up the little clearing where he lay. He was guessing fifteen minutes had passed since the men had left, but he really had no idea. He was normally exceptionally good at estimating time—that came from his quarterback days, years of practice at internally counting down the time between plays. Now, for some reason, he had no feel for the seconds as they passed. He supposed he was slipping into shock, and he made a mental note to figure out how to deal with that condition if it ever happened again. He hoped like hell it never happened again.

He finally rolled to his right side and spit out some of the blood. He tried to get to his knees but threw up before he made it. His left eye was caked shut with dried blood, but from his right eye he could see that Luke had left a phone and a bloody knife beneath him. Win rocked back on his heels when it hit him—the blood wasn't his—it was Luke Bordeaux's. "Oh, dear God," he whispered when it dawned on him how Luke had pulled it off.

He'd seen enough old Westerns to know how to stab the knife blade into the ground and use the exposed blade to saw off hand restraints. Win found that in reality it was much harder to do than it appeared in the movies. The knife was sticky with Luke's drying blood and it was sharp as a razor. His hands were still numb from straining against the cuffs and he couldn't move several fingers. He nicked himself with the knife several times before he even got it firmly planted in the ground. The plastic flex cuffs were more difficult to cut than rope or thinner zip ties, so he had to force himself to work at it very slowly. He could easily slice his own wrist and bleed to death. It was tedious and scary.

Then it got worse. Out of the corner of his open eye he caught movement near the tree line and heard the sounds of limbs breaking. He saw a dark form in the woods fifty yards away. He immediately remembered Luke's words about wolves and bears finding the fresh blood. It sounded like something big was coming through the woods, looking for breakfast.

CHAPTER THIRTY-SIX

Trey Hechtner was beginning to see this as a classic case of too many chiefs and not enough Indians. It was nearly 6:00 a.m., and the early-morning sun was peeking through the low clouds and fog and streaming through the open blinds in the Park Service's conference room. Trey leaned back in his chair and ran a hand over his face while he thought back on the night's events.

The FBI's SWAT convoy with fifteen agents, along with four Park Service Special Response Team members, had finally rolled into Mammoth from the monument dedication site about the time the heavy fog began to roll out at 2:45 a.m. By that time he had a reasonable facsimile of an incident command center up and running out of the park's Administration Building. He'd issued a general alarm to all park law enforcement personnel and support staff; folks had trickled into the command center in reasonable numbers. The crime scene at Win's house had been secured, and the backcountry campers had been brought down from the vicinity of Sepulcher Mountain. One of the rangers had stumbled onto the kidnappers' utility van abandoned in a parking lot near the hotel. It was secured for processing by the FBI Evidence Response Team, but those folks wouldn't arrive until mid-morning at the earliest. Based on an initial inspection, there was no indication Win had been in the van, but much more analysis was required to nail that down.

Trey had rangers physically blocking the highway to West Yellowstone and all hiking trails leading out of Mammoth to the north and west. He wasn't taking the chance visitors would actually obey the *Do Not Enter* or *Trail Closed* signage. Vehicles coming into and out of the park were being checked by rangers and local deputies at all park entrances—not a huge job since a third of the park's roads weren't even open yet, but as traffic increased this morning, it would become more of a problem. He needed more bodies. He'd called the Livingston and Cooke City police departments for additional help and Gus had requested additional law enforcement rangers from several of the surrounding national parks and national forests. It would be hours before most of them arrived, but at least reinforcements were on the way.

His one attempt to get the helicopter up last night hadn't been successful. They'd lifted off around 2:30 a.m. and tried their thermal-imaging equipment on the south slopes of Sepulcher Mountain and down the valley from Swan Lake. The dense ground fog and large numbers of elk and bison in those areas had made the imaging device nearly useless. They'd grounded the ship after less than an hour, when more fog rolled in. As much as he hated to suspend the search, there was a guiding principle he wouldn't violate: He wouldn't risk the lives of the four-man helo crew for one lost soul.

Trey knew Gus and Chief Randall had been waging war through the early-morning hours in West Yellowstone's tactical operations center, with elements of the State Department, Secret Service, Department of Justice, and FBI. Based on his last conversation with Gus an hour ago, no one could agree on anything. The State Department was adamant that the monument dedication go forward. The Secret Service and DOJ were equally adamant that the FBI and the Park Service focus most of their manpower on securing the site for that upcoming event, while the FBI brass were furious they weren't being allowed to shift more resources into the search for Win.

Trey shook his head to try to clear the headache forming behind his eyes—lack of sleep always did that to him. It would sure be nice to have a shower, but that wasn't an option; he was still wearing the grungy tactical garb he'd worn last night on the trail. He stared back up at the big white board he was using to detail the various facets of the incident. He'd set up a flowchart on what was known . . . and unknown. He breathed a deep sigh. *Way, way too much still unknown.* The ubiquitous government clock on the wall hit six o'clock as one of the clerks brought him more coffee. He walked down the hall to stretch and clear his mind. Agent Johnson was on the landline when Trey walked back into the room.

Johnson jumped right in. "Can you get that helicopter up? You've got some thermal-imaging capacity, right? Been light half an hour and they still can't get anything off the ground in West Yellowstone. We've got two teams of SWAT agents flying into Bozeman, that airport opened at 5:30. But their ETA is three hours out—that will put them here after nine. What are you hearing?"

Trey ventured a question before he began answering Johnson's. "Who's in charge now?"

Always the diplomat, Johnson thundered back, "Who in hell do you think's in charge! We're in charge, and from the looks of it, we're doing a damn poor job!" The big man snorted into the phone. "Apparently the State Department and DOJ are yanking everyone's chain and insisting that our primary resources stay in the Cohn Monument area until after the dedication—like it's some big national crisis if a damn piece of granite doesn't get some dead guy's name on it this afternoon! All the while we've got a *real* crisis—one of our men kidnapped by a bunch of raving loons!"

Trey pulled the phone away from his ear and listened as Johnson blew off more steam. He closed his aching eyes for a few seconds, then realized if he left them closed, he might fall asleep sitting at the conference table.

When Johnson momentarily calmed, Trey began talking. "The ceiling's lifting again. Are you authorizing me to get the helicopter in the air? I haven't been able to get authorization from anyone else."

"*Me* authorize something? I don't have any *real* authority. I've got fifteen SWAT agents milling around downstairs, wondering what to do, but I think getting the copter up would . . ." Johnson paused. Trey could tell he had turned away from the phone. "Oh, hell, got to take this. . . . Call you right back." The line went dead.

Helpless. That was Trey's overriding feeling. In his career, he'd worked horrible vehicle wrecks, rappelled down cliff faces to recover bodies, and kayaked through raging rivers to search for drowning victims. He knew what helplessness felt like, but he'd always been able to channel that emotion into action. It was much more than going through the motions—it was trying to make a difference, a positive difference. The primary aspect of his job, as he saw it, was helping people. Trying to save lives. And in those sad times when that wasn't possible, trying his best to provide closure to anguished family and friends. This time, for the first time, he knew the victim. He knew the man who might not come back—that added a sharp edge to the emotions in his heart. He knew he might be finding out sooner rather than later if the concept of closure was just an illusion.

His thoughts were interrupted by the ringing of the secure landline. "All right, finally got something!" Johnson sounded almost excited. "One of our ground surveillance teams lucked out just before daylight and spotted nine men coming down a ravine onto the church's land from the south. Fog was still so bad they couldn't get clear definition with night vision, but the thermal imaging showed eight men armed with long guns and one guy, about Win's size, with cuffs or ties on his hands." He took a deep breath. "Our guys were under orders not to intercept them. . . . They're probably walking into the church buildings about now."

"Thank God he's alive!" A wave of relief swept over Trey. "So now what?"

We've got hostage negotiators from Washington landing at Bozeman within the hour. We've got HRT sending their Blue Unit guys back to the compound—those are the guys you worked with—but they can't fly out until the fog lifts down at West Yellowstone. The Salt Lake City ASAC will take over as the Bureau's on-scene commander outside the church compound as soon as their SWAT Team arrives, hopefully in three hours or so. My stint as FBI honcho on this deal is short-lived."

Something unsettling stirred in Trey's mind. "But it will still be several hours before you hand it off?"

"Yeah, looks that way. . . . What? What are you thinking?"

"Not sure . . . a gut feeling, but this all seems a little too logical, too predictable, considering what Win told me about Daniel Shepherd. Logical and predictable were never that man's MO." Trey stared down at his coffee for a moment. "Why don't we send my best tracker up Sepulcher Mountain and see what he finds? Let him summit it and check the other side—just in case."

"You're thinking some kind of switch-off?"

"I'm not sure what I'm thinking, but something doesn't feel right. Can you spare four or five of your really fit SWAT guys for a seven-mile jog up the mountain with my man? I'm way too shorthanded to send anyone else. They'll have to travel light. Just weapons." Johnson didn't answer right away. So Trey forged ahead. "I'd also like to get my ship up again and snoop around, now that we've got some ceiling."

Trey could tell Johnson was thinking out loud. "I can't authorize your helicopter up . . . but our SWAT guys won't deploy to the church compound for a few hours and they're rarin' to go. We don't have any other air assets that can get up—they can't even fly the drones 'cause the fog's so bad south of us. But hell, nobody's gonna approve any move at the TOC. They're in gridlock down there." Johnson sighed into the phone, but his voice had resolve. "I can retire any damn time I want to . . . so what the hell. Yeah, let's send some guys. Let's see what's out there."

* * *

He held his breath for several seconds because he knew if he breathed, his hands would move ever so slightly. He had to be close to cutting through the plastic cuffs—even a fraction of an inch would matter. He'd been steadily sawing at the same spot for a couple of minutes. He prayed he was still sawing on the same spot. Sweat was mixing with the blood on his face and running down onto his crimson-stained jacket front.

His good ear picked up more movement and a loud snort from the direction of the woods. Maybe a black bear—they weren't so bad. *Please don't be a grizzly.* He hazarded another glance and saw a dark brown head and huge shoulders emerge from a bank of small evergreens. The large hump over the beast's shoulders told him what he'd feared: grizzly bear—real big grizzly bear. *Dadgummit!* The bear's head was up, his nose tilted toward the sky, sniffing the air. The little rounded ears flicked back and forth. Win could see the rusty-brown eyes clearly from this distance. There would be lots of "man" smell in this place. . . . The bear was being cautious.

He continued the delicate sawing motion with his hands against the knife blade. He mentally warned himself over and over against pushing too hard; he could fatally wound himself with Luke's skinning knife. He needed to be slow, steady, and methodical. What he didn't need was a six-hundred-pound bear deciding to make a meal of him. He heard the creature move through the surrounding thicket and out into the open. It was behind two large boulders and he couldn't see it without turning. He couldn't turn—he had to free himself. He remembered Tory telling him a grizzly's sense of smell was seven times better than a bloodhound's, and that the bears could run faster than a thoroughbred in short bursts. He tried to shut out the magnificent attributes of his latest adversary—he tried to focus on cutting those cuffs.

He heard it behind him; it had rounded the big rocks and pushed through the brush. It was probably less than thirty yards away now. He had no cover. He held his breath again and pressed his wrists into the knife blade. The bear snorted sharply, snapped its jaws, and let out a deep, low guttural growl. He heard water splash. . . . It was crossing the stream, it was within forty feet now and still coming. *Please break! Please break!* he silently pleaded with the cuffs. *Please!*

They broke.

He rolled to the right, scooped up the bloody knife, and stood on unsteady legs, waving his numb arms as he came up. He wasn't sure what he yelled at the approaching bear, but it was along the lines of "Whoa! Damn it!"

The bear rose to its full height on two feet and let out a bloodcurdling roar that reverberated through every inch of him. Win's limited hearing didn't matter at this distance. The massive head went back and he could see the huge canine teeth. Four-inch claws ripped the air. Win figured there was a very real possibility he might just die of fright right there. He tried to steady the knife, a pathetic excuse for a weapon against such a creature. The bear threw its head back again and let out another long roar. Then they both blinked. As he tried to aim the knife at the now eight-foot-tall bear, Win realized his hands were shaking so badly that he might not hit it at thirty feet. But the bear's eyes reflected an element of surprise, like a horse that had been spooked. Apparently it hadn't expected its breakfast to offer this much resistance. Both of them hesitated.

For some strange reason, Win's mind flashed back to the advice he'd read on the ever-present warning signs dotting Yellowstone: "If approached by a bear, remain calm. Do not run. Speak to the bear in a conversational voice."

No way! They've got to be kidding! But in view of recent events, Win was feeling a little lucky. *What do I have to lose?*

"Okay . . . okay . . . okay . . . don't want to hurt you . . . go away . . . please go away," he began in an unsteady voice. He didn't move, he tried hard to firm up his grip on his weapon. He was going to go for the beast's eye. "I need you to move on." The bear had cocked its head and seemed to be smelling the air again. Its "arms" were no longer waving. He thought its eyes looked more curious than menacing. He knew he was probably fooling himself, but he was gaining a little confidence. He wasn't trembling quite as badly.

"I'm gonna need you to clear out so I can figure out how to catch some very bad guys . . ." He was now using his best "calm the horses" voice, and to his amazement it seemed to be working. He kept talking. The bear dropped to all fours and wagged its huge head at him a few times, but did not advance.

The dark head turned. It seemed to catch a whiff of something from the militiamen's campsite up the slope. *Have they left some food?* Win knew human food was taboo for wild animals, but at that moment, he was praying someone had left something edible behind. The bear moved up the slope in the direction of its nose, and Win grabbed the phone and forced his still-shaking legs to climb a six-foot boulder standing in the clearing a few yards below him. The big rock would give him some protection from the bear—not much, but some, and he'd still be visible to the drones or search planes. He turned Luke's cell phone on. No service, of course, but the phone's locator might send out a signal. It gave him hope.

*　*　*

"Hey, Trey?" The satellite phone was coming in loud and clear. "We've got an issue up here." Sam Morris had taken off his field cap and was running his hand through his sweaty hair as he spoke. He leaned behind a big whitebark pine with one of the SWAT guys to get out of the wind. "Got nine men, the same nine men from Win's carriage house, all the way to the summit—got nine men coming down the north side. But it's not the same nine men."

Trey didn't know what to say. Sam was an exceptional tracker. He'd rescued dozens of lost hikers during his many years with the Park Service.

"Okay . . . tell me what you've got," Trey finally replied.

"Got some different boot prints going down. We're about a quarter mile off the summit on the north side, we just hit the tree line. It's real flat, slick rock and ice up higher—no real imprints for a good ways. We're going to backtrack and see where the changeup occurred. Our man, Tyler, he came up past the summit, but he's not with them here. Boot treads are different. Also tracking a group of five who came up the north trail. Recent tracks—and you know that trail isn't heavily used. Let me get back with you when I figure it out, but wanted you to know."

"You're sure?"

"Yep, not a doubt."

"Call me as soon as you know more."

"Roger that."

Trey sat for a minute with the sat phone in his hand. His first reaction: *This isn't good.* There were several possibilities, none of them good. He glanced at his watch; it was nine o'clock straight up. He punched in a call to Johnson.

"Whata you got?" The guy was not big on formalities.

"Got an initial report from my tracker. It's not the same nine men. The men who left Win's place with him are not the same men going off the north side of the mountain. And based on the tracks, Win is not with the group on the north side."

There was silence for several seconds. Then a couple of curse words Trey wouldn't repeat. "You're sure? How good is your guy?"

"Sam Morris is real good, and he says there's no doubt. They're hiking back toward the summit to see if they can figure it out. Looks as if five men may have hiked up the north face of the mountain to meet the kidnappers. Lots of flat rock and ice up there, difficult tracking, but it's looking like Win is somewhere else."

Another moment of silence, a few more curse words, then, "Got an army of ramped-up HRT and SWAT agents heading for that church compound right now. We're going to set up a tight perimeter and get our negotiators out there. We should be operational outside the compound within the hour. As soon as Salt Lake's ASAC gets there, I'm off the clock." He paused. "Have you been seeing the Prophet's latest rants on the web? He is really going off on the dedication and on the heavy-handed federal thugs, as he's calling us today."

"Anybody made a visual on Shepherd or any of the heavy hitters today?" Trey asked the obvious question.

"No. No, and that's making me real nervous. If Win isn't in the compound—if that's another of Shepherd's diversions—then I'd really be circling the wagons down at the monument site," Johnson replied.

"Yeah, I'm thinking the same thing. Shepherd's trying to get us to divide our resources, reduce our assets in any one sector, to split our attention."

"Looks like he's not just trying to—looks like he's done it. Which still begs the question, where the hell is Win Tyler?"

CHAPTER THIRTY-SEVEN

Win was trying to keep from falling asleep on top of the big rock overlooking the clearing. He and the bear had settled into an uneasy truce—uneasy for Win, but the bear just went about doing bear things. It had grown bored with whatever it smelled near the militiamen's campsite and had returned to lick and roll in the bloodstained grass a few yards from Win's boulder. It seemed to claim that spot as its own, chasing away the occasional raven that flew down to look for a potential meal. It fended off an incursion by a skinny fox that ventured too near. The bear ate grass, dug several holes, turned over two or three rotten logs, and occasionally rose on its hind legs to give Win the once-over. Win got the feeling it was eating roots and bugs and hoping the main course would give up the fight, come down off that rock, and make things easy. It appeared to be a lazy bear.

It might have been lazy, but it had nearly four hundred pounds on Win, not to mention the formidable teeth and claws. Win was smart enough to stay on his rock and keep the high ground. And keeping the high ground got harder and harder with each passing hour. His watch said 9:00 a.m.—the militiamen had been gone for roughly three and a half hours, and Win was a mess. His mouth was so parched and bitter he could hardly swallow. One eye was still caked shut with dried blood. His left ear was throbbing and oozing blood; he figured his eardrum had burst from the pistol's concussion. There was fresh blood on his wrists, and he ached all over. He desperately wanted to clean off the blood, wash the taste of it from his mouth, and get a drink, but the bear had settled in between him and the stream. Even with his physical discomfort, the sensations of shock were beginning to wear off and his mind was becoming clearer. He'd thanked God a hundred times for his deliverance, but he still couldn't get his head around the fact that if Luke hadn't shown up to carry out the fake execution, there would have been a real one.

He'd managed to unlock the audio and camera apps on Luke's phone and transcribe the *who, what,* and *where* of his kidnapping. He'd also taken a video of the bear, just to prove to himself this wasn't all a horrible dream, if for no other reason.

And he'd played it over and over in his mind—Daniel Shepherd's actions and words. He figured Shepherd had used their white supremacy contacts to connect with Richter. Shepherd's twisted mind had concluded that he'd somehow displeased God with the impersonal sniper approach, then failed with the up-close-and-personal assassin method. So he'd gone for the kill-him-in-person-in-front-of-the-troops move. To what end? Win's gut told him this wasn't just about revenge for Dennie Shepherd. No, this was also a means to tie the men to his cause. They'd all stood by and watched him kill a federal agent; as far as they knew, Win was dead and they were accessories to his murder. No way to step back now, no way to back out—they were all in too deep. All in a very, very bad way.

His mind wandered to questions about their real mission. Had Luke tried to send him a message just before he pulled the trigger? Was there an actual attack planned on the monument dedication today, or simply more "New America" bluster? And what of Two's purported suicide mission? Win knew he wasn't operating on all cylinders just yet, but he also knew those issues weren't nearly as pressing as the huge predator that was currently napping in the grass a few yards below him. His hand flexed as he gripped the knife. He willed himself to stay awake; letting his guard down wasn't an option.

His open eye scanned the sky again. *Someone has to be out here looking for me.* He hadn't heard of any FBI oath to never leave a man behind, like some of the military services had, but with so many Bureau folks in the area, there had to be some rescue effort. He hoped he was worth that much.

*　*　*

"Trey . . . we've got another issue." It had been thirty minutes since Sam's first call from the mountain. The connection on the phone was no longer crystal clear; Trey could tell the wind was howling, and Sam Morris's voice sounded strained. "Nine men headed down the mountain on the north side. Four of them were with the original party that kidnapped Win. The other five came up from the north. Looks like they met about a hundred yards down from the summit. Lots of partial tracks—lots of flat rocks up here, so I'm still working out where the others went—but we found . . . uh—" The wind snatched the end of the sentence away.

"You found what?" Trey asked anxiously.

"We found where something's been buried."

Trey felt his stomach drop; a lump formed in his throat. He took a moment before he asked the questions that needed to be asked.

Five minutes later, after Trey had conveyed Sam's report to Chief Randall and Johnson, he waited by the landline. When it rang, it was Gus Jordon. The Deputy Chief was to the point. "No change in status? Sam and those four FBI agents are still near the summit?"

"Yes, sir. Like I told Chief Randall, the agents wouldn't let Sam disturb the area, where, ah, something's been buried. The FBI wants to wait for their Evidence Response Team to get up there. They're not considering it to be exigent circumstances. Can you believe that?"

"So we've got no idea whether we've got a body there or not?"

"No, sir. Sam found no sign of blood in the immediate area. But . . . that doesn't mean anything. There are other ways—"

"Yeah, yeah." Gus took a deep breath. "Sam followed the other tracks off to the southwest?"

"For a few yards, then he lost them. He could never get good prints on the flat granite. He's trying to find where they came off the mountain. It's slow going and dangerous now. Wind is gusting to forty-five knots at their elevation. I'm not sure how much longer we can leave them up there. With the wind that high on top, there's no way we can get a helicopter to either take that group off or bring in the Evidence Response Team—if the FBI ever gets their evidence response folks here to Mammoth. . . . Could take hours."

The line went quiet while Gus thought it out. Finally, he spoke again. "Well, the Chief and I will be here at the TOC until after the dedication at four o'clock. I suppose the FBI has surrounded that church compound with enough firepower to wipe out a small city by now. You've got next to no one in Mammoth to help you. . . . If you were to decide to use the helo to scope out the area southwest of Sepulcher Mountain—"

Trey interrupted. "I thought everything to the southwest of the mountain was within today's no-fly zone because of the monument dedication."

"That's what they told us, another one of their FBI procedural rules. But I'm hearing that the FBI is only flying their drones and surveillance flights within a five-mile radius of the monument site itself. Leaves a lot of open airspace."

"Are you suggesting we violate their rules and go looking for Win?"

Gus didn't hesitate. "Apparently most of this 'rules' crap is coming down from DOJ in Washington. The FBI folks down here are pulling their hair out. Someone is trying to micromanage the incident from the Attorney General's office. Those lawyers don't care about Win, and they haven't got a clue about the situation on the ground. Lots of the bigwigs in Washington are pushing for a move on the compound to supposedly rescue Win . . . sometime today. We sure as hell don't need a raid on a heavily armed church full of women and kids—especially if Win isn't even there. We need to prove where he is, one way or another."

Trey let out a breath. "You and I have seen plenty of miracles in this job—he could still be alive. If they won't let anyone start digging on the mountain for hours, we need to go with what we've got and get the helo up."

Gus's voice took on an even more somber tone. "The FBI brass here seem resigned to the worst, especially after Sam's find on the mountain. But you're right, we've seen miracles before." He paused. "Trey, I can't authorize you to break the FBI's rules. You'll have to think it through yourself. You're our incident commander up there."

"Ten-four. I'll get back with you."

Trey hung up the phone, walked over to the conference room window, and stared down at a crowd of visitors gathered around two grazing elk. Maybe it was the lack of sleep, maybe it was too much caffeine, or maybe it was just his caring nature. Whatever the cause, he had a nearly overpowering desire to sit down and cry. But he didn't. He sucked in a few deep breaths and turned back into the room, where the others expected him to be calm and in control. He hadn't been a supervisor long, less than a year, and he'd never been involved in a case even remotely this large and complex. He was beginning to understand the loneliness of being at the top.

He knew what he had to do.

*　*　*

Win woke up in a daze. He'd had a terrible nightmare. He tried to blink his eyes open, but something was wrong, he could only blink with one eye. His hand reached his head and quickly pulled away—the side of his head was matted and crusty. His wrists were bleeding. . . . *Lordy!* He sat up with a start and nearly fell off the boulder. He'd fallen asleep. Where was the bear! Had he dreamed the bear? *Uh, nope.* There it was, asleep in the sun, flat on its back, right by the little stream, about twenty yards away. An inquisitive coyote was sniffing at an area of brown-stained grass . . . the blood—Luke's blood. The awful nightmare was real.

He checked his watch. It was just after noon; he'd been asleep for nearly three hours. The coyote had moved on, but he was still watching the bear nap and the ravens pick around in the dried blood about fifteen minutes later when he saw the bear suddenly sit up and stare off to the east. Then he heard a low hum in the distance. *Helicopter? Plane?* With the ear injury it was hard to tell the exact direction the sound was coming from, but he prayed they'd be able to fix on the weak signal from the phone.

The sound suddenly grew louder as a helicopter cleared a mountainside slope to the northeast of him. He could hear the high-pitched whine and the steady thump of the rotors even though he couldn't see it yet. He gingerly stood on the rock, trying to look over the tree line. If the locator on this phone worked way out here, he vowed to be a customer for life.

Before he knew it the bear was sprinting for the tree line and the Park Service's yellow medevac helicopter was above him, with an armed ranger waving down to him. Win gave the guy a thumbs-up, shimmied off the rock, and waited while the ranger rappelled down about sixty feet with an extra harness. The clearing was too small and steep for the copter to land, but the guy was on the ground in seconds and the helicopter lifted higher above them to regain position in the rising wind.

The small man in the green tactical uniform flipped up the dark sun visor on his helmet and grabbed Win by the shoulders. It was Ranger Jimmy, and Win could tell from his expression that he was both shocked and thrilled to find him alive. The ranger's eyes immediately went to the left side of Win's head.

"Head wound? We'll get you to Idaho Falls!" He shouted it over the noise of the returning helicopter.

"No hospital! Back to Mammoth or the TOC! I'm okay—just lots of blood. Need to report in!" Win was shocked his parched lips could still form words as he yelled back at the ranger. Jimmy wouldn't call down the chopper until Win agreed to let him wash out both eyes and shine a light into them. Then the ranger did a quick manual exam of his bloody head. Win impatiently submitted while he washed the blood from his mouth with an extra bottle of water.

Jimmy helped him into the harness and they were both winched up to the helicopter by another ranger and strapped in for the ride. It was hard to communicate, since Win couldn't hear much out of his left ear; he was still bleeding from that side of his head. After he drank two more water bottles and washed more of the blood off his face, he settled for holding one half of the copter's headset to his right ear.

"We kept getting weak pings from the phone locator out here in the Gallatin Bear Management Area. There isn't supposed to be anyone in this area—locator kept coming in and out to our repeaters for the last two hours. Trey kept us on it. We had no idea you'd be this far southwest. When we got over Quadrant Mountain, we were able to lock on the general area of the cell phone pretty good. Used binoculars to spot you. No sign of anyone else around, but there was a bear—a grizzly bear in the clearing!" Jimmy was saying through the headset.

"Yeah, he was waiting to have me for lunch. Thank goodness you ruined his plans!" Win tried to smile and it hurt. "The bear kept me out of the water or I coulda cleaned up a little for you."

He asked Jimmy to relay the coordinates of the clearing to the TOC as he gave their communications guy a quick report that fifteen heavily armed men, including one sniper, had left the clearing for parts unknown just after dawn. Then he tried to focus on not getting too airsick on the bumpy ride back into Mammoth.

He was told to be on a video feed from the rangers' ready room to the TOC as soon as they landed—twelve more minutes of turbulent riding. When the TOC technician signed off, Win handed the bloody headset back to Jimmy and dropped his head down into his arms for the rest of the flight. He knew Luke had left him a clue to Shepherd's plans right before he'd pulled the trigger. He just had to put the pieces of the puzzle together.

CHAPTER THIRTY-EIGHT

Win unbuckled and stepped out of the helicopter as soon as the skids touched the ground. He ducked his head, cleared the rotors, and jogged off the concrete landing pad and up the ramp to the Park Service's Fire Response Building a few yards away.

Trey was standing just outside the building's metal door. "Video conference in five!" he called to Win over the decreasing whine of the helicopter's engine. "Oh, man! It's good to see you!"

Win grabbed Trey's outstretched arm and pulled the ranger to him into a serious bear hug—he wasn't big on hugging, but it sure felt like the right thing to do at that moment. Trey slapped him on the back a couple of times before his EMT training took over and he starting checking him for injuries.

"Good Lord, you look rough! Where did all that blood come from?"

Win was already moving through the door. "Later. Show me your maps, let's talk this thing through."

It was already 12:45—only fifteen minutes until the Israeli delegation's plane was set to land in West Yellowstone. The video feed in the rangers' communications room came up on their 27-inch monitor. Win held the maps and sat opposite the screen in front of the camera. The dark screen blinked twice and then a camera shot of SAC Strickland, ASAC Givens, SAC Lomax from Secret Service, Chief Randall, and Kirk Phillips appeared. Those men were seated at a long table in front of various monitors; there were others in the background whom Win didn't recognize. The higher-ups' body language told him everyone was on edge, even the normally calm Commander Phillips.

The rangers' tech guy hit the feed from his end and Win knew they could now see him. Wes Givens actually sat back and gasped when the feed came through. Win saw Mr. Strickland's heavy eyebrows go up in shock. The SAC began haltingly, "Win, we thought we'd lost you—thank God you're okay. The rangers said you weren't badly injured, but . . . but are you all right?" He frowned, then regrouped. "What have you got for us?"

"I'm fine, sir. The trek toward the church, with me as a hostage, then the switch-off on the mountain, was a diversion to draw us into an attack on their compound. They have some sophisticated video plan set up to use any raid on the church as an online recruitment tool—propaganda. They have a well-established camp, looked like it was within a cave, at the coordinates I sent you. As you can see, it's only about seven miles northwest of the Cohn Monument site." His audience's somber looks became even more grim.

Win shifted in the hard chair and briefly summarized events that were still difficult for him to imagine, much less verbalize. "Luke Bordeaux was at their camp. He pulled off a fake execution at dawn. Most of the blood on me is his. . . . He risked his life to save mine. I've got maybe a ruptured eardrum, lots of dings, no serious issues." *That might not be completely true, but if I have serious issues, at least they're not physical.* He kept talking, "Killing me was to be Daniel Shepherd's revenge for the death of his son in a bank robbery shootout. Shepherd stood in front of me and ordered it. It had nothing to do with their operations today except to tie his men to him, force us to spread our resources, and confuse the situation further." *Which is working out real well for him, from the looks of it.*

Win realized he was talking fast, so he tried to slow it down. "Just before Luke pulled the trigger"—Win saw Wes Givens close his eyes when he said that, and Lomax flinched a little—"just before the shot went off, Luke called out '*La Porte Battante!*' He told Shepherd and Chandler it was a Cajun war cry, but it was actually a clue for me. It's a famous football formation that won LSU a huge bowl game against

Alabama. I think it's Cajun French for 'the swinging gate' or 'the swing-ing door.' It's a designed swing play—you line up heavy to the left, then on the snap you decoy a fourth of your line to the left while swinging the other three-fourths back to the right and into the end zone. Luke knew I would know about it. He figured those western guys wouldn't get it. Luke had me facedown; my head was facing due west. If I'm cor-rect about the clue, there has to be a target of some sort to what was my right, or north. The monument dedication site is exactly 7.1 miles south-southeast, or to the left of that point. Luke mentioned getting to their objective by three o'clock this afternoon. They're mostly using game trails and a few of the park's hiking trails. They could hike as far as eighteen miles to some other target by three.

"The monument dedication is scheduled for four o'clock. I know they have the militia's sniper, Clay Ferguson, and maybe one or two other guys moving toward the dedication site. That group, or at least Ferguson, thinks they're on a suicide mission. I doubt if any of Ron Chandler's men are in the sniper group. Luke Bordeaux went with Chandler's team, as they called it."

Win gave them his conclusions. "I believe the sniper attack on the Cohn Monument is a diversion and their main play is somewhere else. We've been reviewing the maps for the last few minutes, and there are five large private lodges to the north-northwest of their camp, just over the park's boundary. The lodges are all on inholdings within the Gallatin National Forest. They're very remote by road, but any of the five could be reached by the militiamen by three o'clock this afternoon."

Win sat back in the metal chair and let the higher-ups digest it all. Some good-hearted ranger had set a cup of hot coffee near his right hand. He took a slow drink and noticed there was fresh blood all over his wrist and hand. As the blood trickled down onto the white Styrofoam cup, he tried to wipe his bloody hand off on his even blood-ier jacket. He guessed he did look like something out of a horror movie.

Mr. Strickland leaned forward toward the monitor. "You're con-vinced there's another objective—but why would they strike a private dwelling? It makes no sense, Win."

"I don't know, sir. But if Luke's tip to me is correct, there are maybe twelve heavily armed men moving north of their camp toward something or somebody, and two or three men moving seven miles south toward the monument site. I think we've got two situations to counter."

Lomax cut in. "And if you're wrong, and we include Bordeaux and Shepherd, we have fifteen heavily armed men moving toward the site where we'll hold the dedication in less than three hours."

Win's SAC gave Lomax a dark look and took back control. "We got our drones and planes up by 8:30 this morning. We haven't had visuals on anyone moving into our three-mile security radius at this point, but you know how difficult visuals are in this terrain."

The SAC sat back. He glanced over at Mr. Givens. "Wes? What's the latest word from Headquarters since we let them know that Win wasn't in the church compound?"

"The Deputy Director is telling me they don't want to reposition anyone at this point. They want us to leave Blue Unit's HRT guys and our SWAT agents on the church compound. Everyone else and everything else, including our air assets, stays put near the monument site or down at Old Faithful until we get those Israelis out of the park. That word comes directly from the top," Wes said.

"Well, we're in full agreement with that!" It was the Secret Service SAC chiming in again. "We'll be driving the VIPs to Old Faithful and the various sites—it's too windy to make a chopper ride comfortable." He glanced down at his watch. "Their ETA is less than five minutes. I need to get out to the tarmac."

Mr. Strickland turned his attention back to the monitor and Win. "We can't move pre-positioned assets into a new sector without firm intel on what's going down. We can't do that, Win."

"Then let's check in with the lodge owners by phone, see if there's a problem. If we can't reach them, we could send an FBI contingent from here to check the private lodges from the air. The medevac helicopter could hold four of us: Johnson, Hechtner, Emily, and me. Ranger Hechtner knows the area and has technical training. We could at least do a delaying or containment action of some sort if Shepherd's men show up. These guys have a strong criminal element, Mr. Strickland—some of them are killers. I can vouch for that."

Win's big boss seemed to be considering his argument. Win heard someone in the background announce that the delegation's 767 had circled the field and was on final approach.

"Ms. Stuart is on suspension, but . . . but let me reach out to the State Department and see if they know anything about a possible target outside the park. Surely there isn't a potential target we haven't been briefed on." Everyone on the video call was thinking the same thing—something political could be going on, and for some reason the Bureau had been left out of the loop. It was an operation commander's worst nightmare.

Mr. Strickland moved out of Win's sight. "Going to make some calls. Wes, you wrap it up with Win."

Wes addressed his young agent. "You're sitting this one out, Win. You can't even think of going. You've hiked all night and nearly gotten your head blown off."

"Nearly doesn't count, sir," Win replied softly. He saw Phillips actually smile just a bit, as he recognized what he'd told Win after the Richter incident. Win kept talking, "I'm sure there are several of us who've had a long night. The mission isn't over yet, sir."

"Well, get bandaged up. Let us get these folks off the plane and on their geyser tour. We'll conference again in thirty minutes. Be available and ready to go with your plan, in case the boss gets new intel and we move that way."

Win turned away from the monitor as the screen went black. Trey was standing to the side, taking it all in. Win nodded to him. "I just volunteered you. Are you willing to go?"

"You know I am. My guys will gear up while I get with Johnson. I haven't seen Ms. Stuart around. . . . I think she's been suspended or something. Never mind that, you get cleaned up. Our SRT lockers and showers are in this building. Jimmy will take care of you."

Win could have stood in the hot shower for hours, but he knew the clock was ticking. He was stunned watching the hot water turn to a deep pink as it washed Luke's blood from his head and neck. He had to fight back the nausea the sight of it brought on—there was a lot of blood. Luke had certainly made the head shot look convincing. The blast from the pistol had singed all the hair above his ear and burned a streak toward his cheek. No need for a haircut there for a few weeks. It was no wonder he still had a distinct ringing in his ears from the handgun's concussion.

Jimmy showed up with someone's clean ranger uniform that fit him and, more importantly, with dark-green tactical overalls with U.S. PARK RANGER stenciled across the front and back in black. He changed into the clean clothes and had no intention of asking where they came from. He was even more thankful for the toothbrush and antiseptic Jimmy gave him. He had to get the taste of blood out of his mouth. He pulled on his watch, then fished his small Bible out of his grimy cargo pants and slipped it into the borrowed overalls. Jimmy left the steamy shower room to find body armor and weapons.

As Win was walking out of the empty locker room, buckling the black web belt around his waist, he glanced into the long mirror and did a double take at the reflection he saw there. He wasn't sure if it was the buzz he still felt from the militiamen's Gatorade concoction, the shock of his ordeal, or the continuing surge of adrenaline, but the man who looked back at him from the mirror looked older, more confident, and far more intense than Win felt. How had his view of himself changed so much during the last few hours? He saw the angry red stripe of the gunshot blast on the side of his head, but he also saw the deep-blue eyes, the set jaw, and the squared shoulders of a warrior. He was face-to-face with a very capable soldier in the war against terrorism. It suddenly dawned on him: This was the Win Tyler others saw— this was why others often deferred to his leadership. He nodded to the image in the mirror and resolved to make those appearances a reality today. He was going to take this war to his enemy.

* * *

His view of himself as a hardened warrior nearly changed less than five minutes later as Jimmy dabbed alcohol and antibiotic cream on his numerous visible wounds. "Ouch! Ouch! Whoa, Jimmy! You practicing your torture techniques here? Dang! Stop it!"

"Quit whining!" Jimmy was smiling as he slathered on more of the stinging medication. "What wimps you FBI boys are!"

Trey walked into the room and Win bolted free of the paramedic. "Hey, can I use your personal phone? Want to make a quick call before the video feed comes on."

"Yeah, sure. Johnson's on the way over." Trey handed over the phone and gave Win a once-over. "You make a damn good-looking park ranger. Might think about a job change when this little adventure ends."

"Uh-huh." Win grinned back at him and moved to the other side of the room. He turned away from the others as he punched in the number. She didn't answer until the seventh ring.

"Hello?" She didn't recognize the number on the phone.

"Hey, Mom." He felt a lump in his throat and he bit down on his lip just a bit.

"Win! You've got a different number—is everything alright?"

"Sure . . . sure. Everything's fine." *No, it's not, but it's better now that I can hear your voice again.*

"The flowers you sent are beautiful. You boys didn't have to go to such trouble."

Win grimaced. *Bailed out by Blake on Mother's Day—again.*

"You caught me on the way out the door to the church. It's Children's Ministries Week and I'm helping with the six-year-olds' class." She sounded so upbeat.

"I know you're lovin' that!"

"I just finished cutting out three dozen paper diamonds for their little musical tonight. You used to be so cute in the church musicals and plays when you were that age. You had so much fun!" *I couldn't sing, and I always felt like a dork. But if she wants to remember it that way, I'm okay with that.*

"Can't talk but a minute. I, uh, just wanted to touch base since I missed talking to you yesterday." *Could that have just been yesterday? Time doesn't feel the same. . . .*

"I'm so glad you called. We're all looking forward to getting out there and seeing Yellowstone later this summer. We were just talking about it at supper last night. Will is dying to see a wild grizzly bear—he says they're so scary." *You have no idea.* He could tell she was walking as she kept talking. "Goodness! Just nearly left home without some of Malachi's diamonds. Hold on . . . alright, got them." He could tell she was smiling.

Then he nearly dropped the phone. "What did you just say?" It was his FBI agent tone of voice.

"What? The cutouts—the diamonds. They're props for one of the songs the kids are singing at church tonight. It wasn't popular when you were a child. You probably don't know it."

"Sing it. Sing it please, Mom. I have a reason for asking." His voice was urgent.

"Well, okay, hmmm, the chorus goes like this:

> *Noah is coming with his zoo by twos!*
> *Lions, donkeys, zebras—dogs and cats too!*
> *Malachi is coming with his diamonds in chests!*
> *Stores of treasure for us to invest!"*

She laughed. "I don't know all the words. Blake's boys just sing the chorus over and over and over. It drives us nuts, but they sure enjoy it. They have cute hand motions that go with the song. You could look it up on the internet if you need the title." His mother was definitely puzzled.

"It's part of a case, Mom. I can't really say, but why would Malachi have diamonds?"

"Oh, it's in the last part of the Book of Malachi. It says, *'I will make them mine, says the Lord. On that day'*—I suppose Malachi is prophesying about their day of triumph. Anyway—*'On that day, I will make them my jewels.'* Some Bibles translate *jewels* as *diamonds*. I wouldn't know any of this except for the popularity of that silly song. I looked it up myself. Why is it important, Sweetheart?"

"Tell you later, Mom! Got to go. Tell everyone I'm thinking of them. Tell everyone I love them!" He stopped himself from rushing off the phone. "I love you, Mom."

"Love you too, Win. Be careful out there."

He punched in Wes Givens's phone number before he even turned around. He knew what it was now. He knew what Shepherd's and Chandler's code, *"Malachi is coming,"* meant. It had to be a robbery and it had to be jewels.

CHAPTER THIRTY-NINE

After Win's call to his ASAC, the video conference got pushed back for a few more minutes while Win's bosses pushed back on their bosses, who pushed back on their bosses, all the way up the ladder at the FBI and DOJ, then over to the State Department. When the video feed was finally up and running, Win could clearly see the stress and frustration on Wes Givens's face as he spoke. "One of the lodges is owned by the Weinberg Family Trust out of Beverly Hills, California. We've already tried several times to reach out to the phone numbers we've obtained and we're not getting through. That lodge is almost thirteen miles from the camp where you were this morning—it's remote, over seventeen miles by gravel road from the nearest highway, all through the Gallatin National Forest. It's about a mile north of Yellowstone's boundary.

"We've looked at it on satellite maps—not real time, of course—but it's not your typical cottage in the woods. It looks extensive, over twelve thousand square feet in the main lodge building. Two helicopter pads, a substantial guardhouse at the road entrance, and the usual stables, barns, and whatnot. It's on a side ridge overlooking Mill Creek; a national forest steel bridge three miles east of the lodge spans the creek and provides road access to the lodge. We're guessing it's an hour drive from the Gardiner area, at least that far. We've got the Los Angeles office trying to reach out to the owners out there."

Wes raised his chin a notch. "This could be your target, Win. The Weinberg name is big in pro-Israel circles in LA, according to our National Security ASAC out there." Wes rubbed his eyes for a moment, then glanced at someone outside the range of the video camera. "Mr. Strickland wants to get with you."

The SAC sat down at the monitor and laid it out. "Win, we've got orders not to move any assets without more to go on than a hunch. The State Department is stonewalling. The Bureau is trying to bring more pressure to bear on them, but until we have some proof there's another target, our guys and the bulk of the rangers have to stay put."

He shook his head and sighed. "Having said that, your arguments are compelling. Take the Park Service chopper and check out the Weinberg Lodge. If you don't see a problem there, fly on to the High Valley Lodge, it's about six miles further west. We can't reach anyone there either. All the other lodge owners have been contacted and we've found no issues."

"Yes, sir." Win felt the adrenaline kicking back in.

"Do not set that chopper down unless you think it's absolutely necessary—unless you are sure someone is in danger. You pick your team. If you want Ranger Hechtner instead of a Bureau technician, I can't argue with that. I understand that Agent Johnson is ready to go. Emily is under suspension, but if you choose I can lift the suspension if she's willing to go. The other option is to wait until the dedication is over. Your call."

Win quickly scanned the maps he had in front of him. "It's at least a twenty-minute flight from here to the Weinberg Lodge with this headwind. It's almost two o'clock now. If the bad guys do plan on hitting a target during the time of the dedication or thereabouts, I don't see how we can afford to wait."

"If you spot the militiamen, we can certainly get one of the HRT units out there . . . but again, there would have to be compelling evidence there's imminent danger to public safety. We can track them down after the dedication if they're just marching through the wilderness. DOJ has a pretty tight leash on us on this one. Be careful out there, Win." *Heard that from Mom a few minutes ago. . . .*

"Yes, sir. We're on it." He was already out of the chair.

* * *

Emily walked into the ready room just as Win stood up. She stopped near the gray metal door and took in the group gathered there. She wasn't a tall woman, and the black body armor over her tan waterproof parka made her look dumpy. Her frizzy red hair was sticking out from under the green Kevlar helmet in every possible direction. She pushed her thin gold frame glasses up on her nose and cleared her throat. Win saw none of the arrogance she'd displayed the last time he'd seen her—when she'd bullied him in the office hallway early last night.

"Johnson said you might need another agent to ride along. He thought they could lift my, uh, suspension." Her high-pitched voice sounded tentative.

Win took in the Glock on her side and the MP5 she was cradling in her arms. He wondered if she knew how to use those weapons, then immediately tried to force the sexist thought from his mind. Of course she knows how to use her weapons. *Even if I can't stand the woman, I have no business mentally insulting her,* his better nature counseled.

He regrouped and turned to her. "Are you volunteering? There's a chance we'll run into the bad guys. Even if we don't, with this wind, it will be a long, bumpy chopper ride." He was suddenly hoping she'd opt out.

"I'm an FBI agent, Win. Running into the bad guys is what we do. So am I going or what?"

"I'm the case agent. I'm in charge on this trip," Win said.

"I've got that." She shifted the submachine gun to the other arm.

Win shot a glance at Johnson. The big agent just raised his heavy eyebrows and shrugged. There weren't any other agents at Mammoth at the moment—options were limited.

"Alright, then. It's Hechtner, Johnson, Emily, and me. Hechtner is designated as safety officer. Has everyone got two extra magazines for their sidearm and long gun?" Heads nodded. "We're not a SWAT team, but we'll be operating independently, at least for a time. Got to be prepared. Maglites, binoculars, knife, first aid kit, zip ties, cuffs, water bottle, mobile radio?" Everyone nodded.

Johnson spoke up reluctantly. "You need to know . . . our, uh, HTs, the Handie-Talkies . . . these mobile radios are ancient. I haven't upgraded them in years. Not gonna be reliable." He shrugged. "We hardly ever need 'em."

Emily rolled her eyes and Win just sighed. *Probably another one of those issues Johnson got written up for during inspections. One of those things you don't need until you do—and then it could be critical.* Win looked at Hechtner. "Do you have any extra handheld radios?"

The ranger shook his head. Then he added, "And the one I'm wearing wouldn't communicate with your encrypted radios even if yours were actually operational."

Win knew the FBI's internal radio system was designed so they couldn't communicate with most of the other good guys—because occasionally the supposed "good guys" were the bad guys. *Well, then.*

"We go with what we've got." Win nodded confidently to the little group.

He turned to Trey, and the ranger took it from there. "No rounds in the chambers in the long guns—I want to check them." He walked around and quickly checked all three agents' weapons, then held out his rifle for Win to inspect.

"No one's gonna blow a hole in the helo on my watch! I've got the only satellite phone left in Mammoth with me, Win, and I've got extra first aid gear and water. Everyone put on these eye protectors. We're gonna be in the wind." He handed out what looked like Oakley sunglasses with clear lenses. Trey turned back to Win. "We're good to go."

It would have sounded too corny to say, "Let's roll!" but that's what he was feeling. Instead, he just nodded his head toward the door and followed Trey out into the cool wind. Emily looked shaky before she even buckled into the yellow copter. Win was hoping barf bags came standard with this ride.

The colorful buildings of Mammoth and the hundreds of tourists milling around the gleaming white-and-orange terraces came into focus below him as the pilot banked for the trip to the northwest. Win looked down and saw his stone house getting smaller by the second. He looked to the north and saw the distant switchbacks and snow-covered top of Sepulcher Mountain. He looked away quickly. At some point he would relive the events of last night, but this wasn't the time or the place.

Trey tapped him on the knee and signaled for him to pull on the headset and switch to an internal channel. No one else could hear them on the headsets over the roar of the rotors. With the headset on, he was more aware of the ringing in his left ear. He was surprised he could hear as well as he did when Trey's voice came over the equipment's internal speaker.

"Are you really okay? You went a little pale when you were lookin' over the mountain."

"Not into helicopter rides… "

"Aside from that?"

"To be honest with you, I think I'm more okay today than before the ordeal started last night."

"Glad to hear it. . . . Have a lil come-to-Jesus meetin'?"

"Uh-huh." Win nodded and smiled. "I'll tell you about it sometime, once I sort through it myself. Whoa!" The helicopter hit an air pocket and dropped a couple hundred feet. His stomach fought to stay at the higher altitude.

Trey didn't seem to notice the turbulence, but he did hand out airsickness bags to all three agents. Even Johnson was looking a little green around the gills. It was gonna be a long twenty minutes to that lodge.

*   *   *

They flew over seemingly endless miles of dark-green forests, soft-green meadows, and deep-gray granite ridgetops flecked with wide patches of snow and ice. The rushing mountain streams and waterfalls took on a white hue as they crashed down through narrow canyons and emptied into small teal-blue lakes that dotted the high country. Ten minutes into the flight and Win was finally beginning to forget his nausea and marvel at the beauty of Yellowstone's backcountry from the air. He had to remind himself that he was supposed to be looking for domestic terrorists, not elk herds and mountain goats, on the sweeping vistas below them. The landscape was mesmerizing.

It got a little less mesmerizing when they had to detour for miles around severe winds funneling off Electric Peak, a 10,969-foot mountain standing between them and the Gallatin National Forest. Flying far around the mountain rather than over it would add at least ten more minutes to the already-bumpy flight. Win tried to focus on something that wasn't moving violently up and down.

He got more of a reality check when Trey nudged his knee and signaled for him to change to an outside channel on the headset. He was surprised to hear Kirk Phillips's voice.

"HR-1 to FBIY-2. You copy, Win?" The HRT commander was coming in loud and clear.

"Yes, sir. FBIY-2, copy."

"The team intercepted two men at 1435 hours within the tight security perimeter near the monument site. How the hell they got that close . . ." He paused, then, "Our boys engaged them and we have one 10-7 and a second man wounded. No one hit on our side, but they did get off a few shots and one of the rangers has a few broken bones from a bad fall." *A 10-7, the unofficial FBI code for a dead bad guy . . . who?* Win glanced at this watch—it was 2:42 p.m. This had happened less than ten minutes ago.

Phillips kept talking. "The deceased subject was their sniper, he had an M40, and he apparently had a few notes on his person—to relatives, friends. He knew he wasn't coming back. His ID said Clay Ferguson."

Win drew a breath and felt tightness in his chest. *He's made it to the light. I wonder . . .* Win forced his attention back to what Phillips was saying.

"That corroborates what you said about a suicide mission. The other subject is the sniper's spotter. He says they were tasked with taking out the Ambassador—apparently the spotter was not aware this was a one-way mission, so he's talking. He confirmed there's a party of thirteen moving toward some objective to the northwest of their cave camp, as he called it. This just happened, so we haven't really interrogated the guy and he's a little shot up, but our boys in the field don't think he actually knows what the target is. The subject says they were on a *need-to-know* basis. Does that jibe with what you heard?"

"Ten-four. I know they were operating under *need to know* when they grabbed me and when they made the switch-off on Sepulcher Mountain. He's probably telling it straight." Win hit his mic again and asked, "The dedication is cancelled?"

"Hell no! Can you believe that? We have a shootout less than a mile away, within our inner security ring, but the State Department and the Israelis are going forward with the monument dedication—speeches and all. Secret Service is having a fit!" Win heard the HRT commander draw a long breath. The guy still had the mic keyed on. Phillips finished the call. "The wounded guy says he thinks he and Ferguson were the only ones going into the dedication area. If that's true, you've got a real serious problem out there somewhere in your sector and you've got no backup within a reasonable period of engagement. I'll get back with you when I know more. Copy that?"

"Roger that. FBIY-2 out." Win stared out the window of the chopper for a moment, then he switched intercom channels and nudged Trey's leg. He held up his fingers for Trey to change over to the private channel.

"What's up?" the ranger asked quickly.

"What does it mean when someone says, 'you've got no backup within a reasonable period of engagement'?"

"It means you're screwed."

That's what I thought it meant.

*   *   *

At 2:49 p.m. Mountain Time, the State Department finally came clean. Yes, the Israeli Ambassador had a fundraiser planned for this evening, and yes, it was at a private lodge owned by a gentleman from Los Angeles who had ties to Hollywood, who happened to be of Jewish ancestry, and who was a staunch supporter of the State of Israel and certain very powerful members of Congress. And yes, it happened to be called the Triumph of Diamonds, and all the "gifts" to the Israelis were to be in the form of jewels, preferably diamonds. There was a very glitzy cocktail party planned for 6:30 p.m., with the Ambassador and others in his entourage flying in by helicopter for the event to thank the thirty or so well-heeled Jewish American attendees.

The plan was for the Ambassador's jet to make the short hop to Bozeman after the tour of Yellowstone and the Cohn Monument dedication. The Ambassador's plane would be met by a privately owned JetRanger helicopter for the twenty-minute flight to the lavish lodge. After the party, the small VIP group would fly back to Bozeman and the jet would lift off for Washington at 10:00 p.m.

A top-flight private firm had been vetted by both the Israelis and the State Department to provide security. Not only was the FBI out of the loop, but so was the Secret Service. Some honcho at the State Department actually had the nerve to tell the FBI's Deputy Director she didn't know what everyone was so bent out of shape about. After all, she'd said, "We are obligated to provide confidentiality and privacy for our good friends from Israel. This event has the potential to raise over ten million dollars for worthwhile causes in their country and will garner a tremendous amount of goodwill for several very influential Senators and Congressmen."

* * *

Okay, then. They'd just gotten off the chopper's radio with Mr. Givens, who gave the entire team the quickie version of the planned Jewish fundraiser. They were within five minutes of the lodge at that point, and the weather was going to hell on them. At least that was Win's perspective. The turbulence had gotten even worse—he could tell the winds were high—and heavy, dark clouds were on the horizon. The pilot turned, tapped Trey's shoulder, and pointed to the northwest. *Now what?*

Win craned his neck to look forward out the window. He saw a very thin trail of smoke in the distance. It was streaming horizontally over the forest in the wind. The pilot came over the radio for everyone in the chopper to hear. "We've got a little smoke over to our front right. . . . We're still a few miles out from the lodge. Want me to get down lower and check it out?"

"Roger that," Win replied.

Trey was cradling his black helmet in his lap and trying to keep his assault rifle pointing upward as the pilot banked sharply and dropped lower. Emily actually gasped, and Win closed his eyes and tried to keep from groaning out loud. At this point in the ride, he'd gladly fight twenty bad guys just to get on the ground and off the damn helicopter.

The pilot leveled off about five hundred feet above the rugged tree line and slowed the forward momentum of the powerful rotors. Win forced his stomach back out of his throat and looked down. He could clearly see the orange-brown snakelike path of the gravel Forest Service road below them through the gaps in the trees. Then he saw it: the hundred-foot metal bridge, which he'd scoped out on the aerial maps of the site before they left Mammoth, was now dozens of scattered pieces of twisted metal. It looked like someone had dropped a child's set of silver pick-up sticks below them—the steel beams lay at random angles within the rushing creek. A single tree was smoldering on the bank, wisps of smoke rising from it. There was no more bridge, no vehicular access to the Weinberg Lodge, and the bad guys had explosives. *This ain't good.*

The only positive, if there was one, was that there was no sign of any vehicles or individuals near the destroyed bridge. No casualties except for tons of government steel.

As Win looked away from the window, he caught a glimpse of Trey's serious gray eyes. He knew they were both silently praying the same simple prayer. *No casualties. Please, let it stay that way.*

CHAPTER FORTY

Win could tell Wes Givens was a little shaken when he called in the report on the bridge. There was the crackly, static sound of the radio for several seconds, but no comment from his ASAC. Win asked the pilot to hold back from the lodge—with the wind, there was a chance the bad guys hadn't heard their chopper's approach. Win had previously asked for permission to go in, to attempt some form of containment until HRT could hustle out here. *Hustle* was the operative word—any help from the good guys was at least thirty minutes out, and that was if someone got in the air this very second. That wasn't happening. There were lives at stake here, lots of them, and Win thought his small team might at least be able to buy enough time for the cavalry to arrive . . . but it sure as hell wasn't a slam dunk.

Finally the radio came to life again. "Win, you've got authorization to try containment at the lodge. Kirk Phillips is in the field with his guys. He's going to be patching in on your satellite phone reports to us. Get with us as soon as you get on the ground and see the lay of the land. Try to recon it best you can without engaging them. We don't need a hostage situation. Best case: They just want to fleece the jewels and leave. We'd rather have that than hostages, innocent folks shot, or your team in a firefight against overwhelming forces." He paused. "Do you copy that?" Mr. Givens's voice was strained.

"Roger that. FBIY-2, out." He'd had the helicopter's radio channel open so that everyone could hear the conversation through their headsets. He removed his headset and did a quick check of each face. Trey was his usual cool, calm self; he was casually buckling on his Kevlar helmet. Johnson pulled off his headset, yanked his too-small blue FBI cap down tighter on his head, and scowled back toward Win. He raised his shaggy eyebrows and nodded—he was in. Emily was staring straight ahead into space. Her hair was even wilder after the chopper ride. She swallowed hard, then nodded several times. They had a team, such as it was.

Discretion was the better part of valor here, so Win opted for the "fly real low up the ravine" route. The Park Service's pilot was really good—he came in low and fast. He deposited them on a flat spot covered in sagebrush about half a mile east of the lodge. A slight ridge and a big stand of pine concealed the landing spot from the lodge complex. The pilot and copilot gave the little group a thumbs-up and lifted off; Win and the others shielded their faces from the dust storm created by the retreating rotors. The chopper made a perfect 180-degree turn ten feet above the ground and headed back to Mammoth for reinforcements.

As much as he'd hated the helicopter flight, Win felt a heavy, sinking feeling as he watched the yellow chopper disappear above the woods. But this wasn't the time for second thoughts. They were committed to the action, as Luke Bordeaux would say. Win realized that "the action" was becoming an all-too-frequent theme in his life at Yellowstone. He sucked it up and moved behind Trey into the deep forest. The ranger had the topo maps; he guided them through the dense woods and down narrow ravines and gullies toward an area overlooking the huge lodge. Win thought there was still a reasonable chance the bad guys might not have seen or heard their arrival. Unfortunately, they couldn't hear themselves either. None of the three agents' handheld radios worked properly—Win's little team couldn't even communicate with each other.

All four of them finally slumped into a shallow gully that ran parallel to the east side of the big log building. Johnson was already limping and Emily was dragging up the rear. Neither of them would have distinguished themselves in the Bureau's annual fitness tests. Their chosen surveillance post was an eroded ravine only five to six feet deep.

They weren't exactly close to the buildings, maybe eighty yards away, but they could clearly see the east side and parts of the front and back of the immense log lodge, with its glass expanse, long porches, and stone chimneys. The substantial stone guardhouse was over a hundred yards northeast of the lodge. Barns and stables were visible far behind the big house near a sharply rising, wooded ridge. There was almost no cover between their position and the lodge or the guardhouse. The owner's landscaper was obviously into sweeping vistas rather than trees and shrubs. A few aesthetically placed boulders dotted the yard, but that was about it. No one could sneak up on this place very easily.

There were a number of vehicles parked to the rear, near the barns and what Win assumed was the lodge's back door. He counted three caterer vans and an assortment of cars and pickups. He could see several dark SUVs and a sheriff's cruiser on the far side of the guardhouse. They were on the wrong side of the lodge to see the helicopter pads or the swimming pool. The wind seemed to be dying down a little, but he heard no other sound except its movement in the trees on the steep hill behind the barns. His watch said 3:15. If there was going to be a fancy shindig here in just over three hours, where was everyone? There wasn't a soul in sight.

Trey had wiggled under a twisted log at the top of the gully and was acting as their primary spotter. Win crawled next to him and swept the area with his binoculars. Trey's field glasses were focused on the lodge. "Blinds are all pulled on this side. . . . Where could they be?" He scanned the dense forest to the south. "Okay . . . wait . . ." He reached into his body armor for a tiny hooded flashlight and turned it on.

"What are you doing?" Win whispered. He glanced down to where Emily and Johnson were huddled in the shallow ravine. Johnson was alert, with his rifle up. He seemed to be doing a reasonable job of covering their flank. Emily just seemed to be huddling. Win wondered for a second why she'd been suspended. Did it have anything to do with her behavior toward him or this case? FBI personnel issues were like black holes in space—they existed, but no real person ever knew the what, where, or why. The feared Office of Professional Responsibility, or OPR, handled it all—their reputation within the Bureau rivaled that of the Gestapo.

He forced his attention back to Trey; the guy hadn't responded to his question. Trey didn't answer for another minute—he was working the small flashlight's on-off switch. It was pointed in the direction of the woods.

"Luke is at eleven o'clock at a hundred fifty yards in the tree line. He's signaling me that he's coming to us," Trey finally responded.

"Is that a good thing . . . or a bad thing?" Emily whispered from below. Win didn't bother to answer her.

"How are y'all communicating?" Win shifted on the sandy ditch bank toward the ranger.

Trey held up the little flashlight. "Basic Morse code. Didn't you learn that in Boy Scouts?"

"Never was a Boy Scout." Win was embarrassed that even he could hear the regret in his voice.

"Coulda fooled me." Trey grinned at him and pocketed the flashlight.

Win turned the bill of his Park Service cap to the back and kept most of his head behind a clump of sagebrush as he continued to watch the surroundings with his binoculars. They'd been lying there for nearly five minutes. He was beginning to have very real fears for the thirty-some-odd people who were supposed to be at the party. There had been no sounds, no sign of life anywhere on the site, not even sounds of livestock from the barn or stables.

Then, true to his usual form, Luke Bordeaux materialized from behind a low rock on the other side of the gully. He slid smoothly into their ditch and leaned into the sloping dirt wall below Trey. "Good thing they don't have mortars. . . . They could take y'all out with one round." Luke obviously didn't approve of their close positioning in the ravine.

His dark eyes scanned everyone and settled on Emily; he raised a hand to the bill of his camo field cap and tipped it slightly as he nodded. "Ma'am." Win hoped she'd keep her mouth shut at his simple act of chivalry. Win's glance at her confirmed her fear of the man had overridden her instinct to lash out at any civil gesture. She mumbled her name to him and dropped her gaze to study the weapon resting in her clammy hands.

Luke's eyes moved from Emily to Johnson and he nodded a greeting. Trey dropped his left hand and Luke raised his to grip it for a moment. Win caught the gleam of both their wedding rings as their left hands locked—family men; they both had plenty of reasons to make it through this deal in one piece.

Luke's dark eyes turned to Win. "Good to see you, boy."

Win found himself at a loss for words. There was actually too much he wanted to say to Luke, but not in front of the others. He raised his chin slightly to acknowledge the greeting and answered softly, "You too. . . . Thank you." Then he asked the relevant questions. "What's going on? Where is everybody?"

"They herded everyone into the lodge when they got here, little over an hour ago. I wasn't in a spot to see whether they all stayed in the lodge or not—there was some commotion near the stables, but I couldn't see anything. There are bad guys workin' this job from the inside, too. Someone had to have taken out the security team, 'cause no shots were fired when Brother King's group got here—they just walked right in the front door. Couple of King's boys drove off in one of the Suburbans 'bout forty minutes ago, heard an explosion not long after that. Those guys drove back up and went in the guardhouse at three o'clock."

Luke's eyes were gleaming. "It's a big-time robbery, Win. Big-time! King's crew figured I was gonna be tight with 'em after I killed you this mornin' so they told me a little 'bout the job. Before I split from them on the hike over, Billy Thayer told me the haul was over ten million dollars. I followed 'em here and hid so's I could watch. I don't think the regular militia guys know what's going down."

He shook his head like he couldn't believe it. "Prophet Shepherd, King, and five of his men and five of the militia guys are either in the lodge or in the guardhouse. That's twelve, if you don't count the inside men. Right now they're waiting fer another chopper to arrive with more guests—they've done that twice since I've been here. Everyone gets in the buildings . . . chopper comes in, lands, drops off a few folks. One of Brother King's men, Red, is dressed as a security guard, and it looks like they might have another security guard workin' with 'em. Those two and a sheriff's deputy are meeting each helicopter and escorting folks into the front door. They're even bringing champagne out to the chopper pads and carrying the folks' luggage. . . . The arriving guests just think everything is fine until they get in the lodge. There must be another helicopter comin' in soon. It's been real quiet for nearly"—he glanced at his watch—"nearly seven minutes."

"They don't know you're here?" Johnson asked Luke.

"No. Been laying real low, hoping Win would figure out the plan and some help would show up. . . . Was hoping a bit more help would show up." His sharp eyes scanned the meager group. "Y'all need to know this place has security cameras hidden everywhere. And they're flying a drone out of the guardhouse 'bout every twenty minutes to check the area. One of those things comes this way, we're burned." He shook his head again. "There is no way to get a call out, I lifted one of the other boys' phones—I've tried."

"They may have a cell phone jammer. Our people haven't been able to contact anyone here, started trying to call well before two." Win was thinking out loud. He punched in the tactical operations center number on the satellite phone. He could hear a loud roar over the wind even before the call connected. A jet helicopter was coming from the west. It was going to deposit more hostages—more diamonds—and there wasn't a dang thing they could do about it. The fancy blue corporate chopper sat down out of their sight on the other side of the lodge. They couldn't see it until it lifted off and turned to the north less than four minutes later. By that time, Win had already made his brief report to the ASAC; he was on the receiving end of the conversation as the chopper began its departure.

Wes Givens was still talking to Win as the high-pitched whine of the twin jet engines being throttled up filled the air. "If Bordeaux stays with you, get him deputized. I'll get the word out to HRT that he's in a uniform identical to the subjects."

Then Mr. Givens gave him some encouraging news. "All eighteen of Blue Unit's operators and a supervisor will be getting on Black Hawks and heading your way from the Gardiner landing strip. That's just as soon as DOJ gives us the word to release them from their current positions at the church. But that won't likely be until the brass is convinced the dedication is going off without a hitch. Their ETA should be no later than five. That puts them ninety minutes out from you. We're also trying to get the low-altitude drone repositioned from the dedication site—there are thunderstorms between that site and you. We're working on it.

"Win, we'll get a ground stop on all helicopter traffic and a general aviation warning out for the region. Those guests are probably flying into Idaho Falls or Bozeman and being ferried out there from one of those two airports. Those are the closest commercial airports, but there are several small airstrips in the general area that could handle private jets. Lots of really wealthy folks have vacation homes in the mountains. We'll get on that . . ."

Win was concentrating hard to hear his boss over the chopper's engines. "It goes without saying that the Israeli delegation is boarding their plane here in West Yellowstone as soon as they arrive from the dedication site and flying directly back to Washington. We're trying to get a guest list for that party out of the State Department, but you've got at least thirty guests expected, plus numerous employees."

"What about the security detail?" Win asked.

"Amertec Security cannot reach their team. Phones are not working—they're not even answering their sat phones. Amertec says they have an eight-man team at your site, six at the lodge complex and two rovers. They've also got two sophisticated surveillance drones—all their security cameras and drones are monitored from the guardhouse. Their guys last reported in at 1:30 and everything was fine. . . ."

The roar of the expensive helicopter's engines began to drown out Mr. Givens's voice. ". . . not engage them . . . unless you think lives are in danger. Copy?"

"Roger that. FBIY-2, out."

Win leaned back into the dirt bank. He caught a glimpse of the blue helicopter as it streaked off to the north. Even with his damaged eardrum, the roar of the twin jet engines was deafening. There was no chance of anyone overhearing them, so he gave his group the quick version of Mr. Givens's call. Emily perked up at the news that HRT would soon be on the way. But the others were well aware that a ninety-minute ETA was an eternity. Nobody was smiling.

Luke turned back to Win. "Who's in charge here?"

"I am technically in charge, Trey is unofficially in charge, and since you're with the good guys, I would vote for you to actually be in charge until we get some more backup in here. You have by far the most training in this sort of thing."

Johnson spoke up from beside them. "I agree with Luke being in command here, but somebody's got to deputize him. Okay, Bordeaux, raise your right hand and I'll do the deputizing."

"We're going to deputize a man who is out on bail for several federal offenses and who may be one of the terrorists?" Emily interjected.

Win saw Luke's eyes squint real tight as he looked toward her. Emily scooted farther away from him along the ditch wall.

Johnson was not deterred. "This isn't the time to quibble over formalities, Ms. Stuart, since he might be able to keep us from all getting killed. Repeat after me, Luke: I swear to protect America and her citizens as one of the good guys in this operation and as a deputized officer of the FBI."

Luke was smarter than that. "You're just making that up, Johnson."

"Well, hell, it's close enough. Do you swear that or not? This is an FBI operation, not a free-fire zone."

"Alright, I'll swear just what you said." Luke looked like it was almost painful, but he shifted his rifle to his left hand, raised his right, and repeated the oath close enough for it to count.

Win was watching the bizarre exchange play out when Trey called out softly that he'd seen some movement in the sagebrush flats. Trey whispered again, "Got one . . . maybe two men in camo." Everyone just sat there for a second. Then Luke took command.

His voice conveyed quiet authority and complete confidence. The country-boy drawl disappeared. Win understood why men would follow this man into battle. "Johnson, move down this ditch twenty yards and cover our north flank. Ma'am, follow Johnson halfway down the ditch, to that big rock. Hold your position there. Both of you stay low— real low. The rest of us are going south to see who's coming. Win, make sure that sat phone is turned off. . . . Trey, move down the ditch straight on—let them see you just a little, don't make a target of yourself. Win, crawl after me, we're going to flank them. No sounds." They were off.

Win crawled on his stomach in the sandy soil between the scattered rocks and sagebrush. He kept Luke's boots in front of him and his weapon cradled between his elbows. He'd seen soldiers do this on TV, but wearing heavy body armor, with all sorts of gear attached, made it much harder than it looked on television. Luke slid into a deep gulch and was out of sight in seconds. Win dropped into the same gully and was stunned to see two frightened-looking guys in dark camo with hands up against the side of the ravine forty feet in front of him. Two fancy tan assault rifles lay on the bottom of the gully, and one guy had a nasty red welt along his jaw. Luke was leaning against the opposite wall of the gully, with a pistol pointed at them.

"Who the hell are you?" the uninjured one demanded.

"I've got the gun, fool! I get to ask the questions. Who the hell are you?" Luke growled back.

The captives both sent a hopeful look Win's way as he scrambled to a low crouch.

"Park ranger . . . are you a ranger?" the captive's voice was apprehensive. Luke moved the pistol closer to the man's face, but the man in dark camo kept talking. "Be cool . . . okay, be cool. We're, uh, with Amertec Security. For the party. You want to rob the place, hell, rob them! I'm sure they're insured! But there is no reason to kill those people—no reason!" Luke put up his hand. The guy was talking too loudly.

Win blinked rapidly; he took in the small black Amertec logos on the men's uniforms and caps. "I'm with the FBI. So is this man." Win cut his eyes to indicate Luke. "Slow it down, we just got here. What's going on? Where's the rest of your team?"

Luke kept the gun on them and whistled for Trey to join them. The security guard was a pro. He gave them the quick and dirty version of what had been happening for the last ninety minutes. "There were six of our guys in that guardhouse; we were patrolling the ridge. Didn't hear or see anything out of the ordinary. We saw a sheriff's cruiser pull up just before we lost contact with our base. Our communications guy in the guardhouse was able to keep the mic open for a while. We could overhear them, in the guardhouse—several men. They were talking about blowing the bridge. Which I guess they did, we heard an explosion. They said the show would go on at 4:30 and they'd bug out at 5:00. And twice"—he looked to his partner for confirmation—"at least twice, someone mentioned killing all the Jews in the lodge. They were laughing about it." He closed his eyes for a second, then looked down. "I hope to God our men aren't dead, but I did special ops in the military for years. . . . Those voices I overhead, they sounded like killers. Know what I mean?"

Luke nodded. He knew the sound of evil voices.

CHAPTER FORTY-ONE

The report from the security guard that the subjects might kill their hostages was a game changer. Win turned the sat phone back on and immediately called Mr. Givens.

"The security guys had reviewed blueprints and videos of the inside of the lodge before they got out here. They say there are two sets of stairs down to the basement. A large game room or den is down there. The first level is kitchen, dining area, and great room—all separated by huge stone fireplaces. Bedrooms are in separate wings and on a partial second floor. They think the hostages may be on the basement level. The Amertec guy says there's a service door leading into the basement. They'd been scoping it out, trying to figure out a way in. If we get into the lodge, we may be able to secure that building and hold them off."

"Win, that's risky—real risky. You're badly outnumbered," Wes responded.

"Well, we have two more than we had a few minutes ago, and both of these guys were in military special ops. Luke broke one guy's jaw, but he indicates he's still good to go. Based on the descriptions they've given us, most of Chandler's men are in the guardhouse. Those are the really bad actors. We don't know where Shepherd is. Chandler's men have some sort of exit strategy at 4:30 or 5:00—don't know if it's a chopper or what, but the guards overhead them mention those times for a show and a bugout."

"If they're planning on harming hostages . . . it's 3:42 now, and HRT is still well over an hour out." Win's boss blew out a breath. "Okay, do it. Oh, and Win, there won't be any drone surveillance from our end. The HRT drone crashed in a thunderstorm on the way to your position. You're on your own, Win."

"Roger that." He turned off the phone without even saying his call sign. *"On your own." Nope, I'm never on my own. God is with me.*

Win, Luke, Trey, and the security guys crawled back to the original surveillance ditch and Luke signaled Johnson and Emily back in. The group listened to the security guard, Watson, describe how they'd planned to enter the lodge. It wasn't a bad plan, and now that they had six on their team, it might just work. Drawing in the dirt with his knife, Watson made rough interior layouts of the lodge and the guardhouse. Luke quickly divided up assignments. The injured Amertec guard was left in their ditch to lay down fire between the lodge and the guardhouse if the thugs in the guardhouse tried to reinforce their men in the lodge. He could also communicate with Watson on Amertec's state-of-the-art personal radios if anything developed outside of the building. Luke led the others in a single line to the south along the ditch and back into the dense woods. It was slow going, since they had to disable three hidden security cameras along the way.

Finally, they were crouched behind the caterer vans, in position to lift the metal trap door angling into the ground at the rear of the log building. Win was guessing this was some sort of employee or supply entrance; it was discreetly hidden in the natural landscaping. His watch said 3:58. They had a little more than half an hour.

Luke held up his hand and counted down with his fingers. When one finger remained up, Trey yanked the heavy door open and they dove down the concrete stairs, guns at the ready. Luke and Watson split from the group as soon as the stairs hit the hallway leading into the basement. Their job was to take the interior stairway and provide cover if any of Chandler's guys approached from the first floor. Win led his little team down a long, carpeted hallway toward the game room. He was moving fast, nearly at a trot, and Trey was behind him, touching his shoulder; Emily and Johnson were close on their heels.

A close-quarters combat entry is the sort of thing that takes train-ing—Trey had little and Win had less. It could have gone better.

Win and Trey came around the corner into the game room too quickly and ran smack-dab into the giant Eriksson and three other militiamen. Win's heart stopped for a moment as he screeched to a halt in front of four black AR-15 muzzles. Trey had his rifle to the side—he wasn't even in position to fire—but at least Win's borrowed M4 was pointed in the general direction of the bad guys. Everyone was caught off guard. Win's eyes darted past the rifles aimed at him—he could see groups of people huddled in the rear of the large room. The four mili-tiamen were standing directly in front of the hostages. He couldn't fire.

"Hold your fire! FBI! Freeze!" Win shouted at the top of his lungs to everyone in the room—amazingly, no one fired. Johnson swung around the corner in the hallway and had the best position to cover the room. Emily hung behind Johnson.

Win looked into Eriksson's face. The huge man was only ten feet in front of him, surprise registering in his eyes. "You . . . how? Agent Tyler? How?" Win picked up a hint of relief in the low, deep voice.

"God saved my life from that false prophet! Now look where that man has led you! Holding innocent people hostage! Put your guns down, now!"

The big guy wasn't giving up that easily. "These people aren't being harmed! We're keeping them safe down here, from the battle. From your strike force of oppressors! You drop your guns!" There were nods of agreement from the others.

Geez, what a story line Shepherd sold them. Win almost felt sorry for these men. Then he reminded himself that hours earlier, at dawn, all four of them had stood aside while Luke Bordeaux calmly pretended to put a bullet in his head. That made him more than a little mad.

"Look, dammit! We are not the oppressors! This is nothing more than an armed robbery. You're becoming part of a terrible crime! Wake up, men!"

"It's worse than that, Brother Jon." Luke's voice came from behind Win. The man calmly walked into the room and stood between Win and Trey, his assault rifle resting in the crook of his arm, muzzle to the ground.

The big man drew himself up even taller and stared down at the three men in front of him. Eriksson was puzzled; the other three traded anxious glances. Trey sucked in a breath and Win just stood there. *What is Luke doing?*

"There's C-4 or Semtex attached to all the columns upstairs, brothers. It's rigged to go either detonator or timer—I'm not sure. It will bring this entire place down on your heads and on the heads of these people. Prophet Shepherd is trying to commit mass murder to cover the getaway for a robbery. Ron King's boys. . . . We knew they weren't like us. Those boys are killers and thieves. We've all been betrayed, brothers." Luke's voice was genuine and sad. He was including himself with them. His pain was evident.

One of the militiamen spoke up. "That could be right—I heard Red talking about Semtex on the hike in."

It was as if the four gunmen had forgotten about the law enforcement officers who stood in front of them; all of their attention was on Luke.

"What do we do here, Brother Luke? Has Brother King misled the Prophet?" Eriksson asked.

"None of us are outlaws, you know that, Brother Luke," another man stated.

"First off, we've got to get these people out of here, and carefully. There are wires strung everywhere upstairs. We'll get everyone to the kitchen area, just inside the back door . . . then we'll go from there."

"Are there any more hostages?" Johnson's abrupt voice entered the discussion.

"They aren't hostages and we're not criminals!" Eriksson's shock was turning to anger. The big guy shifted slightly, and Win could tell he was looking for options.

"Okay, fine . . . Brother Eriksson. These folks are under your protection. That's even better," Win said. "Let's get them out of here. Let's get to the kitchen. Can we call a truce?" This was starting to feel like sixth grade, except they all had high-powered weapons pointed at each other.

Eriksson was getting nervous. "All right, truce . . . truce till we get everyone out of the building and safely away. Is that agreed?" Almost as one, the militiamen said, "Agreed," or, "Yes," or something along those lines. Win turned his head to address his troops. "Agree to a truce with these four men?" His eyes met Johnson's and the man gave him a *You are totally nuts* look, but everyone said yes.

Win looked sideways at Luke. The man had a peaceful, Zen-like expression. It was an unsettling reminder of how he'd looked this morning right before he'd kicked his legs out from under him. *Is Luke telling the truth? Is the lodge wired to blow?*

* * *

Before anyone even had time to move, Watson came jogging down the corridor toward Luke. His concealed radio was getting a call from the security guard they'd left in the ditch. He gave the militiamen a wary look, but he turned up the volume so everyone could hear. The sound was a little garbled because of the man's injured jaw, but the voice said, "Watson? Just picked some bits and pieces off the base mic in the guardhouse. I think they're playing with it, trying to figure out why they've lost several camera angles. . . . Someone just told one of their guys to set up the video equipment outside and get it ready to feed back to the church—I think he said church? Said something about it needs to go on at 4:30 to catch the national news. That's all I caught. There are three guys in camo outside the guardhouse fooling with some type of camera equipment on a big tripod right now. Will call if anything dramatic happens. Out."

Win was looking at Luke and saw his eyes go wide. *They're either going to kill some hostages on camera or blow up the lodge for the East Coast's national news. A live feed at 4:30 p.m. Mountain Time!*

Luke spun around to the four militiamen. "You heard that! Get these folks herded upstairs. Single file, toward the kitchen. Do not approach any windows. Watson, get to the main level and set up a path through the wires. Trey, you help these men organize these folks. . . . Johnson, you and Ms. Stuart provide cover in case we have company. Watch that front door. Red and another guy are dressed as security guards, and there's a dirty cop, a deputy sheriff—all of them are in front somewhere."

"Billy Thayer is over at the shed by the helicopter pads. That may be where Red and the sheriff's man went to." Eriksson was helping them. "I think Prophet Shepherd went out to meet that last helicopter. He might still be out there with Billy. We don't know where they moved the employees off to, but Bobby Thayer took several of the Jewish men back up to the guardhouse a while ago. Brother Jeffery is up there with them." Win could see the distress on Eriksson's broad face. It had finally sunk in.

"Win, go find the owner, see if anyone else is expected. Then get upstairs and help cover the doors." Luke was confident every order would be followed; he turned and was gone up the hallway.

Win had been so focused on the threat from the militiamen and the explosives that he hadn't even heard the soft crying coming from several frightened women sitting on the floor or standing in corners behind the two billiard tables at the far end of the large room. There were numerous women and a few, mostly older, men.

A petite older woman with a ramrod-straight back, porcelain skin, and severe gray hair apparently heard Luke's orders and moved quickly across the room toward Win. Her flowing beaded gown ruffled as she walked. "I'm Eleanor Kaplan Weinberg. . . . This is my mountain home."

She was so regal he felt like he oughta bow to her or something. "I'm Win Tyler, FBI. Is everyone here? Can you tell me if any other guests or employees are on the place? How many men were taken out of here?" His eyes scanned the group—twenty-four people. Most were dressed for a party or in expensive traveling clothes. Some of the men were in tuxes; many of the women in silk and lace. *Where are the employees?*

She raised her delicate chin and looked him over as you might look over a horse you were thinkin' of buying. Her voice was stilted. She was verbally looking down her nose at him. "FBI? You look like a park ranger."

Whatever! This woman definitely had the "I'm rich and you're not" mentality. Win tried to look deferential. He wasn't feelin' it.

She gave him another dismissive glance, but kept talking. "Yes, all of our guests are here. My husband, Winfred Benjamin Weinberg, our son, and eight other men were taken away well over an hour ago, by these . . . these robbers. They moved all of the Jews, as they put it, down here. I heard them say the Christians—again, their words—were going to be put in the stable cellar." She sighed. "Including the house help and the drivers who were here . . . that's at least thirty people."

"Where?" Win was getting impatient.

"It's a big concrete block storage area under the stable. It's quite secure. As is the entire property." Her voice rose. "We hired the best security! You just cannot get good help these days! I do hope you're getting our diamonds back. Do you have any idea how embarrassing this is to the family!" It wasn't a question. Win was really not liking this lady. The militiamen were doing a good job of moving everyone, and she was one of the few left in the room. He told Mrs. Weinberg he'd do his best and quickly turned her over to Trey.

Win's watch read 4:13 when he hit the top of the main staircase leading to the first floor. Luke was crouched there, moving everyone carefully over several lengths of gray wire that stretched between the massive log columns. Win's eyes took in twelve-foot-tall antler chandeliers, an open dining area the size of his house, and western artwork on the stone mantel that nearly took his breath away. So this is how the other half lives.

Through the thirty-foot-high glass windows, his eyes also took in a redheaded man and a tall, slender man, both in security-company uniforms, walking past the helo pads toward the guardhouse in the distance. Two other men were standing about fifty yards west of the front porch, on the helo pad. They were armed with assault rifles. . . . Something had changed. They weren't pretending to be party greeters any longer. They were watching the house. *Damn!* They'd be able to see both back doors from there. It was now impossible to move the hostages toward the caterer vans—those two guys would have clear shots at them.

"Keep moving, keep moving, come on ladies . . . watch the wires here." Emily was gently leading several of the older women through the maze of detonation wires toward the rear of the house and the kitchen. The traumatized guests were so grateful to be moving toward safety that they were even thanking the militiamen. Emily glanced at Win and whispered, "These are the last ones. . . . Everyone's here." Win wiped a layer of sweat off his face with his sleeve and joined Luke beside the kitchen door.

"All here," he reported to Luke.

Win noticed for the first time how pale Luke's normally tan face looked. The loss of blood must be taking a toll. He could see the tight bandage on his left wrist—the thought of Luke slitting his own wrist to save his life this morning still astounded him.

Eriksson knelt down on one knee beside them and leaned on his rifle. "There are a couple of big rocks out there. If we can get to those boulders, we can keep Thayer and that deputy pinned till we move these folks past the vans to the barns. The vans will provide some cover."

"Whoever tries for those rocks is gonna be wide open," Luke pointed out.

Eriksson sighed sadly. "Me and my boys will handle this, Brother Luke. You people better get to Brother King's guys and those other folks up at the guardhouse. No telling what they're gonna do."

"Alright, brother. You're doing the honorable thing." Luke grasped the big man's left arm and met his eyes for a moment.

"Hey, hey!" Win quickly interjected. "We can't start shooting without giving them the chance to surrender—this is a law enforcement operation." The militiamen and Luke all stared at him as if he were an idiot.

Eriksson scoffed. "I guarantee you them boys ain't gonna give you the chance to surrender."

Emily appeared from behind them without her helmet, badge in hand. "Somebody's got to do this, and they might not expect a woman." She nodded to the big man, who gave a signal, and suddenly they were all gone out the door and onto the wide flagstone patio. Emily faced the two bad guys, held up her badge, and yelled "FBI! Drop your weapons!" She immediately fell to the ground and began crawling toward the house, even before the subjects leveled their weapons. All four of the militiamen's assault rifles fired at the same time. The deputy sheriff went down where he stood, but the Thayer brother rolled to his right and returned fire.

Win watched through squinted eyes—it happened so fast. One of the militiamen fell forward hard into the ground. Eriksson made it to the biggest boulder and sent an automatic burst of at least twelve rounds back at Thayer's position. The other two militiamen made it to cover. While that firefight was going on outside the door, Johnson grabbed Emily's arm and pulled her back inside. "Well, that went well," Johnson quipped. She was white as a sheet, and Win could tell she was shaking—but she'd done what had to be done. Win filed that away in his mind. She might not be the best supervisor in the Bureau, but she was no coward.

Luke quickly turned to Trey, Johnson, and Watson. "Stay with us till we get past the vans, then y'all cut off and go with this group of folks. Get everyone away from this building. Helluva lot of explosives here! Find the people in the stable cellar, make sure it's not wired. Ms. Stuart will go with you. More FBI people will be here within forty minutes. Come back us up when your sector is under control. Got it?"

"Yes, sir," Watson replied. Trey and Johnson lowered their rifles and nodded.

"Go!"

Win knew it had to be nearly 4:30—they all stepped out onto the patio and laid down withering fire toward Thayer's position. The militiamen rose from behind the rock and began firing. The frightened civilians were herded out the door and toward the cover of the vans. Win dropped to his knees behind a fancy barbeque grill and tried to control his heartbeat and his firing angle. *You're a marksman, Win! Ease up . . . take him down!* But Eriksson had a better angle on Billy Thayer, and Eriksson was apparently a marksman too. He put a round just above the guy's body armor, right into his throat. Win was hoping the ladies weren't seeing this. He blinked to clear the sight of the bloody carnage from his mind and realized that Watson's partner was firing toward someone on their flank. The bad guys were apparently sending in reinforcements.

CHAPTER FORTY-TWO

At the *pop! pop! pop! pop!* of automatic rifle fire behind them, Luke and Win both wheeled and glanced toward the east side of the lodge. "Win! Get to that corner of the building and cover us!" Then, "Move!" Win sprinted across the patio, dodged lounge chairs, leaped a low stone wall, and tried to remember how many shots he'd fired from his assault rifle. *More than ten?* He wasn't sure, but this was no time to run out of bullets. The rifle was equipped with the Park Service's standard twenty-round magazine. *More than fifteen?*

Win threw himself on his knees behind one of the decorative boulders near the corner of the log building. He could see two men in the militia's taupe-and-green camo moving toward the security guard's position in the ditch. *Dang it!* It didn't look like they were fearful of taking return fire. They were upright and moving forward with their backs to him . . . *pop! pop! pop!* Their rifle fire sounded so much like harmless fireworks from nearly a hundred yards away. He didn't take time to aim—they were closing on the security guard's position in a hurry. Win squeezed the trigger and got off three short volleys that totally missed his targets, but it did get the bad guys' attention as rounds slammed into the sagebrush-covered ground around them. They both spun and returned his fire. He ducked low behind the rock and pulled out a new magazine—he knew he had to be nearly out. Those guys were pretty good shots; pieces of stone were ricocheting off the boulder. He stayed down and hit the release, detaching the spent magazine, then slid the new one in and heard it lock home.

He caught a glimpse of the partygoers being hurried along behind the house. They were being herded, helped, and even carried by their ragtag rescue team. The colors were a peculiar blend of the bright reds, blues, purples, and yellows of the women's gowns, mixed with the militiamen's camo, the men's black tuxedos, and then Johnson in his blue raid jacket with the large gold FBI lettering across the back. As the running group got closer to the barns and stable and out of his line of sight, Win realized again how surreal this all felt. Too much adrenaline was flooding his system. He knew that battle-hardened troops had to learn to control the surges of adrenaline, that fight-or-flight chemical God gave us for protection and strength in times of danger. Right now, it was too much. Right now it was actually screwing up his focus on the job at hand. He had to be cool and steady—not hyper and frantic. He made a mental note to work on that. . . . If he made it through today, he'd work on that.

His watch read 4:27. Luke had made it to the corner of the lodge and was aiming his rifle with one hand while it rested on a notched log. Win interpreted the closed-fist signal from Luke's free hand to mean *Stay put!* He stayed put. Luke fired one shot. Win peered around the base of the rock just in time to see a black drone shatter into dozens of pieces. The drone hadn't reached the height of the lodge's roof. There was a good chance its camera hadn't picked up the movement of the hostages away from the structure.

Seconds later, Luke moved to his side. "Let's get out of here—this thing may blow any second. Get back toward the trees, then we'll cut to the ditch." He was moving away at a low crouch as he was speaking. They both fired a couple of bursts toward the guardhouse as they streaked across the mostly open yard toward the tree line.

Trey was jogging to them as they cleared the first trees and turned toward the gully. All three crouched low and quickly moved through the thick evergreens toward the ditch.

Trey's breath was coming in gasps as he made his abbreviated report. "Deputy is dead . . . other bad guy is dead . . ." *No doubt about that.* Win knew the image of the Thayer brother taking a bullet in the throat wasn't going to leave him anytime soon. Trey caught a breath and kept talking. "The militia guy . . . took a clean shot through his upper arm, didn't hit the bone . . . and took one into his body armor. . . . Stunned him, but he should be okay. There were a bunch of people in a locked basement up there . . . no explosives. They're getting them out." All three men slid down into the south end of the ditch and began moving forward more slowly. "Johnson or that Watson guy should be coming soon to back us up. . . . It's past 4:30. . . . What's the deal?" Trey asked.

Win was wondering the same thing.

* * *

The contract security guard they'd left in the ditch was not having a good day. First, Luke had busted his jaw when he'd jumped him early on, and now he'd been shot by Chandler's men. But Win was impressed by the man's grit. As Win eased down the shallow gully and dropped into the deeper ditch beside him, the guy's first reaction was to try to aim his handgun.

"Whoa! Whoa!" Win called out as he ducked away from the unsteady Glock.

Trey jumped to the side of the disoriented man. "We're with the good guys, dude! We're here to help!" Win pulled the shaking handgun free and the guy collapsed against the ranger. He'd taken a couple of rifle rounds into his ceramic-plate body armor, and while they hadn't penetrated the plate, they'd caused enough shock trauma to his chest to nearly knock him out. His eyes were dull and blank. He was also bleeding badly from the lower arm. A 5.56mm bullet had done some damage. Trey was pulling out the serious medical stuff from the first aid satchel on his web belt.

Win waited for Luke, and then Johnson, to move in beside him. No one was shooting at them now, and they couldn't figure out why. It looked as if the bad guys had hunkered down inside the one-story stone guardhouse. Why? They were fixing to find out.

They all spotted the second drone at the same time. It was moving from the guardhouse their way at an altitude of about two hundred feet.

"Win, shoot down the drone. If it reaches us they'll know what we've got."

Win was thinking the bad guys had already seen them, they already knew what they had. So why the drone? It was one of the small commercial four-propeller types with a revolving camera. This one was white, and Win was aiming against a grayish-white, cloudy sky. The wind was buffeting the small craft from side to side as it moved toward their position and tried to gain altitude. Win was good with a rifle—actually very good, not that he'd proven it today—but target shooting and even marksmanship competitions were a cinch compared with the stress of knowing the shot could make the difference between life and death. He rested his cheek against the hard, black plastic of the semiautomatic's short stock, found the drone in the metal sights, held his breath, and gently squeezed the trigger.

"Bingo!" Trey called, as the bullet broke the sixteen-inch-wide craft into dozens of pieces, which floated toward the ground in the wind. It occurred to Win as he started to lower his rifle—the drone's camera was pointed away from them, not toward them. It was filming the lodge. His watch said 4:42. Then Trey's cell phone buzzed a message alert. The cell phones hadn't been working . . . *Crap! The explosives aren't on a timer, they're on a cell phone trigger. The bad guys have just turned off the cell phone jammer!*

It occurred to Luke at the same moment. "Get down!" he yelled, dropping over the top of Trey and the injured guard. Win fell forward into the bottom of the ditch just as the entire roof of the lodge blew out in every direction. The shock wave from the explosion and logs the size of grown trees blew over the top of their shallow ditch. It was over in seconds, and as flaming pieces of debris began falling all around them, Win clung to his bit of earth and covered his head with his hands, praying that nothing would land on them. While he was at it, he prayed for his and everyone else's protection in this whole awful mess. He was too stunned to get too specific. Win knew the Holy Spirit could sort it out and the angels were watching over him . . . still, he wished he had a helmet.

Luke was up before the last pieces of the roof hit the ground—mostly in front of them, thank goodness. A massive fire was raging in what was left of the center of the lodge, and thick, black smoke was blanketing the grounds. Luke seemed oblivious to the destruction of the spot where they'd all been standing less than thirty minutes ago. He was rapidly giving commands. "Johnson, get down to those three big timbers—get there while they're wrapped in smoke. Win, go halfway down with him. Lay in at that roof beam and give Johnson cover the rest of the way in, then get back here to the ditch while he covers your back. That's our first move. Everyone got that?"

Heads nodded.

"Trey, you follow Johnson down to those timbers once you finish patching up this boy. Your cover fire will allow Win to take out the guy in front of the guardhouse. You and Johnson keep pinging at 'em, but conserve your ammo—we don't have any to waste."

Wait—what? Did he just tell me to take out the guy in front of the guardhouse?

"Win—you and me, we're moving down the ditch after you get back up here. So don't piddle around down there. Win and I will hit the front and rear of the guardhouse at the same time. That will be five minutes from the time we leave this point. I will whistle the start. Use your stopwatches, be exact. At the five-minute point, I want some cover fire for us. Everyone clear?" Luke's eyes swept faces. "Alright, I'm gonna scout for a few minutes. . . . Johnson, you and Win get on it fore the smoke thins out." He disappeared into the sagebrush.

Johnson had the blue ball cap with the gold FBI letters pulled down low over his face; he'd lost his protective glasses somewhere and was squinting into the blowing smoke. The older agent pulled his heavy frame up and out of the gully and started down the slope at an angle to the guardhouse. Win waited a few seconds, then followed him out of the ditch. He felt the heat on his face the moment he cleared the ditch bank. The inferno in the center of the big lodge was sending flames almost sixty feet into the air—it looked as if the front and east sides of the building were totally blown apart. The fire's roar and the shattering of glass and cracking of timbers were nearly overpowering his senses. Dense smoke was rising hundreds of feet into the air in twisted columns; it was fanned through the sky and across the side yards by the wind. HRT wouldn't need GPS to find them, that was for sure.

Johnson was making a beeline for a pile of jumbled timbers that had recently been part of the roof. They had blown about fifty yards northeast of the house and were about the same distance from the front of the guardhouse—they'd provide an ideal shooting platform to cover the front of that building. The drawback was getting there. The bad guys couldn't see them moving in the swirling, black smoke, but the smoke was so thick that the good guys couldn't see where they were going. Win immediately tripped over several large stones that had been part of a chimney. He nearly went down. Just as he recovered and made it to the pile of logs, someone realized they were hidden by the smoke and began firing indiscriminately into the billowing cloud. *He's wasting a bunch of ammunition,* Win thought, *but he could get lucky.* And he nearly did. Johnson was right in front of Win when he fell hard. The big man's rifle crashed to the ground and he let out a loud groan.

"You hit? Where?" Win got down in a low crouch, slung his rifle over his shoulder, and tried to drag Johnson toward the cover. He could only see through thin gaps in the smoke. It had an acid, bitter taste; it was burning his eyes and lungs. He was blinded and choking at the same time. He used all his strength to half-carry Johnson to relative safety behind three massive timbers just as the gunman let loose with another volley in their general direction.

The smoke swirled away to the south for a few moments and Win started patting Johnson down to see where he was hit. He roughly pushed Win's probing hands away. "I'm not shot, damn it! Stepped in a damn prairie dog hole! I hate those things—couldn't see where I was goin'. Twisted my knee. . . . I'm too damned old for this!"

Win was taken aback. "You're what? Mid-fifties?" He was thinking that was about his dad's age. "That's not old!"

Johnson leaned against the shattered timbers. He was shaking the sand out of the MP5 and checking his magazines. "Don't you know that FBI agents age in dog years after the age of fifty! That makes me, what? Eighty-five! Hell, I shoulda retired last month!" Then his gruff look changed for a moment. He almost smiled. "Glad you made it back today—I know I haven't had much to say to you. But you've done a good job here . . . and, honestly, no one thought you were comin' back." His quota of sentiment apparently spent, he abruptly turned from Win and took up a defensive position in the jumbled logs. He changed the topic. "I'm down to one spare magazine and my handgun. Our backup sure as hell needs to get here. Chandler's boys are gonna push back any second. Bordeaux's right to go on the offensive. This is gonna get ugly."

Like it isn't already?

"Get back to Luke before the smoke clears. Go! I'm covering you!" Johnson bellowed. He fired a couple of shots, drawing the bad guy's return fire, as Win sprinted back through the cloud of black smoke and cleared the top of their little ditch.

The satellite phone buzzed just as he slid down the dirt bank. Win pulled it free of his vest and punched the connection on. It was Commander Phillips.

"HR-1 to FBIY-2. Win, you copy?"

"FB-2 . . . here, I copy!" He stammered as he tried to catch his breath. His radio protocol was falling apart under the stress.

"What the hell just happened?" Phillips asked. "We just picked up a significant anomaly on our security sensors down here in West Yellowstone."

They could pick up the big explosion on their whiz-bang, high-tech sensors forty miles away, but they couldn't get some good old-fashioned boots on the ground to back them up! Win was angry and his answer showed it. "They blew up the lodge. We got the people out by the skin of our teeth! Where is HRT!"

"Calm down . . ."

Calm down? Calm down! He wants me to calm down!

"Sounds like it's a little hairy up there. . . . Their ETA is 1715 to 1720, maybe twenty minutes out. The choppers are having to dodge some weather—thunderstorms. What's your status? Do they still have hostages?"

"Ten-four. There are two dead subjects, one's a deputy sheriff. We have a militiaman wounded and a security guy wounded—neither wound appears life-threatening. Ten hostages we know of, they're being held by Chandler's men in the guardhouse. Haven't located six of the security team. We have a truce with four of the militiamen. They are protecting the freed hostages near the stables, well over fifty people. Running low on ammunition."

"Did you say 'truce'?"

"Yes, sir." Win was sure Phillips was closing his eyes and shaking his head in disbelief.

"Make *sure* none of them are armed when our guys land—our boys will be coming in hot. We'll sort it out when we get the situation under control. Copy that?"

"Roger."

"Since they've got hostages, you've got to keep them contained." Phillips paused for a second. "Who's actually running your operation there?"

"We put Bordeaux in charge, sir."

The HRT commander considered that for a moment. "Probably smart, considering everything. Win, keep them contained until our team gets there."

"Roger that. FBIY-2 out."

Luke had appeared and eased closer to him in the ditch. Win started to speak, but Luke put up a hand. "I overheard it. What if Brother King doesn't want to be contained? He's still got us outnumbered by my count. He'll figure your boys are comin'."

"Uh, just to be real clear . . . your plan . . . that is containment?" Win asked haltingly.

Luke's eyes were bright. He raised his eyebrows slightly and flashed a cagey smile. "Active containment, boy. We can contain them a damn sight better if they ain't shootin' at us or killin' hostages."

Win couldn't argue with that. It was obvious Luke feared the bad guys were fixing to make a bold move. Evidently he was an aficionado of the "take them out, before they take you out" notion of combat.

Luke checked the cartridge caliber in the security guard's extra magazines and then handed one of the fresh magazines to Win. He glanced over at Trey. "We're just waiting on Trey to get the lead out . . ."

Trey shot Luke a humorless grin as he finished up the bandage on the security guard. The man seemed to be improving, but he was in no condition to help them. Trey had removed the guy's mobile radio and laid it beside him. It suddenly crackled to life. "Copy? Do you copy? This is Watson."

Win grabbed it and hit the mic. "This is Win—I copy. Your man is being treated. He'll be okay. We could use some more backup over here."

"I'm a little shorthanded myself right now. Uh, your gal . . . Ms. Stuart? She informed our allies that none of them would ever see the light of day again after HRT got here in a few minutes and shipped them all off to federal prison." Win could hear him sigh. "Not the best timing."

Win's heart sank. He hit the mic. "Sooo . . ."

Watson clicked in and interrupted. "They got her weapons—I'm shocked they didn't shoot her—but apparently they don't shoot women. Even stupid ones. They just cuffed her to a pole in the stable. Anyway, they faced me down and I told them I'd stay and guard the partygoers. That's all I was paid to do. It coulda got real bad. But they left—said the truce was only on till they got the innocents out safely. That's how the big guy put it."

Well, that is just great! They could rejoin the bad guys! "What's their twenty?"

"Heard one of them say they were going home. They took their wounded man with them and headed into the woods to the southeast. I doubt they'll rejoin the fight."

Hope not! "Roger that. You stay there and keep everyone in the stable. Can you get Emily free?"

"Maybe, maybe not. I'm not in the mood to look too hard for a handcuff key."

Win understood his sentiments entirely.

*   *   *

Trey made it over to Johnson's position, but only after all of them laid down heavy cover fire on the front of the guardhouse. The lodge fire was burning fiercely, and another section of the log wall crashed down, but the smoke was now blowing away from them. They could no longer use it for concealment. Brother King, as Luke kept calling Ron Chandler, still had at least six heavily armed gunmen plus Prophet Shepherd, and near as they could tell, they were all holed up in that one-story rock building.

As Win followed Luke down the ditch, Win replayed Watson's layout of the guardhouse over and over in his head. The crude drawing had shown a double doorway into a reception area, which separated two large front rooms. Those rooms contained the communications equipment and monitors and a ready room with separate offices. The rear of the building consisted of a large equipment room, a break room with lockers, and a two-bedroom apartment. Not your basic guard shack. The front of the building, facing what remained of the lodge, had a covered stone patio with large rock columns. Win's job was to neutralize, as Luke put it, the gunmen stationed there and to clear the two front rooms.

Win crouched low and gingerly moved down the narrow, rock-strewn ravine. His rifle was in his right hand and his left hand touched the sandy side of the narrow ditch for balance. The old Kevlar vest, which was fitted with ceramic plates, was heavy and cumbersome. It weighed more than thirty pounds, and it kept him from bending freely at the waist and threw him slightly off-balance. But he'd seen the damage done by the 5.56mm bullets that hit the security guard's newer body armor—the guy was down . . . but not dead. The weight and lack of flexibility were nuisances, but he'd take the protection over the annoyances any day.

Luke signaled him down with his left hand, and as soon as Win slumped into the dirt wall, Luke edged back up the ditch beside him. "Security building is just ahead of us," he reported softly. "This ditch cuts right behind it. We've got three minutes before Johnson and Trey open up on them to give us cover."

They lay there in silence for about a minute, and it occurred to Win that Luke was likely continuing to cover his back because of his promise to protect Luke's family. That would explain why the man would risk his own life to save Win's—Luke didn't know that promise had long since been handled with reams of Bureau paperwork. Win suddenly felt guilty for keeping it from him.

"I took care of Ellie and the kids with the Bureau days ago, Luke. You don't have to worry about that anymore. If something happens to me, it will stand. . . . They'll be okay. The poaching and firearms charges will be dropped, and they don't have anything on you for shooting Bronte. You, uh, you don't have a dog in this fight. You don't have to risk this—to keep me alive. You can just disappear and go home. No one will blame you."

"You think you're with me 'cause I'm lookin' out for you?"

"Why else? Trey's got the tactical training—"

"Trey's a healer. He's got a gentle spirit . . . more of a peacemaker."

Win was a little offended and a whole lot puzzled. "So what's that make me?"

"You? You don't quite know it yet, but you're a fighter. There's no backing down in you. You're still a work in progress, I'll give you that, but you're with me 'cause you'll pin your ears back and keep goin' after 'em."

Whoa. So Luke can see it too. His spirit soared for a moment, then he got real—they were gonna try to rescue those hostages before Chandler had them killed. Just the two of them against at least eight men, and it wasn't gonna be pretty and they might not succeed. Luke had concluded it was do or die. And it could very well be do and die.

Alright, then.

Luke was suddenly talkative. He was lying real close to Win against the ditch wall. He spoke in a low voice. "Your word to me, to take care of my family, as important as that was early on . . . it wasn't the big thing in me decidin' to get back in this last night. Gotta be able to look at myself in the mirror every mornin'. Here I'd trained and worked

with men who were goin' on a damn killing spree. Woulda never have
been a part of that—just wanted to be a part of somethin' positive, and
it come to this. . . . Knew there'd be hell to pay as it went along." He
paused and looked up toward the blowing gray clouds. "What it come
down to was my values—my faith. I couldn't let you die over on that
mountain iffen there was any way to stop it, no more than I kin let
these innocent folks die if there's anything I kin do about it. If I don't
come out of this . . . well, I want my kids to be able to say I was a good
man . . . that I done my duty." He took a deep breath and kept staring
up into the unsettled sky.

They lay there in silence for another several seconds. Win thanked
God for getting them this far and said his final prayer again. He was
thinking it might be lingering shock or a lack of sleep, but in addition
to the relief he felt after coming clean with Luke, he felt no fear of the
coming firefight. He shifted slightly on the sandy slope to keep the
wind from blowing dust into his face. "Luke, I don't have the words to
thank you for this morning . . . and I'm sorry I swore at you."

"You thought I was fixin' to blow your head off." Luke turned his
face toward Win and grinned a little. "No problem, you were angry."

"Angry and afraid. Thought you'd betrayed me."

"You had to believe I was gonna kill you or it wouldn't have worked.
And just so you know, I come close to movin' to the other side after
that meetin' with HRT—awfully close. But I didn't know they'd taken
you till Trey called me at midnight from Mammoth. Figured where
they'd go, and got to Prophet's camp 'bout a hour ahead of you and
the boys. I didn't know anything about this plan till I got there." He
took another breath. "Can't even imagine what you've gone through. I
admire your courage. I was scared I couldn't pull it off this morning—
God's provision fer both of us."

Win laid his head back against the hard sand. He was humbled
Luke thought he was a warrior—that he had courage. He'd never gone
into battle, but he was also thinking it might be a bad sign that they
both seemed to want to confess everything to each other.

"Luke, if we get out of this alive, I'd like to take you and Trey fishing," Win said.

The man kept his face to the sky and smiled. "Alright, that sounds real good. *When*, not if, we get out of this, we'll take them fish and have us a fish fry at my place. Kids, and wives, and all." Something made him frown at the thought of that, and he added, "Need to find you a girl, though. We'll have to work on that."

The beep from Luke's watch was barely audible. Time was up. Win took a deep breath and closed his eyes tight for just a second. He said, "Remember, this isn't Afghanistan, this is an FBI operation. We have to give them a chance to surrender if they aren't actively engaging us. We have to identify ourselves."

Luke met Win's eyes. "Yeah, I'm thinkin' they know we're with the Feds at this point. You take the guy out in front. I'm takin' the guy out in the back . . . then comes the challengin' part. Use your handgun in close quarters." He took a final long breath. "Here we go." He said it quietly, but with firm resolution. "Let's show 'em how southern boys can fight."

CHAPTER FORTY-THREE

The borrowed Sig Sauer handgun jammed as Win pulled the trigger. The man in camouflage was less than two yards in front on him, behind a rock column at the front of the guardhouse. The guy had just fired a burst back toward Trey and Johnson, and his clean-cut face registered shock as he swung the AR-15 toward Win. Win hit him square in the chest with 2.3 pounds of useless pistol, and went for his knife as the man staggered back from the blow. They went down together in a heap on the guardhouse porch, the man using the rifle as a brace to block Win's attack. Win got him with an elbow to his jaw as they rolled, and the assault rifle dropped to the porch's concrete floor. Gunfire was coming from somewhere close, but Win was so focused on his struggling foe that he never looked up. The guy had both hands around Win's right wrist, trying to slow the steady drop of the black commando knife. Win was bigger and stronger—the outcome wasn't in doubt.

"Don't kill me! Don't kill me!" the frightened voice whispered—it jolted Win back from the rage enveloping him. He willed the knife to stop its descent inches above the man's throat. He saw the fear in the wide blue eyes below him.

"You're under arrest—FBI! I wasn't gonna kill you!" *Yes, I was, damn it!* He forced himself to draw in a breath. *Get a grip, Win! What are you doing!* His left hand pulled the man's handgun from its holster. *A Glock. Better armed than I was.* He recognized the man as the militia's corporal, Jeffery Shaw, just as another burst of gunfire erupted from somewhere nearby. Fragments from the concrete floor stung Win as he rolled off the prone fighter and sent several rounds from the Glock back toward the two muzzle blasts inside the guardhouse. Now he knew why the Bureau put such emphasis on shooting with either hand—his left-handed shots brought a garbled cry from someone inside the doorway. He scooted behind the rock column and sent two more rounds toward the location of the shooters as he sheathed his knife and realized he no longer had possession of his prisoner.

"I'm shot . . . I'm shot." *Why is the guy still whispering?* Win fired again through the open doorway as he crawled across the concrete, grabbed Jeffery's coat sleeve, and dragged him and the rifle back to cover. A trail of blood followed the man's boots across the bullet-pocked porch. He pulled the younger man into a sitting position behind the column as a retreating shooter sprayed it with bullets. Several volleys of gunfire erupted from the rear of the building as he turned his attention back to his wounded captive.

"Where you hit?" The fear in the man's eyes had been replaced by panic. Win absently wondered how many Bureau rules that were meant to protect him he was breaking as he pushed the guy back into the rock pillar and began checking him for wounds. Protocol required handcuffing the subject and leaving him for a medic to deal with later. The problem was they had no medic and the guy would probably bleed to death before anyone arrived to help them. The motto *"First, do no harm"* floated through his mind—not the Bureau's motto, but it seemed to apply.

"Help me! My leg . . . my leg! . . . It hurts bad, real bad!" The guy was gasping for air through clenched teeth.

"Okay, be still. Put your hands behind your head." Win kept shifting his eyes between the captive and the threat in the guardhouse.

The young man groaned. "Why? It hurts bad!" He was bent forward with both hands still grasping at his wounded leg.

"Just do it! Will make me feel better, okay? Do it!"

Win stole another glance toward the shooter's location, stuffed the pistol in his web belt, and pulled the knife again. He slit the lower part of Jeffery's blood-soaked pants leg. The guy was bleeding heavily from what looked to be two places in his calf and one just above his knee. The gunfire in the distance, on the far side of the building, had become sporadic, but Trey and Johnson were still firing single shots toward the guardhouse, giving Win cover while conserving ammunition.

The ranger's first aid pouch contained the same basic medical essentials Win had spent all of two hours learning about at Quantico. He sprayed the clotting solution on the militiaman's three wounds and applied a combat tourniquet above the highest wound above his knee. Win dragged an overturned lawn chair over to them, eased the man onto his back, and used the chair to prop the wounded leg up above his heart level. Jeffery gritted his teeth and struggled to keep his hands locked behind his head as the pain from the leg's movements hit him.

Okay, cuff him and move on—no, someone has to release the tourniquet every ten minutes or his leg can be permanently damaged . . . geez. Win was no medic, but he remembered what he'd read.

"I don't wanna die. Do . . . do you know what you're doing?" the militiaman whispered.

"No, but I'm trying. Okay?"

"You're FBI. . . . You guys can do anything, right?" His voice wavered, and he winced as the pain hit him again.

"You watch too much TV—or you got us mixed up with the park rangers. Apparently they *can* do anything!" Win made a final adjustment to the tourniquet, wiped his bloody hands on his pants, and sat back on his heels. *Time to switch gears.*

"Listen to me, Jeffery! Look at me!" The militiaman's wide eyes met his; he was blinking back tears from the pain. "If I handcuff you behind your back, like I ought to, you won't be able to release that tourniquet. It has to be released for three minutes every ten minutes. You got that? You got a watch? Okay—check it. I'm gonna cuff you in front so you can help yourself here—you don't want to lose that leg or bleed out. Wait nine more minutes, then release it for three. Got that?" Win slapped his metal cuffs on the man's wrists as loose as they would go. The guy was still gasping for breath, but he nodded that he understood.

"Where is Shepherd?" Win asked. "Where are the hostages?"

The man looked confused. "The Prophet and one of his men left in the helicopter . . . over an hour ago. He left with a man they called Pedee. He isn't here. . . ."

Oh, man! Shepherd's gotten away!

The kid kept sputtering. "And those Jewish men . . . we're waiting for the jet helicopter to come back . . . to take them somewhere. . . . That's what Brother King said."

"That corporate chopper only holds seven people and a pilot, Jeffery! Where do you think that's gonna leave the hostages? King, or Chandler—that's his real name—is probably gonna kill them!" He heard shouts and gunfire from inside the guardhouse. He had to get in there and clear those first two rooms. He had to help Luke. "Okay, then—you're under arrest. Lay still. HRT will be here to help you soon."

"I . . . I haven't done anything wrong. . . . I'm a soldier of the Lord!"

Win was quickly transferring extra ammo from Jeffery's gun belt to his own. He made sure the militiaman's rifle was empty and heaved it toward the open area far out into the yard. He swung his M4 off his back and checked the chamber of the appropriated Glock—one jammed gun was one too many today. He glared down at the wounded man from a crouch. "For Pete's sake! Ron Chandler's—uh, Ron King's guys are nothing but thugs and killers! You better be rethinking your life and know the God you serve! My God doesn't stand with murderers and thieves!" With that lecture hanging in the air between them, Win lowered his rifle and sprinted toward the door of the guardhouse, praying he was getting there in time.

*   *   *

One of the gunmen who'd been firing from behind the open guardhouse door was no longer a threat. Win's three left-handed shots with Jeffery's Glock had struck him square in the face. He was sprawled on his back in the reception area, his head resting in a pool of dark blood. Win kicked the black AR-15 away from the man's limp hand. He fought the urge to gag, to be sick. He quickly turned away from the lifeless form, and his eyes swept the room for others. He'd caused another death. *I'll deal with it later . . . later.*

He heard a muffled cry for help over the humming of the room's bright fluorescent lights. The solid door to the ready room was locked. That large, windowless area would be the most logical place to stash hostages. He heard the cry for help again—a voice called out the name Winfred Weinberg. *I've found them! They're alive!* He heard more shouting and gunfire from somewhere in the building's rear. *I have to save these people first!*

"FBI! Stand back!" Win sent two rounds from the rifle downward into the lock and kicked the door open. He swung his rifle into the doorway and stepped into the brightly lit room. He silently counted ten men in formal wear, tied hand and foot, sitting against the far wall. He heard more gunfire from the rear of the building. *I've got to hurry!* He pulled his knife and cut the zip ties on the ankles and wrists of an older man who was saying he owned the place.

"Free the others, barricade the door, and stay in this room. Our Hostage Rescue Team will be landing any minute." Win handed the knife to the man. "I need to get back out there." He turned and caught an unexpected sight. Several men were prone on the carpet in an adjoining interior office. They too were hog-tied, but none appeared conscious.

"Are they . . . ?" he began.

"It's my high-paid security team!" The older man fairly spat out the words. "No, they're alive. The robbers drugged them with something, but they're starting to come out of it. We've seen them moving around. One of our security men was in on this. So was my new foreman, Peter." As he began cutting the others free, the man leveled a harsh question at Win. "What happened to the barbarian who was guarding this door?" The other men were rubbing their wrists and staring at Win.

"I killed him."

"Well done! Well, I'll get his weapons—I hunt big game, you know. You are retrieving our jewels, I hope. I would think that's why you are here."

Well done? Win flinched. A man was dead on the other side of the door and all this man was concerned about was his diamonds. Win didn't even want the Good Lord to know the thoughts going through his mind at that moment.

"Get those other men free and tend to them. There are other gunmen in this building. Stay in this room!" Win retrieved the dead man's AR-15 and handgun and shoved them into the estate owner's hands. Several of the men started to offer him their thanks, but he abruptly turned away from the group, slamming the metal door behind him. He wasn't in the mood to be polite.

* * *

The windowless communications room appeared to be deserted, but Win ducked through the door, his weapon at the ready. It was dark as pitch. He ran a hand along the side of the doorframe but couldn't find the light switch. He paused and stilled his breathing. He didn't hear a sound from inside the cavernous room except for the low hum of a dozen dark security monitors. He knew there'd been another gunman at the front door when he subdued Jeffery. *Where'd that guy go?* There was still sporadic gunfire coming from somewhere in the back of the building. *Have to make sure this area is clear.* That was his assignment from Luke. *Can't let them flank us.*

Watson's rough building layout had shown a door to the equipment room somewhere in this area. He turned on his Maglite, held it against his rifle, and moved cautiously between two desks. The door had to be near the rear, to his left . . .

The blow to the back of his head came out of nowhere—everything went completely black. He went down on his knees hard. For a second, he couldn't see, he couldn't breathe, he couldn't think. For some reason he could hear, and for the second time today, he heard Ron Chandler's gravelly voice. "Should have popped you this morning, boy. Would have saved me some trouble." Win could picture the evil grin behind the thick voice. He sensed the man behind him, but his limbs wouldn't obey his commands to move.

He felt himself sway from the effects of the blow, and he fought to remain upright on his knees in the heavy body armor. As his vision began to clear, he saw a figure move awkwardly into the room twenty feet in front of him. Someone had hit the lights, and Jeffery's bloody hands, still in handcuffs, were pointing that damn Sig Sauer handgun right at his head.

The voice behind him was directed at the bleeding gunman. "No need to waste a bullet on him—we need to conserve our ammo. Get with the other boys. We've got that traitor Bordeaux cornered in the back room. Our chopper shoulda already been here—it'll be here any-time." He laughed that short, evil laugh. "I'm on my way to finish our Jewish problem. This here won't take a second!"

Win sensed movement behind him, but he still couldn't make his arms or legs obey.

"No, Brother King! I've got a score to settle with this Fed!" The guy wasn't whispering now. He shouted the angry reply. Win's eyes locked on the pistol. It was shaking as Jeffery tried to balance on one leg.

It was one of those moments that froze in time. He saw Jeffery lean back into the stark-white wall of the security room; as he did, a twisted pattern of bright-red blood streaked the wall from his bloody coat. Blood was pooling at the bottom of the man's boots. Win saw him set-tle the pistol into a solid two-handed grip. The black muzzle seemed to be trained right between his eyes. He saw the militiaman's ashen face take on a hard look; his blue eyes narrowed, his jaw was set. He saw the flashes of the muzzle. *One, two, three . . . damn thing didn't jam that time!* He wondered if he had blinked, if he had flinched. He wasn't sure.

Ron Chandler gasped in shocked surprise—"What! What the hell . . ."—and dropped facedown beside him without another word. The heavy shotgun clattered to the floor. Win saw blood and dark hair on the long gun's wooden stock. A leather satchel dropped beside the shot-gun, and the jewels spilled out onto the dark linoleum floor. Dozens of the tiny stones scattered and bounced across the floor in front of him, gleaming and sparkling in the bright light like, well, like dia-monds. This was the loot, their haul—this was what all this senseless bloodshed was about. Who'd said greed was the root of all evil? Win couldn't remember the paraphrased Scripture.

Then it was as if the air had been sucked out of the room. Jeffery let himself slide down the wall to the floor. He grimaced with pain and dropped the pistol and his cuffed hands onto his lap. "We're even now. . . ." He sighed and closed his eyes. "You may be right. I hate that you may be right. I just wanted to be part of something good."

Win realized he'd somehow staggered to his feet. He moved to Jeffery's side and eased the 9mm out of the younger man's shaking hands. Win heard his voice, or at least he thought it was his voice. "Stay here. Help will be here soon. Tend to that leg . . . come out of this alive. Someone needs to . . . to come out of this alive."

* * *

Win found himself back in the main hallway, moving toward the rear of the building. He had to get to Luke. He still had the assault rifle in his hands, but he didn't remember picking it up. He pulled the bolt back quickly and released it to clear a cartridge and chamber another round—he didn't remember how many rounds he had remaining. There was a low roaring in his ears. Maybe the helicopter Chandler had mentioned? Maybe HRT? Maybe the blow to his head? A bullet thudded into the wall beside him as he eased around an open doorway. Before he could react, a strong hand pushed him to the side and someone sent three quick shots back into the open office. *Who's beside me? Who's firing?* Win heard himself call out, "FBI! Drop your weapon!"

"Don't shoot! It's down! It's down!" a shaky voice responded from inside the open door.

The man beside Win was yelling commands at the bad guy, "Hands up—completely up! Turn around! Get on your knees!"

Win fumbled for a set of zip ties from a pocket and handed them off.

"Seen them do this on TV," the very capable bald guy in the tux was saying as he cuffed the man wearing an Amertec Security Company uniform. He pulled the bad guy's handgun, kicked the rifle across the room, lowered his pistol, and turned his head back to Win. "Hi, Aaron Weinberg. Thanks for what you're doing here. They were going to kill us—and film it! Sorry my dad was such a . . . well, he can be . . ." He shook his head.

"Met your mom too."

The man raised his eyebrows and grimaced. "Ouch! And you stayed to help us?"

Win grinned a little. "God doesn't let us choose our relatives."

The sharp crack of gunfire from somewhere in the rear of the building got Win's attention. The man in formal wear was still talking. "Big helicopters landing, we could hear them. Two of your guys were getting us out of the building through the front. They said everyone else was okay. That's why I came back here. Thought you might need some help."

Win tried to focus. "Appreciate that. . . . Uh, you stay and cover this guy. I'm going to the equipment room. Uh, lose the gun before our guys get in here, okay?"

He turned out the door to move on down the hallway. He heard the man call after him, "Do you know you're bleeding? Do you know you're hit? Hey . . ." The sounds were fading in and out for some reason. He kept moving down the long hall.

Luke Bordeaux was pinned down in the front of the building's big equipment room and running out of options when Win appeared from a side door. Win heard Bobby Thayer yell "Ranger coming in!" just before a half dozen rounds slammed into the door he'd just walked through. Win threw himself behind a stout wooden worktable and flipped it on its side. He sent two bursts back toward the far side of the big room, more to make his presence felt than to hit anything. It occurred to him that he had to stop firing and locate Luke or he was liable to end up hitting his own man. He tried to take a deep breath, and it startled him when he realized he couldn't . . . he couldn't catch his breath.

"Comin' to you." Win heard those words and recognized Luke's Louisiana accent.

"Come ahead." He heard his own voice softly reply.

Luke slithered like a snake across the short expanse of concrete floor between them and drew himself up behind the heavy table. "Damn glad to see you." He was slipping another fifteen-round magazine into his Beretta; he was down to his backup handgun. "Got Red, Bobby Thayer, and one of those white supremacy boys in here—it's damn crowded. We're between them and the loot—apparently Brother King has it." He stole a glance around the table. "What took you so long?"

"Been a little busy. . . . A few of their men are down, including King, uh, Chandler. Hostages are free, and guards were just drugged—I think they're all okay. I can go home now . . ." *What? What did I just say?* Win paused and blinked a couple of times. It was odd—he still couldn't catch his breath.

Luke's eyes narrowed as he glanced at him. "Have you checked your magazine?" He tried another quick look around the table. Two rounds came in and took chunks of wood off the top of their barricade. Luke was giving orders. "Got to go for head shots, some of them are wearing level 3 body armor. Are you okay? Win? Are you hearing me?" Luke slapped him hard across the face. "Roll!"

Win snapped out of it long enough to roll and fire the rifle. He saw the large, black-headed man he was aiming at stumble forward and drop a pistol. The man grabbed for the steering wheel of a big riding lawnmower and slumped across it. The front of his camouflage jacket was shredded from Win's three-round burst. Maybe the body armor had saved him. *Maybe . . .*

Win caught a glimpse of the redhead, still in the security guard uniform, lunge between two tables. He was firing an AR-15 and shouting something at someone, but Win didn't know what. The redhead dipped down below a metal bench covered with tools. Luke was still behind the wooden table, but he was standing now, firing back at someone—Win could see the flashes of the muzzles. The booming sounds of the rapid pistol and rifle fire echoed off every surface in the prefabricated metal room. It was too loud to think, even if Win had been capable of thinking. Across the room, a man in camouflage dropped backward. The man was still firing an assault rifle, but he was falling and it was firing wildly into the ceiling. The red flashes from that muzzle formed a bright halo above a camo cap that was flying through the air. Luke had hit him with a headshot. Win could see blood, lots and lots of blood.

Out of the corner of his eye, he caught sight of the redhead moving toward them. The man rose and fired toward Luke before Win could swing his rifle up. As Win lay on the floor, he pointed and pulled the trigger, held down the trigger, but couldn't tell if he'd fired. . . . It had all gone real quiet. He needed to get to his feet, but he was floating again. He saw Luke stagger backward and grab for the wooden table with his free hand. He was firing the Beretta back across his body with his right hand. Win saw the redhead's rifle let loose another long burst. That man was almost on top of him. *Why am I not hearing the sound?* Then the redhead seemed to freeze. The evil smirk on his face froze in place. . . . A dark spot had appeared above his vacant eyes. He pitched forward and didn't move.

Win tried to get up on all fours, but it wasn't happening. He still couldn't get his breath, and just when he was beginning to realize that could be a big problem, he felt a wonderful peacefulness come over him—he was floating above the room. There was bright-white light. The brightest light he could imagine—the deepest peace he could conceive. It was moving toward him . . . or he was moving toward it. . . .

Then he saw Luke's prone figure on the concrete floor, and the tape covering Luke's wrist. The man had cut his own wrist to save him this morning. He saw Luke try to raise his head. *I need to help him!* He forced himself back; the glorious light began to recede. *I'll just be a minute,* he thought. *I need to tend to Luke—he gave me another day. I'll just be a minute.*

Win couldn't figure out how he'd gotten up. He stood over the redhead and had enough awareness to kick the rifle away. But there wasn't really any need to secure that gun. He forced his eyes not to see the gaping exit wound the 9mm bullet had left in the back of the man's head. He realized he could hear again. He moved slowly to Luke's side and knelt down. Luke was alive. He reached up and grabbed the back of Win's collar.

"The vest saved me . . . I'm . . . I'm just down from the shock of the rounds hittin' it." He spit up a little blood and his dark eyes widened slightly. His words became more breathy. "Then again, maybe I'm wrong 'bout that." His bloody right hand fell away from Win's collar and his eyes focused sharply on Win's face. "He got ya from behind. . . . What'd I tell you . . . situational awareness. . . . You're gonna have to work on that . . . some more."

Win tried to pull open Luke's heavy camo jacket to expose the light body armor, but his hands weren't steady and every movement seemed to be in slow motion. *This body armor wouldn't stop 5.56mm bullets—* something in his mind registered that fact. The wounds were below the left shoulder, and he pressed down hard with the corner of the jacket he'd pulled free. Luke choked a little and spit up some more. *God help me! There's so much blood.*

"I kept my promise to you! I took care of Ellie and the kids. You have too much to live for—don't go!" He heard himself saying those words at the same time he felt himself slipping away again. He kept pushing on the seeping wounds, but realized he wasn't feeling his hands anymore.

Luke's breathing was suddenly raspy and quick; his eyes had taken on a glassy look. The voice was softer and low. "We . . . we may have to . . . do that fishing trip in Glory, brother. . . . You tell her . . . you tell her I love her. . . . You tell her I done the best I could."

"She knows that! But you tell her yourself! Don't go!" Win tried to blink the fog in his mind away, but it wasn't working. "I've . . . I've got to get help . . ." *God help me!* He tried to rise from his knees, but once again his legs wouldn't obey his commands. He saw shapes moving into the room. He started to reach for his handgun, but he had no idea where it was. Trey's calm voice was telling him to lie still. He didn't know he was lying down.

They were in the olive green of HRT. There were several of them suddenly there. Win's vision was blurred. He was trying to lift himself from his side. "It's a ranger down! Medic!" someone shouted.

Trey's voice in the background—sounds were becoming more distant. "Stay with me, Luke! Luke, stay with me!" Trey's voice wasn't calm any longer. Trey's voice was pleading.

Someone above him in olive green was calling into a radio, "Got 10-7s in this building. Got several men down! Got two down here: one blow to the head, one with gunshot wounds to the chest. Got two red tags here!"

Win's mind was floating. . . . He was wondering what a red tag was. *It doesn't sound good.* Thoughts kept swimming in and out of his consciousness. *Why can't I get up? Are they talking about me?* Matt Smith's Georgia drawl came from somewhere nearby, as Win tried to rise again. "He's not a ranger—he's one of ours. Win, don't try to move. Medical choppers will be here any minute."

Win felt a firm hand on his chest, holding him down. In the background he could hear Trey begging Luke to keep fighting for his life. He willed himself to see Smith, who was kneeling beside him. He tried to focus on Smith's shoulder patch, which was right above his face. It said *Servare Vitas*—HRT's motto. *What does the Latin mean?* To Save Lives. A noble motto. A noble calling. They were living up to their motto. *Have I lived up to mine?* He tried to say something, but no words would come. He heard Smith command him sternly, "Agent Tyler! Don't close your eyes! Look at me! I'm answering your question, Win! You're on our team! Our team!" Then it all went quiet and dark.

Where is the light? Is the light not coming back for me?

EPILOGUE

It was like a deep, warm fog, with a heaviness to it. He couldn't quite open his eyes, but he had to keep trying. A swirling haze, then harsh light, then sounds. A hushed female voice, and a steady, low beeping. Another voice, a familiar voice. He tried to blink toward the light. . . . He finally saw him standing there. It was Trey in his standard uniform, the gray shirt and the dark-green tie, the gold badge over his heart gleaming in the bright lights. Trey was standing near the side of his bed, holding his flat hat. Win felt someone take his hand. *I can feel my hand.*

"Yup, he's coming out of it. . . . Easy, Win, don't try to move—they've unhooked you from Lord knows what all and moved you out of ICU this morning. Your mom and dad are here, Win. Tucker Moses flew them out the night it happened. They just went down to get a bite to eat, be back up here in a few minutes. And a friend of yours came in, she's . . . ahh, she's still here, and some of your college buddies too. They're all downstairs with your folks. I'm in town picking up one of my guys they're releasing today."

He tried to talk but couldn't quite form the sounds yet.

Trey seemed to understand that. "You've been in an induced coma for over three days—trying to keep the brain swelling down. Was touch and go for that first forty-eight hours. . . . You must of turned just as he hit you. Glancing blow, thank God. That militiaman, Jeffery Shaw, made sure Chandler didn't get a second lick in on you. But your tests are all coming in real good now. Still got you really doped up, will be that way for a couple more days, but you're gonna be fine. Doctors now say you're gonna be fine. Lotta people praying for you, Win."

It was coming back to him now, in tiny pieces—trying to get those people out, the gunshots, all the blood, trying to stop the bleeding. Trying to make sure Luke knew he'd kept his promise. Smith's words: *You're on our team . . . our team!*

Win's eyes closed, but he forced them open again. Trey was next to him; he felt him holding his hand. "Partner?" *There, I can talk.*

"Yup. You bet, and proud of it, Win."

He fought for words, through the fog. His heart heard Trey's desperate cry over and over again: *Stay with me, Luke! Stay with me!* He finally found the word. "Luke?" he whispered.

"He's gonna make it too. Been through two surgeries. Bullet got a small piece of one lung, lost a huge amount of blood. He'll probably be in here another week, but they say he'll be good as new. Now there's a scary thought! I sat in with Ellie when your ASAC told her you had it fixed for the government to pay all the medical expenses and so much more. She's still in shock about it all. You done right by them, Win."

Win still felt the pressure on his hand, and he tried to force himself to hear his friend. He realized he was thinking of Trey as his friend. That pleased him and he tried to smile, but he couldn't quite make it.

Trey was still talking. "An agent named Murray asked me to tell you there's some loose ends to tie up on this case and he has a new lead for you on some missing persons cases. He wants you outa here ASAP to handle all that. I think he was kidding, but you know those FBI types—maybe not. And hey, I brought over several cards. There's a card from your bear girl. Be glad to open and read it for you."

Win was able to smile at that, but the dense fog was closing in again. It was warm and his eyes were so heavy. He was floating above it all. It was peaceful, the light was fading. He was drifting away again. But he still needed to know . . . he still wanted to know . . .

He finally found the two words he was struggling to say. "Who . . . won?"

"The good guys."

ACKNOWLEDGMENTS

Writing a novel, I've discovered, can be a bit of a solitary calling, but it is certainly not a journey taken alone. For me it was an exercise in humility—so many contributed to the book, both directly and indirectly.

First, I thank God for the generous blessings He has given me that allowed me to have the time and resources to pause my life and follow my grade school dream of becoming an author. Foremost of God's blessings in this regard was the leading of the Holy Spirit in nudging me forward to write Win Tyler's stories.

I also want to thank my husband, Bill Temple, whose thirty-one-year career in the FBI provided practical insight into the workings of the Bureau and its agents. Several of Bill's former colleagues at the FBI, both retired and currently employed, contributed to the realism of the text. They have asked not to be acknowledged by name, and I respect that request. You know who you are—thank you so much for your help! Several park rangers also made significant contributions and helped me understand, and hopefully convey, the hardships, hazards, and joys of a career in the National Park Service. A special thanks goes to Rangers Kevin and Melissa Moses, who spent hours answering questions and letting me tag along on fast-water and mountainside rescue training. Kevin is a tremendous encourager who read the book's first draft; he offered wonderful advice. All the men and women in the FBI and Park Service provided excellent and detailed technical advice. Any errors on those issues within the novel are mine alone.

The book could not have been completed without the invaluable input from my band of twelve readers. Special mention goes to Barbara Mills, Anna Anthony, and Annette Maples, all of whom read three drafts of the book! Suzie James, my very best friend, read the first chapter years ago and told me I had to write the story. She never stopped encouraging me.

Thank you to all the associates at Girl Friday Productions, whose professionalism and enthusiasm helped me navigate the intricacies of the publishing process. Heartfelt gratitude also goes to my outstanding editors, Allison Gorman and Brittany Dowdle, who greatly improved the text while kindly allowing some deviation from the *Chicago Manual of Style*.

Lastly, I want to thank you, the reader. I hope you enjoyed this glimpse into Win Tyler's world in Yellowstone National Park. I would encourage you to go there and visit—as Win discovered, it's a magical place. Most of the locations mentioned in the book are real; a few are fictional or were modified to accommodate the story. Join me on my website at www.rhonaweaver.com and I'll fill you in on which is which. Let's go have a little adventure!

ABOUT THE AUTHOR

Rhona Weaver is a retired swamp and farmland appraiser who had a thirty-five-year career in agricultural real estate and founded a program for at-risk children in Arkansas. She is a graduate of the University of Arkansas, a Sunday School teacher, and an avid gardener. Growing up on a cattle farm in the Ozarks gave her a deep appreciation of the outdoors and wildlife. Her ideal vacation spot is a state or national park. Her novel draws on her love of the land and her deep admiration for the men and women in our law enforcement community who truly share a noble calling. Those park rangers, FBI agents, and other first responders are her heroes. Rhona's husband, Bill Temple, is a retired Special Agent in Charge and Deputy Assistant Director of the FBI; he helped immeasurably in researching the book. Rhona and Bill live in Arkansas on a ridge with a view with three contented rescue cats. *A Noble Calling* is Rhona's debut novel and the first in the FBI Yellowstone Adventure series. Please visit her website, www.rhonaweaver.com.

Made in United States
North Haven, CT
18 January 2024

47610701R00300